THE PARADOX HOTEL

THE
PARADOX
HOTEL

A NOVEL

ROB
HART

BALLANTINE BOOKS NEW YORK

Published in the United States by Ballantine Books, an imprint of Random House, a division of Penguin Random House LLC, New York.

BALLANTINE and the HOUSE colophon are registered trademarks of Penguin Random House LLC.

Library of Congress Cataloging-in-Publication Data
Names: Hart, Rob (Fiction writer), author.
Title: The Paradox Hotel: a novel / Rob Hart.
Description: First Edition. | New York: Ballantine Books, [2022]
Identifiers: LCCN 2021015892 (print) | LCCN 2021015893 (ebook) |
ISBN 9781984820648 (hardcover) | ISBN 9781984820655 (ebook) |
ISBN 9780593499085 (international edition)
Subjects: GSAFD: Mystery fiction.
Classification: LCC PS3608.A7868 P37 2022 (print) |
LCC PS3608.A7868 (ebook) |
DDC 813/.6—dc23
LC record available at https://lccn.loc.gov/2021015892
LC ebook record available at https://lccn.loc.gov/2021015893

Printed in the United States of America on acid-free paper

randomhousebooks.com

1 2 3 4 5 6 7 8 9

First Edition

Frontispiece and title-page images © Goettingen, iStock

Book design by Elizabeth A. D. Eno

For Tom Spanbauer

It's a poor sort of memory that only works backwards.

—the White Queen in *Through the Looking-Glass*
by Lewis Carroll

THE PARADOX HOTEL

QUANTUM ENTRAPMENT

Droplets of blood pat the blue carpet, turning from red to black as they soak into the fibers. The drops come slow at first, before turning to a trickle as the bones of my skull squeeze like a hand around my brain. My body yearns to release the tension in my shoulders, to let the pressure off my knees, to lay down and go to sleep.

Except it won't be sleep.

It won't really be death either. Something more in-between.

A permanent vacancy.

This moment has been chasing me for years. The third stage, when the strands of my perception unravel and my ability to grasp the concept of linear time is lost.

More pats on the carpet. But the blood from my nose has stopped flowing.

Heavier, from the other end of the hallway, getting closer.

Footsteps.

Maybe I can fight this. A handful of Retronim. A cherry lollipop. What if I scream? I open my mouth. Nothing comes out but blood.

The footsteps get closer.

This is the moment when my brain will short-circuit. That's the third stage of being Unstuck. No one really knows why it happens. The prevailing theory is your mind finds itself in a quantum state and can't handle the load. Others think you witness the moment of your death. I don't give a shit about the "why" of it. I just know the result doesn't look pleasant: a glassy-eyed coma that'll last as long as my body holds out.

The pressure increases. More blood. Maybe I'll bleed to death first. Small victories.

In a moment I'll be gone. Probably reality too. The timestream is broken and I'm the only one who can fix it, but instead I'm dying on the floor. Sorry, universe.

I slip again, memories rattling around my brain like rocks in a tin can. Sitting in my bed, the smell of garlic and chili paste frying in the kitchen, wafting upstairs. Graduating the academy, walking across the gymnasium stage, new heels tearing at the skin of my feet while I scan the sea of folding chairs.

The first time I let Mena kiss me, the two of us alone on the balcony overlooking the lobby.

That taste of cherries, and everything I ever needed.

The footsteps stop.

I feel it, the displacement of air, the gravity of another person, standing there, watching me writhe on this dumb blue carpet. Nothing I can do now. It's over. But I'm not going to die on my hands and knees.

With the last of my strength I push up . . .

Tap-tap-tap.

Doctor Tamworth is holding his pen an inch above the flat expanse of his desk, looking at me like I might bite him. Which, the day is young.

I take a second to situate myself. The fluorescent light is so white it's almost blue, to match the sky-blue walls and dark blue linoleum tile. So much of this place is blue, which is calming, or so I've been told. The room is otherwise bare, save a small tablet on the desk, a diploma on the wall from a university in his home country of Bangladesh, and a half-eaten deli sandwich in a cardboard clamshell container. I can smell the sting of the vinegar, the funk of the cheese. My stomach growls at it. Ruby is hovering in its usual spot over my shoulder, too close by half.

"Where were you just now, January?" Tamworth asks.

"Right here, Doc," I tell him, which is only mostly a lie, because the place I slipped to is gone. Something about carpet? I reach for it, but it disappears between my fingers like smoke. Probably not important.

"It didn't look like you were here," Tamworth says, his voice an airy, nasal pitch that seems determined to match the creak of his desk chair. "It looked like you were somewhere else."

"Your word against mine."

Tamworth sighs. "No behavioral changes. That's a start."

He heaves his blocky frame to a standing position and turns to the cabinet. The rattle of the pill bottle lifts my soul. He places the orange tube of Retronim on the desk, just next to the sandwich.

"I'm increasing your dose," he says. "Ten milligrams. One pill in the morning, one at night. If you're slipping a lot you can take a third, but no more than that in a twenty-four-hour period. Your weight." He raises his hand, spreads his fingers, waves them back and forth. "Figure by the time we get to twenty milligrams in a day, there might be a problem."

"What kind of problem?"

Tamworth slumps in his chair. "Aggression, irritability . . ."

"I must be OD'ing right now."

He frowns. "Heart palpitations, confusion, hallucinations. Not to mention your kidneys won't be too happy."

"Got it," I tell him, nearly snatching the sandwich, but instead palming the bottle and stuffing it in my pocket. "Take as needed. Like candy."

His face goes dark. "Do you ever get tired of this?"

I offer him a shrug in response.

"Your latest round of scans came in. Let me show you something."

He reaches for the tablet, opens it, and tilts it toward me. The mushy oval on the screen is lit up in greens and blues and reds. "This is the brain of a woman your age who has never stepped foot in the timestream." Then he swipes, showing another scan with slightly less color around the center of the mass. "This is your brain. Do you see the difference?"

"I'm not a doctor," I tell him.

"There's clear degradation in the hypothalamus. We're still not sure exactly how this works, but we believe the problem is related to the suprachiasmatic nucleus, which regulates the body's circadian rhythms . . ."

I put up my hand. "Doc, don't tell me you don't know how this works, and then tell me you know what's wrong. I told you. I'm still on the first stage."

He taps the screen of the tablet with his pen. "Nobody with this much loss of function . . ."

"Except you don't know how this works, so how do you even form a benchmark?"

He stops and stutters. "January, I'm doing this for your own good."

"I've got my pills, Doc," I tell him. "And if I hit the second stage you'll be the first one to know."

He slaps the tablet on the desk. "Retronim isn't a cure. All it does is forestall the inevitable. I have serious concerns about you being here. I know it's supposed to be safe, but look at the clocks. There's clearly radiation leakage. You ought to be somewhere far away. Why not retire? You hit your tier. Find a beach community. Read books. Meet someone."

I put my hands flat on the desk and lean forward, taking time to enunciate each word: "Don't tell me what I need."

"If you're on to the second stage of this, you know what that means," he says, pleading.

"First."

"January, I'm not an idiot."

"You may well be. And I like it here."

"Really? Because it doesn't seem that way." Tamworth peers over my shoulder. "What's your take on this?"

Ruby whirs a little closer. I consider whacking it against the wall. Not for any particular reason, just because I consider that a lot. It gives a soft beep and, in its genteel New Zealand accent, says, "Nothing worth reporting, Doctor Tamworth."

Tamworth rolls his eyes. I don't have a good insult, nor do I care to formulate one, so I stand and pat the pill bottle in my pocket. It gives another optimistic shake. "Thanks for the lift, Doc. I'll see you around." I wave to the drone hovering at my shoulder. "Let's blow, Ruby."

"January . . ." Tamworth starts.

"What?"

He looks at me again, ready to say something deeply caring and meaningful, probably. Then he thinks better of it.

As I leave, I realize I could have handled that better.

Could have taken the sandwich.

I should feel bad. It's not like he's not wrong. I shouldn't be here.

But how could I be anywhere else?

I walk to the railing overlooking the hotel lobby and survey my domain.

The swooping lines and rounded corners of the midcentury modern space give it the feel of being simultaneously retro and futuristic. The lobby is cylindrical and dizzying, starting a hundred feet below me and continuing up another hundred above me. Concentric rings of walkways start at the top—the restaurant, the bar—and continue down, level after level of offices and amenities. All of it linked by elevators and sloped walkways, like a shopping mall built vertically. The focal point is a brass rod hooked into the ceiling, which plunges into the depths of the lobby. At the end of the rod is a massive, brass astrological clock, hovering a few inches off the floor.

Mena comes out of the spa across the chasm, in her black and white waitress uniform, carrying an empty drink tray. Her wavy hair is pulled back into a tight ponytail, and the precise swing of her hips reminds me of how a panther moves. My heart lurches across the empty space between us and I consider calling to her, but before I can open my mouth she turns a corner and disappears.

Mena.

I know she's not really there.

But she's also the reason I could never leave this place.

Because what if I do, and I never see her again?

How do I explain that to Tamworth? To anyone?

If I do, they'll make me leave for sure.

And for the briefest moment, I think the same thing I think every time I see her: a five-minute tram ride. That's all it would take. I just have to be willing to break the rules I've sworn to uphold and maybe destroy reality in the process.

Some days, it seems worth it.

"Big snowstorm about to roll in," Ruby says. "Blizzard warning. Hazardous travel conditions."

Snatched from my daze, I exhale and turn to the drone, which looks like a floating pair of binoculars. It turns to me, rattling the googly eyes I glued to its lens.

"You ruin everything," I tell it.

"Just doing my job."

I should get to work. The lobby clock reads 9:17 A.M. I watch the second hand marching across the face.

9:17:24
9:17:25
9:17:26
9:17:25
9:15:26
9:15:27
9:15:28 . . .

Movement around the lobby draws my attention. Lots of people dragging roller bags through the tunnel from Einstein. The lines at the three desks surrounding the clock are deep and getting deeper. Cameo is at concierge, and all the check-in slots are staffed. Still, everyone is in the weeds. Which is not something that makes me happy.

"What's with the crowd, Rubes?"

"It seems there are some issues at Einstein that have grounded flights," it says. "Also, I have a message from Reg that he needs to see you."

"About what?"

"That's all it says."

"Haven't I asked you to not let people leave incomplete messages? You should have pinged him back and asked for more information."

Ruby floats for a few seconds before responding. "I didn't really care to."

"Thanks."

"You made me like this."

I swipe at it, but it dodges out of the way.

"It would help if you were a little faster," it says.

Whatever. I skip the elevator and take the winding, sloped corridors down to the lobby, where my canvas sneakers squeak on the marble floor. Hanging on one wall is a large oval screen displaying the upcoming trips.

QR3345—Ancient Egypt—DELAYED
RZ5902—Battle of Gettysburg—DELAYED
ZE5522—Triassic Period—DELAYED
HU0193—Renaissance—DELAYED

Today is going to be a day.

As I'm crossing to Reg's office, I clock a guy standing at the coffee urn. My antennae go up. He doesn't have a bag with him. He's surveying the room as he sips on a cup of coffee, looking for someone. Tall, movie-star handsome, motorcycle boots, a leather jacket he actually manages to pull off. Could be a guest, but he's a bit too scruffy for this lot. His clothes are sharp but not designer. The men who stay here tend to look like they're dressed for an emergency yacht club meeting.

"Ruby, see the pretty boy over there?" I ask.

"You understand that as an artificially intelligent construct I don't grasp beauty standards?"

"By the coffee, dummy," I tell it. "Keep an eye on him."

"Any reason?"

"Gut."

Reg's door is cracked so I push it open and find he's on the phone. He looks up from his disaster of a desk—paperwork, food wrappers, who knows, maybe a cat?—and shrugs at me, like, *why can't you knock?*

I give him a little shrug in response, like, *you're really asking me that?*

He goes back to the call, listening intently as I survey the clutter, focusing on my favorite piece: the Sicilian flag he keeps tacked to the wall. Red and yellow, with a woman's head surrounded by three disembodied legs, which, as I have told him many times, really ought to be the lesbian pride flag, but he does not agree.

"Yeah, I understand that," he barks into the phone. "Right, but we're understaffed as it is and . . . no, you listen . . . okay, fine, fine. Fine!" He taps off the call, slams the phone on the desk, and leans back, pressing his hands into his face like he wants to crush it.

Reg played offensive line in college and while those days are long behind him, he still carries an intimidating thickness. And usually, his charm and personality match his size. Not today. His skin is gray and his white hair, normally gelled into slicked-back spikes, is disheveled. His lavender button-down shirt is wrinkled and he smells like he bathed in aftershave. He's giving off some real walk-of-shame vibes, but since the only thing he's married to is his job, I know a hammer is about to come down on both of us.

"Jan, what was the biggest, bloodiest battle in all of human history?" he asks.

"I had to track someone down after D-Day in Normandy," I tell him. "That was pretty gnarly."

"I'm going to book a one-way ticket. It'd be preferable to this." He sighs. "Those assholes moved it up to tomorrow."

"Moved what up to tomorrow?" I ask.

"The summit."

I breathe out a large portion of my soul. The summit. A logistical nightmare that'd been keeping me from sleeping restfully the past few nights, but at least I had until next week to prepare for it. Anger shoots through me like an electric current and I consider digging my thumb into his eye to make myself feel better, but there's no point taking this out on Reg. The poor guy is just the hotel manager. And clearly, he's no happier about the change than I am.

This was a TEA call, so I know who to be mad at.

"Does Danbridge know?" I ask.

"He said to take five minutes to calm down before calling him."

"I'm giving him two, and that's generous."

Reg leans back in his seat. "I need a drink. Is it too early for a drink?"

I spot a lottery ticket on the corner of the desk. Reg likes to bet on horses, though he doesn't do a very good job of it. I give the ticket a tap and say, "You know, you'd be better off putting your money in a pile and burning it. At least it'll keep you warm."

He snatches the ticket with one hand, and with the other reaches for the tape dispenser, then affixes it to the bottom of his monitor. "You gotta have dreams, kid. This is the one that's gonna change my luck. I know it." He glances from side to side. "Big jackpot. If I win, I'm going to retire. Someplace down in Mexico. Beautiful women, colorful drinks. Never putting on a pair of full-length pants again." He laughs to himself. "You should come with."

That earns a laugh in return. "You think a few drinks with umbrellas in them are going to improve my disposition?"

"I expect you to have the personality of a battle-ax until the day you die. But you can't stay here forever, you know."

"I can try," I tell him.

Leather daddy is gone. The lines at the desks seem longer than they were before. Still plenty of blue bloods, but now flight staff too, in their sparkling red and green and purple uniforms. Which means we're going to hit capacity real quick. At least staff tends to be polite. Hooray for class solidarity. I slide up to Cameo, who as per usual, looks like a sculpture come to life, with their sharp, angular features, bald head atop a nearly seven-foot frame, and heavy jade earrings.

"How do we look?" I ask, craning my neck to look up at them.

Cameo smiles at the elderly woman they're helping. "I'll be with you in one moment, dear." To me, they say, "We're a little over half full already, but I'm hearing flights are grounded for at least the day, so it won't be long until these people resort to cannibalism."

"Excuse me," the elderly woman says.

We both turn to her, and her pearl necklace and designer luggage and pink velour tracksuit.

"Ma'am, I'm very sorry, as I've said, these are not normal circumstances . . ." Cameo starts.

Her voice is like a squeaky toy shoved into a garbage disposal. "I've already been told that the trip I planned more than a *year* ago has been postponed and they can't tell me until when, and now you're saying I can't have the room I booked either. I reserved a superluxury room and I want a superluxury room."

"I understand that," Cameo says, with the patience of a saint, which is impressive because I already want to kick over this lady's expensive bag. "I'm deeply sorry for the inconvenience. I can comp your room as well as your meals for the duration of your stay."

"I'd like to speak to your manager."

Cameo touches their ear. "Reg? A Miss Steubens would like to speak to you. Send her over? Right away." They raise a delicate hand, palm flat and unthreatening, toward Reg's office. The woman huffs, takes her bag, and trudges over.

"Did Reg really say to send her over?" I ask.

"Of course not," Cameo says, offering a sly smile.

And then their face drops, like they were digging around their teeth with their tongue and came across the squished remains of a bug. I turn again to find an old white man in a linen tunic, a gold-woven band around the neck and a gold-colored rope holding it together at his waist. Probably prepped for that grounded trip to Ancient Egypt.

To see people in period garb around here is not uncommon.

The problem is the bronzer he's used to darken his skin.

The costume designer, Fumiko, has a hard-and-fast rule about not doing any kind of skin alteration. The "no blackface" policy, she calls it.

The worst part is he seems so proud, smiling like a kid who drew on a wall. Even with the way the makeup cakes and cracks around his wrinkles, the way he missed some spots on his neck, highlighting pale patches of skin.

I glance at Cameo. With their aquiline features and almond skin, they could be from that region of the world. Or, like me, they're just wildly offended at a sight like this in the year twenty-goddamn-seventy-two.

The old man seems to detect our discomfort, which isn't surprising because the two of us are frozen still as statues. He gives a little shrug and says, "When in Rome, right? Or, Thebes I guess will be the case."

I can see Cameo's jaw working as they chew on the words they want to say, before forcing a smile onto their face and nodding. The trouble with the clientele here is, push back too hard and they remind you that they "know someone," and the worst part is, none of them are lying.

"Yes, sir," Cameo says, pushing the words out. "How can I be of service?"

"Well, it says my trip is delayed, and I'm hoping you might be able to give me an update, or at least call up to my room when something changes . . ."

I turn to Cameo, give a big *I'm sorry* shrug, and leave them to suffer. Not much else I can do. The withering look I get in return, it could be for the old man or it could be for me. Makes no difference.

I wave to Ruby and don't have to ask—a little compartment in its side opens and my earpiece sticks out. I place it in my ear, then twist to ensure a tight fit. "Danbridge."

He picks up almost immediately. "Was that five minutes?"

I make my way toward the coffee urn. "What in the hypotenuse fuck is going on, Allyn?"

"That's funny."

"What's funny?"

"That you think I have any say in this."

I grab a paper cup and hold it under the urn, my reflection in the gleaming surface distorted and pencil-thin. When I pull the lever nothing comes out. I tilt the urn toward me, and not even a drip. As I'm putting it back in place, a sconce on the wall gives a little flicker. God, this place is falling apart. "You run the TEA," I tell him.

"Right," he says. "And Vince Teller cares about that. So does the Crown Prince of Saudi Arabia. You know all those groups that were planning to protest? They found out the date and were organizing a demonstration, so we had to pivot."

"I thought we were friends."

"Don't worry, I'm sending someone over to help."

"Okay, I guess we never were friends . . ."

"Jan, you need a right hand."

"Then you come do it. Don't foist another trainee on me. Most of them can't count past ten without taking their shoes off."

"Don't worry, this kid is good. He reminds me of you actually, if you weren't a huge asshole every single second of every single day."

"I sleep sometimes."

Allyn laughs. "You're probably an asshole when you sleep. You probably dream of kicking people and taking candy from babies."

I consider disagreeing but it's not like he'll believe me. Or that he's wrong?

"Tell the kid to meet me in the Tick Tock. I need about six gallons of coffee. I'll send you the check."

Before he can respond I pull the earpiece out and stick it back into Ruby. I give one last look around the lobby, my stomach twisted into a tight knot, because I know this is going to get far, far worse before it gets even a tiny bit less worse.

And now I have to go upstairs to get my coffee fix. I whisper a little prayer, that Mbaye isn't in yet, but then realize, what's the use? That son of a bitch is always in.

I reach into my pocket, pull out a cherry lollipop, and stick it in my mouth. Savor the sweetness—there won't be a lot of free moments to savor anything in the next two days—and head upstairs.

The Tick Tock is mostly empty. Just a few folks scattered throughout the grid of tables, swiping through tablets, sipping on coffee while they pick at ornate breakfast plates. Mbaye is sitting on the other side of the bar with an espresso cup and a half-eaten croissant. His hand is on his chin, like he's lost in thought, and the way his muscular frame strains against the white chef's apron, he reminds me of that statue. What was it called? The Thinking Guy?

Not long ago, I would have called Mbaye a friend.

I don't remember much about those days.

As I approach he jumps to his feet and smiles. "Good morning, January! How are you today?"

"Fine," I tell him. "Coffee."

A mug appears on the countertop as I pull out a stool, and by the time I'm settled he's pouring steaming black liquid from a stainless-steel carafe.

"Leave the bottle, am I right?" he asks, giving me a wink.

"Yup," I tell him, making sure to sharpen the word as it passes my lips.

His smile falters, but he pushes it back onto his face. "What can I make you for breakfast? I have some specials I could tell you about, but it's slow so I'm happy to whip up just about anything you'd like." He points a finger at me. "You like blueberries, right? I just got a fresh batch. Beautiful. I could put out some blueberry pancakes, with a fresh bowl on the side."

Mbaye is a world-renowned French-trained chef. His pancakes ruin all other pancakes. And Tamworth's sandwich definitely got my stomach's motor running . . .

"Not hungry," I tell him.

He nods, starts to say something, but stops and turns away. As he's walking toward the kitchen I ask him, "Could I have another mug, please? I'm meeting someone."

He nods, his mouth a flat, frustrated line, and he rummages under the bar, coming out with another ceramic mug, which he places down next to mine, like it might shatter. He fills it, then puts the carafe down. He lingers in the space and I pick up my coffee. It's still too hot to drink but I sip it anyway, singeing my lips, putting my focus into it entirely, so that he will take the hint and go away.

After a moment, he does.

I sit in silence for a bit, then hear a *clack-clack-clack* sound. It makes me think of a roller coaster going up the tracks. I don't need to look around to see what's causing it; the little electric shock that leaps across my brain tells me it's a slip. Briefly, I wonder what it is, but ultimately can't be bothered. I'll find out soon.

I'm halfway through my cup and reaching for the carafe to warm it up when I hear, "January Cole?"

The white kid weaving through the tables looks more like an eager-for-applause musician than he does a federal agent representing the Time Enforcement Agency. Medium height, medium build, his blue polo shirt neat and tucked in, the stodginess of it offset by intricate tattoos down both forearms. Lots of flowers, some fish. All very colorful. He's wearing thick-framed glasses and his dark hair has that swept-back style that looks effortless, but probably takes all morning. He extends a hand. "Nik Moreau."

"Nik," I tell him, returning a firm, brief handshake. "Coffee?"

"Thanks." He picks up the mug and presses it to his mouth, testing the temperature, not even bothering with the basket of sugar and creamers to his right, which I take as a sign of good character.

"Danbridge warn you about me?" I ask.

He takes a long sip before responding. "He said you were prickly."

"He did not use that word." The next few moments are going to be make-or-break. I'm feeling generous so I give him a hint. "Honesty counts. What word did he use?"

Nik laughs, a little burst of air through his nose. "He said you're one of the best agents he ever worked with, and I was lucky to be paired with you. He also said you were a huge bitch."

I slap him on the shoulder. He's not anticipating it so he jerks forward. "If anything, he's understating." I turn a little in my seat and wave my arm around the empty restaurant, like a bored magician. "Welcome to the Paradox Hotel. Been here before?"

"Nope," Nik says. "First time."

"We'll get the lay of the land in a second. First, do you know why you're here?"

Nik nods. "Danbridge briefed me. The summit."

The summit. More like a goddamn fire sale.

Turns out, time travel is expensive. And this whole place—the hotel, the Einstein Intercentury Timeport, all the land that comes with it—is costing the government more than it's earning. Even with richy-rich assholes ponying up hundreds of thousands of dollars to see the first-ever public showing of *Hamlet* or visit the Library of Alexandria, it's not turning a profit. So the feds invited a bunch of trillionaires to make their pitches for taking it private.

"But it was going to be next week, right?" he asks. "Why did they move it?"

"A bunch of groups were planning a demonstration," I tell him. "Saying the timeport shouldn't go private. And I'm sure nobody involved with this thing wants to drive through crowds of people holding signs and yelling at them. It's now a variable I don't need to worry about, but it was also the thing giving me the least stress, to be honest."

"You're not bothered by a bunch of hippie lunatics trying to push through the doors?"

That's an interesting choice of words, and makes me wonder about his politics. The last thing I want to deal with is some thin-blue-line bullshit. "Those 'hippie lunatics' have every right to protest such a boneheaded move. It's insane that we're going to hand the keys over to someone whose only goal with this place is to turn a profit."

Nik shrugs. "But right now, aren't we just subsidizing a bunch of rich people's vacations? That's not sustainable. And anyway, the TEA will still be regulating it, right?"

"It's not just about vacations," I say. "There's a lot of world-changing technology across the way there. And yes, the TEA remains in place. I'm sure whoever wins will make all the right promises about respecting the timeline and playing by the rules. But there's no way these guys don't look for any which way they can find to maximize their investment."

"And yet"—Nik says, searching for his words—"you're going along with it."

His body shrinks a little after he says this, and I don't know if he's feeling me out or directly challenging me. "Our job is to babysit the toddlers trying to wreck the playroom."

"So what's my role here?" he asks, a little too eagerly, showing me his belly.

I throw him a little eyebrow before I say, "Given the complexities of all this, Danbridge decided I needed a hand. There are few people I trust in this world and Danbridge is one of them, so if he backed you, consider that a high compliment."

His cheeks flush. He's an approval seeker. Good to know.

At this point Nik notices Ruby hovering a few feet away. He tilts his head at it. "AI drone." He leans forward in his seat to see the undercarriage. "Why does it have googly eyes?"

"Aftermarket upgrade," I tell him. "Gives me something to focus on when I talk to it."

"And it impairs my visual acuity," Ruby says.

"You always manage to get out of the way when I throw my boot at you, so clearly it's not that bad," I tell it. "Say hello to Nik."

"Hello," Ruby says.

"Don't these things usually have female voices?" Nik asks. "And why does it have an accent?"

"Because it's sexist that an assistant drone would come bundled with a female voice, so I changed it. The accent, I just thought that would be funny. Ruby, show him your party trick."

Ruby whirs a bit closer. "Nik Gaston Moreau. Age twenty-seven, graduated at the top of your class from Stanford, degree in criminal justice. Two years with the TEA. Currently living in Watertown. You're allergic to shrimp, and you are currently participating in an online auction for a pair of vintage Air Jordan 13 sneakers, which for the record, I believe are counterfeit. You're active on a dating app, which you haven't logged in to recently, but you should, because you have a match with someone who seems to fit your profile quite well—I predict an eighty-one percent chance of compatibility. I could tell you what kind of pornography you prefer, but I imagine it would make you uncomfortable. Or, more uncomfortable, given the current rate of your pulse."

"What kind of middle name is Gaston?" I ask.

"That's . . . I mean, my mom's dad. But . . . that's creepily accurate. I know there's no such thing as privacy anymore, but shit."

"That's artificial intelligence for you," I tell him. "Ruby is like a floating secretary. Answers questions and reminds me of appointments and keeps notes and is just generally a pain in my ass."

It also helps sometimes to let me know if I'm situated in time or not, but I don't tell Nik that.

"I'm only a pain in your ass because I do my job," Ruby says.

I wave it off. "Let's start the tour." I stand up and hold out my hand. "The Tick Tock. Headed by chef Mbaye Diallo, who designed the menu and all the food offerings in the hotel. Make sure to have the thieboudienne. Fish stew from Senegal. Out of this world."

"I've been to Diallo's restaurant in Queens," Nik says. "Had to wait three hours to get a seat."

"Three hours?" I ask, with a laugh that's probably a little condescending.

He shrugs. "I'm a food guy."

I glance toward the kitchen. "Introduce yourself later. Don't tell him I sent you."

Nik doesn't say anything to that, which is good. I lead him out the glass doors to the circular balcony, the highest point above the lobby, so high it makes me a little dizzy to look down, but I do anyway, and those lines at the check-in desk are still pretty long. Fantastic.

I lead him on a winding path and point out the various amenities, level by level. "A lot of this is normal stuff you'd find in a hotel. But we also have some things unique to the Paradox. There's a costumer on-site for period-specific clothing. We have a doctor and a medical suite that handles vaccinations and screenings. No sense in coming back with a plague. And we have a linguist, who hooks you up with an earpiece translator. With me so far?"

"Linguist, doctor, costumer," Nik says.

We make it to the lobby. Cameo gives me a glance as another old man—this one, at least, not a walking billboard for racism—is arguing for another room. "You don't understand," the man is saying. "My room is *haunted* . . ."

"Sir, I assure you . . ." Cameo responds, but the rest of the conversation tumbles into the din as we make our way toward the security office.

I nod over my shoulder. "That tall drink of nonbinary water over there is Cameo. They know everything. If you need something, ask, you'll get a decent answer." I point across the way. "That's Reg's office—he's the manager—and next to it is the security office, which we will get to in a little bit."

I point down the two hallways that lead to the wings. "To the right is the Atwood wing, and to the left is the Butler wing. Each wing has two hundred and six rooms. The room numbers in Atwood are even, in Butler they're odd. Got it?"

"Atwood even. Butler odd. Four hundred and twelve rooms total."

"All right, kid, you can math," I tell him. "Downstairs is next."

We get to the next level down—underground now—into the circular hallway around the ballroom, the outside of which is lined with hallways and meeting rooms and bathrooms and storage rooms. The inner circle is a giant oak wall that leads into the heart of the hotel. I take Nik inside the curved space, which is huge, empty, and dim.

"This is Lovelace, where we set up for events and tomorrow, for the summit," I tell him.

"Is this the bottom level?" Nik asks.

"There's a bunker below this, because when they built the hotel they wanted someplace safe to go in case the timeport blew up. Now we mostly use it for storage."

"What time does the party start?"

I try to remember the plan I was putting together, which until an hour ago was preliminary, but now I guess we're going with it. "I'm going to tell them ten A.M. and they'll respond however they like."

"How many people in here?"

"Room has a stated capacity of four hundred fifty-two and I'll tell them I want no more than a hundred max and they'll tell me how many they want."

"You know what Danbridge didn't tell me?"

"Hmm?"

"That you were such an optimist."

"Do this job long enough and you and I will be on the same page."

We return to the lobby and as we step off the elevator, another electric spark jolts my brain. Then three dinosaurs roughly the size of chickens run across our path, their black claws clacking on the unforgiving floor.

They look like baby velociraptors. One of them stops and looks up at me, tilting its head. I turn to Nik, who is surveying the lobby, and clearly does not see any dinosaurs. When I look back, they're gone.

No sense in playing coy. "I have a party trick too," I tell him. "At some point later I'm going to make three dinosaurs appear."

"That's a weird trick."

"You work with what you got." We head toward the security office. "Danbridge told you I was Unstuck."

"He did," Nik says.

"What do you think about that?"

He shrugs. "I know it's rare. And I've heard it sucks." He pauses, considering whether he should ask the question I know he wants to ask. And then he does. "What is it like?"

"You remember the idiot's guide to time travel from the academy," I tell him. "Time conforms to the block universe model—everything that has happened or will ever happen already exists in a three-dimensional cube. We perceive events as linear because we travel through the cube on a straight line."

"Arrow of time," Nik says.

"Arrow of time. So when you're Unstuck, your arrow gets a little less straight. It zigs and zags, putting you in contact with past and future moments. It feels a bit like déjà vu. You see something that you feel like you've seen before. Then it's gone. The flashes only last for a couple of seconds. Sometimes up to a minute. It's not so bad. You get used to it."

"And you're only on the first stage."

"That's correct," I tell him, incorrectly.

You also get used to stage two, eventually, though it's a lot less fun. And a lot more confusing. Because the zigs and zags get more severe, and your perception jumps entirely into past moments. You'll be going about your day and—*bam!*—suddenly you're wandering around the halls of your high school, or on a bad date that still haunts you, or filing papers in the office where you worked ten years ago. It's hard to distinguish those slips from reality, and it's easy to get lost in them. When you snap out, no matter how long you were under, time hasn't really passed in the present. To anyone watching, it looks like you zoned out for a second.

Sometimes your brain jumps into future moments too, but those are harder to remember once you come out of them. It's like waking from a dream, the memory dissolving the more you think about it. Because it's not really a memory since it hasn't happened yet.

After that it's not long before you hit stage three. Your perception of time gets so out of whack that your brain fries. And there's not much you can do except stay away from the timestream, pop your Retronim, and wait for it to happen.

Nik asks, "Do you think it's safe for you to be here?"

"Are you asking because you care, or because Danbridge brought it up?"

He doesn't reply, which is answer enough.

A voice from behind us. "January."

We both turn to the source. Brandon the porter. A goofy Black kid whose uniform, as always, is a little rumpled, one tail of his shirt untucked. He's got one earbud in, pumping music so loud I can hear the tinny thump of it. He's unwrapping one of the little candies he uses to combat what I figure is a near-constant state of dry mouth, popping one between his lips as he shoves the small square of wax paper into his pocket. He does a bad job and it falls to the floor, so he stoops to pick it up.

"What's up?" I ask.

He comes up alongside me and eyes Nik. I do a quick intro and the two of them shake. Then Brandon asks, "Is it true?"

"Is what true?"

"That we're all going to be out of jobs soon?"

"Who told you that?"

"Just the word going around."

I've heard that rumor too. Whoever wins at the summit tomorrow is obliged to play nice with the TEA, but the hotel and its staff don't get the same deference. Brandon nods to Nik. "So, uh, are you taking over?"

"I'm just here to help," Nik says, eyes narrowing, picking up on the nervous vibe.

"Don't get too worried," I tell Brandon. "No matter what happens, these assholes are still going to need people to change their diapers and tuck them in at night."

His eyes narrow, like he wants to say something, but then he shakes his head. "Well listen, lots of folks coming in today. I have to go."

Brandon hustles toward Atwood and Nik waits until he's out of earshot before asking, "Drugs?"

"Dude has never not been high. But he's good at his job. That a problem?"

"Nope," Nik says, and I believe him. It makes up for his "hippie lunatic" comment earlier.

I hold my watch up to swipe into the security office and tell Ruby, "Make sure you update Nik's clearances, okay?"

Ruby beeps. "Already done."

"Good dog."

"That is belittling and inappropriate."

We step into the office and I give Nik a quick tour—the video feeds, the computer equipment, and the hologram table in the middle, where I pull up a 3-D schematic of the hotel. The main building looks like a bucket, wider at the top and narrowing slightly as it reaches the bottom. The two wings sprout from the sides, curving slightly away from the center in opposite directions, like if they continued all the way around they would create an infinity symbol. I push and pull the image with my hands, rotating and zooming, as we run through the basics of the floor plan.

Once Nik has the hang of the table I let him play with the model to get a feel for the space. He zooms in on a superluxury suite and is examining the layout. I turn to Ruby and snap my fingers.

"Put word out to whoever is here already. Lovelace in one hour. I want to start meeting the chuckleheads we're going to be dealing with. Then pull a list of guests who have traveled to or will travel to . . . which era had velociraptors?"

"Late Cretaceous."

"Do that. And keep a close eye on the camera feeds."

"Done," it says. "One trip yesterday and another scheduled for tomorrow. I'll check the itineraries and look for anything suspicious."

I'm going to have to interview all those guests with tickets for the Late Cretaceous. Which is nice because I didn't have enough to do. I leave Nik to his study time and head into the lobby, walk past a long line of people, which is being jostled out of shape by porters dragging large pieces of shrink-wrapped furniture toward the Butler wing. It never ceases to amaze me that people will show up with their own furniture for stays that never last more than a few nights. It must be nice to have money.

I make my way to the elevator bank of Atwood. An older white couple is waiting to get on: a man with silver hair and a silk navy blazer, and a woman who looks like she covered herself in glue and took a dive into a room full of pearls. I look down at my torn jeans and white T-shirt and battered red blazer. I don't look like staff. I don't look like I belong here at all. I'm pretty sure they cannot see me. I may as well be a ghost.

"For what we're paying I would have expected more," the man says. "And the staff here does not seem to be very responsive."

"Oh, it's quaint," says the woman.

"This is what happens when you let the government run things," he says. "Do you know how much this is costing me?"

"I know, honey. But it's time travel. It's not like we're going to be late."

She says it like she wants him to laugh, but he doesn't. "And the menu. The reviews are good but the food looks a little too . . ." He glances in my direction. "You know."

"Just say 'ethnic,'" I tell him. "That way you get to maintain a façade of decorum."

"Excuse me?" he asks. Less at what I said, and more that someone of my station would address him. The wife turns away from me, beet red, not wanting anything to do with our exchange. At this point I bail and head for the stairs. I don't want to be trapped in a confined space with these people, even if it's just for a few moments. The way things are going, the elevator would get stuck.

As I'm walking away I hear her comforting him with the kind of tone you would use for a disappointed toddler. "I'm sure they'll make you just a regular steak, sweetheart."

The fifth-floor hallway is empty. I trudge across the blue carpet toward my room at the end, but stop halfway. Feel a little twinge outside room 526. Kind of like when I'm slipping, but different.

Instead of a bolt of lightning, it's a dull thrum. A toothache in my brain.

The door to the room is cracked, so I give it a little knock. There's a shuffling sound from inside and Tierra opens the door, black hair pulled back into a tight ponytail, carefully put together in her gray maid's uniform. She looks me up and down, confused.

Then I get confused, because when I look past her, in the empty space between the doorjamb and her flank, I see someone lying in the bed.

Why is she cleaning the room with someone still in there?

Then I notice the trail of crimson blood spilling down the white sheet.

"Is everything okay?" Tierra asks.

Blood. Definitely blood. And Tierra is standing there like her biggest concern is that I'm distracting her from whatever she's listening to on the buds crammed in her ears.

"Everything okay with you?" I ask.

She looks around and shrugs, eyes sliding right off the body, then turns back to the room, wiping down the dresser with a rag. She leaves the door open, so I step in after her, navigating around her pushcart of cleaning supplies.

Yeah. There is a dead body in the bed.

And it's the guy. The leather daddy from the lobby.

"Can I help you?" Tierra asks, getting annoyed.

It takes me a second. "Guest says they lost an earring in here. Have you seen it?"

She knows I'm not accusing her, but still she gets a little steamy, her Jamaican accent coming on stronger. "I found a phone charger in 470. And a wallet in 312, but I took that right down to the front desk."

"Okay." I pretend to poke around, like maybe she overlooked it, which annoys her too, but it allows me to get closer to the body.

The image is hard to process. The bed is clearly made and the guy is sprawled out on top of the sheets, staring at the ceiling, blood having seeped from a dark gash in his neck. But it's a bright, crimson red, a fresh kill, so it should still be oozing.

This must be a slip. I'm seeing a future moment. He's probably still in the hotel.

Which raises a fun ethical question. The rules of time travel are rooted in the idea that we cannot and should not interfere with anything that's already happened, lest we mess with the timestream, which could cause ripples and fluctuations that would be dangerous to the fabric of reality. But there's no rule for interfering with something that hasn't happened yet. In part because we haven't cracked future travel, at least not beyond the occasional semischizophrenic mind trip. And according to the block model, any change I make to the future is one I've already made anyway, right?

Which raises a lot of disconcerting questions about free will and determination, but I'll leave those to the guys wearing leather patches on their elbows. I'm just here for a good time.

And I may be a miserable bitch, but I'm not going to do nothing.

"I'm about finished in here," Tierra says. "If I find the earring I'll bring it down."

"Great," I tell her. "Thank you."

I leave and make my way down the hallway to my room, and when we're out of earshot I ask Ruby, "Where's the guy? The one I asked you to follow."

"Still searching."

"You don't have eyes on him?"

"There . . . appears to be some kind of interference."

"Find him, now. If he goes near an elevator or stairwell to this wing, lock him out."

"Why the sudden interest?"

"Do what I told you to."

Baby dinosaurs and a soon-to-be-dead body and grounded flights and the summit. A recipe like that usually calls for the addition of tequila, so it bums me out that I don't drink anymore.

I need a million more gallons of coffee. I need another Retronim.

I'm a little on edge when I step into 508, so I survey my room, just to be sure it's the way I left it. I usually take stock before I leave in the morning—a good mental exercise to keep me situated—and find everything as I left it.

There's a fresh pile of towels and toiletries stacked just inside the door, thanks to Tierra. The towel I used after I showered is still hanging from the door. My toothbrush is lying across the drinking glass sitting on the edge of the sink. The bed is unmade, because what is the point in making a bed if you're just going to get into it again? The shades are drawn and the small armchair in the corner is sitting on the hem of the curtains, so they don't accidentally get undrawn. The pile of dirty clothes in the corner is roughly the same size, my favorite red hoodie still in a crumple at the top of it. Stuck in the frame of the bathroom mirror is the worn, weathered postcard showing the Georges Seurat painting A *Sunday Afternoon on the Island of La Grande Jatte*.

And like I do every time I enter the room, I cross over and touch it. Just to remind myself it's there, and to ask myself the question I still don't have the answer to.

What are all those people crowded on the bank of the water looking at?

Ruby asks, "What did you see?"

I jump a little. The damn thing is so quiet it's easy to forget it's there. I take the fresh bottle of pills out of my pocket and set it on the corner of the sink. "Nothing."

It knows I'm lying. It can track my pulse, intonation, phrasing. Every single indicator it took me a lifetime to learn so I could tell a truth from a lie, it has built into an algorithm.

Not that it matters. One of Ruby's jobs, which I didn't mention to Nik, was to report back to TEA Medical if I reached the second stage of being Unstuck. But when I was upgrading the voice, I managed to make it so it won't tell anyone anything I didn't give prior approval for.

In the process, somehow, I made it lazy and sometimes annoying.

"Charge," I tell it.

It floats down to its station next to the TV, and I toss my wallet and phone onto the bed, then replace the torn jeans with some dark slacks, and exchange the sneakers for a pair of boots I can run in. In the bathroom I throw on some mascara, then consider doing something with my hair, but find I don't have the energy. I run my fingers through it to work out the bigger knots, but in the end pull on a wide-brimmed boho hat.

I stick my knife into my boot. A black lockback that can still remove a fingerprint ten years later. Then I readjust my watches: on the left wrist, my security watch, which gives me swipe access to every door in this place. On my right wrist, the silver and black chronograph watch I got for graduating from the TEA. This one I rotate so the face is on the inside of my wrist.

So you never forget the importance of time, the proctor said to me, his voice heavy with sincerity, as he handed it to me along with my diploma.

Yeah, until you forget to replace the battery, I said, and he did not laugh at my funny joke.

I load the pockets of my blazer with cherry lollipops out of the plastic industrial bin under the desk, then hear a faint rattle in the bathroom. It takes me a second to figure out what it is: the pill bottle.

It's still sitting on the corner of the sink, where I put it.

I must have heard the sound of putting it down a few moments ago.

Part of being this far Unstuck is that sounds will sometimes be out of sync, or I'll catch random snippets of conversation in empty rooms, shortly before or after they happen. I've gotten used to it, but it's proof I'm slipping today a lot more than usual. Plus the weirdness with the body.

I haven't taken my pill today. That must be it. I pop one and slide another into my breast pocket. I can have up to three in a day, right? I add a third, just in case.

Then I check myself in the mirror and decide I look presentable enough to meet my low standards. Now I need to find leather daddy. A murder might mess with proceedings. I'll get myself pretty later.

I open the door and see movement down the hallway.

The wings curve slightly, so you can't see the ends of the halls. A cool effect from a design standpoint, an absolute nightmare from a security perspective. There's a figure all the way at the end of the viewable space, peeking around the bend. It takes me a moment to figure out what it is.

A girl, I think, long dark hair obscuring her face. She's wearing a green shirt and dark jeans and battered sneakers, which seem slightly out of step with the hotel's fashion trends. My heart stutters in my chest, because there is nothing on this green earth creepier than a little girl with dark hair hanging in her face. But the fear is quickly replaced by frustration.

I hate when parents let their kids run wild in this place, like we're a bunch of babysitters. I'm a goddamn law enforcement official. I turn to Ruby and tell it to follow, then make my way down the hallway, ready to wrangle the kid and send them back to their room—with a stern talking-to for the parents.

Then I pass room 526, and I get the same toothache feeling.

Which . . . should not be happening.

The body should be gone. This was a stage one slip. The longest one I ever had lasted maybe a minute. It's been at least ten. I step closer to the door. Put my ear against it. Give it a knock. No one answers so I swipe my way into the room.

Motorcycle boots. Crimson blood. Limbs stretched out. Staring at the ceiling.

The body shouldn't still be there. And slips *move*. But as I lean down close to the body I see something I didn't notice before: a fat bead of blood suspended in midair, in the inch or so of space between his neck and the bedspread.

This isn't a slip. I'm not seeing a past or future event.

It looks like a moment frozen in time.

I've never seen anything like this before.

And that's a problem.

SCHRÖDINGER'S CORPSE

"January?"

I turn to Ruby, who is floating on the other side of the room. I forgot it was here.

"Why are we in an empty room?" it asks.

"So the room is empty?"

It makes a lazy loop around the perimeter, probably running an array of scans. I hold my breath, hoping it comes back with something, anything, but then it stops and says, "Is this a new way for you to mess with me? Because I don't quite understand it."

"Wait in the hallway."

"What?"

"I need a minute."

It hovers for another moment, then silently floats away. I close the door behind it and put my hands against the frame. Breathe deep. Can't tell Ruby. Can't tell anyone. Not until I figure out what this is.

I return to the bed and brush my fingers against the dead man's shoulder and meet no resistance. I push my hand in and it slides through, coming to a stop against the bedspread. But I can feel something around my hand. It reminds me of being in a pool, when the temperature of the water is so close to that of my skin, it's hard to tell it's there. Just the slightest bit of drag.

That's not much, but it's better than nothing.

It says to me this is not an outright hallucination.

So I can't interact with the body. Which means I can't go through his pockets to find something that will ID him. No markings on his neck. No visible scars. He's wearing long sleeves. It would have been nice to see his arms. But the sleeve on his right arm is pushed up a little, and there are tendrils of ink on the delicate skin on the inside of his wrist. Some green, a bit of purple. Maybe a petal? Something to add to Ruby's search algorithm to help narrow this down.

With my half-ass examination of the body done, I comb the room for anything around the bed or on the floor that might be useful, but considering the room was being serviced when I got here, and oh right, this is some weird quantum phenomenon, I don't get too upset when I end up with nothing.

So I sit back on the carpet, against the other bed. The man's face is tilted toward me, his eyes vacant, his mouth hanging open. I shuffle myself a little to the side so he's staring right at me. The toilet flushes, though the buzz in my brain tells me it's a slip.

"Who are you, dude?" I ask.

He doesn't answer.

Oh well. Could have saved me some trouble.

Ruby is hovering so close to the door when I open it that it startles me.

"What were you doing in there?" it asks.

"Working."

"It's my responsibility to say that your behavior is making it very clear you're hiding something from me, and . . ."

"You are a flying toaster. Save the commentary."

It doesn't respond. I hope I hurt its feelings. Does it have feelings? Should I program in some feelings so I can hurt them?

A project for another day.

Nik is where I left him, pinching and pulling at the schematic of the hotel. He doesn't notice when I enter the room, so I give it a second and clear my throat.

"We don't have toys like this at Einstein," he says, glancing over his shoulder. "I could play with this thing all day."

"Nothing beats walking the floors," I tell him. "Give you a feel for the space. Half hour to go until the first meeting downstairs. Go wander a bit, meet me there. I have some busywork to do."

He doesn't seem to pick up the chips and cracks in my voice, or else he does and doesn't want to say anything. "Sure thing, boss. Meet you downstairs."

I wait for the door to close behind him and turn to Ruby, back in its charger. "I don't want the following logged or recorded. That includes any and all searches. Got it? This is completely dark."

"Understood."

"Bring up the camera feeds. Every moment before and after I saw leather daddy at the coffee urn."

Ruby beeps and whirs, and the grid of tiny video feeds expands to six large ones, and they show the man's movements, with time stamps. He came into the hotel around the time I was meeting with Tamworth. Skulked around the lobby, trying to look relaxed about looking for someone, then went to get coffee. I watch myself cross in the corner of one of the videos, headed for Reg's office. I notice him but he doesn't notice me, until I'm out of his field of vision, and then he watches me very intently, until I close Reg's door behind me. Either my ass looked good in those jeans or he knew who I was. And those weren't my ass jeans.

From there he tosses the coffee cup in the trash, checks his phone, and leaves toward Atwood. I watch him from feed to feed, disappearing off one screen and appearing on another.

Until he doesn't appear.

He's just gone, when he should be showing up at the elevators. I wait, like maybe he bent to tie his shoe in a blind spot or something, but the video keeps going. He doesn't show up again, and there's no place in that hallway for him to disappear to. It's a bare tunnel from the lobby to the elevator bank.

"Ruby, what's wrong? Where did he go?"

A few seconds pass. "There appear to be issues with the time stamp. The numbers are jumping around. I'm trying to figure out how it affected the video recording. I'm . . . not sure."

Never a fun answer to get from an all-knowing machine.

"Has anything like this happened before?"

"We've lost single frames in the past due to time fluctuations, because of the way the data is encoded. But a few milliseconds at a time. Never for this long."

"You never told me that. Why have you never told me that?"

"Because it wasn't statistically relevant."

I put my hands flat on the hologram table and breathe deep, so as not to pick up the nearest thing and throw it. "It's relevant now. Run a diagnostic on the system. And run every feed for the past few weeks, to see if he appears on any of them. And I want you running facial recognition. I need an ID. Every database you have access to, and if that fails, break into the ones you don't. I noticed a tattoo on his forearm. Couldn't make the whole thing out, but it looked like flowers. See if that helps."

"That's a lot of processing. It's going to take time. And I can't promise I can hide all of that from the network."

"Then get started. Face the corner while you do it."

"Am I in a time-out?"

"Yes."

Ruby whirs indignantly and turns away, giving me a little privacy. I slump into a roller chair, glide to a computer terminal, and open an incognito browser. Something that won't log my searches. Ruby probably assumes I'm looking at porn, because that's usually what my incognito searches are for. Instead I look up Unstuck case studies. Play with keywords, looking for anything I can find about longest recorded slips. Thirty or forty clicks later, I can't find anyone who experienced a first-stage slip longer than two minutes.

Next up I search for slips along with references to frozen moments. I come up with nothing, but I'm not surprised about that either. I could talk it out with Ruby and see if its searches can do better, but what would be the point?

Because this is just confirming my worst fear. If I'm this far gone, someone—Danbridge most likely, but Tamworth has his eyes out too—will force me to leave the hotel. And medically speaking, they'd be right to do so.

Which means I can't tell anyone what I saw.

And I have to limit myself in how I figure this out, because the wrong question or search might ring a bell that ends with me on the curb, my bags packed, waiting for a cab.

No more Mena.

This hotel is the only place she knew me. I know that when I see her, I'm just reliving past moments. Conversations she had with me, maybe sometimes with someone else. Home movies in 3-D. But that recognition in her eyes, when it's there, it's enough to keep my heart beating a few moments longer.

To my right is a legal pad and a red pen. I slide it toward me and turn so I'm out of Ruby's field of vision, then jot down some notes.

> *John Doe enters hotel, 8:57*
> *Coffee urn, 9:23*
> *Disappears in Atwood hallway, 9:37*

It's not a lot. But I need to keep track of this and I can't trust Ruby to do it. I tear off the page, fold it tight, and shove it into my inside breast pocket, along with the pen. Pull out a cherry lollipop and put it in my mouth. The stick juts out the corner of my lips, and I grip it between two fingers, take it out, and blow. If I can't smoke at least I can satisfy the oral fixation.

"We should head downstairs," Ruby says. "I'll keep the searches going in the background."

"Yeah," I tell it, squaring my shoulders. "Let's dance."

Nik is waiting outside the Lovelace ballroom, walking and talking to a lithe woman in a flowing black burka who doesn't so much stride as float. I approach them and ask the woman, "You work for the prince?"

"Prince Mohammad al Khalid bin Saud," she says, in a way that is not terse, but still corrective.

The Crown Prince of Saudi Arabia, colloquially known as MKS. Trillionaire number one.

"My name is Eshe," she says. "And you are January Cole, the head of security."

"That is correct." I turn to Ruby. "Any other bidders or staff joining this shindig?"

"Nobody else responded," it says.

That's annoying. It would have been nice to get all four, or at least their reps, into the space now, but I already walked all the way down here, so, may as well get started. "Take the minutes and send them to everyone involved, as well as Danbridge and Senator Drucker, and file requests as needed," I tell Ruby. Then I turn to Eshe and Nik. "Let's head inside."

Nik opens the door to Lovelace, which is now a flurry of activity. The lights are on and there's a team of people setting up: tables, seating around the room, a podium, a large video screen, a hologram table in the center. Wires spill in every direction, like they were thrown down with little care for where they landed. I lead us to a corner where it seems like we'll be the least in the way.

"Once the room is set up," I tell Eshe, "you're welcome to check things out and let us know if you have any special requests or accommodations, which we will meet, if they are within reason. We're going to close all entrances to this level but one, and I'm going to have TEA agents stationed here until this is done. They'll be checking IDs, and roaming the hallway and ballroom. You will be responsible for providing a list of who is allowed down here. If someone wants to come down and they are not on the list, it's not happening. Nik, you'll run point on that."

Eshe remains silent.

"There will be a scanner set up and everyone will be required to come through it. Even your boss. You will be given access to my direct comms channel," I say, holding up my watch. "If you need me, buzz me. If you ask me a stupid question or wake me up, so help me god I will spend the rest of my life ruining yours. Don't make me regret being accessible. I want your attendance list by twenty-two-hundred tonight. Any questions?"

"How many guests are we permitted to have?" Eshe asks.

"Everyone gets ten names so we can keep things manageable. Obviously your name doesn't count since you're running point. You can come and go."

"We have more than ten," she says.

"Prioritize."

Her eyes narrow but she doesn't protest.

"Good talk," I say. "You're welcome to check out the room now."

She nods and glides away, scanning the room as she goes.

"Nik, remember that little spiel, because if you run into someone who needs to hear it, you can give it to them." I turn to Ruby. "Put those requests for a scanner and TEA agents to Danbridge. And when you send the notes out to everyone else, be sure to underscore when I want those names. Okay, dummy?"

Ruby gives a whir and says, "Done. Despite your incessant name-calling and your unending list of requests."

"That thing is pretty useful," Nik says. "You're awful hard on it."

"It's a machine. It doesn't have feelings."

"Right, but it takes effort to be mean," he says.

"I know it takes effort," I tell him. "It's how I get my exercise."

Snowflakes whip against the sliding glass doors of the hotel, loud enough that I can hear them. I pray the forecast is wrong and we only get a dusting, but with the way things are going, those doors will be completely buried in the next ten minutes. I know this because as much as I want things to be quiet in the lobby, they are very much not.

"The nearest hotel is forty-five minutes away. Do you see what it looks like outside? I want a room *here*."

The man making the racket is shorter than Reg, by a head and a half. And Reg has a good hundred pounds on him, only some of it fat. Still, he's practically genuflecting in fear. Besides being short, the crybaby is wearing a very sloppy suit for a rich guy. I have a theory about that: if a guy with money can't wear a suit that fits, then he has no one in his life who cares about him enough to provide an honest opinion. Which says an awful lot about his character.

"I told you, we are fully booked," Reg says, his palms out in a calm-down gesture.

The man makes an annoyed sound in his throat and walks up to a nice young couple who look like they pose for the stock photos that come with frames when you first buy them. "How much did you pay for your room? I'll triple it."

"Sir . . ." Reg says.

"Lord," I say, starting toward the scrum, but Nik puts his hand on my shoulder.

"Let me earn my keep."

He raises an eyebrow at me and smiles. He's eager to cut loose a little, and I think he's picked up on my general disdain for the clientele. So I put out my hand, give him the go-ahead. He gets between the man and the now-terrified couple. He speaks softly, but puts his hand on the man's shoulder to exert dominance.

If I can slide some stuff onto his plate, it'll make my buffet of bullshit a little easier to get down.

I head for the coffee urn, hoping someone has refilled it, but no, chaos continues to reign. I consider pushing the urn onto the floor so maybe someone will notice, but then I do the adult thing and look for someone to wave down and tell them. No one is looking in my direction.

"Ruby, put in a note for someone to refill this."

"Is there anything else you'd like me to do for you, master?" it asks.

"Drop the attitude. Find anything yet?"

"Not yet. And I won't if you keep giving me more to do. Is coffee a priority now?"

"Figure it out or I'm going to recycle you."

I head for the security office, so I can have a bit of quiet, and I can arrange time with the other bidders. But there's a high-pitched shriek from the Butler elevator bank, and a woman screams, "What *are* those things?"

Godfuckingdamnit I forgot about the dinosaurs.

"I thought I told you to keep an eye out," I tell Ruby. "How did you miss that?"

"I'm . . . not sure," it says.

Not comforting, but something we'll need to come back to.

I sprint for the elevators, glad I wore my running boots. Nik falls in alongside me, the two of us dodging people who want to see what's happening, or are trying to run away.

We find a bottle blonde in red fuck-me pumps on top of an empty luggage cart, clutching onto the railing like she's at risk of blowing away. A chicken-size velociraptor is nipping its tiny little jaws at her feet, and she's trying to keep away from it on the narrow surface without tipping the whole thing over.

For a trained security professional it is inappropriate to laugh, but I do anyway.

The scene becomes slightly funnier when I see her other half: a very large man with a pug-dog face, who is standing with his head in his hands, unable or, more likely, unwilling to act.

He sees us run up and points to the tiny, scaly beast. In a heavy Greek accent he yells, "Do something!"

Nik turns to me and whispers, "This might be weird, but that thing is actually kind of adorable."

"Ever cross a big one?" I ask.

"Nope."

"I did once. Breaking up a poaching ring. I'd show you the scar, but it'd involve me taking my pants off, and, kid, we are not there yet."

"What's the play?"

The woman kicks at the dinosaur and makes contact but doesn't do much damage. In the process she nearly tumbles off the cart, but manages to catch herself. The pug-faced man is now trudging toward us, waving his arms. "Will you please do something before she breaks her neck?"

I try to suppress the eye roll and fail. "Well, there should be three, so that's . . ."

There's a scream from the lobby.

"Number two," Nik says. "I got it. What are we doing with these things?"

Good question. We have a holding cell in the back of the security office, but I don't want them this close to the lobby. Can't put them downstairs in one of the meeting rooms because I'm sure someone will complain about storing dinosaurs so close to the trillionaires.

But the bunker underneath the hotel has a big heavy door and is just being used for storage. I relay that to Nik, tell him to grab his and meet me downstairs. Getting two down will make the third easier to deal with. Nik takes off for the lobby, and I move toward the luggage cart. The woman sees me coming and says, "Oh thank god, finally, doing your job."

The little dinosaur is still somewhat intently trying to eat this woman's foot—which, Nik was right, it's adorable to watch, like a kitten trying to eat a giraffe—but I want its eyes on me, so I clap my hands hard and yell, "Hey."

It turns. I can't be sure, but I think it is the same one who looked at me when I had my slip getting off the elevator. Same little weird tilt of the head, its beady eyes focused uncomfortably on mine. It lingers for a moment before charging. The thing is fast and my heart leaps into my throat, because even though it's small it's still a damn dinosaur. And it could probably take off a finger if I'm not careful, so I sidestep, let it dive past me. Figure I should be grabbing it from the rear, away from the end with the teeth.

I was hoping it would double back and focus on me, but it keeps going, straight toward the lobby, so I chase after it, yelling to Ruby, "Lockdown. All guests to rooms, all staff to offices."

The fire alarm goes off, filling the hallway with bursts of white light, and Ruby's voice comes in over the intercom, soft and calm.

All guests please proceed to your rooms. All staff please report to the nearest office with a secure door. We apologize for the inconvenience. This will be over shortly.

The message repeats a few times as I duck and dodge my way past scattering guests. And Brandon, who is standing off to the side, laughing his stoned ass off. The lobby is a bad place to do this; it was designed to be circular, to evoke the eternal nature of time, according to the woman who designed it. Really that means there isn't anywhere for me to corner the tiny lizard, so we're just going to run around in circles.

I catch a glimpse of Nik running into Atwood as the dinosaur I'm chasing makes a leap onto the concierge desk. Cameo is folded underneath it, which is impressive considering their height. The dinosaur turns in a circle, surveying the room, and gives a soft little screech. It's lost interest in me, so I stop, circle slowly, and as I'm trying to get behind it, it hops off and tears toward Atwood.

As I make it to the elevator bank I nearly trip over another dinosaur, and Nik nearly knocks me down, before taking off in the opposite direction.

"This is like a Benny Hill video," I yell over my shoulder.

"I don't get that reference," he yells back.

I watch as my dinosaur runs into an open elevator, and an old woman tears out screaming. I put a little effort into it and manage to make it to the doors just as they're closing, throwing my hand in as I fall to the floor.

And then realize my mistake.

The raptor clamps down on my pointer finger and I pull back, find it rimmed in blood. The wound isn't deep, and the adrenaline is doing a good job of keeping away the pain, but the damn thing has a taste for flesh now. I roll to my side, and kick at it as I try to get to a standing position. It lunges at me while I regain my footing, and I slam my back into the wall of the elevator, then step over and around the dinosaur. But before I can grab it, it wriggles away and heads back into the hall-way.

At least it runs away from the lobby. I can corner it at the end of the hall.

It seems like a good plan.

Except I see the open door coming up on the left, and pray that the dinosaur keeps going straight instead of veering off.

So, of course it veers off.

It crosses the threshold of the room and there's a scream from in-side, and when I turn the corner, I find the blonde from the luggage cart, who is now standing on the bed. She's barefoot, her pumps on the floor. Her paramour is nowhere to be seen. My guess is: behind the closed bathroom door. The dinosaur, at least, has finally stopped run-ning, and is now chewing on one of the woman's shoes.

"I think it has a shoe fetish," I say.

"That's a *Louboutin*," she hisses.

"Shut up," I whisper. She falls to her knees and goes silent, hugging a pillow like it's a shield.

The closet next to me is open, two terry-cloth bathrobes hanging from hooks on the inside. I move slow, careful not to draw the thing's attention, and pull one of the robes down, then crouch and move as close as I can. It finally stops tearing at the heel, which is all but ruined now, and looks up at me just as I throw the robe over it and smother it with my body.

It's strong, and it writhes hard beneath me, but it's trapped.

The pain in my finger is lighting up now. Need to get that looked at. I make sure I have a decent grip on the thing and turn to leave.

"I expect to be reimbursed for those shoes," the woman says.

"You're welcome," I tell her.

The bathroom door cracks open and the man peeks his head out.

"Is it over?" he asks.

"A third of the way, cowboy," I mutter, and I bring the jerking, screeching package down the hall. In the lobby I find Nik holding his dinosaur, his arms outstretched, as far away from his body as he can get them. The thing is snapping at the air, furious, but contained.

"Thought you said there were three," he says.

"Means we're not done. Let's stash these and . . ."

"So is this the kind of operation you're running around here?"

I turn to find a young white guy with big shoulders and an aggressive buzz cut, like his barber uses a hammer and chisel. He's holding the last raptor, one hand on its neck, the other on its leg. The animal is writhing, clearly in pain, and I am flooded with a mix of being very thankful and really annoyed. It's not like the thing is evil. It's just following its biological imperative.

"And who are you, exactly?"

"Grayson," he says. "I work for Vince Teller. Thanks for starting without us."

Vince Teller: real estate magnate, world-renowned racist asshole, and bidder number two.

I give Grayson a proper once-over. He's got a corn-fed Midwest farm boy face to go with the ten-dollar haircut, but he's wearing an expensive custom gray suit and a checked orange-and-white tie. And he's got that *I'm the toughest guy in the room* sneer unique to football players and Marines.

"You should have gotten here on time," I tell him. "Follow me."

We take a pathway to the lower level, then down another hall, to an unmarked room at the end. I hold the raptor tight to my chest and twist so I can press my watch against the keypad. It beeps and I push the door open, to where there's another door—this one large, gun-metal gray. I give the pad a swipe with my watch and the door slides up. White emergency lights flicker to life, revealing a spiral staircase leading down into darkness.

I put my dinosaur on the top step, the creature struggling to free itself from the robe. Nik lets his go gently to run in after it. Grayson tosses his in carelessly, and it bounces down a couple of steps. I hit the button to close the door before any of them can get their bearings and run back out. There's scratching and commotion from the other side, but otherwise, it's secure.

"What the hell was that about?" Grayson asks.

I look down at my hand. The bleeding isn't too bad and I consider sticking my finger in my mouth but I don't know where that dinosaur has been.

Grayson takes a step closer. "Are you going to answer my question?"

Nik puts a hand on his chest. "Calm down there, chief."

Grayson pushes his hand away. "I want to know what's going on right now."

Another fun detail: there's a bulge at his side that indicates he's carrying a firearm. Do not like that. "Dinosaur poaching is a big industry. But only ever eggs. Never seen someone get out with live ones." I turn to Nik. "What the hell is going on over at Einstein? They asleep on the job over there?"

"There is no way someone got through security with those things," Nik says.

"Well, someone did." I turn to Grayson. "Thanks for the assist."

He crosses his arms. "You're January?" He waves his hand around. "You're in charge of this place? I have to say, this is not the best first impression."

"Right, because I made three dinosaurs show up and wreak havoc," I tell him. "It was a welcome gift, specifically for you. You're not impressed?"

"Since you started without me, I will now formally request a list of every person staying in the hotel so we can vet them."

"How about you give me the name of the place you get your hair cut. I want to see if I can pull off that look."

He squints, confused. "I want to speak to your supervisor."

"Go ahead. Tell him I said hi."

Grayson turns and leaves, probably to go tell on me. Nik takes my hand and looks at it close. "You need to get that seen to."

"I just need a minute," I tell him.

"Okay," he says. "Sure. Take a minute. I got things covered."

We step into the hallway, where Ruby is waiting for us. "Call off the lockdown," I tell it.

It assures guests that the problem has been contained and they are welcome to move freely about the hotel, then to me says, "Would you like me to alert Tamworth about your injury?"

"Yeah, please," I tell it. "Just . . . need to take a breath."

Ruby floats stupidly as I step into the women's bathroom.

My footsteps echo off the hard gray-and-white surface. I glance under the stalls to make sure I'm alone, and head for the line of sinks, twist a knob to cold, and hold my finger underneath. Red coils of blood swirl down the drain. It stings, but once the wound is clean, I can get a good look at it. The little monster barely got me. A little bandage and I'll be fine.

I pump a big glob of soap into my hand and hear the toilet flush, which makes my heart stutter. I look into the mirror as the door of the stall directly behind me swings inward.

Out steps Mena.

She sees me and smiles.

That recognition. My insides catch fire.

"You look like you are having a day," she says, in her Brooklyn-by-way-of-Puerto-Rico accent.

Is this something she said to me, or to someone else? It was not an uncommon thing for her to say to me. I have a lot of days.

Her brown hair is long, down past her shoulders, and she has blond highlights, which means I can roughly place which version of Mena this is. Six months before she died.

Not that I know she's dead. Not right now, not in this moment.

Because, yes, this was her talking to me. I see it in her eyes, reflected in the bathroom mirror. That recognition that cuts to my core. I'm ready to throw my arms around her, to say the things I only said when we were alone, to beg her to hold me tight, so tight it hurts, but when I turn, the bathroom is empty again.

Just me and the bright lights and the sound of the water running in the sink.

I cross to the door and lock it, then sit on the floor with my back against it. Wrap my hands around my knees. There's soap on my hands. Now on my pants. I don't care. I just want to sit for a minute. Look at that stall door, still cracked open. She was just there and I feel like my chest is contracting and then . . .

. . . Mena interlaces her fingers with mine. She says: "This is the most important thing you will ever see."

The Art Institute of Chicago is almost impossibly crowded, people jostling for space, peering into the expanse of the painting hanging in front of us on the eggshell-colored wall. The horde makes me feel claustrophobic, but as I look into the painting, I feel them dropping away.

"*A Sunday Afternoon on the Island of La Grande Jatte*," she whispers into my ear, her breath so warm on my skin it sends a trickle of cold water down my spine. "Painted by Georges Seurat in the late 1800s. His most famous work. Dead at thirty-one."

It's a painting I know. One of those paintings I've seen before, I just didn't know the title or the artist. A verdant slope covered in people wearing fancy clothes, many of them holding umbrellas, looking to the left, out over the water. As the crowd shifts, Mena grips my hand and we step closer.

With each step, the image becomes more grainy. The green of the lawn, the blue of the water, the deep, deep shadows. They reveal themselves for what they are: an accumulation of dots.

"This is probably the most famous example of pointillism," Mena says, extending a long finger, tipped by a nude-painted nail, toward the center of the painting. "Pointillism is the contrast of tiny dots or small brushstrokes that, from far enough away, the brain processes as a single hue. The space in between all those little dots makes the picture more vivid. I think it's because you have to work harder for it."

We take another step and the breadth of the scene disappears into a collection of smaller parts.

"That's the great thing about the human brain." Mena snakes an arm around my waist, pulls me close. "It excels at taking all this chaotic information and smoothing it out, so you can comprehend the entire picture. But that makes it easy to forget the really beautiful thing."

Another step. The crowd closes in on us, people holding up phones and digital cameras, searching for the perfect angle, the best lighting. Leaning into their own shots to prove they were here.

"The beauty is in each individual dot," she says.

She pushes into me when she says this and the sharp bone of her hip presses against mine.

"Something so small, but so precious. Without it, the picture isn't whole. And that, *mi reina*, is the point. The majesty of life can be found only in the present moment." She doesn't take her eyes off the painting, but she lifts my hand to her mouth and kisses my knuckles, then takes my wrist and twists it, so both our hands are against her heart, and I can feel the *thump thump*. "Right here."

Her voice is like the purr of an animal that stalks its prey from the shadows of a forgotten jungle. Somehow that purr, and all the danger it suggests, makes me feel safe. An evolutionary trait.

"It's not how we're meant to see things," she says. "We spend too much time worrying about what's next, rather than what's happening in this moment. But I believe we should try."

A man steps in front of us, holding his phone nearly in my face. On the screen, the dots of the painting are rendered into pixels. It snaps me out of my gauzy trance, and Mena, noticing I'm about to smack the phone out of his hand, pulls me back, toward the refuge of empty space.

We stand there for a little while and watch. The crowd moving and shifting, as some people grow bored, or satisfied with their digital facsimiles, and new people come to take their places. I imagine what it must look like from above. The colors of their hair and hats, their heads like little dots. The pictures they must be creating. I want to tell Mena this but I'm afraid it'll make me sound maudlin.

"You're characteristically quiet," Mena says.

"It's a nice painting," I tell her.

"Eloquent as usual, too." She leans forward and presses her lips on the corner of my mouth. "Thank you for humoring me. I know you don't like crowds. Or traveling. Or much of anything, really."

I kiss her back, harder, in the center of her mouth, and taste cherries. "I love it. Now tell me why this painting is the most important thing I'll ever see."

Mena raises an eyebrow at me, offers a little half-smile. "Did I say that?"

I know this look. It doesn't mean I won't ask a million more times in the next week. She knows that I can't abide an unanswered question. She also knows she is the only person on the planet I will tolerate this from.

"I want you to think about one more thing," Mena says. She points to the painting again. "This is even more important. All those people, on that shore. Looking out over the water. What do you think they're looking at?"

For a moment I think she wants an answer. But then I realize it's another one of her kōans, so I let her have it and take her hand. Feel the smoothness of her skin against mine. Take that and let it consume me. I'll come back to the question later.

Later.

I look around the museum. The people. Mena in front of me.

This isn't now.

Now is the bathroom. I close my eyes. Concentrate.

As much as I want to surrender to this.

As much as I want to live in this moment forever . . .

. . . There's a knock at the door. Then a banging.

"January?"

It's Reg.

The sink is still running. The stall door still open. The tile cold and hard under me. I reach into my breast pocket and take out a Ret-ronim, toss it back, and dry-swallow. Close my eyes. Breathe in deep the reason I could never bear leaving this place.

I check myself in the mirror. Mostly to make sure I didn't cry like a big baby and puff out my eyes. And for once, something today breaks in my favor, because I did not.

Outside the door I find Reg with Nik, Ruby floating between them.

"You okay?" Reg asks, looking down at my hand.

"Peachy," I tell him. "What's up?"

"We got the guy," Nik says. "The guy who brought in the dinosaurs. Found video of them coming out of his room. He's in the security room."

"I said to put him there," says Reg, like he wants a pat on the head.

"Good." I point to Ruby. "And we are going to discuss this later."

It doesn't answer.

The holding room is generally empty, but for our purposes, someone dragged in two chairs and a small folding table. Seated at the table is a young Chinese man who is so handsome it looks like he could make an entire career talking old ladies out of their savings. He's wearing a shiny blue suit, his shaved head gleaming in the overhead light. He's also trying to put out cool-guy vibes, but it's not really working, because every muscle in his body is clenched.

I pull out the chair across from him, letting it screech across the floor. Ruby comes to rest by my right hand. I drum my fingers against the table, which is dumb because I tap hard on the bitten finger, and a sharp pain shoots down my arm. The man stares at me and at Ruby, then focuses on the wound on my hand. He's waiting for me to speak. He doesn't realize I have an intermediary.

"You were booked under the name Joe Chen," Ruby says. "A high-level forgery, and it was solid enough I didn't catch it. But your real name is Zhang Shou. You're thirty-two, a resident of Beijing, with three previous arrests for smuggling, but no convictions."

Shou blanches at first, but then he smiles. Whatever uneasiness he was feeling is covered up by the knowledge that he's good at skating.

"We'll get into the legalities of this whole thing in a few minutes," I tell him. "First I want to know: how the hell did you get three live dinosaurs out of the timeport and over into the hotel without anyone noticing?"

"What's your name?" he asks.

"What does it matter?"

He shrugs. "You know my name."

Great. I'm trying to interrogate and he wants to speed date. "January Cole," I tell him.

He nods sagely, like this tells him something about me. Then he leans back in the chair. "I want a lawyer."

"Ruby, are you recording?" I ask.

"No."

"Any recording or listening devices in here?"

"No."

"This is all off the record, Shou," I tell him, dropping my voice, try-ing to lull him into playing ball. "I just want to know how you did it. I don't give a shit about the rest. I've got a lot hanging over my head right now and I don't have time to play games. If there's a security hole I need to know about it."

He doesn't say anything.

But there's a little bead of sweat forming on his brow, and that's an opening.

"This isn't your first rodeo," I say. "If you've gotten off three times, you have deep pockets and good connections. Trust in that and tell me what I want to know."

"Lawyer."

I lean forward on the table. Consider putting my head down and taking a nap, because that's about all I can handle right now. Even with the little charge the Retronim is giving me, I'm exhausted. I need more coffee. I consider offering him some, maybe to loosen him up, when Ruby pipes in. "Your visa is expired."

His eyes go wide at that.

"Finally good for something," I say. "Okay, Shou. I could get you in a car and on the next plane to Beijing before your lawyer makes it out of whatever bathroom he's currently snorting coke in. So how about this. I won't make that call, and I'll let you have your lawyer, and you can play whatever games you want. But you're going to tell me how you got three live dinosaurs into my hotel."

"They weren't live," he says, the fight leaving him.

"What do you mean?"

"They were eggs." He holds up his hands, palms out. "They hatched."

"You mean to tell me you managed to smuggle three close-to-hatching eggs out of the . . . what period, Ruby?"

"Late Cretaceous."

"Out of the Late Cretaceous period, and you weren't smart enough to get some fresh ones? I've got to tell you, that's some sloppy work."

"I know the difference between eggs," he says. "These were fresh."

"Ruby, what's the incubation period on raptor eggs?"

"Four months."

"Clearly," I tell Shou, "you don't math good."

He shifts in his seat. "They were fresh when I picked them up fourteen hours ago. And then I brought them here. And I was taking a shower and came out and found them tearing up my room."

"So you let them out?"

"I was trying to get out of the room," he says. "But I panicked and they got past me."

"Nice," I tell him.

There's a knock at the door, and a sharp-faced man in a suit barges in. He looks at me like he wants to light me on fire. "Bracken Abrams," he says. Then to Shou, "Not another word until we're alone."

I put my hands up and stand, clear out of the room while the two of them huddle up. Truly and frankly I do not care. I mean, I do a little. My whole job used to revolve around chasing down pricks like that. But right now the hotel is my job and I have enough to worry about.

It's not surprising the first person I see when I step into the main security room is Allyn Danbridge.

And as per usual he looks like someone answering a casting call for the role of TEA director in a made-for-TV movie, the exact kind of buttoned-down WASP who plays great at a congressional hearing. His lean figure is wrapped in a government-gray suit, and he's clearly keeping up with his Pilates. Tight shoulders and strong back to accentuate his stupidly handsome face. It's been awhile since I've seen him, and his dark hair is showing a bit more gray. It's also getting long, so it's curling a little around his ears. His face is covered in stubble. I'd put his stress level just edging up on "coronary event."

But his eyes light up when he sees me.

"January," he says, and Tamworth appears at his side. Before I can say anything, the doctor has got my hand in his, examining the bite.

"Minor puncture wound," he says.

"Think I caught anything from them?"

"Probably not," he says, leading me to the darkened hologram table, and an open first aid kit. He disinfects the wound and bandages it so tight I can feel my pulse in my fingertip. He promises to follow up shortly. Allyn nods to him, then holds the door open for me.

The lobby is quieter than it was before, most guests having retreated to their rooms, or probably upstairs getting a drink. Grayson is standing at the edge of the room, talking to Reg, as well as an older woman with immaculate makeup and a black bob that looks like a helmet. Senator Drucker. As they talk they throw stray glances at me, so I figure I know who the subject of their conversation is.

"I think I figured it out," I say to Allyn.

"What's that?"

"You went to Boston U right? I looked it up, they have an exchange program in Germany. That's where you learned to speak the language?"

He laughs hard and deep at this. The running gag between us. He speaks fluent German, with no apparent Germanic ancestry, and I know he was born and raised in Wisconsin. For years I have been trying to figure out where he picked it up. For some reason, he has refused to tell me, and he gets a kick out of the fact that I can't let it go.

"Wrong again," he says. "So what did Shou say? How'd he get them in?"

"He insists they were fresh eggs and they hatched here."

"He must have misjudged."

"Must have," I say. "How's Mary?"

"Mary is at her sister's. Giving me some space while I handle all this."

"Hmm."

"What?"

"That all it is?"

He shrugs. "You know how it gets. Long hours. How are you doing?"

"I'm doing the best I can with a plate full of shit," I tell him.

"January, if I had any say in this . . ."

"I get it, I get it. Above your pay grade. Listen, I don't have a good feeling about this. There's a hole in the security somewhere. Whether it's here at the Paradox or over at Einstein. You have to postpone the summit. At least give me another day while we sort this out."

Because it kills me to admit it, but that meathead Grayson was more right than he knew. I'm losing my grip on this. Between the snow, a smuggler waltzing in here with three velociraptors, a corpse that shouldn't exist, and issues with our video surveillance, I'm getting some serious Hindenburg vibes.

I've got no idea what to do about any of it.

And if I told Allyn everything, maybe he'd listen, or maybe he'd get me fitted for a pretty new white jacket with arms that go all the way around.

He purses his lips and shakes his head. "Everyone is coming out, and the weather is complicating things. It's easier to hunker down here than it is to leave and come back. And of course everyone's time is more important than ours. I think they see it as a bonus. If word does get out, it's not like anyone is going to be able to make it out here to mess with the proceedings."

"Snow supposed to be that bad?"

"Three to four feet," he says. "We've got cleaning crews ready. We keep moving forward. How's Nik working out?"

"He's sharp."

Allyn comes to a stop and braces himself. "Okay, give me the rundown. I'm ready."

I lay out the basics, including the dinosaur chase, which earns a few chuckles, but not at my expense, which is why I don't feel compelled to pop him in the jaw. The way the hotel is filling up and how that's putting people on edge. I don't include the part about the body. But when I'm done he can see I'm holding something back. We have enough trust built up over the years that he lets me have it.

We'll see how long that lasts.

"So what are the next steps?" he asks.

"I'm hungry. I need to eat something. Then we need to figure out what to do with three dinosaurs, which is not the kind of question I ever thought I'd have to ask. Maybe we should . . ."

In the corner of my eye I spot Cameo, standing about ten feet away from us, staring at the clock in the center of the room. They're en-tranced and, it seems, slightly confused. Which sets off my alarm bells.

"Hold on a second," I tell Allyn. I walk over to Cameo and ask, "What's up?"

Without moving their eyes, they ask, "Is the clock supposed to be doing that?"

It takes a few seconds to figure out what's happening. But then I see it. The minute and second hands stuttering and whipping.

    12:32:22
    12:32:23
    12:30:44
    12:29:14
    12:33:09
    12:32:44

"Because I'll tell you something, darling," Cameo says. "I've been working next to that thing since this place opened, and I've gotten used to seeing a second slip here and there. But I'm sure I have never seen it do that."

EVENT SYMMETRY

"Is something wrong with the clock?" Nik asks.

The words jerk me out of a trance. There's a crowd of people standing around us, transfixed, all staring at the stuttering hands. The answer is, yes, something is wrong. That is very much not a normal thing. But I can't get the words out.

Allyn glances at his phone. "No reports of radiation spikes at Einstein."

"Probably just broken, like half the shit around here," Reg says.

I step away and head to the elevator bank of Atwood. This is getting weird, and I want to see if the body is still in 526, or if anything about it has changed. I can't think of anything else to do right now and I don't want to be in the lobby. Ruby floats behind me. "Stay here," I tell it. "Monitor things."

"Where are you going?"

"Bathroom."

"You just went to the bathroom."

"Do you need to track how often I use the bathroom?"

"For health reasons, yes."

I put up a finger. "That's gross. Now, stay." It floats there silently and I keep walking. When I reach the bank I hear a throat clear behind me. It's Brandon, a look on his face like he just walked in on his parents engaged in light bondage.

"That's an atomic clock," he says.

"Do you want a medal?" I ask.

He holds his hands up, turning them, like he's cradling what he wants to say, presenting it carefully. "Atomic clocks are regulated by the frequency of the electromagnetic radiation of the quantum transition of atoms."

"I'm impressed you know so many big words, but also, no shit."

Brandon steps closer. "So you know these clocks are insanely accurate. Like, with a quartz clock, the crystals can vary slightly in their frequency, because of temperature or manufacturing"—he holds up a finger—"but every single cesium atom in the entire universe resonates at the exact same frequency. If the frequency is changing that drastically, something is doing it. We know flights are grounded. Why do flights at an airport get grounded?"

He's right. Whatever Allyn's reports are telling him, the odds that timeline radiation *isn't* to blame here are roughly equal to me getting through the day without punching someone in the face. It's going to happen.

"There's a storm coming," I say. "Why are you telling me this?"

"Because all anyone cares about right now is this meeting. They're all so focused on the messaging and on getting what they want, they're ignoring the obvious. It's like a mini-Chernobyl."

I wasn't expecting this deep a conversation with our resident stoner porter, and it must show, because he gives a shy half-smile and says, "I know I may not seem like the best resource, but I do have a degree in particle physics."

"And you're working here?"

He shrugs. "The market sucks and entry-level jobs pay shit. Between this and my side hustle I make better money."

"Fair enough," I tell him, pressing the button for the elevator, which lights up blue under my fingertip. "Get back to work. I have to check something."

As I'm about to step inside, Ruby buzzes me on my watch. "I hope you're done because we could use you over here."

And the lobby is back to being absolute lunacy.

It's crowded with a large group of men in flowing tan robes and red-and-white checked shemaghs, accompanied by burly men in expensive suits. I catch snippets of conversations in Arabic. It takes me a minute to find Eshe, who is silently standing by the concierge desk, hands clasped in front of her. She's listening to Grayson and Senator Drucker. Cameo and Reg are there too, and they both look like they wish they could climb onto a rocket and blast themselves into the sun.

Ruby appears next to me.

"There aren't enough superluxury rooms to go around," it says. "The prince's party was checked in and Vince Teller was locked out and downgraded."

"How did that happen?"

"Simple human error. But there also seem to be some anomalies within our system at the moment."

"Is that why you can't seem to accomplish a single thing I ask you?"

"January, this is serious."

There are voices on the rise across the way from us and I point toward the ruckus. "That's serious. But we'll come back to this once I get it settled."

I spot Grayson's dumb haircut peeking above the scrum. ". . . unacceptable," he's saying to Reg and Cameo. "You can't set aside a superluxury room for . . ." He looks at MKS's entourage, and seems to have a couple of words in mind to describe them. Then he looks at Eshe standing so close, and cools. "You can't set aside that kind of room for staff and then leave my boss in an inferior room."

"Surely there must be some kind of compromise we can make here," Drucker says, her voice with that little bit of gravel that comes from a lifetime of smoking. Her tone tells me her sense of compromise is: put Teller in the room he wants.

"Does it have a bed?" I ask, walking into the conversation. "What difference does it make?"

"This isn't something you need to have an opinion on," Grayson says, not hiding the eye roll that comes with hearing my voice.

"I don't give a damn what you think and frankly I'm a bit exhausted by you," I tell him, the words gushing out of me like water broken free from a dam. "You and your boss should stop being such crybabies about this and . . ."

"January," Reg says.

"What?"

"This is Senator Drucker." Like, *cool it, sis, not around the fuzz.*

Drucker smiles, a little too smartly for my taste. Like her presence is going to impress me so much that I will suddenly toe the line. I give her a big smile back and ask, "Cool. Do you have a problem with your room, too?"

Drucker nods, deciding everything she needs to know about me in that moment. Reg presses his hand into his face. Cameo betrays a hint of a smile, and seems to want to give me a high five. This is why I tend to like Cameo.

"Senator, this is January Cole, our head of security," Reg says. "She'll be point for the conference."

Drucker does not offer her hand. "Very nice to make your acquaintance. I assume you're already monitoring all ingoing and outgoing calls and texts from staff? It doesn't help us if someone tips the press off to this."

"I am not," I tell her. "And I have no intention to. I like to think in terms of reasonable requests and unreasonable requests. Metal detectors and extra staffing? Sure. A full-throttle reenactment of *1984*? Not so much."

Allyn appears. His deepest fear is written all over his face: *I'm talking to someone important without a chaperone.* "Senator Drucker," he says, "I see you met January . . ."

"Yes, she was just telling me that she's not monitoring staff communication, which I believe we discussed, what, three weeks ago?"

That rings a bell. I turn to Allyn. "I do remember you bringing that up now. What was my response? Abso-fucking-lutely not." Back to Drucker. "I assume he passed on the message."

Drucker makes a thin line with her mouth, pulls her phone out of her pocket, and taps away at the face. "Luckily, some of us are prepared. My office will monitor all messages . . ."

"Ruby," I say. "Send a memo to the entire staff letting them know that they're being monitored for the duration of this."

Drucker doesn't look happy about that, but she swallows whatever she's going to say. "Fine."

She pulls Allyn aside and leads him away, and just before Allyn turns I catch a look on his face that tells me I will pay for this later. I turn back to Grayson. "So where were we? We're going to make this hard?"

"It doesn't have to be hard as long as my boss gets the room he was promised."

"This," I say, waving my hands widely around the lobby, "all this bullshit, we call it 'extenuating circumstances.'"

"Look, okay, I get it, Teller is who he is, and I'm sure your"—he looks in Cameo's direction and spits the word *staff*, then gives it a beat before continuing—"is delighted to make him feel unwelcome. But I promise you, he's not a guy you want to mess around with. Especially since he's got this place in his pocket."

What if I just kicked Grayson in the nuts and let them take me off this assignment? Allyn could handle it with Nik, I could spend the next two days in my room watching movies and getting off and ordering room service. No more dinosaurs, no more corpses, no more imploding reality. Let someone else worry about it.

That seems like it's worth seeing him collapse in a groaning heap on the floor.

I take a step forward when I hear, "Perhaps I can help."

We all turn to the voice: an older Black man in a gray suit with a light purple checkerboard pattern. Floral purple tie, purple pocket square, brown leather shoes. A nice, but not extravagant, watch. Very sharp, very simple. He's carrying years in his face and in his voice, but I'm not sure if it's confidence or time. It takes me a second to place him.

Osgood Davis, tech and data investor, and bidder number three.

He doesn't have an entourage, which is both surprising and a little refreshing. I'm tired of dealing with lackeys. He reaches his hand for mine. His grip is warm and comfortable, and I can see at least one ingredient of his success—he's one of those people who smiles at you like he's known you for years. "Osgood Davis. You can call me Oz. You must be the head of security. Miss . . . Coral?"

"Cole, but close enough. I respect the effort," I say, returning the shake and feeling a firm grip.

He snaps his fingers. "My apologies. Been a lot to brush up on, and the old noggin"—he taps his head and laughs—"not what it used to be. So I've got one of those fancy-pants supermega, high-end, whatever-you-want-to-call-them rooms. How about I move on down to a smaller room, and Teller can have mine."

No one speaks. We're all waiting to hear what he wants in return, but he just folds his hands behind his back.

"Frankly it feels a little too big for me. Myself"—he touches the breast of his suit, his fingers rustling the pocket square—"I like to feel a little cozy. Now would that be amenable?" He looks at Grayson, and he says it kindly, but also firmly, so even though it sounds like a question, I'm not sure that it is.

"Yeah," Grayson says. "Yeah, it would be."

Davis smiles and waits for the thank-you that he knows isn't coming. Grayson turns around and walks away. Eshe leaves too. A woman of few words. I like people who don't talk too much, but people who don't talk at all, that's proving to be a little complicated as well.

"I heard you held a meeting without me," Davis says.

"We waited, but . . ."

He puts his hand up. "Not an admonishment." He nods to Reg and Cameo and leads me away from the group, toward a quiet corner of the lobby. Ruby follows, and Davis notices, but doesn't seem to mind. "Did I miss anything important?"

I run him through the notes, which he should have gotten, but still. When I'm done I ask him if he has any questions.

"Funny thing," he says, looking back toward the main desk.

"What's that?" I ask.

"They don't care about the rooms. It's all about who got the biggest toy."

"And you're not competitive at all, I bet."

He nods and rubs his hands together. "Maybe I'm above the fray because I already know I'm going to win."

I snort-laugh at the bravado, and he holds a finger up, though he doesn't look upset. "I didn't get to the funny thing yet."

God, this is frustrating. I'm actually starting to like him. "Oh really?"

"Did you know a few weeks ago, down in New York City, Teller and Smith and the prince all got together at the Waldorf for dinner? Private room, catering, lobster tails and caviar, the whole nine."

"Not you?"

He shakes his head. "I wasn't able to attend. But that's not the point. In private they get together and wine and dine each other, but as soon as they get in front of a crowd, it's a blood sport."

"That's what it's starting to feel like, yeah."

"Anyway, I won't take any more of your time," Davis says, giving me another shake. "Let me know if there's anything you need from me, or anything I can do to be helpful. I suspect this is going to be an interesting few days."

"Yes. That it will be."

"And thanks for all your hard work."

It stuns me a little, just to be thanked, so I have to push out a "you're welcome" before he walks away.

Yeah, I know he was working me. But at least he knows what a normal human being sounds like.

Okay. The lobby is still packed, but temperatures have cooled. Grayson and Eshe have gone, Allyn is glancing in my direction while talking to Drucker, but the look he gives me is a little softer. Nik is nowhere to be seen, but I suspect Allyn has him on something. We're getting to all-hands-on-deck, and I expect the boss man will now be here for the duration.

I'm actually thankful for that. It gives me a little space to work.

So, what next?

I need to have a serious talk with Ruby, away from distractions. But I've also touched base with at least a rep for each bidder, except for one.

"Ruby, has Kolten Smith or someone from Axon arrived yet?"

"He is currently in Fairbanks's office."

"Perfect," I tell it. "Then that's where we're headed."

The lobby of the Paradox is misleading. It doesn't give you a true sense of the place. All the smooth lines and gentle curves, the way all the shops and amenities dotted along the walkways seem to spiral toward the cathedral ceiling. Go beyond those and there are branching pathways and alcoves and hidden hallways. Easy enough to navigate, now that I've been here, what, six years? But a few times a week we have a guest head for their room and end up back at Einstein.

My favorite part of the hotel has always been the office of Melody Fairbanks.

Fairbanks designed the Paradox, from the font of the logo to the dreadful carpet underfoot. And through the entirety of the construction, she maintained an office on the second floor, down a hallway and past the gift shop, near some restrooms that no one ever seems to use. It wasn't behind a door—it was a drafting table and a desk out in the open, so she could be accessible. As the story goes.

She disappeared shortly after the hotel opened. No one knows why. Some think it's because she considered it her greatest achievement, so she hung up her hat and left for some remote beach to live out her days. Others say she went nuts, that the weight of her career finally caught up with her.

A few people have said they've seen a woman who resembles her roaming the hallways at night. Which any other day I would call bullshit, but I see my dead girlfriend in the bathroom, so who am I to talk?

Regardless, the office remains, preserved in amber, like maybe she might come back and it'll be ready for her. It sits on a platform now, tucked into a corner, and guests are allowed to wander around the space, to look at the hotel renderings on the drafting table, the paperwork on the desk, browse the books on the floating shelves along the wall. Flip through her notebook, the contents of which were used to write a book about her after she disappeared.

Some folks have tried to swipe souvenirs, so most things are bolted or glued down. Except the books on the shelves—design manuals and studies on physics and time travel classics. For some reason, no one ever seems to take the books. And while the spot is not exactly secluded, it's usually a quiet place to sit. So hopefully, once I'm done with Smith, I can sit down for a quiet confab with Ruby.

Because I don't like all this talk about anomalies and issues with the system. I know I'm giving it a lot to do, but it should be picking up on things faster. Even though Shou was checked in under an assumed name, it should have caught the forgery. Hell, it should have caught the dinosaurs the second they left his room.

But I wait to broach it, letting Ruby follow me up the ramp to the second floor, past the gift shop, which is now filled with people picking up food and supplies, like suddenly a little snow and a few delays and the world is ending. I take the final turn and the lights flicker again. I need to talk to facilities about this, and I consider paging Chris but then get distracted by a gap, like a missing tooth, in the row of books. Guess someone finally got brave.

Kolten is perusing the shelf, hands clasped behind his back, slowly contemplating the spines. He's wearing an AC/DC T-shirt—that's a hell of a deep cut—along with tight jeans and sandals. He looks less like he wants to buy this place and more like he wants to play hacky sack on the quad.

It's easy enough to pick him out with the amount of time he's spent on TV lately, serenely avoiding questions in congressional hearings about Axon's data collection methods. But I've only ever seen him sitting at a table. Standing, he looks like a bird of prey. All long limbs and gawky gait. I wonder if he pulled the book off, but he's not holding anything, and there's not one sitting nearby.

He's not alone either. He's accompanied by a white dudebro in a checkered blazer who recently lost interest in running but gained interest in beer. His tucked-in shirt is straining against his gut, but he carries it well. He sees me and barrels over.

"You must be January," he says, his diction so precise it feels practiced. "I'm Warwick Smith, COO of Axon." Kolten hasn't moved from where he was standing on the office platform, and even though it's only a step, it feels like he's looking down from above us. "I'll leave the two of you to talk," Warwick says, glancing between us.

Kolten descends from the platform, coming down to my level. As he gets closer I notice the mala beads on his left wrist, small little spheres of sandalwood. Buddhist, for concentrating on meditation and mantras.

Mena had a bracelet like that, though she never wore it. She got it as a gift. Turns out she thought the practice of meditation was cheapened by something that could be bought in a gift shop. So they lived on the doorknob of our room, on the inside, so she could touch it every morning on the way out the door.

I appreciated the effort she put in, placing it somewhere special.

Still, I got better at giving gifts after that.

Kolten looks at me like he knew I was coming. He puts his hands together in a prayer gesture and bows slightly. "Miss Cole," he says. "Namaste."

I choke back a laugh. He gestures toward the desk. Behind it is a roller chair—Melody's—and in front of it is a wooden chair for guests. "Would you like to sit?" he asks.

Before I can tell him that, no, I am not sitting in the guest seat at my own hotel, he circles the desk, offering me the roller chair. And my feet are a little tired, so I go to the chair and put them up, kicking against the pen cup, which stays in place. I get myself comfortable and lean back, the chair creaking.

"So?" I ask.

He nods solemnly, then notices Ruby floating over my shoulder, and says, "Suitcase four-six-nine-two."

Ruby comes to a soft landing on the desk and powers down, the constant hum of its innards going silent. A lump rises in my throat but I try to hide it from my face, though I'm sure I do a terrible job.

"What did you do?" I ask.

He shrugs. "Turned it off."

"Why did you turn it off?"

"I don't like being recorded."

"Says the guy whose whole stock and trade is recording people's entire lives," I tell him. "I guess the better question is, how did you turn it off?"

He points at the silent drone. "I own the company that developed them. I have a back door. And for what it's worth that command only works for my voice." He laughs. "Wow, that is creepy, isn't it? I'm sorry. I feel like I am setting a bad tone. Look, the reality is, the reason I wanted to see you is because I'd like to offer you a job."

It takes me a minute to figure out how to respond to that. I settle on "This is weird."

"I have a campus in San Francisco," he says. "I'm not a huge fan of the man running security right now. He's not . . ." He folds his hands again and looks up at the ceiling, like there's an answer written on it. "Efficient. And I hear good things about you. I checked into your background. A celebrated TEA agent. That's an elite agency."

"Have you seen the jokers working at Einstein?" I ask.

"You were in the stream," he says. "You busted more than a dozen major smuggling operations. And I know about the assassination attempt you thwarted."

Another lump. This one I nearly choke on, because that was top-level classified. "I don't know what you're talking about," I tell him.

He smiles, satisfied to see he's right. "Point is, I'd like to offer you this job, because I think you'd be good at it. It would be five times your current salary, plus benefits, stock options, housing, moving costs, everything. Top medical care."

That last bit hangs in the air, deliberate, bold. Glaring.

"Why would I need top medical care?"

He doesn't speak for a few moments. Then he says, "Your condition."

"My condition."

"I own a biotech company that's doing promising research into being Unstuck," he says. "We can't cure it. Not yet. But we can slow the progress. We're currently testing an improved version of Retronim. And there are some holistic treatments that I hear are very effective."

"You know," I tell him, dropping my feet to the floor and putting my elbows on the desk, leaning close, which causes him to lean in, matching my posture. "First you screw with my pet. Then you make a bananas job offer to someone you haven't said more than a hundred words to. Then you tell me you know my personal and private medical history. And the worst part is, I know it's not over, because there's a 'but' coming, isn't there? What do you want in return for your remarkable generosity?"

He shuffles in the seat. Brings his leg up to cross over his opposite knee. Folds his hands. Looks at everything around us except for me.

"Yeah," I tell him. "There it is."

"The room."

"What room?"

He tilts his head a little, reading my response, like he's trying to decide whether he believes me.

"I know about the ghosts," he says.

"People think the hotel is haunted." I shrug. "So what? People think every hotel is haunted. It's how hotels work. They're creepy. Sound carries."

"What do you believe?"

"I'm a nihilist. I don't believe in anything."

Kolten nods and smiles. "Let me tell you a story."

"Oh god."

He sits back in his chair and says, "When this hotel was being planned out, they picked Fairbanks for two reasons. One was, she really did have a very good design sense." He glances around him. "The blue aside. It should have been red. Like the old TWA Hotel. Anyway, she was also a woman. And the federal government knew that naming the timeport after Einstein instead of Dorothy Simms was a misstep."

"Damn straight," I say.

He nods. "Did you know Simms spent a lot of time here during the construction?"

"I hear she was around a lot while they were building Einstein, yeah."

"Yes, but," he says. "She also worked closely with Fairbanks. The two of them collaborated on the design of the hotel. Unofficially. And I guess the prevailing attitude is that the two of them were acquaintances. But I think it's more than that. I think Simms was weighing in on the actual construction. I think she was helping. And not picking out décor. She was doing something inside the hotel. I don't think those ghosts are a coincidence. I think they're a sign of something."

"Of what?"

"I don't know. But based on some research I've done, I believe there's an unmapped room in this hotel. And I feel like if anyone is going to know about it . . ." He waves his hands toward me.

I sigh, hard, just in case there's any question about how I feel here. "I do know every inch of this place. And I would know if there was a secret room."

He sits up in the seat and looks around, making sure we're alone, then tugs at the mala beads on his wrist. "Had you applied for the job I would have given you serious consideration anyway. It's not like . . ." He trails off.

"You can say 'quid pro quo,'" I tell him.

"It's not that," he says. "But if you can get me into that room, if you can get me access to internal documents on the hotel—maybe the original print schematics . . ."

"Like you haven't gotten access to that stuff already. You knew my medical history."

He gets up, looks at the books, paces the platform. "There's a crucial piece of information here that's missing. Something that'll make the whole thing fall into place. I'm asking you to help me find it."

"Why?"

He stops, turns to me. "Why?"

"That's right, why? Why do you want this place? Why does anyone want this place, if it's a money-losing operation?"

Kolten gives a pained little smile. "It's not always about the money."

"Yes it is," I tell him. "And don't you dare tell me it isn't. I don't give a shit how much you give to charity. I don't give a fuck about your education programs, or all this gobbledy-gook about changing the world. It all comes down to money for you people. I spent years chasing down assholes like you who thought the rules didn't apply to them. Why would you be doing it otherwise?"

Kolten sits back heavily in the chair. "Because the planet is dying."

Well, yeah. We'd long since accepted that we couldn't turn back the thermostat. We broke off the knob by not taking appropriate action decades ago, when it would have counted. And now populations are shifting away from the equator and toward the poles. Florida is under three feet of water and New Orleans is a modern-day Atlantis. At this point we're the frog in the boiling pot of water. No one's doing anything about it, just adapting the best they can.

Tomorrow, they say. We'll get to it tomorrow.

"And?" I ask.

"The prevailing science says we've got, what, two generations left? And the Mars resettlement plan is not going well. This hasn't been publicized, but the radiation shielding on the habitats isn't working the way it's supposed to. So where does that leave us? Stuck on a dying planet? No. So many of my predecessors . . ." He pauses. "Contemporaries? Whatever." He waves the word away. "They were so concerned about getting off the planet. But what if we could *fix* the planet?"

"You're going to make me say it, aren't you?"

"Say what?"

"The TEA has one and only one goddamn rule related to time travel . . ."

He gets up again, back to pacing. And as he does, his words tumble out, like he can barely keep up with them. "Yes, look, don't touch. I get it. But what if that's a mistake? What if we should be touching? What if there's a way to get us to invest in clean energy initiatives when it actually matters, decades ago?"

He stops. Closes his eyes and pinches the bridge of his nose.

"Warwick is going to kill me. I'm not supposed to be telling you this." He looks at me with sad puppy-dog eyes. *Please don't tell on me.*

I shrug at him. "And if you blow up the timestream in the process of saving the world, doesn't that sort of defeat the point?"

"That's just a theory," Kolten says. "The timestream adapts to little changes here and there. Just by standing in a room in the past we're altering things, because something is happening that hadn't happened. But people have been traveling in time for years now without any major repercussions."

"Yeah. Because we have rules. And people like me."

"But what's the point of a theory if no one is going to test it? These past few years have been the beta test. Isn't it worth finding out what kinds of changes it can bear if the end result is saving the human race?"

"Maybe you ought to book a trip back to the nineteen forties so you can hang out with Oppenheimer. I'm not a big history buff, which I know is probably a little funny, but I do recall he had a few regrets about playing god."

"The timestream is hardier than anyone thinks."

"Based on what?"

"I believe it to be."

I point over my shoulder. "I got a lot of grounded flights and a wonky clock in the lobby says different. And what makes you think the TEA is going to let you run roughshod over history?"

Kolten puts his hand on the desk and collects himself, thinking carefully over his next words. "The offer is on the table. The job. We can help you. And you can help me. Just think about it. And I trust this stays between us."

I shrug again, but don't say anything. I don't feel the need to give him the satisfaction.

He nods and gets up to leave.

"Hey," I call after him.

He turns, something like hope on his face.

"The new timeline design on Axon sucks," I tell him. "I can't figure out where to access my old photos. Also, fix my robot."

"Rave nine-nine-three-one," he says.

Ruby powers back up and it floats into the air, spinning around in fast little jerks, getting its bearings. Kolten disappears around a corner and Ruby says, "That was unsettling."

"How does a robot get unsettled?"

"By having someone verbally take command of programming infrastructure it didn't know it had. What did I miss?"

I explain the conversation I just had with Kolten, after which Ruby says, "His plan would be highly illegal and also very dangerous."

"Kinda my job to know that, bud."

"And I really do not think there is a secret room here. We would know about it."

"Correct," I say. "Now spill. You said something about anomalies. What is happening here?"

"One of the main tasks I have at the moment is determining the identity of the man in the lobby. You also asked me to conceal my searches, which makes them more difficult to perform. I have found, while conducting these searches, that there are . . . blocks in place. Something is preventing me from searching for him."

"What does that mean?"

"It means every time I try to perform a facial recognition search, the data doesn't transfer. It freezes."

Freezes. Do not like the sound of that.

"Let's forget who is he, for just a second," I say. "Focus on the video feeds. Go back a month. Maybe he came in, bought something, took out his wallet, and you can get a shot of his ID. Anything. Are you able to find out if he was here any time besides today?"

"Hold on," Ruby says. Then: "That's odd."

"What's odd? Don't hit me with odd right now."

"There's more video missing," it says. "In fact." It jerks from left to right, like it's looking around the room in confusion, even though the way it makes the googly eyes rattle is pretty funny. "A lot of video is missing. Our backup system is failing. It seems like we've been losing bits and pieces all day. Not just related to him. Going back historically.

There are suddenly big holes in our records. But randomized. Like they're . . . dissolving."

"And you've just been waiting until now to tell me this?"

"I didn't notice . . . whoever is in our system is tearing it apart and I can't even detect their presence."

"How do we stop it?"

"A shutdown and reboot will likely . . ."

"Do it."

"But we won't be able to recover any missing . . ."

"Do it!"

Ruby pauses and then says, "Done. I've altered the security structure just enough that they won't be able to regain immediate access. But now they know we're on to them. And if they got in once it's only a matter of time. I'll do the best I can to hold them off."

"What the fuck is happening?" I ask.

"Should I inform Danbridge?"

"No, I'll do it."

I lean back in the chair, try to center myself.

Things have been weird enough, but this is the first indication that someone is deliberately screwing with the summit. And the body? They have to be related. Times like this, I would talk about the problem with Ruby, but I'm not ready to show that card.

What do I have? Bits and pieces.

It could be any one of the four bidders messing with the proceedings. Could be all four in a shadow war with each other. The dinosaurs getting out of the room doesn't feel related, but it can probably get lumped in with the clock . . . if time is starting to stutter, maybe those were fresh eggs that just suddenly aged up?

Maybe it's not even one of the four bidders. The whole reason the summit got moved was the protests. Drucker seems intent on clamping down on leaks. Maybe someone caught wind of it, and it's an outside party.

Then there are the cameras. The way Kolten was able to take over

Ruby makes me think he has some familiarity with TEA tech, if not outright ownership of it.

There's only one thing I know for sure at this moment. We need to call this damn thing off. Too many variables. I can't keep the people here safe. There's already one dead body.

I think.

Can't wait to have this conversation with Allyn.

I glance down to Fairbanks's journal. It's open, and I wonder if Kolten had been reading it.

Much has been said about the nature of time, with endless analogies and metaphors trying to make it so we can understand it. I don't get caught up in all that. Call time a river or a stream or a path or an arrow. It's all the same to me. Whenever I hear someone try to explain it I go a little cross-eyed.

But while designing the Paradox, of course I read all I could about the nature of time.

One thing I kept coming back to was something Aristotle said, that time doesn't actually exist. Which, if you think about it, is true. We invented it. The universe does not consider the minute. Rather, he said time is like an empty container, into which events may be placed, and that container exists independently of the things inside it.

I like that. Time as a container. A container of things, like this hotel is a container of people. A container for the energy that we generate. Apparently this is called Reductionism with Respect to Time. The name is the only thing I don't like about it.

What's reductive about the events and the people that make up our lives?

There's a framed photo on the corner of the desk. A dozen people in fine clothes standing in front of a freshly dug hole, wearing gleaming silver hard hats, holding up golden shovels. Pretending they themselves were the ones who dug the hole, and not the laborers they shuffled to the side for the photo op.

Melody Fairbanks stands on the far left. A tall, busty white woman with a megawatt smile and silky brown hair that catches the sun. Dorothy Simms is to the right, cradled between two men who look like melting ice cream. A tall, lithe Black woman with a shaved head, who probably has a smile as brilliant as Fairbanks's, but hers isn't turned all the way up for the picture, and I suspect I know why.

The Einstein Intercentury Timeport should have been named after her.

The woman who actually invented time travel.

There's a flutter on the edge of my vision. A vaguely humanlike shape ducking out of view. I turn to look, at the empty expanse of hallway.

I'm alone. I know I'm alone. Not counting Ruby.

Kolten was right about the ghosts. I mean, the whole reason I'm here is so I can keep seeing my dead girlfriend, though it's not so much her ghost as it is flashes of her from previous moments in time.

But isn't that a kind of ghost?

"Picking up anything in the vicinity, Rubes?" I ask.

"Anything what?"

"Temperature fluctuations. Movement. Whatever."

A few whirs and a second of silence. Then: "No."

"Fine," I tell it. "Miles to go, as they say."

I give another look over my shoulder, wonder whether I need sleep or a drink or both, and head for the ramp that'll bring me back to the lobby. The room suddenly feels claustrophobic. I can't shake the feeling that there's something following me. Probably just the bad feeling. I'm on edge. Hypersensitive, probably picking up on the movement of people who've been through here recently.

The joys of being Unstuck.

Just as I'm feeling a little better, I see it again. Movement in my peripheral. I turn, and at the far end of the hall is the little girl, peeking around a corner. Again, my heart leaps into my throat. God, that kid is quiet. She's a little closer now.

I call out to her. "Still looking for the dinosaurs? They're locked up now, but if you don't get back to your parents I'm going to throw you in there with them."

The kid darts around a corner and disappears.

Now I'm annoyed. I run after her, but by the time I reach the corner, all I find is an empty hallway.

"Damn it," I say. "Ruby, send a note to Cameo. Tell them to find whichever family is staying here with a kid, and then tell me what room they're in, so I can go give them some shit."

"What do you mean?"

"The kid at the end of the hallway."

Ruby is silent for a moment. Maybe it's only a few seconds but it feels like about three hours, and then finally it says, "Didn't pick it up. Must be more camera issues."

I glance back down the hallway. Hoping the girl will peek her head back out.

Just to confirm I'm not losing my mind.

No such luck.

I head back for the lobby, wondering what fresh hell awaits me this time, and as if on cue, Grayson and his two-dollar buzz cut step out from around the corner.

He's wearing a different suit than he was earlier, and when he looks at me, he is somehow angrier than before. The light catches his silver tie clip as he pulls a gun from the inside of his jacket, points it at my head, and fires.

From the accompanying jolt in my brain, I know this is a slip.

I know this is a future moment.

I know he is not actually shooting me.

But he will. And I don't know when.

So it's not exactly a great comfort.

CONSERVATION OF SUFFERING

Allyn is alone, pacing outside Lovelace, tapping away at his phone. When he sees me approach he shoves the phone in his pocket and says, "We need to talk."

"We do, because . . ."

"What was that shit you pulled with Drucker?" he asks.

I shrug. "She was being an asshole."

"She's a senator. She's practically our boss. She could have either of us reassigned or fired with a phone call. I don't like this surveillance nonsense either, but we've got bigger things to worry about right now."

"That's right," I tell him. "We have to move the summit."

He runs his hands through his hair like he wants to pull it out. Given how long it's gotten, it ends up in disarray, like he just got out of bed. He says, "Not happening."

"Allyn, we've been compromised," I tell him. "Someone is in our system."

"What are you talking about?"

I point over my shoulder at Ruby, who says, "Someone broke into our video feeds and has been erasing data. I've locked them out for now but I don't know why they were doing it. The obvious theory is someone is trying to hide something."

Allyn exhales. "Okay, that's not great . . ."

"No, it's not," I tell him. "And I just had a conversation with Kolten Smith. You know why he wants this place? So he can go back in time and fix climate change. It sounds like a nice enough idea, except for, you know, the potential it has to destroy reality. Which I think underscores a larger point: you think any of these knuckleheads are here to play nice and follow the rules?"

"The TEA isn't going anywhere," he says. "That was made very clear before we even considered taking bids. We're still the enforcement arm of this place, and we will continue to operate under the authority of the federal government. I'm not worried about them screwing around with stuff."

· "You trust these guys? You trust Drucker? Because I sure as hell don't."

"No, I don't. But we don't exactly sit around all day with our thumbs up our asses. There are checks and balances in place."

"Like what? What if Drucker decides to replace you, or . . ."

Allyn puts his hand on my shoulder and locks me in a tight stare. "January, I need you to trust me on this. It's complicated, and . . . need-to-know. That's all I can say. But trust me, no one's going back and changing anything, okay? Our system is secure."

"You know I trust you. But how secure is secure, exactly? What do we do about the video feeds?"

He sighs. "I'll talk to Jim Henderson in digital ops. I'm sure someone is just playing dirty pool, which honestly, I expected. But until something turns up dead, it's not a priority." I must twitch a little at that because he narrows his eyes and hyperfocuses on me. "Unless there's something else you're not telling me?"

Yes.

"No," I say.

He sighs. "I'll talk to Jim."

We're at an impasse. It feels like he's holding something back too. I don't like the way we're standing, with some invisible thing between us.

"Teller and the prince are en route," he says. "I know it's hard, but try not to deliberately offend either of them. Please. I'm asking as your friend. Just toe the line for twenty-four hours. Hell, at this point I would take five minutes. Five minutes of good behavior."

I'm about to say something when he puts his hand on my shoulder.

"Jan, there are a lot of moving parts here," he says. "I'm doing my best and I'm still drowning. You being you doesn't help. So please, make my life a tiny bit easier."

I laugh. I can't help it. Because for some reason, the memory that comes back to me right now is being three weeks out on the job, me and Allyn junior agents, blowing off steam with some co-workers at a bar, and we ran into each other in the hallway, him going to the bathroom and me coming back. He gave me that look, the one every man wears when he's four beers into the night and he sees a woman by herself. He asked if I wanted to get another drink somewhere quiet. When I told him I was gay, I expected the same reaction you get whenever you're a woman who says you're into women—you become repulsive or you become a challenge. Allyn just smiled and apologized, and we carried on after that like it never happened.

Plus, he did save my ass back in 1945.

Allyn joins me in laughing, though he's not sure why. "What's so funny?"

"Nothing," I tell him. "Just, I know I can be a lot. You're a good friend."

"Shit, a compliment from January Cole? Am I dying?"

"I'll be good," I tell him, putting my hand on his arm. "C'mon. Let's go get yelled at by rich people."

"You go ahead," he says, holding up his phone. "Few more calls to make, and then we meet the last of the VIPs. And, January . . . thank you."

I pat him on the arm and head for the lobby, hoping my trust isn't misplaced.

The departure-arrival screen is lit up red. That's new. New things hap-pening all over. I do not like it.

QR3345—Ancient Egypt—CANCELED
RZ5902—Battle of Gettysburg—CANCELED
ZE5522—Triassic Period—CANCELED
HU0193—Renaissance—CANCELED

This isn't going to help the mood among the guests. It'll be a fun distraction from the rest of this nonsense, up to and including the fact that I've got a bullet marked for my brain. Which raises an interesting thought experiment: I had already considered the ramifications of keeping my John Doe out of death's path, back when I thought seeing his corpse was just a glimpse of the future.

But close as Grayson was standing, he'd have to have been half drunk and blind to not make that deposit directly into my dome. Of course, I don't want him to. But am I destined to die? If I dodge out of the way, take the gun, and feed it to him, will the universe course-correct, and then I'll fall in the tub the next day and break my neck?

Would saving my own tail risk damage to the timestream?

Would the safe and smart thing be to accept my death?

How does the look-don't-touch policy apply going forward instead of back?

Or does it even matter?

Time travel!

I hate to say it, but there's more important shit to worry about in this moment than the potential end of my life.

No sign of Teller or the prince, so I may as well check into the crowding issue. I go looking for Cameo, who I find ducking through the front doors of the hotel, not even caring enough about appearances to go out one of the service doors. I tell Ruby to wait and follow them.

It's cold outside, but not bitter. The snow is coming down hard, but the air is still, so the snow floats in lazy circles on its way to the ground. Narrow pathways are cut underneath the overhangs, the most trodden one leading over to the standing ashtray. The sky is a heavy blanket of gray, and the vista, which on a sunny day can be quite nice, is washed out. The circular drive is covered with snow, plowed a short time ago but already filling back up. The fields rolling away from the hotel are white curves that accentuate the squat gray buildings and flashing lights of Einstein in the distance.

Cameo is standing by the ashtray, tense against the cold, a cigarette clamped in their lips. They see me and give a pained little smile, then pluck the cigarette free, holding it up.

"You still quit?" they ask. "Or about ready for a relapse?"

I can feel the tug of it. That slavish devotion to smoking never goes away. Lucky for me I had the best kind of aversion therapy.

"Not enough nicotine in the world right now," I tell them. "What's the story indoors?"

"The story indoors is that the world is coming to an end," they say. "That is, if you ask any of our guests. Flights are officially canceled until further notice. Something is up. Not that anyone is telling us a damn thing. And now . . ." They wave the cigarette toward the drive.

There's one car headed away, slowly, navigating the snow. Another seems to have spun off a bit down the road, but not far enough they need help.

"Lots of people headed on the tram back to the timeport right now," Cameo says. "Get while the getting is good. But the closest airports are Rochester and Syracuse and those are both an hour with no snow or traffic." They take a deep drag, exhale a large plume of smoke. "Getting might not be good anymore. With all the Einstein staff on their way in, we're talking about cots."

My stomach drops. "Where?"

"I thought maybe the meeting rooms?"

"Well, we can't do the meeting rooms, because they're still setting up downstairs for this stupid summit."

"So where do you suggest we put them?"

"There are plenty of alcoves on the second or third floor accessible to bathrooms," I tell them. "And there's the gym."

"What if people want to use the gym?"

I sigh, fold my arms. "Well, thanks for ruining my day." It builds up in me, the pressure making my skin bulge, and then it comes out. "We're at DEFCON Level Holy Shit. You didn't think, Oh well maybe this isn't the best idea? C'mon."

I know I shouldn't be dropping this on Cameo, and there's a little voice in the back of my head—*stop, no, what are you doing*—but it's not as loud as the voice currently scorching my throat. Thirty seconds of serenity after my talk with Allyn and we're back to the damn churn.

"Excuse me." Their eyebrow is arched into a knife blade. "I did not ruin a thing. External forces are intruding and it's up to us to address them."

They flick the cigarette into a pile of snow, where the cherry sizzles and dies. "I get it, sweetie. You loved her. We loved her too. And sure, yours was a different kind of love. But it was all love nonetheless. We all feel the vacuum she left behind. Maybe instead of being such an asshole about it, you can remember that this is a thing we all share."

I know there are many right answers to this.

I'm sorry.

You're right.

Thank you.

My anger is misdirected and I'm taking things out on you that I shouldn't.

Instead I say, "This isn't about that."

"Everything you do and say is about that. And that, my love, is the problem."

I spin on my heel. "I have to find Reg so we can fluff a bunch of trillionaires. Oh, and Ruby was supposed to send you a note about this but there's some kid running around the hotel without their parents. Find out who they are. I don't need it getting eaten by a dinosaur."

"Hey."

I don't turn. I can't take any more of that knife-blade eyebrow. But over my shoulder I ask, "Yeah?"

"We're here. We're always here. But there's only so many times your hand can get batted away before you decide to stop offering it."

I consider telling them that if you don't need anybody, you can't lose anybody, but it's cold now, and I want to go back inside.

Reg is pacing outside his office, muttering to himself, and when he sees me approach he gives a very audible sigh of relief.

"Teller is on his way," he says.

"Where do we keep our red carpet?" I ask him, as Ruby rejoins me.

"We need to go welcome him."

"Did we welcome Kolten Smith? Do we have any plan to welcome the guy who is a literal prince? What's so special about Teller?"

Reg looks around to make sure we're alone. "I think he's the one who's going to take it."

"Who says that?"

"My gut."

"Reg, if you gut was any good you wouldn't come home from the track with empty pockets so often," I tell him. "Or spend so much time in the bathroom."

He grimaces. "I got a gluten thing."

"You got a nacho cheese and coffee thing."

He rolls his eyes at me, from somewhere between annoyed and embarrassed. "No one trusts Smith because he makes Zuckerberg look like Gandhi. Davis is a self-made man, but old money always beats new money, which stacks the deck in favor of Teller and the prince. The United States government isn't going to sign American tech over to a foreign government. Especially the Saudis. This is all not to mention that Teller and Drucker go back a long way, and you know what those relationships count for."

That is lucid and concise. I think I've decided my favorite too, for the moment. Though the thing about money is, as much as we all pretend to understand it, it operates on a level beyond our comprehension. At least, the comprehension of mere mortals who don't have a lot of it to spare.

"I feel like a betting man would have given the same level of welcome to all four players, just to play it safe, but who knows," I tell him. "I don't go to the track."

Reg starts to say something, but we see movement from the carpeted tube leading down to the tram station that comes in from Einstein. Grayson and Teller. Coming up behind them is Drucker.

"Told you," Reg says.

"Congrats," I tell him.

We make our way to the trio, and Teller is looking around the lobby like a kid on Halloween, conditioned to wait for someone to give him something. His face is set in a perpetual frown, and he looks like the kind of man who has a couple of dead sex workers in his past.

Just seeing him kicks my blood up a few degrees.

People with money, man. They can do whatever the fuck they want.

Like use every ethnic slur under the sun—and a few it seems he made up on the spot—in a series of voice mails leaked to the press by his ex-wife during a messy divorce. And it really ran the gamut, from which ethnicities he thought were the most lazy, which members of his cleaning staff he thought were stealing from him, and which he thought would be the most fun to choke out during rough sex.

But one "I don't have a racist bone in my body and I'm sorry if anyone was offended by my language" statement later, and the world pretty much moved on. He still gets to party with the president. The joys of being in the trillionaire club. Dude could eat a baby, probably, and most folks would look the other way as long as they were getting paid.

He doesn't seem to notice, or care, that me and Reg are approaching, but then Reg makes a big show. "Mister Teller! Such an honor to have you at the Paradox. I'm Reginald, the manager . . ."

C'mon, Reg.

Teller gives him a nod and a fuck-off handshake and asks, "Has the prince arrived?"

"Well I'm not sure . . ." Reg starts.

"You're the manager," he says, finally zeroing in. "I would think you should know that."

"Sorry, sir," Reg says, bowing, which makes my stomach gurgle a little. "His people are here. Did you want to see them, or . . ."

Teller puts up his hand to quiet Reg. Done with him, forever. He turns to Drucker and says, "I'm going to say this one last time. It was a mistake to even involve them in the process."

"That decision was made above my pay grade."

"You're a U.S. senator," he says. "It's the same thing I told Everett, and if he could get off the golf course long enough to listen, he'd agree. I don't know why I wasted my time and effort bundling for him if this is how he's going to treat me . . ."

"We are going to handle this in a fair and expeditious manner," Drucker says, but there's something about the way she floats over *fair* and lands hard on *expeditious* that makes me feel like she has a strong preference between the two.

"And this place," Teller says, sweeping his arm, nearly clipping Reg. "It's a dump. The blue carpet? Are you kidding me? It clashes with everything. First order of business. Carpet comes up. I'm thinking green." He glances at Grayson. "Always been my favorite color." Then he turns to me. "You. I want to unwind a little. Have something sent up to my room. Steak, well done, and whatever scotch you have that's older than fifteen years. What movies do you have playing in the rooms?"

For the first time in a long time, I am momentarily struck speech-less at the audacity, which frankly, is probably a good thing.

"God, is everyone here so useless?" Back to Grayson: "Get that taken care of."

Grayson turns a little red, to be treated like a secretary in front of me, of all people, whom he not only dislikes but will soon attempt to murder. I take a little solace in that.

"The process . . ." Drucker starts.

"Don't hand me that," Teller says. "We know how this is going to end."

God, he is unpleasant. And I can hear Allyn's voice in the back of my head. Telling me to just keep my mouth shut. Which is kind of funny, because it would take no exertion or effort to just smile and nod and let Teller go watch a dumb movie.

Because what does it matter? These people who live in their golden castles, what can I do to bring them down?

Nothing. I can do nothing to hurt them.

But that doesn't mean I shouldn't try.

"Wow," I say, snapping the word like the end of a towel.

Everyone stops and turns to me. I turn to Reg and say, in a very loud stage whisper, "It's like they don't even know we're standing *right* here."

"You," Grayson says, and my heart skips a half beat. "You and I have something to talk about . . ."

Yeah we do, motherfucker.

But his eyes slide off me, to something over my shoulder, and a voice booms, "My friend!"

Prince Mohammad al Khalid bin Saud is making his way across the lobby, flanked by his security lead, Eshe, the pair of them surrounded by his entourage, all of them carrying the kind of nervous energy that, at any second, they might be called on for an important task, like fetching him a soda or getting on their hands and knees to serve as a footstool.

Except he doesn't really give off that vibe, despite the fact that he is huge. Not heavy. Just . . . big. Enough of it is muscle that you wouldn't want to say the wrong thing to him. But his hands are open, palms outward, calm and peaceful. He's young, and handsome, and his smile is the kind of smile that comes with willful practice. Not like Teller's, something you rush to learn at the last minute because someone told you to.

And he's the one I would expect to be the most disagreeable of this bunch, considering how the Oil Wars a decade ago leveled half his country and wiped out a good portion of his people. If he's holding a grudge it's not against anyone in this room.

Davis said the two of them and Smith had dinner recently. It seems like they have very different recollections of how that dinner went. The prince reaches us and extends his hand. Teller takes it, begrudgingly, and the prince's face falls—the dynamic is not what he expected. He turns to me and nods. "You must be the head of security Eshe told me about." He offers his hand. "Salam alaykum."

Ruby had briefed me on how to respond but now I don't remember, and I can't exactly ask as it hovers over my shoulder, so I respond with "January Cole. Good to meet you," and the prince does not seem offended.

Of course, with so much net worth standing in one spot, Allyn and Nik are now jogging up to us, which I'm thankful for, because I feel something heavy and fragile is about to topple over.

And then it does.

"The Saudi government should not be given control over American land and technology, and it's insane that he's even been invited to participate," Teller says, like he's on a stage, projecting to the back of the room.

"I have to confess," the prince says, "that I'm a little surprised by your reaction. The audience hasn't assembled yet. You have nothing to gain by posturing."

"It's not posturing," Teller says. "I'd say it's something else."

"What's that?" the prince asks.

"Patriotism." The way he says it, he means it to be dramatic and stirring. Really he sounds like a clown.

The prince, though, is game. His lip curls and he says, "From what I hear, there are questions about whether you can even afford to place an opening bid."

Teller's face scrunches up in fury, but before he can speak Drucker jumps in. "Okay, let's all just settle . . ."

"If we could just . . ." Allyn says.

It's Teller's camp versus the prince's, and while the prince has the numbers, Grayson is strapped, which I need to keep reminding myself. Voices rise and twist into a loud jumble. I step into the middle of the whole thing and shout, "Hey!"

Everyone shuts up and looks at me.

"This is not the time, nor is it the place, okay?"

"She shouldn't even be here."

Grayson. He takes a step forward. His turn to be the center of attention. "I checked your file," he says to me. Then he turns to the crowd, making sure it lands. "The head of security for this hotel is Unstuck."

That changes the subject right quick.

And it sends a whole gallon of blood rushing to my face, making me a little dizzy from the sudden attention and embarrassment. Because I see it spread through the crowd, immediately. The pity. The fear. The assumption that I am damaged or crazy. Which hell, maybe it's true. But it still doesn't feel nice.

"Someone like *this* . . ." Teller says, and I'm not sure if it's because I'm Unstuck or just a woman in a leadership role, "should not be in charge of security. Are you kidding us with this, Allyn?"

Allyn. They're on a first-name basis. Swell.

"January has a long and impressive service record," Allyn says, his voice strong, sharp, and borderline furious. "One which, I might point out, includes saving my life on a few occasions. She is in charge because there's no one I trust more."

Teller actually blinks. The tension drops from the prince's shoulders. I'm not sure anyone really trusts me that much, but they trust Allyn enough to leave it alone.

Except Grayson. He's still not a member of my fan club.

Me, I'm a little annoyed that Allyn had to step in to defend me, but what was I going to say? *No, it's cool, I'm not crazy, but will you all excuse me so I can investigate the dead body that only I can see?*

"Now everyone split up, because I don't like the look of a crowd like this," Allyn says.

The scrum unlocks and drifts apart. Teller with a look of satisfaction—he made his point. Grayson is disappointed that he didn't get me off the case. I almost wish he did, because then there'd be less of a chance he'll end up shooting me?

Who knows.

Time travel!

And the prince looks genuinely sad, in that way when you thought you'd figured something out about someone, and ended up being wrong.

Allyn leans into my ear and says, "Reg's office. Now."

The way he says it has the distinct feel of being called to the principal's office. We break off and head inside . . .

. . . I'm supposed to be in a briefing, but instead I'm sitting in a half-empty office in an all-empty building. There's a computer in the corner, still in the box, and the filing cabinets have blue tape over them, to prevent the drawers from rolling out during shipping. Allyn waves his hand at an empty chair in front of the desk. "Take a seat, January."

My stomach twists. I'm not sure what he wants to talk about, though I have an idea. I also want to portray myself as relaxed, so I put my feet on the desk, and he grimaces at that. Though the grimace turns into a smile because it's not like this behavior should be surprising.

He settles in the roller chair behind the desk, adjusts it to his liking. Then he runs his hands through his short, dark hair, smoothing it out. Taking his time. Which I do not like. Allyn is usually direct. If he's hesitating, that means he doesn't like what he has to say. And neither will I.

"How are you feeling?" he asks.

I scratch behind my ear, give him a shrug. "Fine."

"Your test results came in."

"Yeah, well, what do doctors know, am I right?"

"January, this is serious."

"Just get it out, okay? You know I hate dancing. I hate even more to watch you do it."

He smiles. "I'm a decent dancer."

"Mikayla's retirement party? I almost called an ambulance. I thought you were having a seizure."

"You're being reassigned."

I knew it was coming. I tried to convince myself it wasn't, but also I knew.

"Where?" I ask.

"Here."

"This heap?"

He looks around the empty office, the bare walls, like he's looking for something to defend himself with and, finding nothing, turns back to me. "You're three years out from your pension. You hang here, you get your ten, you retire with some modicum of security. Don't you want that?"

"Tell me when and where my job performance has suffered," I say. "Just last week I broke up a plot to kill Lincoln before he could run for president. Which, if it didn't destroy the timestream outright, would have been a bit of a mess if we suddenly had slavery again. And this is my reward? For stopping slavery?"

"January . . ."

"Or remember the guy who was going to go back and invest in Betamax and then game the videotape format war to kill VHS? Who stopped him? Me. Think of all the ripples that would have created."

I hold up a finger. "I have stopped a dozen big game hunters from going after a *T rex*."

Another finger. "The guy who wanted to warn Hitler to get out of Berlin? We got him."

Another finger. "The woman who . . ."

"You're Unstuck, January."

I give the word a minute to settle. The sharp edges and dark valleys of the letters.

Again, not a surprise. For weeks now it felt like I was having moments of extreme déjà vu. A few times a day I'd see things I thought I'd already seen. Someone would walk into a room and I could have sworn they'd already been there.

And then a few days ago I heard someone tell me to duck, so I dropped to the floor on the concourse of Einstein. Nothing happened. Ten minutes later someone told me to duck for real, and I was so confused over hearing it again that I didn't. One of those dumb little AI drones was having a navigation malfunction and flew right into my head.

I knew it.

It just sucks to get it confirmed.

I hold up the third finger. "The woman who tried to board the *Titanic* so she could warn them about the iceberg and, I quote, 'save Rose and Jack.' As much as I wanted to let her follow through so I could see the look on her face, I stopped her."

Allyn gets up and walks to the wall, turning away from me. I'm frustrating him. Which is the whole point. It's the only card I have to play right now. Because I know how this hand ends.

"Have you ever seen it?" His voice is quiet. "Have you ever seen someone who hit the third stage?" He turns to me, his eyes almost misting. "It's horrible. They're there, but they're . . . not. Like shells. I know it's a risk we all face doing this job. I know if I gave you a choice, you would be back in there today."

I try to respond and he puts up his hand.

"You'll be the house detective," he says. "Frankly I think it has a nice ring to it. You get a room and an unlimited tab. There's still plenty of bad shit here to break up. Where do you think that *Titanic* woman was staying? The Paradox Hotel will be your own personal fiefdom." He knocks on the desk and I look up at him. "I'm not asking you to come here and put on a guard's uniform and let your ass grow fat. I'm putting you in charge of this place. It's yours."

I sag in the chair, lean my head back, stare into the light until it hurts. "Can I think about it?"

"Sure," he says. "Have yourself a walk around. Go up to the bar and get a coffee. We can talk about it tomorrow. Two or three days if you need."

"Okay." I get up, push in the chair, and pause at the door.

"I'm sorry," Allyn says.

"I know."

I don't wait for a response. I let the door close behind me and stand there, taking in the lobby. The sunlight spilling down through the skylight far above, shattering on the shiny brass clock hovering above the floor. The bustle of the employees. The movement and the sound of it. The smell.

Coffee.

I could use coffee.

I go to the urn and it's kicked, so I amble over to the wall, where there's a map of the hotel. There's a café on the second floor but the restaurant and bar are on the top, so I figure on walking my way up there. Get the lay of the land. Sit. Maybe it'll be quiet. What a bonus that'd be.

It's after breakfast but before lunch, so by the time I make it up there, it's mostly empty. I consider taking a table, but decide on the bar, which doesn't have anyone working behind it. I pull out a stool and wait.

I'd have to give up my apartment. It's not even a very nice apartment, but I've lived there for six years now, which is the longest I've lived anywhere since I was a kid. I won't get to ride the stream anymore, which has been the greatest thrill of my life that didn't involve two bottles of wine first. And I'll have to come here. Live in a hotel.

I feel hollow. The plight of being a workaholic. You lose your job and suddenly you find yourself with nothing. As much as I could use that pension, maybe I should go. Being this close and not able to play the game—that'll hurt. Maybe I'm not prepared for it, to stand at the window and look at the lights of Einstein and wonder what's happening over there, the fun I'm missing out on.

The worst part of being Unstuck is, drinking can supposedly exacerbate it. So I can't even order my coffee with a few licks of whiskey. I have to navigate this sober.

It's real now.

Allyn saying it makes it real.

"What'll it be, honey?"

I look in the direction of the voice and when my eyes land on the woman in the sleek white blouse and the black apron, just about every drop of blood in my heart squeezes out, before rushing back in and making me light-headed.

Her skin glows, and the gentle curve of her Adam's apple catches the light even in the dim confines of the bar. But it's the smile that does me in. She smiles from the top of her head down to the points of her toes, and she's not just smiling, she's smiling for me.

With me, like we're sharing something.

"Coffee, black," I tell her, finally making my throat work again.

She sees me stumble, and she likes it, giving a little grin as she glances down at herself, like she wants to make sure her apron is clean and her shirt is tucked in. She disappears around the corner and comes back with a steel carafe and a ceramic mug on a plate. She places the mug down in front of me and pours perfectly from the carafe without taking her eyes off me. Then she sets it down and leans her elbows on the bar. "You're troubled."

"That obvious?" I ask, trying to sound cool. Failing.

"What's troubling you?"

I take the mug, place it to my lips. It's a touch too hot but I take a sip anyway. "Change."

She leans a little closer to me. I can smell her. Cherries? I like the way she leans close to me, and when she speaks her voice feels like sunlight on my skin. She takes a deep breath and says, "There was once a student who went to his meditation teacher and said, 'My practice is horrible. I feel distracted. My legs ache. I'm constantly falling asleep.' And the teacher said, 'It'll pass.'"

I put down the mug. "I'm not one for parables."

She holds up a finger. "Not a parable, but we'll get to that. So the next week the student went back to the teacher and said, 'My meditation is wonderful! I'm so peaceful! So alive!' And do you know what the master said?"

"Good for you?"

She shakes her head. "It'll pass."

I laugh a little. The kind of laugh that makes me vulnerable and I would have rather held it in, but when it manages to get out, I don't feel so bad anymore. "And what's that supposed to mean?"

She shrugs. "You tell me."

"All things pass."

"A bit of a surface read, but it's a start."

"What is it, if it's not a parable?"

"A kōan. They're a little different from parables. Parables are supposed to teach you a lesson. Kōans make you think. A good tool if you feel your Zen practice needs a little centering."

"Ah," I say. "Buddhist?"

She nods. "You?"

"Nihilist."

She gives a bemused smile, teasing me for my attempt at clever-ness. It is both maddening and wildly attractive.

"I'm Ximena," she says, offering a long, slender hand. "But every-one calls me Mena."

"January."

"Janus. Roman god of beginnings and endings."

"You are full of trivia," I tell her.

"I'm full of a lot of things. Do people call you Jan?"

"Some people," I say. "But I like it when you say my full name."

She leans close to me again. So close that the next thing she says, I can feel it. I can feel the movement of the air and I can feel the way it reaches through my skin.

"Good," she says. Then she narrows her eyes and nods. "You should take the job. Come work here."

"Why's that?" I ask, flushing. Not caring.

She shrugs. "You'll like it here. This place"—she gestures to the empty bar around her—"it's sort of like a family. It's my sangha."

"What's that?"

She nods her head toward the far wall. "It's better than a family. I used to work over at Einstein. I was a stewardess, back when they first opened up to tourists. I would come stay here sometimes and there are a lot of great people who work here. So I made the choice to stay. Your sangha is the family you choose, not the one you're stuck with."

Suddenly I know why I am so wildly attracted to this woman. The two of us bear scars from our childhoods. Wounds that were inflicted so long ago it feels like another life and, at the same time, yesterday. Those scars are invisible to most people who would look, but we can see them in each other. Even as strangers, that binds us.

That was the moment I knew I was going to stay, so I could get to know this woman. Which may be shallow. Yeah, she was superhot. But there was something about her that felt magnetic. Something in-side me pulled toward her.

Even in this moment, feeling that pull again, I know it isn't real. Or at least, it isn't real anymore.

It's an echo. And as much as I want to wrap my fingers around it, pull it close to my chest, live inside it—you can't hold an echo.

An echo can't hold you . . .

. . . "January?" Allyn asks.

The mess of paperwork is back on Reg's desk. The computer is unboxed, set up, and collecting dust. Allyn's hair is longer and graying again. Ruby is floating dumbly next to me.

I'm back, the echo faded into the air.

The way it filled my heart, gone with it.

"Do you know what Drucker is doing right now?" he asks.

"Giving Teller a handie in the bathroom?"

"No, Jan, she is telling everyone I answer to that I'm employing someone who is stage two Unstuck. I had to fight to get you this job when you were stage one, and they only went for it because you were good at your job and three years out from your pension."

"I'm not stage two."

"Damn it, January, I know what it looks like. You were sitting there *just now* in a daze." He sighs and leans forward, and doesn't bring his eyes up to meet mine. "There's nothing I can do. It's time to retire."

"No."

"What do you mean no?"

"I mean no, Allyn." I stand up, having gotten my bearings. "You gave me this place. You said it was my fiefdom. You said I could have it. So it's mine until it's not. Do you understand me?"

The decision is causing him pain. It's all over his face. He doesn't want to do this. I should give him credit for that. "It's out of my hands," he says. "You're the one who took a swan dive directly into Drucker's bad side. It's happening whether you want it or not."

"You know what, fine. Retire me. I can always get a job here."

"Damn it," he says, slapping a pile of paper on the desk. "What is it about this place anyway? You have no friends. You're miserable. You were always a pain in the ass, but now you're like a heat-seeking missile for trouble. You're not the January I remember. Do your job. Keep shit in order. That's all I ask. Instead you're wandering around pissing people off like I pay you to do it."

I get up. Push the chair in hard, knocking a pile of papers onto the floor. Pause like I'm going to bend and pick them up, and realize that's not me.

"And you're not the friend I thought you were," I say, slamming the door behind me.

Make me go. I'd like to see him try.

I grip the railing, look down into the lobby from my spot—from our spot—and resolve to ask Reg as soon as possible about keeping me on in some capacity once this is all over. I'll clean rooms. I'll do laundry. Whatever.

Though if someone is going to come in and clear house, does it even matter? Maybe I should wait. Either way, they'll have to take me out of this place on a stretcher, my brain a pile of wet leaves. And it'll be worth it if until then, I can see Mena.

I catch Ruby in my peripheral vision and ask: "Where's my intel on the guy?"

"Still working on it."

"What good are you?"

"I'm doing my best, and . . ."

"Fine fine fine."

This is a jigsaw puzzle someone dumped on the floor and then kicked a handful of the pieces under the couch. And they won't show me the box, but they still want me to put it together. Quickly and in the dark.

Someone is inside our system. That's happened before. Foreign governments. Bored hackers. But again, I don't believe in coincidence.

Too much shit is happening in conjunction with a bunch of rich people trying to buy this place out.

I think Teller is my favorite right now in Pin the Tail on the Bad Guy, but that might be his track record clouding my judgment. It'd be dumb to rule anyone out. Everyone's hiding something. So is Allyn. What did he say before? Checks and balances?

I'm considering what those might be when a gentle buzz leaps across my brain and Kolten crashes through the front doors of the Tick Tock, grasping his throat, face red. Anaphylaxis. Behind him I hear a voice. His brother Warwick? "Where's the pen. *Where's the fucking pen?*"

I watch as Kolten falls to his knees, people suddenly rushing around him, trying to revive him. Warwick is cradling his head, screaming for someone to help, asking if anyone has an EpiPen. But it's too late. Kolten's chest stops moving. His eyes go glassy. It's painful, but it's also quick, and that much is a mercy.

Great. More to do.

It seems like an easy enough task: stop Kolten from eating whatever he was planning to eat. But when I open the glass doors I don't see him. Instead I'm hit with a wave of shitty music. It takes me a second to place it: "Walk Like an Egyptian" by the Bangles.

And the place is packed with people dressed in Egyptian garb. Many of them, just like the guy in the lobby earlier, are wearing bronzer to darken their skin. They must have gotten ready for their flight, it got canceled, and they all ambled up here to let off some steam. Because there's serious drunken energy in the room. Old folks flailing their bodies to the music, hoisting glasses of wine and light beers, smiles stretched to capacity as they try to make the best of their terrible, horrible, no good, very bad situation.

Standing just inside the door is my new trillionaire bestie, Osgood. He's staring at the crowd, dabbing at his forehead with his little purple pocket square. His face is flat. He turns to me and just shakes his head a little, and even though I know he doesn't hold me responsible, I feel embarrassed to be associated with this place.

The shit these people get away with.

Okay, Kolten.

I glance around and don't see him, but the crowd is thick, so I dive into the middle of it, scanning the room. I spot him sitting with his brother and Drucker. She's having a red wine, they both have beers. No plates yet.

But Cin, the tight little Dominican waitress covered in tattoos who I've considered making a pass at, is wending her way through the tables, her arms laden with food.

And there are a lot of people between us.

I move toward them and call out, "Hey."

They're not paying attention, or maybe they don't hear me over the music, which is playing much louder than it should be. Cin puts down the plates. The social media wunderkind is having a sandwich. I cut through the grid of tables, dodging around drunken racists, but it's not a straight path, so I'm hopping from foot to foot.

As I'm about to call "hey" again, an old man in a white robe and an Egyptian headdress bumps me into a table, setting me off course and knocking the wind out of me.

I push him away and scramble to my feet, yell, "Hey!"

Kolten still doesn't notice me, so I pick a saltshaker off the nearest table and wing it at them. It catches Warwick in the chest, and he gets up, not sure what happened with all the chaos around him, but Kolten already has his sandwich in his hand.

I start pushing tables out of the way. Warwick sees me now, and I point at his brother. "Stop him right now."

But he doesn't get what I mean.

Stop him from what? Eating a delicious sandwich?

Finally, though, Kolten pauses, mouth open, sandwich halfway there, and it gives me enough time to reach him and knock it out of his hand. The sandwich flies through the air and lands on the floor, and he pauses, before standing up and screaming, at the top of his lungs, his face red with rage, "Why the *fuck* would you do that?"

I can't help but notice he's still wearing his Buddhist beads.

"Are you allergic to anything?" I ask, catching my breath.

"What the *fuck* is wrong with you? You tell me right now why I shouldn't have you fucking fired and carted out of here like a fucking *criminal* . . ."

Warwick grabs his brother's shoulder, and Kolten seems to calm a bit. "Peanuts," Warwick says. "He's allergic to peanuts. But we told the waitress . . ."

Kolten is still sputtering but I ignore him and go around to the sandwich. It's a vegetarian banh mi, with a sauce that, when I dip my pinkie in and taste, may as well be full-blown peanut butter. I take the sandwich and toss it on the table and ask, "Where's Mbaye?"

"Right here," he says, standing behind me, wiping his hands with a dish towel, probably drawn by the commotion.

"Dropping the ball back there?"

"What are you talking out?"

I gesture to the sandwich. "Guy has a peanut allergy."

"Okay, whoa," he says, hands up. "I made and plated that on a station I cleaned myself. I double-checked everything. I always do."

"Try the sauce."

He dips a tentative finger in, sticks it in his mouth, and his eyes go wide. "That's not the sauce I put on."

"Well it's the sauce he almost ate," I tell him. "How did it get there? Fairies?"

"I don't . . ." He falters for a minute, allowing that maybe he did mess up. But then he steels himself and looks me clear in the eye. "I prepared that myself. I double-checked everything."

"Well you don't always, do you?" I ask, my voice cracking.

The words are acid. They splash on his skin and burn. And it feels good to see how much they hurt him. It brings me comfort. It's like a pressure-release valve, letting out a little of the steam that lives in my chest. I don't care what that says about me.

Mbaye drops his head. He doesn't look up at me when he says, "January . . ."

"What?" I ask. "January, what. What do you have to say to me?"

He sighs.

We have an audience. Mbaye gives up and turns to Kolten. "Mister Smith, I cannot apologize to you enough. This mistake is unacceptable."

Kolten has cooled a bit. I think because of the way his brother is gripping his triceps. He no longer looks like he wants to rip someone's head clean off their shoulders. He nods slightly and says, "Yes, it is unacceptable."

Then Warwick says, "Huh."

We all turn to him. He's patting his blazer, his face twisted in confusion. "I had it when I left the room. I remember switching it because I changed jackets . . ."

"Had what?" I ask.

"The EpiPen," he says. "I always carry one. That's impossible." He looks up at me. "Thank god you were here. How . . . ?"

"She's Unstuck," Drucker says, taking some small degree of pride in being the one to inform them.

"Thanks for the reminder," I tell her. "Yes, everyone, I am Unstuck, and I watched Kolten here choke and die a few minutes ago and thankfully I got in here in time." I turn to Kolten. "So, you know, sorry I put my unwashed hands on you."

"Thank you," he says, because he knows he needs to say it, not because he's in the proper emotional state to mean it.

Warwick steps in, and I am beginning to understand the dynamic of their relationship much better. "We owe you so much. Thank you for this. Seriously. I just . . . I can't believe I forgot the pen. That seems impossible."

No, it doesn't.

There's a bad feeling worming in my gut. The music has stopped, mercifully, so I leave them to sort out the aftermath and take Ruby to a quiet corner and ask, "How are the video feeds right now?"

"They seem fine," it says.

I take out my phone. "Show me their table for the past ten minutes. Double speed."

The video appears on my phone, but the view sucks. There are too many people moving. I only have a view of Warwick's back.

"Okay, now show me the kitchen, and Mbaye preparing the sandwich."

Again, not the best view. I can see him working on it but the image cuts off what he's actually doing at the station.

"What exactly are we doing?" Ruby asks.

"My job," I tell it.

Next I go looking for Cin, find her standing at the bar, unsure of what to do after all the commotion. "Hey," I ask her. "You got a second?"

She smiles a little, like maybe she's hoping I'll flirt a bit, but I don't have time for that. She nods. "Yeah?"

"Did you notice anything weird about that table while you were serving them?"

She shakes her head slowly, unsure of what I'm asking, which is fair, because I'm feeling it out myself. "No, nothing."

"Did you notice anyone at any of the surrounding tables taking photo or videos?"

"Yeah, there was a big party next to them, celebrating a birthday. They all had their phones out."

I glance over at the next table, which is abandoned, but I see the trail of people heading out of the restaurant. I go chasing after them and manage to catch a guy in a white silk shirt with a shaved head and an obnoxious gold chain around his thick neck.

"Party over so soon?" I ask.

He smiles a very drunken and lascivious smile and responds in a thick Russian accent. "We are headed back up to my suite for the after-party. You are welcome to join."

"Thanks, but it's been too long since I've had a tetanus shot. Were you taking any video during your meal?"

He suddenly goes cold. "Why do you ask this?"

"I'm the head of security. As you can see we just had an incident here and for insurance purposes I need to collect as much data as I can. Since you were seated across from that whole incident, I'd like to review whatever footage you might have."

He takes his phone out of his pocket, but then hesitates.

"Ruby, comp their meal," I say.

"They ordered four bottles of Dom Pérignon, Reg isn't going to be happy . . ."

"Do it."

After a moment Ruby says, "Done."

"You're welcome," I tell the Russian, then put out my hand. "Phone."

He shrugs, cues up something on the screen, and hands it to me.

And it's perfect. He's filming two people sitting across from him, and they're singing "Happy Birthday" to someone else seated at the table, doing a horrible job. Between them is a fairly unobstructed view of Warwick. I watch him in the background, gesturing to Drucker and his brother.

"How long is this going to take?" the man asks.

"Shut up," I tell him.

There.

Just as the people he's filming are finishing the song, Warwick's jacket seems to rustle. I stop the video, rewind it, and watch it again, wondering if maybe it's a trick of the light, or just the way Warwick moves.

No. He's listening to something that either Drucker or Kolten is saying. He is sitting nearly perfectly still. And his jacket seems to lift for a moment before falling back down against his chest.

Like his pocket was being picked.

"I need a copy of this video," I tell the Russian.

"I'm not so sure . . ."

"I just comped your damn meal. Consent to sending me the video."

He nods, so I hold the phone toward Ruby, who handles the data transfer. Then I give it back to him. "Thanks."

He takes the phone, crams it in his pocket, and stalks away. I suspect I am no longer invited to his party.

"Warwick's jacket," I tell it. "Just after the three-minute mark."

Ruby pauses, and says, "What are you implying?"

"Doesn't it seem like his jacket moved? Like someone was reaching inside?"

"January, this is hardly conclusive . . ."

"Is it common knowledge that Kolten has a peanut allergy?"

Another moment. "Yes. There was a profile in *Wired* three years ago in which it was cited, along with the fact that he tended to forget his EpiPen, which is why his brother always carries one."

"Shit."

I cross to my perch above the lobby and look down. It's less crowded now, some level of stasis having been achieved. Cameo is back at concierge, Reg is standing by the coffee urn, which seems to have coffee now, because of course it does. As soon as I get down there it'll be empty again.

A few other guests mill about.

But I'm not looking at them. I'm looking at the space between them.

Looking for the ghosts.

Kolten asked me about them. Yeah, my brain is broken and I'm slipping in time and it allows me to see my dead girlfriend roaming the halls, which means I have to be open to the fact that the universe is a big, complicated place, to which I do not have all the answers. And I know that other people see things in this place too—the rumors of haunting have persisted from day one—so it's not just me who experiences this stuff.

Figures roaming the hallways. Conversations in empty rooms. The occasional brush or nudge that comes from nowhere.

As much as I want Mbaye to feel like an asshole, like he might have screwed up, the reality is, I know he takes this kind of thing seriously. He wouldn't have overlooked that.

So yeah. Ghosts. Who else was going to dose Kolten's food with something that would kill him, and manage to swipe the thing that would save him from his brother's pocket?

. . . I'm sitting in bed, feeling the heat radiating off the steam pipe next to me. The smell of garlic and chili paste frying in the kitchen. I want to go downstairs. To be seen, to hear my mother's voice.

No . . .

I'm in the gym. The skin on my knuckles is raw because I didn't bother with hand wraps or gloves. I just needed twenty minutes of beating the shit out of something. It gets the blood flowing to my brain. I can't just keep throwing back Retronim, which it seems like I'm building a tolerance to. And I can't even remember if I took one or two today. Ruby says I took one but what if I took a second when it wasn't looking?

So off to the heavy bag I go. Fighting has always helped center me. My own holistic remedy. Throwing punches and the occasional roundhouse kick is the closest I've ever gotten to a meditative state.

Which I always thought made for a pretty good joke. Look at me relax as I try to bust open this heavy bag. But Mena explained that meditation isn't about sitting in lotus and closing your eyes and humming. It's about finding your center, your inner peace, and inhabiting that.

That's what I'm inhabiting.

This is my inner peace.

The pain in my knuckles. The ache in my lungs. The sting on my shins.

And within that pain I can find a little focus.

Unfortunately, there's a lot to focus on. And before I can settle into that, the door of the studio opens behind me. In the mirrors running along the walls, I see Nik come in. I'm midcombination—jab, jab, cross, hook, uppercut, low roundhouse—so I finish before I turn. All the blows are quick and snappy, which makes me feel good, that he saw me at my best. Because I haven't been feeling at my best since I woke up.

I turn to him, rubbing my knuckles, feeling where the skin is abraded—it was careless to not wrap—but at least I took the time to put on a pair of yoga pants and a tank to sweat through.

Nik surveys the studio, which branches off the main room of the gym. Heavy bag, speed bag, lots of gear and equipment for just about anything you might want to do, from rolling out some sore muscles to a step aerobics class to sparring. All the equipment is pristine. This room doesn't get used too much. Mostly it's just the ellipticals out in the main section.

"You don't see this kind of stuff in a typical hotel gym," Nik says, touching the ballet barre. "Usually just a few machines and a shitty treadmill."

"Welcome to how the other half lives," I tell him, trying to hide that I'm a little out of breath. "What's the situation outside?"

He glances at Ruby floating silently in the corner. "That doesn't keep you updated?"

"It does. I want to hear it from you."

"Well," Nik says, slapping his hands together, making his way across the studio to me. "Cots are being distributed on the upper floors, though, funny thing. A couple of the luxury rooms are empty, in case any more"—he puts both hands up and does finger quotes—"VIP guests arrive."

"Again, welcome to how the other half lives," I tell him. "Meanwhile the people who actually do the labor of shipping these assholes through time and keeping them safe have to bunk out in a goddamn hallway."

"What do we do?"

I laugh at him. "What do you mean, what do we do?"

"It's not right," Nik says.

"That's life."

I don't have to look at his face to tell he's disappointed in me. Whatever. After a few moments he says, "Silver lining."

"What's that?"

"We've got some extra TEA agents in the fold. Danbridge set up the shifts downstairs, and he deputized a few more just to roam around and keep an eye on things. But they all know that you're in charge."

It's starting to feel like that isn't the case, but I tell him, "That's good."

He's eyeing the bag. I see the look. I put my hand up, palm flat, offering it to him, and take a step aside. From what I've seen today, he carries himself tight in the shoulders, but in front of the bag his body unfurls and he throws a couple of quick jabs, testing distance. Then he dances around it, sending out a flurry of very sharp, very accurate shots, the bag barely swinging. He finishes and turns to me with a smile, like he wants my approval.

"What do you train in?" I ask.

"Mostly boxing, though I've been getting into Brazilian jiu jitsu," he says. "You?"

"Krav Maga," I say. "Muay Thai. Could never get into BJJ. Too much time getting up and down from the floor."

Nik shrugs. "I like it. It's like playing chess at a hundred miles an hour."

As he's talking I throw a quick low roundhouse at his shin. Not even going for power, just to see how he reacts. He checks it, and hops to his other foot, ready to throw a push kick, and then stops himself.

"Really?" he asks, falling back into a loose fighting stance.

"Just curious."

He glances back at the gloves. "Into sparring at all? It's been forever."

"You're okay sparring with a woman?" I ask.

"Women have better form. Guys can sort of muscle their way through shit. All the women I train with, when they're good, it's because they have the technique down cold."

I laugh a little, hoping it doesn't sound like flirting. "Do you like getting hurt by women?"

"I like learning, and getting hurt is the only way you learn."

I glance at the wall of gloves and wraps and headgear. Feel the itch to fight with someone. "Not today, kid," I tell him. "Too much work to do."

"Danbridge wants you gone," Nik says, almost blurting it out.

It hurts to respond: "I know."

"He's feeling me out on the house detective position. He told me not to tell you."

It's kind of him to say that. But still, I walk over to the wall rack holding the sparring equipment, select a pair of gloves that don't smell too much like feet, and toss them his way. He catches one and drops the other, asks, "Changed your mind?"

I pull on my own pair of gloves, which I keep in the gym, but pushed toward the back of the shelf, so no one ever uses them. I get them on nice and tight and ask, "Do you want the gig?"

He doesn't answer. Which feels like an answer. But then he says, "I've been working the stream for a year now. I'd rather be there."

"It's overrated."

"Really?"

"No."

We tap gloves, and then move slowly around each other. "Nice and easy," I say. "Let's not go back to work bruised up or missing teeth."

As we make our way around the floor, feeling out how we move, I figure on being bold, which is usually my jam, so I give a little duck, move in, and throw a fist at his midsection. He blocks with his elbow and taps me on the head with his hook. He's not built for power, but he's fast and he's got reach.

He steps back and lets me shake it off. "It doesn't seem like a bad job. Being here. The test for full field agent is coming up in April. I've been studying."

"The test isn't so hard," I tell him, moving back into my rhythm. "I guess the real risk is on your health. I know plenty of people have done it and haven't exhibited symptoms. But there's no way to tell how you're going to react. Which has got to be a little scary, right?"

"A little," he says, dancing out of the way of a jab cross, but not responding with anything. "No one lives forever."

"No," I tell him, hopping back. "No they do not."

I think he's going to say something, and then he doesn't. His chin dips, elbows get tighter to his sides. He's in it now. Good. I move in, let him throw a few, and put up some blocks, waiting for an opening. When I see it, I take it, and my fist glances off his cheek, but I opened myself up; he comes in under my chin and it snaps my head back, my teeth clicking. Stupid to do this without headgear, but even more stupid to do it without a mouth guard.

Nik steps back, puts up a glove. "Good game. Let's get back out there, okay?"

But now I'm seeing red. I move toward him, not even worrying too much about my guard. At this point I just want to hurt him a little. I go for speed, thinking I can best him there, and I make him defend himself as he steps back. Then I play it a little dirty, throwing a roundhouse at his floating ribs, knowing he'll drop his arms enough that I can put my fist square into his forehead.

And I do, a little too hard. His head snaps back and I can imagine he's seeing stars, so I back off, let him regain his composure. Thinking maybe I should apologize but not really wanting to. Hitting the bag may be my meditative state, but hitting another person, that's the real medicine I needed.

He puts his gloves up in surrender, smiling. "Okay, before you kill me, we should get back down there."

"Damn right," I mutter, then I shake off the gloves and return them to their secret spot on the shelf, glad to have gotten that out.

Over my shoulder I hear Nik say, "Huh."

"What?" I ask.

He's staring out the window.

"What time is it?" he asks.

Before I can even check my watch Ruby answers, "It is currently four-oh-six."

"And what time is the sun supposed to set?" Nik asks.

"Five twenty-eight," Ruby says.

"Then what's the deal with that?"

I join him at the window and find out why his jaw is practically unhinged from his mouth. Not because I hit him. Even though the snow hasn't stopped, the clouds have thinned out, just enough to see the sun setting on the horizon.

BROKEN ARROW OF TIME

The ballroom is still coming together—a lot of half-set-up furniture and wires spilled across the floor—but this was the only place it made sense to do this.

We have the core security team: me, Allyn, Nik, plus a whole bunch of TEA agents in their standard-issue blue shirts, milling about like someone is about to serve free cupcakes.

There are most of the summit players, all of whom bring their own crews, and for MKS, that means nearly twenty people. Plus Reg and Cameo, a few other folks I don't recognize, clearly not from the hotel. They carry the self-serious air of midlevel bureaucrats. More TEA, probably.

No Kolten though, or Warwick, so I guess Axon doesn't require a seat at this table.

We're assembled in a loose circle around a white guy standing on a chair. He has wild hair and thick plastic-framed glasses, his paisley button-down tucked tight into a pair of mustard khakis. He's the kind of person I would have taken seriously if not for the fact that he's also wearing a bow tie. Some things are hard to forgive.

Everyone in the room is talking, the din of it filling the space, and the man on the chair puts his hands up and says, "Okay, okay," and everyone quiets down.

"So here's what's happening . . ." he starts, his voice trembling a bit.

"Introduce yourself," says Allyn, standing at my shoulder, mildly annoyed.

"Right, sorry." The man adjusts his glasses, looks momentarily confused about where he is. "I'm Adrian Popa, chief science officer for the TEA. So here's what we know. The uh, the sun was due to set tonight at five twenty-eight P.M., but obviously it did so more than an hour early."

He pauses for effect, or out of nervousness.

"There's a TEA office about ten miles from here," he says. "When we tried to confirm our data over there, they reported something entirely different. The sun hadn't started setting yet."

Murmurs from the crowd.

"And no radiation spikes from Einstein, correct?" Allyn asks.

Popa closes his eyes and pinches the bridge of his nose. "Not . . . exactly. There have been, uh . . . ripples that have made it impossible to calibrate our instruments correctly. That's why we're grounding flights. It's like fog conditions are so great we can't see through them. Though I guess most airlines can detect through fog so maybe that's not the best analogy. But, after what happened with the Aztec incident . . ."

He stops himself, his hands hovering in the air, almost like he's going to clap his palm across his mouth. Allyn winces, then tries to hide the fact that he winced.

Uh-oh.

"What Aztec incident?" someone calls from the crowd.

Popa looks at Allyn. Allyn looks at the floor. Then he waves his hand. *Go ahead.*

"There was an expedition three days ago that was meant to visit Tenochtitlán in fifteen nineteen, during the reign of Montezuma, shortly before Cortés arrived. We . . . overshot. The trip arrived during the Spanish siege of the city."

"And?" comes the same voice from the crowd.

More looks between Allyn and Popa, before they both admit defeat. "Two people died. A steward and a client."

The crowd erupts. Allyn looks like someone bought him a dog, gave him long enough to fall in love with it, and then shot it in front of him.

I'm speechless, which for me, is pretty damn rare. I can't believe they managed to keep the news of that under wraps. They must have gone into a hard lockdown. I sort of don't blame Allyn for playing this close. Besides a dump truck full of money hanging in the balance for control of this place . . . something like that has never happened before.

The early days of time travel were rough, and in total five people died before they really nailed down the process. Turns out you can't cross your own timestream, which is a lesson we learned pretty hard. One of the first test "pilots" went back to visit himself as a kid. Not to interact, just to watch himself play on a playground. Soon as he saw himself, he had a brain aneurysm, and the kid had a seizure. Some kind of grandfather paradox feedback loop. It was not a good day.

But the time radiation only affects people who spend too much time in the stream, like me. The occasional trip isn't supposed to be dangerous.

Since the tourism aspect was introduced, only three people have died. One woman suffered a heart attack in the field, but that wasn't related to the travel burden. A man succumbed to a disease that shouldn't have been fatal, but he'd paid his doctor to falsify his medical waiver, covering up an underlying condition that left him immunosuppressed. And another guy got killed looking for Jack the Ripper, presumably by Jack the Ripper, but no one is really sure about that.

This, though, this is all very terrible.

Drucker steps up, stern but not surprised. She knew about it. "What's the prevailing theory? What do you think is happening here?"

"Look . . ." Popa takes a deep breath. "There are a lot of things we still don't understand about time travel. For example, why we can go backward but not forward. We know time conforms to the block universe model that . . ." He pauses, sees that he's losing the room. "Okay, think of it like this. Time is like a pond. When you drop a pebble in a pond it creates ripples. The ripples are temporary. It's not long before they dissipate. When we move through time, we create some ripples."

"And?" Drucker asks.

"What if we dropped something in that was too big and too heavy? What if what we're doing . . ." As he's sounding this out I can see Allyn in physical pain. "What if we're splashing all the water out of the pond?"

Popa seems like he wants to say more, rubbing his hands together, licking his lips, but he picks that as his ending point.

"Okay, okay, hold on," Teller says, appearing at Drucker's side. "The past happened. Nothing can change that. I find it very hard to believe we could do something that would actually create a problem." He looks at Drucker. "I have spoken to expert after expert and they've used a lot of big words I don't understand, but it all always comes down to one thing: the timestream fixes itself. It always has."

"Right, but . . ." Popa starts.

"Excuse me," Teller says, his hand up. "I've spoken to dozens of experts. They've all told me the same thing."

A bold claim from a guy who got into Harvard because his dad agreed to renovate half the campus. This is the guy Drucker wants to hand the reins to?

"Yeah, and how much were you paying them?" I ask, under my breath. "Enough they'd tell you whatever you want?"

Nik, who seems to be the only person who hears me, lets out a little laugh, which draws a few curious looks but, much to our luck, nothing beyond that.

"What happens now?" Drucker asks.

"We need to wait a little bit," Popa says. "See if this smooths out. And meanwhile we're running tests to see if we can find the exact location of the disturbance."

"Wait," Teller scoffs. "How long do we need to wait?"

Popa's skin is glistening with sweat now. His glasses slide down his nose and he pushes them back up. "We're not really sure."

"You're telling me you don't even know that?" Teller looks around the room, incredulous, before settling on Allyn. "What kind of people are you employing here?"

"The best," Allyn says, not even attempting to cover up the disdain in his voice.

At this, Osgood steps toward the center of the scrum and puts up his hands. "Vince, I do believe they're going to figure this out, and we have to let them, okay? You said yourself you don't understand half the words they use, and neither do I. We have to allow that certain things are beyond our understanding."

"Speak for yourself, *Davis*," Teller says. "My family didn't get where it is by waiting around for so-called experts to get their senses together."

Osgood smiles, glances at the floor, and looks back up. "You're right about that. My family wouldn't know anything about listening to experts. My momma was always more concerned about putting food on my plate. I learned that you do the best with what you got, and you learn a little patience in the meantime."

Teller goes red at this, which I think is exactly the reaction Osgood was going for. At this point I wonder when MKS is going to weigh in, because if these two are making themselves the center of attention he can't be far behind.

And right on cue, he says, "Perhaps we should delay the meeting."

"We're not delaying anything, okay?" Teller says, momentarily losing interest in Osgood. "I didn't come all the way here just to go home. It's snowing, we're trapped, we may as well do the work."

MKS raises his eyebrow. Like, *who put you in charge?*

"I agree," Drucker says. "This thing with the sun could be a fluke. Everything else seems fine, and as long as we're all stuck here, I don't see the point in moving things. Do you disagree with that assessment, Allyn."

It is very pointedly not a question. Allyn catches the drift and nods.

"It's settled," Teller says. "We get this done tomorrow." He points to Popa. "And in the meantime, do your job." Then he nods toward Grayson. "Maybe he can put you in touch with some of the folks we talked to. People who actually know what they're talking about."

At this point the room breaks up. Osgood steps to Teller and the two of them lock into a heated discussion. I want to talk to Allyn, but he's already pulling Popa aside, likely to ream him out or tell him to hurry up. No sense in getting in the middle of that. MKS's entourage closes around him like a football huddle, with him at the center. I point to Reg and Cameo.

"Gather the team," I tell them. "Conference room three."

As I exit the room I hear it again.

Clack-clack-clack.

Can't wait to find out what that is.

Fifteen minutes later, a good chunk of the hotel staff is crammed into conference room three, the largest of them, but still slightly too small for our needs. I would have preferred the ballroom for this, but asking everyone else to clear out probably would have been met with a blank stare.

There are more people standing than there are sitting around the shiny, oval oak table. I focus in on the people I need: Reg, Cameo, Brandon, and Mbaye, as well as Tierra, who is currently point on housekeeping, and Chris, the facilities manager. I didn't invite Nik to this one, leaving him to keep an eye on the ballroom, make sure nothing silly happens, and so that Allyn has a little backup if he needs it.

The room is filled with nervous energy. Lots of clasped hands and darting glances, as they wait for me to weave through the crowd and move toward the head of the table, underneath a television that's playing a silent montage of the photos on the website—glamour shots of the gym and the pool and the restaurant, the photos angled so those things look bigger than they really are.

I take my spot and look out at the room; everyone is wide-eyed, tense, looking at me like they're children about to be scolded.

Is it because of the circumstances?

Or is it me?

Whatever. Not the time to worry about that.

"Here's the situation," I tell everyone. "We've got a full house, plus some. The roads out are no good, and it's not like we can send anyone to another hotel down the road. We're stuck here for . . ." I turn to Ruby. "How long?"

"Snow is due to end sometime later tonight. Expected accumulation currently at three feet."

"Why is it always so much?" Reg says, to no one in particular.

Ruby rotates slightly toward Reg. "It's lake effect snow."

"I hate lakes," Reg says, like that means anything.

"We will have our revenge on the lakes later." I turn to the group. "What are we low on? What do we need?" I point to Tierra. "Housekeeping, go."

Tierra looks around, hating that she was the first called on, and says, "We're low on soaps. We have a shipment that was due, but the truck didn't arrive today like it was supposed to."

"Easy enough. Ration them. We probably give out too many as it is. Next, Mbaye." I pretend like I didn't just tear him apart a little while ago, though he has clearly not forgotten, because when I make eye contact, he looks away. "How are we on food?"

"We're okay for now," he says, speaking to the table. "I may reduce portion sizes on anything we're low on, but we've got more than enough for a few days."

"Good. Cameo, any major issues we need to be aware of?"

Cameo nods. "There are still a few people arriving from Einstein. Either staffers or people who had trips scheduled and were holding out that things would change. We had to move a lot of people around, so there are some hurt feelings. Who didn't get the fancy room. Who missed their trip and is now taking it out on us."

"Reg," I say, "can we finally implement that policy I've been suggesting?"

"What's that?"

"To call them whiny babies and tell them to march into the sea?"

Reg sighs. "This is why you don't work in the hospitality industry."

"One other thing," Cameo says. "I'm a little concerned with the people we had to stick on cots. It's mostly staff, and they understand, but it still feels unkind. Can we have a housekeeper assigned specifically to them, and then see about some comps? Drinks and snacks at least?"

I point to Tierra. "Let's set that up. Make sure they're getting what they need. And Reg, any objection to treats and goodies, keep their spirits up?"

"No objection," Reg says.

"Good. Chris. Any issues?"

Chris starts to stand, then realizes he doesn't really need to stand and sits back down. He smooths out his mustache, the same red as his thinning hair. "We're just trying to keep the ground clear right now. Working on the drive, but as soon as we clear it, it's like we barely touched it."

As if on cue, the lights in the room give a little flicker. I point a finger to the ceiling.

"And what the hell is that about?"

"Still trying to peg it down. I think there's some faulty wiring somewhere but I don't feel good about ripping the walls apart. Last thing I want to do right now is knock out the power with this many people here. Even if it's just for a few minutes, it's going to cause a panic."

"Keep an eye on it."

Chris raises his hand, like he ran out the clock but needs a few more minutes. "Also."

"Yeah?"

"You know we have dinosaurs in the basement, right? Should we call the CDC or animal control or something?"

Lord, I actually managed to forget about that. And it's a good question. I was so worried about getting the dinosaurs contained that I didn't consider what we were going to do with them. Can't exactly just give them to a zoo.

"They're small," Reg says. "Can we just, you know, put them in a bag and throw them in the lake?"

"We are not killing them," I say. "They're fine for the moment. Now listen, everyone, the next two days are going to be a huge pain in the ass. You come across a problem—something, anything—you let me know. I don't need to be missing things right now. As for the guests, in the spirit of hospitality, I'm not saying you have to tell them to fuck off, I just think that you should."

"Do not tell anyone to fuck off," Reg says, raising his voice.

"Fine. Okay, everyone. I've got a million other things to do, so . . . break."

They all get up. Mbaye leaves the room like a shot. Everyone is very specifically moving away from me except Brandon, who practically pushes me into the corner. "I couldn't get in the ballroom," he says. "What's going on? Something with the sun?"

I run him through the basics of what Popa said, and he nods, taking it in. After mulling it he says, "You know what this sounds like?"

"What?" I ask.

"Like being Unstuck. Like . . . the way time slips for you? Something happens a little before it's supposed to happen? It sounds like that. Except, with all of us."

That's a fair assessment.

Also, not fun to hear.

I need to eat something. But more than that, I need the peace of my own bathroom. I need five minutes where I don't have to look at someone. I stop into the security office and after Ruby returns to its perch I tell it: "Stay."

"Where are you going?"

"Jealous? Do you think I have a date with a tablet?"

"It's just helpful for me to know where you're going."

Sigh. "I need a minute. And you need to focus on the pile of crap I've given you. I'll be back in fifteen."

I leave before it can respond, wend my way through the lobby, and get to the Atwood elevator. I punch the button for the fifth floor, lean against the back wall, and close my eyes. Feel the small lurch in my stomach and the press of gravity as the elevator moves up.

All day long, I've been hearing the dull chatter of past or future conversations, to the point where it just generally sounds like radio static to me, but a familiar voice cuts through and grabs my attention.

"You're sure you can make this happen for me?"

Drucker.

Interesting.

I wait for more, but that's all there is. It pings my radar enough that I pull out the sheet of paper in my pocket and scribble it down, then almost immediately forget it as the doors open and I feel a buzz radiating in the air.

It draws me toward the room with my maybe-dead friend. But the buzz seems to get a little stronger before I even make it there. As I'm passing the storage closet between rooms, something seems to grab at my skin.

Something magnetic.

It's just a closet. Painted dark gray, compared to the doors of the rooms, which are a light gray, set against the beige walls of the hallway and the blue carpet.

I punch the code into the door: 5-4-9-2.

The room is small, able to fit four people, and even then they'll all be best friends by the end of the ordeal. The walls are lined with industrial shelves, laden with toilet paper and individually wrapped soaps and towels and anything else you might find in your hotel room that isn't bolted down. I step inside and move some things around, look at the back wall. Nothing looks different about it. It's just a closet, like every other closet.

Except, I can feel something.

This little tug at the core of me. At first I thought it was nerves or anxiety. The feeling of being stressed out, and in a place alone, and looking for something, though you're not sure what. But it's not that. The more I think about it, the more I can feel it.

A physical sensation.

It's got to be the dead body in the room next door. Except, again, it feels a little different. Like electricity on my skin, moments before a thunderstorm.

I step out of the room, and as I do, brush against the doorframe . . .

. . . The floor of the holding cell is cold and hard underneath me. It makes me feel bad for all the people I've put in here. Not that it's been a whole lot of people. Mostly just drunks who need a little while to cool off, or that one time, a guy we found beating on his wife at three in the morning, and we needed to keep him contained until the cops showed up.

Not just cold and hard, but gritty, too. Like someone spilled sand in here before painting over it. I wish there was a bench. Even just a chair. I should put one in here. I reach my hand out and press the white painted wall, find there's blood on the back of my hand. Crimson red. Fresh. I check my hands and find no wounds. The blood isn't mine.

The blood matches the color of my blazer.

What is this?

Wasn't I just somewhere else?

The green door at the far end of the holding room opens and Allyn comes in. The look on his face is so grave it may as well be etched. *Here lies the career of January Cole.* He stands for a few moments, unsure of what to say. He keeps his distance, like I'm a wild tiger chained to the wall. After a beat he steps forward and leans down so he's more on eye level with me.

"I need to know why you did that."

The words spring from my mouth like a script. It's like watching a movie of myself. I want to say, *Allyn, what the hell is going on?* But it's like I know what to say, even though I don't know I'm about to say it. "I don't even know if I can trust you. I don't even know who you are."

What?

"January, it's me. I am here to help you. But after what you just did, I'm not sure if I can. You've been holding shit back since I got here. I know that you have been, and I let you, because I trust you. Now I need you to trust me."

What did I do? I don't even know.

"You didn't see it?" I ask.

"See what?"

"The ghost," I say. "It was going after him. It was going to kill him. I was trying to save him."

"January," Allyn says, starting a thought, but then dropping it. He looks away, and his face falls. He's resigning himself to some level of defeat, and I can tell that I've let him down. That something he believed about me has been broken. It hurts in a way that I haven't felt hurt since the day Mena died. I know I can be a prick, but Allyn, and his trust in me, was always a rock. Something to be sure about. I've worn it down to a grain of sand, and the tide is taking it away.

And I don't even know how.

Ghosts?

Who died? What happened? Where are we? What day is it even? I can't get the words out. They ring in my brain but my mouth operates independently of that. "It was going to kill him," I say, my voice dropping, to a place where it sounds like I'm not even sure I believe myself.

"This is my fault," he says, pressing his hands to his face, standing. "I knew you were in the second stage. And I figured—you're January Fucking Cole. You'd handle it. That's what you do. But your behavior the last few days. We should have pulled you from this when we found you tearing up that wall."

What wall?

"Allyn, I know this is hard to understand," I tell him. "I know I've been . . ." I drop my head. "I know I've been me. But you have to believe me. There's something at play here and I think I'm finally seeing how the pieces come together."

And? Say more about that!

"Just cool your jets here for a little," Allyn says. "I'm going to do everything in my power to protect you. I feel like that's what I owe you. I feel like I failed you." The corner of his lip curls, like he's about to offer a smile, but then he pulls it back. "I'll do the best I can."

He crosses to the door and leaves.

I touch the floor. Think hard about where I'm supposed to be. Somewhere else. Except my brain is all twisted.

My body moves of its own accord. I get up and pace. Touch the walls. Peer out through the small security-wired window into the office, where Allyn is talking to Nik. The panel is soundproofed so I can't hear them, but Allyn is doing most of the talking. Then they both leave. I pace the room, looking for something. But it's just an empty box. A big box holding me, but me not now.

Where was I?

Focus.

Concentrate.

I close my eyes. My own eyes don't close but I close my eyes on the inside, and retrace my steps. I know nothing before this room, but I know the last time I saw Allyn, something about the sun.

The sun. Then the meeting. Going to my room.

The closet.

I was in the closet.

How did I get from the closet to here?

How do I get from here to the closet?

Now I'm sitting with a match clenched between my fingers, the flame slowly marching down the wood. Where did I get matches?

Is this it? Is this my brain crackling and popping, surging with the electricity of being Unstuck, about to blow out?

The door opens.

The person standing there is the last person I wanted to see in this moment. The worst person to see, and it . . .

I hit the floor hard and just barely save myself from cracking my head.

Blue carpet. Closet.

Must have stumbled into the doorframe and fallen. How did that happen?

I get to my knees, shaking. Feel something wet on my nose, touch my nostril, and my fingertip comes back red with blood. I fall back onto my knees, take a Retronim out of my pocket, and dry-swallow it. Consider taking another, but figure I'll wait. Pull out a cherry lollipop instead and press it to my tongue. Try to find my center.

There's something else too. Something earlier today. Tamworth's office comes back to me. I don't remember why. I didn't slip while I was there, did I? It's like there's a big arrow pointing to it. To what? Tamworth's warning? The brain scans?

God, I am not here for this quantum bullshit.

I sit against the wall, try to remember details for the cell, anything that could be useful, but already they're fading. I pull out the paper in my blazer pocket and jot down what I can remember: *ghosts, blood, cell, when? killed someone? can't trust Allyn?*

And someone came in the room. Who?

Damn it. Already gone.

All I've got are words on a page. I can't even conjure the memory. Because it's not really a memory if it didn't happen yet.

The nosebleed wasn't bad, but I go to my room to indulge in a hot shower. Needed it after the gym anyway. The water feels nice pelting my skin—I took out the restrictor cap on my first night in here. The heavy flow distracts me from the way my brain feels like a truck has spent the afternoon backing up over it.

I step out of the shower and lean toward the mirror, wiping my hand across the condensation, and see a small figure behind me, long dark hair hanging in front of her face.

I yelp and nearly hop onto the sink as I turn around.

I'm alone.

Shit, how many Retronims was that? Tamworth said it could cause hallucinations. I need to cool it for the day.

Once my heart rate has returned to normal, I pull on a pair of pink jeans, a black T-shirt, and strappy boots, then pull my hair into a half-wet ponytail. I cram extra cherry lollipops into my pockets. After that, a quick cat eye. Casual day at the office, by decree of me. I just want to solve crimes and for my eyes to look good while I do it.

Still hungry—need to do something about that.

I head back down to security and find it, mercifully, empty, though as soon as I step inside Ruby pops out of its little stand and hovers up to my face.

"I got a hit," it says.

"On what?"

"The body."

"Finally," I say, relief washing over me. "Can you pull it up for me? Incognito?"

It floats over to the wall of video screens, which flashes off for a few moments and then comes back red, before turning into a profile of the dead John Doe.

Whose real name is John Westin.

The picture is a mug shot, from a pop on petty larceny. He's thirty-eight, originally from Staten Island, NY, and is carrying a couple of B and Es, one felony assault, and a few attempted robberies.

"This is a start," I say. "Next question, what was he doing here?"

"I anticipated that," Ruby says, and an employment history pops up. Mostly odd jobs—bartending, shipping, driving for a rideshare. But he also worked for a couple of years as a driver and cleaner for Teller Properties, which Ruby helpfully highlights in red, just in case I am a complete and total idiot.

"The file has been flagged by someone within the TEA. He was a person of interest in an ongoing investigation."

"Whose ongoing investigation?"

"I can't access that information."

"Anything else you want to tell me to ruin my day?" I ask Ruby.

"That's all I have for the moment," it says.

So, great, I've got a new piece of the puzzle. Problem is I have no idea what to do with it.

Ruby floats stupidly in my field of vision. This thing, full of computers and processors and information. This thing I hacked specifically so it would keep my secrets.

Isn't that a little like trust?

Maybe it's time to open the circle a bit.

I knock on the door of 526 and there's no answer. I swipe into the room, and if whoever is staying here is on the can or in the shower, I do not sufficiently care. But the lights are off. There's some luggage in the corner, a laptop on the corner of the bed, and a few wads of tissue on the bedside table next to the moisturizer, which, gross.

The body, though, that's here. Same condition, like it was killed moments ago. Blood still seeping down the bedspread.

"There's a body over there," I tell Ruby.

It beeps. "No there isn't."

"Well, I can see it. Clear as day."

"John Westin?"

"Bingo."

Ruby floats to the bed and hovers. A little red dot appears on the bedspread, expanding out until a frame of flashing red light covers the mattress. "I detect nothing. But I suppose this is why you've been having me search for him."

"Correct. Add that to the frames of video that are missing, and you can see why I've been a bit more tense than usual."

Ruby floats for a moment. "To be honest it didn't initially register as any different from your usual level of acerbic and antisocial behavior."

"Thanks." I move toward the bed. Touch the body again, my hand sliding through and meeting the mattress. "The crazy thing is it looks exactly the same. The blood is still red. It's been hours now. It should be showing signs of rigor. The blood should be drying. But no."

"How did he die?"

"Exsanguination," I say. "Throat cut. Left to right. Sharp blade. No defensive wounds on the hands, so whoever did it snuck up on him. Or maybe it was someone he knew, so he dropped his guard." I shrug. "I'm not a forensic expert and I can't even examine the body, so that's really the best I got."

"We know he was a criminal, with a tenuous connection to Teller," Ruby says. "He's dead and whoever killed him likely tampered with our video. I haven't been able to find any record of him being here on the remaining feeds."

"This sucks," I tell Ruby.

"Are you open to suggestions?"

"At this point?" I wave my hand, welcoming it to proceed.

"Have you considered examining the crime scene?"

"You mean the crime scene that, when I first found it, was being cleaned by housekeeping?" I ask. "The crime scene where I can't touch the body, and no one else can see it?"

"I guess you could just sit there and do nothing then. Would you like me to set the mood?"

Ruby launches into a recording of the chorus of "All by Myself" by Céline Dion.

"I wish you were a real person so I could murder you," I tell it.

Not that it's wrong.

I stand up. Survey the room. Wonder how much longer I have before the occupant comes back. The room looks like just about every other room in this place. Granted, they're of different sizes and shapes, but the general design scheme is the same. Lots of bronze fixtures and brushed wood. Gleaming black surfaces. Blue carpet. The closets are small, because no one's coming to stay here for more than a few days.

The bathrooms are simple: subway tile and Hollywood lighting around the vanity, with more gleaming black surfaces—the sink, the toilet—to offset all that white.

I drop to the floor and check under the bed and the desk. Nothing. The dresser is flush to the floor. Run my hand behind the TV, then pick up the lamps. Next I check the drawers, pulling them out to see if anything is written underneath.

Which is one of the fun secrets of hotel rooms. People leave odd messages in unseen places, for someone else to stumble upon. The inside of my toilet tank, someone wrote in black permanent marker: *This hotel wasn't half bad. It was all bad!*

How droll.

In the bottom drawer of the desk, I find a name carved into the wood. Sam Seidlinger.

"Ruby, did a Sam or Samuel Seidlinger ever stay in this room?" I ask.

"Three years ago."

Probably just someone marking their territory. I slide the drawer back into place. Check the toilet tank and find nothing there.

Last place to look. The painting over the bed. Every room in here has a different one. They're all stock bullshit, all of them having some-thing to do with clocks. Too on the nose for my taste. The one above my bed is a series of watch faces that melt until the last one is a pud-dle. Obvious Dalí rip-off. This one is an hourglass, perched on the sand of an expansive desert, the sky blue behind it. But the hourglass is empty. Someone smarter than me could probably interpret it. I grip the painting by the sides and tug. It's stuck to the wall. I stand on the bed, look down, and realize John Westin's dead body is now staring at my crotch. I try to not think about that. I run my fingers underneath the painting, manage to get it loosened a bit, then pull it down.

It's written in thick black marker, in beautiful swooping text:

> In the garden of memory
> In the palace of dreams
> That is where you and I
> Shall meet

"Ruby? What do you make of that?"

The drone hovers over my shoulder and scans the back of the painting.

"Make of what?"

"This right here," I say, pointing. "The text."

"There is no text."

Well, I'd call that a clue. A corpse only I can see, text only I can see. I read it off and Ruby says, "That's a quote from the Mad Hatter in the film *Alice Through the Looking-Glass*, based on the book by Lewis Carroll."

"Didn't see it, never read it," I say. "What's the gist?"

"Alice steps through a mirror and ends up in a world where up is down, backwards is forwards, and the future is remembered," it says. "That's from the description I found online. Would you like me to download the movie and order you a copy of the book, in case they contain anything relevant?"

"Why not. Haven't read a book in ages."

"You haven't read a book in the entire time I've known you," Ruby says.

"Shut your vents."

I put the painting back and I'm just getting it into place when I hear, "What the hell are you doing?"

I turn to find a young, handsome guy in a sweater and a pair of slacks. He's standing at the door, a small bag in his hand, slightly agog at me on his bed and messing with the painting. Oh, how much more entertaining this would be if he could actually see the corpse between my legs.

"Security check?" I say. I drop my voice and say to Ruby, "Couldn't have warned me?"

"I was running a scan," it says, making no attempt to be quiet.

As I'm hopping off the bed, the man crosses to the desk, puts down the bag, and picks up the phone. "Security."

My watch buzzes. "January, you free?"

I smile at the guy when he realizes the implication, so he hits the tab on the phone and redials. "I need a manager up to my room right now. It's important. I caught one of your staffers going through my things." Pause. "Yes, I contacted security. Apparently it's one of your security people who was doing it." Another pause. "Fine. Thank you." He hangs up and turns to me. "The manager is coming up."

I nod. Look around the room. Relax my shoulders. "So . . . where ya from?"

He doesn't answer.

"What were you doing?" Reg asks outside the elevator bank, breathing hard, his face red. He's still that way after making it to the guy's room, hearing him out, and comping the rest of his stay. Because the only way to truly satisfy people with money is to give them stuff for free. Frankly I think it's a con and that's how they keep their money. They've convinced people they're too good to spend it.

I fill my lungs until they feel overstretched like balloons, and let all the air out. Try to think of something to say. Where do I even start? I don't know that I can. Telling Ruby is one thing. It's not going to report me. Reg might. Or he might say the wrong thing to Allyn. Who knows? I settle on: "I'm looking into something."

Reg waits, tipping his head toward me, showing me his ear. "That it? You're looking into something."

"Yes."

"What something?"

"A thing."

"A thing," he says, nodding slowly. He looks at Ruby. "What thing?"

My heartbeat picks up, but then it answers, "Do you honestly think she tells me anything?"

Reg nods, frustrated but accepting this is how it's going to be, and says, "Follow me."

He leads me into the elevator and we ride it down. Aside from the heavy breathing he's silent as a palace guard, not looking at me, trying very hard to not say anything. I can feel the strain of it. And as much as I want to break the silence, I don't. I'm just exhausted. I need a nap. I need coffee. I need to see Mena right now.

We get to the lobby, where there are a few more TEA agents floating around, plus Nik is standing at the concierge desk talking with Cameo. Reg leads me to the elevator that runs up through the lobby, parallel to the brass pole suspending the clock, the hands of which are still stuttering and jumping.

As the elevator ascends I ask, "Taking me to the roof to murder me? There's so much snow we won't be able to get the door open. You might be better off throwing me over the railing of the lobby. The guests won't like it. I mean, I'm going to hit that floor and splatter open like a tomato. Then again, who knows what half of these weirdos are into . . ."

"Stop it," he says.

We make it to the top and he leads me to the Tick Tock, where we proceed to an empty table and sit down. As if he was expecting us, Marc, the waiter with the ear gauges who is always wearing artfully done eyeliner—it's so good I've been meaning to ask him for a lesson—comes over and waits for his command.

"Macallan, the twenty-five, splash of water," Reg says, then looks at me, like he wants to know if I mind.

"Seltzer, splash of lime," I tell Marc.

He nods and disappears.

"Isn't that a hundred bucks a glass?" I ask.

Reg bores a hole in me with his stare. "It's my hotel. And it's been a long day."

"What are we doing here?"

"Getting something to eat."

"Why?"

He leans back. Looks around the restaurant. MKS is hunkered down with Drucker in a corner. A few members of his entourage are having dinner on the other side of the room. Warwick is sitting at the bar nursing a beer and pecking at a laptop. The place is reasonably crowded, though we have a nice little oasis around us. A few empty tables that make it feel like we're sitting alone.

"How are you doing?" he asks.

"I'm fine," I tell him. "I'm always fine."

"Look, I'm not dumb . . ."

It zips right into my head—*really, coulda fooled me!*—but he sees it and puts his finger up.

"Stop actively trying to be a dick for like two seconds," he says.

"Nothing active about it. It's a reflex."

Marc shows up with our drinks. He sets them down and waits for a food order. Reg gets a banh mi on gluten-free bread and I go for the thieboudienne. Been craving that ever since I suggested it to Nik earlier. Marc disappears without writing it down, and Reg says, "You've been on edge. More so than normal. Now I get a call from a guest that you're going through his things?"

"I wasn't going through anything."

"Doesn't matter exactly what you were doing, because the point remains, you were in someone's room, unsupervised and without permission."

"I was supervised," I say, pointing over my shoulder at Ruby.

Reg sighs. Picks up the scotch. Takes a little sip. His body relaxes as soon as it hits his lips and I can smell it from here. It makes me wish, deeply and desperately, that I could have a drink, but that's not in the cards. Not usually, and especially not now, with where my head is at.

"January, I know you went through a lot of shit," he says. "We all did. And I know it's a little frou-frou, but . . ." He looks around again. "This is a family. It's a weird little family. I get that. But we're here for each other. I mean, when we held the memorial for Mena you didn't even show up."

I take a big gulp of my seltzer. Too fast and hard, so that it goes down the wrong pipe and sears my lungs. "Someone would have asked me to talk. Not my jam."

He's halfway to sipping his scotch but he stops, points a finger at me. "See? That right there. We all know that. You think we don't know that? No one would have expected that of you. It was you projecting your insecurities on us."

"Whatever."

"What can I do?" he asks. "Just tell me, what can I do?"

I don't know what to say, so I say nothing.

"You think I don't see what this is?" He looks around, makes sure we're alone, that Marc isn't making his way over with the food. He leans forward and drops his voice. "You shouldn't be here anymore. You should be safe away from this place. Seeking treatment. You stay here, you know what happens."

"Did Tamworth say anything to you? He's not supposed to."

"Tamworth didn't say shit. We all see it. We all know. It's not a secret. It's like you're running toward the third stage of this thing, full speed. At this point I gotta ask, how's that different from putting a gun in your mouth, other than the time it takes?"

He sits back, satisfied at having said the thing he's clearly been meaning to say for a while. I let that one sit in the air. Not really willing to take it in. Because of course I have thought that. Of course I have considered that. I know what I'm doing. But how do I explain it? That it's worth it? That every time I see Mena, even for those few moments, I am filled with so much sunlight it practically bursts out of me? That it heals up all the hurts and leaves me stronger for long enough that I can survive until the next time I see her?

"Me and Allyn have been talking," he says.

"Yeah, about that," I tell him. "When Allyn turfs me, I want a job here. Whatever you need. I'll clean toilets. I don't care."

"January . . ."

"What, you think I can't do it?" I ask. "I know everyone's names and I know where everything is. That's a pretty good start."

Reg looks away from me, steels his voice. "January, if you cannot get with this, we are going to have your things removed. We don't think it's safe for you to be here anymore. They thought it was. But look at what's happening."

That one knocks my heart into my spine and it comes back bleeding. I push out from the table, see Marc approaching out of the corner of my eye. "Family, family. Everyone keeps calling this a family. Throwing me out on the street is how you treat your family? Fuck you, Reg."

I get up and snap my fingers at Marc. "I'm taking mine at the bar." Then I turn and head for the far end, where there's an empty handful of seats, and sit there, stewing, until the plate appears in front of me. I mumble a thanks, probably not loud enough to be heard over the jazz, and then I breathe in the scent of tomatoes and fish.

I adjust myself on the stool and catch another glimpse of Drucker and MKS. Drucker is leaning in now, their faces almost touching. She's speaking intensely. I can't see MKS's face from here but his body language looks tense. I tell Ruby, "Amplify their conversation."

"I can't."

"Why not?"

"One of them seems to be utilizing an audio mask."

Could be either of them, though my money would be on the prince. Devices like that are expensive. Maybe above government pay grade. Which means the prince has a toy that's designed to screw with security measures. Good to know.

After a few moments of staring at the back wall, I catch Mbaye standing toward the middle of the bar, talking to an old white man in a seersucker suit, a straw hat perched on the bar next to him. I do make note that, yes, he is drinking a mint julep.

"Sure thing, this place is haunted," Mbaye says. "I see them in the kitchen sometimes. Down in the hallways. In the bathroom once, too."

"The first time I stayed here," the man says, in a syrup-thick southern accent, "and now this is a few years ago, I saw a woman. She was walking down the hallway, away from me. Then it was like she heard me. She turned a little, and then she was gone. Long brown hair. Very"—the man glances around—"well endowed."

Mbaye nods. "Let me guess, fourth-floor hallway? Butler?"

The man smiles and snaps his fingers. "How'd you know?"

"Rumor was that's the designer of the hotel. She went missing after this place opened, you know? A lot of people think this place burned her out and she moved on, but I'm not so sure." He takes a deep breath, exhales. "This is the thing, about places like this . . ."

At this point, Mbaye turns and notices me. It annoys me that he's talking to someone. That he's standing there. That he feels any kind of joy or happiness in this life.

I ask, "Why didn't you check the gas?"

He stops. Stands there. Then smiles and apologizes to the man he's talking to and heads toward the back of the house. I say it louder.

"Why didn't you check the gas?"

His shoulders sag and he turns to me.

"I did."

"Like you checked Kolten's plate today. Like you're always on top of things, right? All you had to do was check the gas line, and you didn't and she died. Right in there. On that floor. Alone. Why are you even still here? How do you live with that?"

The music is still playing but I realize that I am screaming, practically standing on the stool, and people are staring, which should probably encourage me to shut up, but it does not. In fact, I dig deep. The three words that have been trying to burst out of my chest since the day of the explosion.

I didn't so much hear it as I felt it. A little shudder in my room. Something amiss. It was late, and I was just getting out of the shower, waiting for Mena to show up, so we could lie around and watch some bad TV and she could tell me about her day while I struggled to stay awake.

But I felt the shudder and then I pulled on my clothes and by the time I got out of the room I was getting calls about it. Explosion in the kitchen of the Tick Tock. Fire and smoke. No reported injuries.

Yet.

I was halfway up the elevator when it cut through the chatter: "Shit, there was someone in here."

And I knew. In that moment, I knew, so that when the elevator doors opened I was already on my knees, weeping, and refused to go any further, because I just could not. And since that night, since it became clear it may have been due to a problem with the gas line, I have held these three words in reserve.

"It's your fault," I tell him.

And I can see that the words landed as accurately and sharply as I intended.

Tears spring to his eyes. He clenches his jaw to keep it from quivering.

Reg is at my side. His hand on my arm. I brush it off. I don't want to see how it goes. I stamp out of the now-silent restaurant, every eye on me, and make it to the railing. I stare down into the lobby. My stomach lurches a little as I gauge the distance between here and the marble floor below . . .

Marc comes out from the kitchen, cradling a birthday cake, the mess of candles on it making his face glow amber in the dim glow of the restaurant lighting. I take a swig of the mescal I know I shouldn't be drinking, the smoky goodness burning my throat, and watch from my perch at the bar as he carries it toward a large table on the far end, where the staff has assembled around Tierra.

The hotel is mostly empty; construction at the timeport, so no flights in or out for the next few days. Tierra's birthday isn't today, but it's close, and it's a rare moment where there's not much to do, so most of the staff is here, even the ones who aren't on shift. They crowd around her and when Marc places the cake down they launch into the "Happy Birthday" song.

And I watch, my heart twisting and contorting, trying to remember the last time someone did that for me. Then I feel silly for caring.

When the song is over, I turn back to my drink, but then someone pulls out the stool next to me.

"Don't you want some cake?" Mena asks.

"Not really a cake person. I prefer pie."

"And yet, I love you anyway," she says, leaning into me and kissing my neck, sending a shudder down my spine.

We sit there for a few moments in silence. I take another sip and put my glass down, staring at the back wall. This feeling inside me that I haven't felt in a long time, that I thought I'd pretty much extinguished a long time ago.

Want.

"They're your family too, you know," Mena says.

"Never been much for family," I tell her.

Mena picks up my glass, throws back the rest of the drink, and stands, then grabs my stool and pulls it away from the bar top. I nearly fall off. "C'mon. Have some cake."

I sit there for a minute, planted on the stool. I'm overwhelmed by this feeling that, by going over there, by taking part in that, I'd be intruding. That I wouldn't belong. I'm not one of them. Two months here, and besides the connection I've made with Mena, I still feel like it's just a matter of days before I have to pack up and go home, even though this is supposed to be my home now. I want to say this to her, and I can't, but also, I don't have to, because she takes my hand and says, "It's okay."

She leads me to the table, and everyone looks up, almost all at once, and their faces erupt in smiles.

"There she is!" Reg says, pulling out the chair next to him. "Thought we weren't cool enough for you."

"I'm a little disappointed we didn't get to hear you sing," Cameo says, "but, maybe next time."

I want to say something clever, but truly, I got nothing. I just sit. Mbaye is cutting the cake, a large sheet with delicate pink and purple frosting florets, placing them on the expensive plates that are usually reserved for the guests, but tonight, it's for them.

For us.

He slides a plate toward me and smiles. "My mother made this kind of cake for me when I was a child. It's not as good as hers, but I try my best. I hope you like it."

I take the plate and pick up the fork perched on the edge, but before I carve off a piece I look up, and everyone is staring at me. Waiting for me.

Is this what it feels like?

To be a part of something?

It's so much I can barely breathe, but I don't want them to see that, so I nod toward Tierra and say, "Happy birthday."

"Thank you, love," she says.

Mena hovers behind me and she gives my shoulder a little squeeze. I take a bite, and the cake is sublime, flooding me with this feeling of . . .

My hands are on the railing, my heart feels like a bottomless pit, the slip extinguished by a cry for help.

GENERAL RELATIVITY

The cry came from somewhere below, so I take off for the ramp and make it down to the next level, where I find Osgood, his smart gray-and-purple suit disheveled, holding himself up against the wall outside of a bathroom, clutching his temple. Blood seeps from between his fingers.

There's a flash of movement and a black-robed figure ducks around a corner.

Eshe.

And I start running again. I don't have time to worry about Osgood—his call for help has drawn attention and while he's clearly injured, it doesn't seem life threatening.

By the time I make it to the corner, to a long hallway that constitutes the business center, it's empty.

She had a good start on me so she could have ducked into one of the offices lining the hallway. Twelve doors on either side, all closed.

I make my way down the line slowly, swiping the locks on the doors, pushing them open, checking the offices inside without taking my eyes off the hallway.

Each office is fairly small—a desk, lots of outlets, no windows. They all seem to be empty at the moment, and there's not much room to hide.

It gives me a second to wonder what the hell is going on. Why would Eshe attack Osgood? It seems out of character, though in fairness, I don't know much about her.

As I make my way down the hall I hear something nearby. A scratching sound. I wonder if it's a slip, but I don't feel the accompanying charge in my head. After a few moments it happens again.

It sounds like it could be coming from above me? Then I open an office door and find one of the ceiling panels slightly askew. I scale onto the desk and move the panel aside, and as I'm about to pull myself up, a robed figure darts across the hallway. I drop down and head after her, catch her turning the corner, and by the time I make it to the end of the hallway, she's disappeared, with three potential directions she could have gone. There's no one around to tell me which way to pick.

Ruby catches up to me and I ask, "Got eyes on her?"

"The cameras are, once again, giving me problems."

"Great, so whoever got in is back inside?"

"Actually the system has been shut down for routine maintenance. Though it usually only happens at night, and only when they detect that there is nobody out in the hallways and there's nothing to currently make a record of. It's not supposed to happen at a time like this."

"Do you think it's an accident?" I ask.

"No," Ruby says. "I believe our infiltrator is just getting creative."

"Lovely."

I jog back to the bathroom, and find Osgood is now surrounded by a large group of people. Someone has passed him a handkerchief, which he's holding against the wound on his head. The front of his pants is soaked in either water or urine, I can't tell. Nik is jogging from the other side of the hallway, and we arrive at the same time.

"What happened?" I ask.

Davis squints his eyes at me, confused for a moment, then says, "I was using the facilities and someone grabbed me from behind. Put their arm around my throat. I didn't even see who it was. I struggled, threw some elbows, and then it sounded like someone came in and scared them off . . ."

"C'mon," Nik says, taking his arm. "Let's get you down to the doc."

I watch as Nik leads Osgood away, and, none of this fits. The guy is, what, fifty? Sixty? Eshe is a professional, with no clear incentive to just randomly attack one of the bidders. Two plus two is currently equaling fish.

"Ruby," I say. "Find Eshe for me, now."

Ten minutes later and I'm sitting across from Eshe in the security office. Just me and her, no table between us. Her hands are neatly folded in her lap. Her entourage, along with Allyn, is crowded outside in the lobby, but I insisted on having a moment alone with her.

I don't want to call it an interrogation. Because none of this feels right to me. Starting with the fact that Eshe voluntarily walked into the room.

She waits for me to speak. I know that I could sit here for the next hundred years and she'll never say the first word, so I don't concern myself with trying to get the upper hand. I don't have the patience.

"Did you try to kill Osgood?" I ask.

"If I tried he would be dead," she says. "Nor would you suspect me."

I believe her, and that pretty much sums up why I don't think it was her. We sit in silence for another minute, listening to the raised voices arguing outside. Mostly members of MKS's entourage arguing in English and Arabic about the hostility of our reaction. I can hear Teller, too. Of course he got involved. He's probably thrilled.

"Someone attacked Osgood, and they were wearing a burka."

Eshe nods. "And whom do you suspect?"

She's confident, I'll give her that. "Not sure yet. My mind goes to Grayson, but he's a big dude. The person wearing it was slim. Body type closer to yours."

Eshe nods again but doesn't speak.

"You have an alibi for the last hour or so?"

"No."

"That doesn't help me," I tell her. "Or you."

Eshe gives a little shrug. "I did nothing wrong."

"Yeah," I say, throwing a thumb over my shoulder. "Tell that to them. Everyone's going to want to believe what they want to believe, until I can hand them something that convinces them to believe something else. So, work with me on this. What were you doing?"

She doesn't answer.

"So obviously it was something you don't want me to know about," I say, leaning back in the seat, crossing my legs. "Reconnaissance? Checking in on the other bidders?"

"Don't you have video showing my movements through the hotel? I'm sure that could exonerate me."

Is she taunting me? Does she know our system has been compromised? Even if she doesn't, I don't want to tip her off that it has been.

"It doesn't," I say. "But I did have another idea." I raise my watch and page Allyn. "Is Fumiko here?"

His voice comes back, nearly lost in a sea of jabbering voices. "Yes."

"Bring her in. Just the two of you."

The door opens and all the muffled voices spill into the room. Allyn gets the door closed and leads in a small Japanese girl, her orange hair in a bob cut. She's wearing pants that match her hair and a green velvet top, tapping away on her phone without looking up. The hotel's costume designer, responsible for outfitting travelers in period-specific clothing.

"Fumiko," I say. "Tell Allyn what you were about to tell me."

Her eyes are glued to the phone and I wonder if she even heard me. But she puts up a finger and her phone makes a little *whoosh* noise. Then she looks up.

"There's a burka missing," she says.

I raise a finger in the air, glad that my timing was on. Eshe seems to untense a little. It would be easy enough to steal something from Fumiko's collection, but I also figured it wouldn't be long before she noticed.

"So you think the attack on Osgood was staged to throw suspicion on MKS?" Allyn asks.

"Yes, thank you for catching up. But it begs the question of who. As I was just telling Eshe, logic says it would have been Teller, because he's been expressing the most animosity about MKS being involved in this, but again, it wasn't Grayson under there and they don't seem to be traveling with anyone else." I turn to Ruby. "Keep an eye on the two of them, let's make sure there's not a third member of their entourage. Someone they've been meeting with on the sly."

"Sure thing," Ruby says.

"And"—I turn to Allyn—"how is Osgood?"

"Didn't even need stitches," he says. "Obviously he wants answers, but he is conspicuously absent from the mob outside the door."

"Speaking of, go take care of that, and let's square it with Osgood that it was someone else. Then we have to figure out exactly what is happening."

"Can I go now?" Fumiko asks, back on her phone.

"Yeah," I say, and she exits, the voices bursting through the door. Allyn follows her, and it's just me and Eshe again.

"Thank you," she says.

"Well, like I said, it didn't track," I say. "You struck me as more professional than that. Whoever did that was sloppy."

She stands and gives me another nod, then leaves the room, where the voices have softened significantly.

I lean into the seat, lean my head back, and close my eyes, but it's too bright in here. I don't like it. Take a few deep breaths. Pray for a break in all this. That maybe the chaos is enough at this point for someone to say, yes, let's move this stupid meeting because everything that's happening right now is just too much.

There's a silver lining here. This isn't a ghost stealing an EpiPen.

It's a clear attempt on the life of one of the bidders, plus an incursion on our security system to cover the killer's tracks. Even Drucker can't say it's a good idea to keep after this dumb auction.

And then my watch lights up with reports of a fire in the kitchen.

When it rains.

The fire suppression system kicks in before I'm even halfway to the restaurant, so when I get there foam is already seeping around the corner of the bar. That much is a mercy because I haven't been in the kitchen since the night Mena died and I have no intention of going back in. Not that there's even much for me to do.

How am I going to handle a fire? Investigate it into going out?

Mbaye is talking intently with Reg, and I consider getting closer to join the conversation, but realize now is not the time. I don't really regret saying what I did to Mbaye—it's been a long time coming—but I know it'll just make things worse to push myself into his orbit right now. I hang back until they're done and wait for Reg to come over to me, Mbaye disappearing into the back to assess the damage.

"That's weird," Reg says, jerking his head toward the kitchen.

"We don't have enough of that going around," I tell him.

"Chickens roasting in the oven. Mbaye says he put them in ten minutes ago. Suddenly they're black as charcoal and the oven catches fire."

"Motherfucker can't cook chicken now?"

Reg looks around at the guests, some of whom are lingering, unsure what to do. Others are still eating like nothing happened. "Said it's like they'd been in there for hours."

The clocks. The sun. Now the ovens. Time has always been a bitch, but now it seems to have a vendetta.

"So what's the plan?" I ask.

"Mbaye wants to shut down the kitchen to make sure it isn't some kind of mechanical issue. But we're both thinking the same thing. He's had issues with cook times before. Things taking slightly longer or slightly shorter than they should. Figured it was a hazard of being here. But this." He shakes his head. "This is dangerous."

"What's going on?" Allyn is cutting through the restaurant, Nik at his side.

I put my hands up to slow them down. "Fire. Currently under control."

"What happened?" he asks.

I run him through it, along with the time theory. He closes his eyes and bows his head, then says, "Downstairs, now."

Popa again holds court, but this time it's just me, Allyn, Nik, and Reg. And we skipped the security office in favor of the chapel, a room which I am sure has never once been used for praying, but has most definitely been used by older couples looking to "spice things up" by smashing their wrinkled parts together in a semipublic place.

It's a small room and there's not much to it—three rows of wooden pews, gorgeous never-lit candles in sconces along the walls, and a large window overlooking what's supposed to be a rolling field, but right now is covered in a blanket of white.

Things are spiraling and I know what Allyn is doing. Tightening the huddle so we don't have to deal with pricks like Teller.

We all sit awkwardly in the pews—Popa at the front, then me and Allyn, with Reg and Nik in the last row. Popa is twisted around, listening with his eyes closed as I recap the whole kitchen thing—again—and when I'm done he turns his head, gazing out the window. Then he picks one foot up and drapes it over his other knee, trying to get comfortable on the hard wooden surface. A look on his face like he's contemplating what topping he wants on his pizza.

"Earth to smart guy," I say, snapping my fingers. "What's going on?"

"I don't know."

"Aren't you paid to know?"

He arches an eyebrow at me. "There's not exactly a rulebook here. I would love for it to be an Occam's razor thing. The stove malfunctioned. But based on what you're saying, I have to allow that, yeah, we're getting time leaks."

It seems like there's supposed to be more than that, so I raise my hand and prod him to keep going.

"We're pretty far from Einstein," Popa says. "Two miles, at least. We've got sensors on the hotel exterior, and on the surrounding land, to watch for exactly this. This place is built to keep radiation out. Two-foot-thick concrete walls with three inches of lead sandwiched in the middle. The windows are made of lead glass. Nothing is making it through that." He clears his throat. "And even then, we're getting some weird data from Einstein, but no spikes."

"So if radiation isn't leaking over, why is time acting like a drunken sorority girl?" I ask.

Popa leans forward, clasps his hands together. "I don't know."

"Great," I say. "Great thing to hear from the smartest guy in the room."

"Technically, as an artificially intelligent construct, I'm the smartest thing in the room," Ruby says, from its little floating spot in the corner.

I take off my boot and throw it at the drone. It glides out of the way and my boot smacks against the eggshell-painted wall, leaving a little scuff. As I retrieve the boot and put it back on, Allyn says, "We need to figure this out. Get as many people here as you can."

Popa nods and gets up to leave.

Then Allyn zeros in on me. "The rest of you, give us the room."

Reg and Nik exchange a look, but now I don't want to break Allyn's stare. The two of them get up and follow Popa. We wait for the door to close, and then we wait a little longer, next to each other, turning to look out the window. It's so quiet you can hear the flakes hitting the glass.

"John Westin," he says, breaking the silence.

Ah. So he flagged the file.

"Person of interest," I tell him.

"In what?"

I wonder what I would say, if I didn't know that at some point in the near future I'd be in a cell and Allyn would be there and I would suddenly find myself questioning his allegiance. We had that relationship, once. I could find it again. But right now I know the safest thing to do is keep this close. The first half of the story.

"He was in the lobby," I say. "No luggage, not the usual vibe I get from the clientele. I told Ruby to pull a face scan and tell me who he was. That was before we found ourselves in the middle of a hurricane of dicks, so my interest in him has waned. Who is he to you?"

"A person of interest."

"Go on."

"In an investigation."

"Stop being cute," I tell him. "Something is going on."

"Understatement," Allyn says, with no inflection.

"I'm serious," I say. "Someone went after Osgood. At what point are you going to admit that we need to move this thing?"

"January . . ."

"And Kolten. Someone tried to kill him."

"That was an accident," Allyn says.

I pull out my phone and sit next to him, queue up the video of Warwick. After the jacket flutters I rewind so he can see it again. "What does that look like?"

Allyn shrugs. "What am I looking at?"

I rewind and let it play again. "Right there. His jacket moves. Like someone is reaching inside. He said the EpiPen was missing. Whoever tried to poison Kolten also tried to make sure that he couldn't be saved."

"January . . ."

"Look, I know it's weird, but given how things are playing out right now . . ."

"January, they found the pen. It was under the table. The thing fell out of his pocket."

My mind goes blank. "Wait . . . what?"

Allyn gets up and moves toward the window. "You know who I just got off the phone with?"

"Who, the president?"

He turns and raises an eyebrow at me. "Yes, actually."

"Oh," I say. "Shit."

"Yeah. And he was very insistent that this go forward. As in, I will lose my job if it doesn't." He pauses and sighs. "I'll be taking lead on this, starting now."

"Allyn . . ."

He sits down next to me. "As your friend, I'm asking you to not show that video to anyone else."

"Why?"

"Because I'm going to do everything I can to protect you. And that doesn't help."

My stomach drops out. I suddenly want to hide my face from him.

He doesn't believe me.

That one actually hurts.

What if I'm seeing what I want to see? What if it's just a trick of the light? Why would someone steal the pen to drop it at his feet?

I'm starting to not believe myself.

"How about this," I tell him. "You had a German nanny. So you were raised in a bilingual household. That's how you know the language."

"January . . ." he says. And there's a weight to it that makes me think now was the wrong time to make a joke. But then he gives a little laugh and says, "Wrong again."

At the elevator bank I punch the button and close my eyes and feel a little spark across my brain and look up and watch as the doors explode outward, flames and debris flooding around my feet, and within the carnage I see mangled bodies, Eshe and MKS among them.

The slip doesn't last long. Once it's done and the hallway has re-turned to normal, I ping Chris on my watch. He comes back, "Yeah?"

"Take elevator five out of service."

"Why?"

"Because I told you to. Give it a safety check."

"The elevators were just inspected a month ago . . ."

"Do it," I say, cutting him off and ending the call.

I consider paging Allyn to let him know, but I'm pretty sure at this point he thinks I'm crazy. Still, I'm getting real tired of saving people's lives and getting no goddamn recognition for it. It makes me want to march up to whichever luxury suite MKS is staying in and tell him, *You know what I just saved your ass from? I don't even need a hug. Just a high five.*

"Well, hello there, Miss January."

I turn to find Osgood ambling my way, flanked by two TEA agents, following at a respectful distance. He's changed into a fresh suit and has a neat, white bandage on his temple.

"Making some new friends?" I ask.

He glances over his shoulder at the agents. "Since I'm the only one without a crew, Danbridge decided I needed one. Especially after what happened."

"Speaking of, how's that noggin?" I ask.

He touches the bandage softly. "Could be worse. Thank you again."

Well, at least someone is gracious.

"Hell of a thing," Osgood says, as the elevator door opens, but he makes no move to step on. Maybe he's staying on this floor, or else he just feels like making conversation out here. Not the worst idea. It gives me an opportunity to poke him a little.

"So we know it wasn't Eshe who tried to ace you, but someone wanted you to think it was," I say. "What do you make of that?"

"You're the detective," he says.

"You seem unbothered by an attempt on your life."

"Got myself a nice big glass of brandy upstairs, and that helped," he says. "Certainly not my favorite way to spend the evening. But the thing about bullies is, if you run away when they push you, next time they just push you harder."

"Still, it makes me wonder, what's your play?"

"Hmm?" he asks, understanding the question but pretending he doesn't.

"Why this place? What do you want it for?"

He gives me a little smile. He steps closer to me, like he wants to get out of earshot of the agents.

"Do you ever wonder if the world we're living in is the right one?"

"The hell does that mean?" I ask.

He shrugs. "If you could be anyone, do anything, what would you be?"

"I like my job just fine."

He smiles. "But you worked the stream, right? I imagine that's a hell of a high. Travel all over time. Do you miss it?"

"Of course I miss it."

"And what does the Time Enforcement Agency do, exactly?"

"It's sort of in the name. And, shouldn't you know that if you want to buy this place?"

"Humor me."

"We prevent people from fucking up the past, which is mostly about stopping rich assholes from doing whatever the hell they want, whenever the hell they want."

"Right," he says, clapping his hands. "Time cop. So you're saying that if you could be anyone, do anything, you'd still want to be a time cop? Why?"

Because . . .

I don't have a great answer. But rather than flounder I tell him, "I've always liked to travel, and that's the only way to hop around time and get paid for it. Plus I like telling people what to do. Or, more specifically, what they can't do. I kind of get off on it."

"And in all this running around and telling people what to do, how do you know that you haven't already failed? Who's to say that someone didn't change things already?"

"The prevailing theory is that reality would implode."

"That's the theory, yes."

God, I am tired of this. Everyone acting like it's worth testing a theory where you get either super-rich, or super-dead. Russian roulette might give a similar high without screwing things up for everyone else.

"If you're so worried about whether we do the job or not, why not just give your fortune to us?" I ask. "More resources, more agents?"

"Who watches the watchmen?" he asks.

"You, I guess."

He smiles. "I'm sorry. I just like asking questions. Feels like I learn more that way."

And with that, he turns to leave, the agents tailing along, raising their eyebrows like, *we dunno, we're just doing what we're told.*

Then Osgood stops. "Pity an old man with one last question."

Sigh. "What?"

"If you could go anywhere in time, where would you go?"

I know the answer without having to think about it. The answer lives in my chest. It's all I think about.

"I'd go hang out with Cleopatra," I tell him. "I bet she'd be fun at a party."

"I want to visit Atlantis," he says, a twinkle in his eye.

Ah. There it is. The genial attitude and the obtuse questions are there to cover up that he is a nutball. Just another Atlantis truther.

"I believe it was wiped out in the Thera volcanic eruption," he says. "Which happened sometime between fifteen hundred and sixteen hundred B.C. That's a lot of time to explore. On top of that, we're still not entirely sure where it was, though I believe in the Strait of Gibraltar. I'm never going to find it if I have to keep calling for cab rides. It'd be nice to have the keys to the car."

"And what if it ends up being a myth?"

"I have faith."

"Faith enough to ignore someone trying to kill you in the bathroom?"

He gives a little huff-laugh. "You seem to have things under control."

I'm not entirely sure about that. I wonder if his faith is misplaced.

But I don't correct him either.

He gives me a little wave and heads down the hall, the agents following, to his modest room on the first floor.

Ruby floats closer to me. "Of course you know Plato was using Atlantis as a metaphor, and according to the original text, it wasn't the utopia the currently accepted mythos makes it out to be . . ."

"Shut up."

As I get on the elevator it happens again. A little flash on the edge of my vision. That way when you turn your head and you think you might have seen a figure walk by, but then you stop and realize, no, it's just your brain playing tricks on you.

Then there's that noise again.

Clack-clack-clack.

I'm tired. That's all it is.

But the unease lingers, and when I get to my room, something feels wrong.

I stand there for long enough, on the patch of tile inside the door, before the carpet starts, that Ruby has to ask: "January?"

It snaps me from the spell, and I move into the room like the floor is the surface of a frozen lake that might crack if I step down too hard.

Nothing seems amiss. It looks the same as I left it. The towel I used after I showered is in a heap on the floor. My toothbrush is perched on the sink, next to the drinking glass. The bed is unmade, because what is the point in making a bed if you're just going to get into it again? The shades are drawn and the small armchair in the corner is sitting on the hem of the curtain, so they don't accidentally get undrawn. The pile of dirty clothes in the corner is roughly the same size, my favorite red hoodie poking out from the bottom.

But there's something in the air, like someone was just here. A disturbance, or maybe an odor, but so faint I couldn't tell you what it was: sweat or perfume or just an unfamiliar laundry detergent. Enough molecules in the air that I can detect them without discerning them.

"January?" Ruby asks again.

I search the room. Check my belongings. Look behind the bathroom door in case someone is wedged there, waiting. All this thought of ghosts is making me feel not alone. By the time I'm done it feels like, okay, maybe it's just me being jumpy. Maybe it's the way my brain is firing like an old wire. I know I said I would take it easy, but I take out the bottle of Retronim, place a tab on my tongue, and down it with a glass of water. Thirsty. How many was that today? That's only my second, right?

"January?"

"Shut up and go charge," I tell it.

"I'm worried about your current state of mind."

"You should be," I say, falling to a hard sit at the edge of the bed, letting the mattress and the tangle of sheets envelop me. One thing I will say about this place: the bedding is pretty rad. Focus on the positive.

"There's more that you're not telling me," it says.

"I slipped into the future. Apparently I'm going to kill someone. Also, Grayson is going to kill me. So. Got a lot to look forward to."

"Do we know for sure it's going to happen?"

"What do you mean?"

"The block universe model and free will are not necessarily incompatible," Ruby says. "Remember, we are as yet unable to travel into the future. Some, including Dorothy Simms, have speculated that's because the future isn't set the same way the past is. It is possible that the future timeline is a little more fluid. And it is also possible that the timeline will adjust—or rather, has already adjusted—to incorporate any changes you might make."

"Doesn't that throw the block model out the window then?"

"Yes and no. It is possible that all future possibilities exist until a decision is made. So what you see in a slip resembles a possible course of future events. Yes, changing that course of events in response to that stimulus is intuitively incompatible with the block model. However, that apparent lack of simultaneity is an artifact of our linear perceptions."

"What if the pathway doesn't matter as long as you reach the same outcome? I watched Kolten go into anaphylactic shock, and he died. I stopped it from happening. Who's to say the universe won't find another way to slit his throat?"

"It could," Ruby says. "Or it could not. There's no real way to tell until it happens."

So maybe Grayson doesn't shoot me in the head?

Or else I'll avoid it, and slip in the shower later that night, breaking my neck.

Different pathway, same outcome.

I throw my hands into the air. "Time travel!"

"Indeed," Ruby says.

At this point there's too much rattling around in my head, including now whether or not the elevator was even going to fail, so I put it aside and move over to the whiteboard installed on the wall. Allyn wants me to take a step back? Fine. Let the foot soldiers deal with the shit on the ground. This is a chance to consider the bigger picture.

This whiteboard is my happy place. My space to think. I need visuals. I need information in front of me. I pick up the red marker and yank the cap off with my teeth, the chemical smell of it stinging my nose in the most pleasant way possible.

Start at the top. The most pressing issues.

Summit, Westin, snow, time.

It's not worth ranking them, because they all suck in different and unique ways. I feel like there's something missing and then remember, oh right, there are dinosaurs in the basement. So I add that to the list.

Summit, Westin, snow, time, dinosaurs.

Next, the suspect list. Someone broke into our system. Someone is erasing video and trying to hide a thing they did. Someone is trying to kill the other guests.

Teller, Davis, MKS, Smith.

Then, *Drucker.* I'm not naïve. Government and trillionaires are intertwined at their roots. If one of them is trying to game the process, I fully expect to find that she's at least aware, if not involved.

So who broke into our system? I'm sure any one of these four could afford a threat-level nerd capable of the task. But the fact that Kolten is a computer whiz—besides him taking control of Ruby—makes me wonder about him a little more.

I add x's next to Smith, Davis, and MKS, because I've thwarted attempts on all of their lives. Nothing with Teller though. Which is interesting. There's still time. Or maybe he's the one orchestrating this.

The next name, I don't feel good about adding. I consider whether or not I even should. But I realize I have to. The Westin thing demands it.

Danbridge.

Money can do strange things to people. It can make them compromise themselves and their values. Maybe he's tired of a hard day's work for a half-ass government paycheck. Or maybe it was something else that's getting tied into this, but until I can prove otherwise, I have to be careful about what I say around him.

I add: *Eshe, Grayson, Warwick.* Just so I keep them on my brain. I roll over my desk chair and position it in front of the whiteboard. Sit and lean back and put my bare feet on the wall. Stare at the board for a little bit. Like the letters are going to re-form into some kind of answer. Something to tell me what's going on.

They don't. But they never do.

So what else do I know?

Davis is a nut. Smith wants this place to mine the past for data or save the planet or something, but he also thinks this hotel has a secret room. There's a lot he's not telling me. Didn't MKS say something about Teller not being able to afford this place?

"Hey, Ruby, what's the deal with Teller's finances?"

Ruby responds: "A recent report in *Forbes* says his net worth is not nearly as high as he is reporting. It's possible he may have actually lost his trillionaire status. He, of course, insists this is inaccurate."

That goes on the pile of things.

"Do you suspect him?" Ruby asks.

"It's trending that way," I say. "Though he's a piece of shit, so his reputation is probably shading my judgment. Same with Kolten, and his little freak-out in the restaurant. That didn't exactly score him any points. I get a good vibe off Davis and the prince. Which makes me suspect them less. But that's always a mistake."

Ruby says, "Despite bin Saud's genial nature, there is the issue of Nura Fayed, a Saudi dissident and journalist who was critical of his leadership and suddenly went missing two months ago. And Davis did make his fortune through private equity investment."

"What's that?"

"He invests in companies, then essentially strip-mines them. Eliminating departments and outsourcing production. While a few of those companies have gone on to be quite successful, for most of them, it means employees are laid off, and lose their healthcare and pensions. Even then, he creates quite a bit of debt but still walks away having made a profit."

"Well, I was right about one thing," I say. "No such thing as a nice trillionaire."

I stare at the board a little more. The words go fuzzy. My head tilts forward, and then I jerk it back and it wakes me up. I'm tired. I should sleep, but I don't want to. Not now. The hairs on my neck are standing. Like there's someone hovering behind me. I'm being ridiculous. There's no one in this room but me and Ruby. And Ruby barely counts.

But still, I hazard a peek over my shoulder . . .

Nothing.

The springs creak as I lean back in the chair and stare at the ceiling.

"What's the value of this place?" I ask Ruby.

"Monetary value? Do you mean in terms of current operating costs?"

"Why buy this place?" I ask. "Where's the profit, if you can't go back in time and invest in Google? Is the tourism market really big enough?"

"Well." Ruby comes floating down to the table next to me, almost like it's tired, or maybe it just needs to conserve its energy. "It could hold a great deal of value in ways that we haven't even considered. Look at the space industry. It started as a government venture but was eventually privatized. And tourism was an aspect of that. But manufacturing and shipping were improved by zero-g environments. The typical asteroid that reaches earth contains billions of dollars in platinum. Not to mention access to communication and satellites. A private investor could charge scientists to use the facilities and sell data that's collected here. There are probably countless ways to innovate and profit."

"Right. And that's assuming they're doing everything aboveboard. Which I don't believe they will, no matter how much Allyn believes the TEA won't get gutted in the process. He said something about safeguards, but honestly, what else is there besides us? It always felt like a mad scramble, trying to oversee these d-bags. And I'm sure little things have slipped through the cracks here and there."

Ruby doesn't answer. I wonder if maybe it did run out of power. Wouldn't be the first time. For something that's supposed to be intelligent it can oftentimes be a little dumb.

But then it keeps on not answering.

"Ruby? Are you still on?"

"Yes."

"Why the silent treatment? I didn't even insult you."

It doesn't respond.

What did I just say. Safeguards? Was that it?

"Rubes, is there some kind of backstop in the system I don't know about?"

"You do not have the required security clearance."

That's new.

"Who does?" I ask.

"You do not have the required security clearance."

"I thought I hacked you. What was the point of that?"

"You do not have the required security clearance."

"But someone does . . ."

"You do not have the required security clearance."

"Okay, I get it, I have to work this out on my own," I say. "Well, if anyone does, it's Allyn. But I don't know what I don't have the security clearance *to*, which means I don't know what question to ask. Don't suppose you could help me with that, could you?"

"You do not have the . . ."

"Mute."

Ruby falls silent.

So there is a safeguard.

The whole point of my job used to be to keep people from changing things. Which I wouldn't have needed to do if there was something preventing it.

But if someone did go back and change something, how would we know? Like, if that guy successfully went back in time and made it so that Betamax beat out VHS in the videotape format war, we'd just always have Betamax, right?

I'm so caught up in the thought, I don't notice Ruby until it's floating so close to my face I can feel the breeze of its propellers.

"Unmute," I say.

"'Twas brillig and the slithy toves, did gyre and gimble in the wabe. All mimsy were the borogoves, and the mome raths outgrabe."

"What is that remarkable nonsense?"

It doesn't respond.

"Tell it to me straight, is your robot brain broken?" I ask.

It floats back to its charging perch.

"Ruby, I know the cameras are compromised, but do I have to worry about you too?"

It doesn't respond.

"Asshole," I say.

"Funny thing to say to your only friend."

I consider arguing against that, but it isn't exactly wrong.

"I have a question," it says. "About your interaction with Mbaye earlier."

"I don't really . . ."

But before I can finish it asks, "I have access to all recorded knowledge of psychology and human behavior, and yet something I continually fail to understand is, why do humans process pain by inflicting it on others?"

It floats there, its dumb eyes glaring at me, and I wonder if it's asking me out of genuine curiosity, or if it's some robot way of admonishing me. I don't care. The room suddenly feels very small and I don't want to be in it anymore. I pull my boots back on, not even bothering with socks.

I don't have time to be psychoanalyzed by a calculator. I've got too much to do. I need to get out of this room. Which means I should go looking for someplace else to hang out. Like a secret room that may or may not exist.

And for some reason the thought pulls me toward that stupid supply closet.

"Stay here," I say.

"Are you sure that's the best idea?" it asks.

"I want to be alone."

"And right now is exactly when you need me, if there are problems both with the video surveillance system and your own cognitive abilities."

"Fine," I tell it. "But keep a little distance and stay quiet so I can at least pretend you aren't there."

"You're not going to answer my question?"

"If you're going to spout nonsense at me, then no."

I duck out of the room. At the end of the hallway I'm bracing myself for when I pass the murder room of mystery, where Westin continues to wait for me. But he's not the only one.

Kolten is hovering outside the supply closet, tapping numbers into the keypad, methodically, like there's a list in his head that he's running through. Each time a code fails there's a soft little angry *buzz*. I whisper to Ruby, "Stay out of sight," so Kolten doesn't try to shut it down again. Then I come up behind him. He's so wrapped up in trying codes that he doesn't even hear me approach.

After he puts in a code that doesn't work I reach past him and type in the correct code, and he jerks back.

The lock makes a happy *ding*, and I push down on the door handle, letting him in. He stares at me for a second, like, *is this okay?*, and then he steps inside, like a kid running into a playground.

Except this playground sucks. He surveys the contents of the industrial metal shelves, starts moving things around, looking at the back wall, knocking on it, searching for hollow points. After a fairly thorough sweep, he steps outside.

"If you needed shampoo you could have just called down to reception," I tell him.

"Hmm," he says, not listening. Then he turns to me. "Where's your sidekick?"

"Felt like a solo excursion this evening."

He nods, too trusting. Then he rubs the doorframe, like it's an old friend he hasn't seen in a while.

"Would you let me open up the walls?"

The laugh explodes out of my chest before I can even consider containing it. "Why in the hell would I let you do that?"

"Because I believe this is where the room is."

I give something away at this. A little jerk. An inhale of air. His secret room next to my room with a secret. His eyes slide toward me, and rather than let him press, I tell him, "You so much as scratch the paint I will drag your ass out of here myself. Anyway, dude, look around. It's a closet." I point to the far wall. "You want to knock a hole in there, you end up outside. This room isn't any smaller than the other closets. I can tell you that by looking. Want to know how? Because I know every goddamn inch of this place."

"You don't get to where I am without dreaming of impossible things," he says.

He smiles a little when he says this. A tilt of his lip, like he's letting me in on some universal truth. All it sounds like is he's trying too hard to be clever, and it's totally not working for me.

"I'm sorry about before," he says. "In the restaurant. I was afraid, you know, and my anger got the best of me."

I wave it off. I'm sure he takes it to mean that I don't mind. The truth is, he showed me exactly who he is.

"Have you considered my offer?" he asks.

"Haven't really had the time, what with everything that's going on."

He tugs on the beads on his wrist and says, "You have to understand, we can help you."

Right. Help. I wonder if he'll even remember my name after this is over. I pat the wall and ask, "Why are you fixated on this spot?"

"Because this is where the clues pointed," he says.

"What clues?"

"The ones left by Simms."

"Simms is Unstuck. She's lying in a bed, dead to the world. What is she telling you?" He doesn't answer that, which annoys me, so I square to him and ask again. "Where are you getting this intel? Because maybe if you were to just—I don't know, tell me?—maybe I could shed some light on this. You're the one who's desperate for information. I can't help you unless you give me something, okay?"

"I'm still not entirely sure where your loyalties lie."

I clap my hands to my face and press my cheeks. "God with this bullshit. I'm tired of people wondering about my loyalties. I'm loyal to doing my job and not dying. How about that?"

"I asked for the chef to be fired," he says. "The one who almost killed me. Management refused."

"Well, you were being a baby," I say.

He gives a little shrug and heads for the elevator bank. After he's gone I stand in the hallway for long enough that the elevator closes and opens a few more times, people coming from and going to their rooms. Headed out seeking drinks, coming back with heads full of them. I just stand there. Thinking. Because there's something he said before. Something maybe I didn't consider in the broader picture.

I hustle back toward my room, find Ruby hovering just out of view.

"Anything to add?" I ask.

"Nothing of note, but I recorded the conversation. I'll be recording all conversations going forward."

"You don't do that already?"

"Not unless I believe they're important."

Once inside I go looking for the red marker, uncap it, then under the list of names, add *Simms, Fairbanks*.

He said it earlier. That Fairbanks built the hotel but Simms may have consulted.

Fairbanks, missing. Simms, Unstuck.

Those things did happen around the same time.

"There was a book written about Simms, right? Using her notes? Can you scan that? Anything in there?"

"Yes, there is a relevant portion, and it was derived from a video. Would you prefer to watch that?"

"Television," I tell it, and fall into the chair.

The TV winks on and the video starts playing immediately. It's Simms, doing an interview with a goofy white guy in a sharp suit who is trying desperately to sound as smart as she is. She's wearing a yellow sundress, along with plastic-framed glasses and Converse sneakers, both of which match her dress.

GOOFY WHITE GUY: So you've been consulting on the design of the Paradox Hotel, correct?

SIMMS: I've always admired Melody Fairbanks's work. The design of the new Metropolitan Museum of Art in New York City is incredible. I met her at the groundbreaking and we had a lot of good conversations about the hotel. About the nature of time.

GOOFY WHITE GUY: And tell me, what does time look like to you?

Simms smiles. Takes a breath.

SIMMS: To be clear, there's so much about time we don't understand. I know everyone likes calling it the "block model." I prefer to call it "eternalism." (Simms winks.) It sounds a little nicer.

GOOFY WHITE GUY: The block model, or eternalism, says that the past and the future have already happened. If the future is there, why can't we go there?

SIMMS: I know what I had for dinner last night but I don't know what I'm having for dinner tomorrow. Right now I could say I'm probably having pizza, but by the time we get there, maybe I'll order sushi. Was I always going to have sushi, or was it undetermined until I opened up the app to place my order? It's something I'm working on.

GOOFY WHITE GUY: Does that mean there's no such thing as free will?

Simms smiles again. This smile, though, seems a little tighter. A little less easy than the previous smile.

SIMMS: I'll leave that one for the people who are smarter than me to figure out.

"Anything else in there that seems relevant?" I ask.

"I do not believe so," Ruby says.

"Who was around during construction?"

"A few staffers have been here since before opening, but I suspect that Cameo might be useful to you in this instance."

"Why?"

"Cameo likes to gossip."

The other problems suddenly seem a bit less important. "Let's go find them."

Cameo is the only employee who maintains a room in the hotel besides me. The housing options around here suck, so I don't blame them. They live on the far end of the first floor, close enough to the concierge desk that they can get there quickly if something happens. There are people to handle nights and weekends, but Cameo, to their mind, runs the show and, to my mind, knows more than anyone else how this place is put together.

They've always been valuable and I've always tried to be less of an asshole with them. Not that I've been great about it.

See also: our conversation outside earlier today.

So it's with a touch of trepidation that I knock on their door, and when they answer, towering over me, in a bathrobe and sweatpants, I know this won't be the most fun conversation. Because what I see on their face is a bit of hope, like maybe I've come around to sharing my feelings.

But I'm not here for that.

"To what do I owe you darkening my doorstep?" they ask, stepping aside to let me in the room.

I've never been in here before. It's cozy. Painted, for one, a soft sea green. The carpeting is a complementary forest green. The bed frame is brass, ornate. The bathroom hasn't been altered, but it feels more lived-in. It feels like a proper apartment, even though, like mine, it's the smallest room model. There's even a hotplate set up above the minifridge. Cameo points me toward the far end of the room, to two handsome wingback chairs facing each other next to the window, a tree stump table between them.

"Tea?" they ask.

"Actually, yes."

"Oolong?"

"That works."

"Ruby, would you like something?" Cameo asks. "Perhaps a touch of motor oil?"

"Thank you for the offer," Ruby says. "Out of curiosity, what would you have done if I'd actually asked for motor oil?"

Cameo shrugs. "Called to the front for it." They busy themselves with the electric kettle, and in short order come over with two steaming mugs, tea bag strings hanging over the sides, and place them down on the stump. They sit, and given Cameo's height it looks like they're sitting in a child's chair.

And I realize this is the first time I've seen them in repose. It's a different kind of intimacy to see someone in their pajamas. Even in my T-shirt and dirty jeans and boots with no socks, I suddenly feel overdressed.

But also, like I'm intruding, so I get to the point. "Dorothy Simms and Melody Fairbanks."

They pick up their mug and take a tentative sip.

"You knew them?" I ask.

"Not well."

"What can you tell me about them?"

"Hmm." They make another go at the mug, so I pick up mine to take a sip. It's too hot but I cradle it anyway because the warmth feels good on my hands. After a few moments of contemplation they say, "Simms spent a great deal of time here during the construction, and I know she consulted on this place a little, but her purview was mostly Einstein." They raise an eyebrow. "What is this about?"

"Honestly, I don't even know where to start, but as you can imagine"—I give a little wave to the rest of the hotel—"there's a whole lot of nonsense going on right now. And I'm trying to put some pieces together. It's just . . . weird, right? One goes missing, one goes Unstuck, both around the same time?"

"Always wondered about that."

"Do you believe in coincidences?"

"They happen." Cameo puts down their tea. "What exactly are you looking for?"

"I don't know. Someone who knew them both. Any correspondence between them. Maybe material that didn't make it into Simms's book."

Cameo shrugs. "Ask the husband."

"Whose husband?"

"Simms. He's the one who put together that book about her. I met him a few times while they were here and have spoken to him a few times since. He's caring for her while she's . . ." Cameo trails off, not wanting to say it. "You should give him a call, tell him I suggested it. And now"—they place down their mug—"there's something else we need to discuss."

Uh-oh.

They take a breath. "I heard about what you said to Mbaye. You understand that was both needlessly cruel and completely unfair, correct?"

"Look, I . . ."

Cameo puts up a hand. "I need to know *you* know that what you did was wrong."

"Why?"

"Because if you can't see that, you might be too far gone."

"He was supposed to check the gas lines that day," I say. "That day. What do you want me to say? I mean, do you know how hard this is? I am a five-minute tram ride away from a machine that'd let me go back in time and check it myself. To tell Mena not to go in the kitchen that day. Anything. But I can't because of the goddamn rule I have dedicated my life to protecting. Every day it's a struggle to not touch."

Cameo leans forward. "Loss is an injury. Like any injury it triggers a pain response. And that pain can be overwhelming. But injuries are supposed to activate a healing response, too. That's why loss hurts less over time, and one day it's just a scar. The evidence of it never goes away, but the pain does. Unless it gets infected. And then it doesn't heal."

I take another sip of tea, filling my mouth with something other than the words I want to say.

"Grief is normal and healthy," Cameo says. "But there's something called 'complicated grief.' It's when you lose the ability to think rationally. You might think the person is going to reappear . . ."

I grip the mug a little tighter at that one.

". . . numbness, bitterness, lack of trust in others. What you need is some kind of professional help." Cameo puts up their hand before I can open my mouth to protest. "And I get it, you're a badass, you don't need nobody, but the fact remains, the wound is infected. It's not going to get better if you stay here."

I take another sip. Put down the mug. Uncross my legs and stand.

"You and Reg ought to form a support group, since you're so clearly obsessed with my shit," I say. "We done here?"

Cameo slumps in the chair and sighs. "I guess so."

"Thanks for the intel," I say, fighting to keep my voice steady, but not doing a great job. As I get closer to the door I turn again. "Ever hear anything about a secret room in this place?"

Cameo doesn't look at me, just shakes their head, but whether it's in defeat or to answer the question, I can't tell. I open the door when Cameo says, "One other thing."

I don't turn around. "Yeah."

"I checked the log and asked around. There aren't any children staying here."

"You sure?"

"Almost positive. Even if we missed it, with kids come requests for cots and chicken fingers and complaints from guests when they run around in the halls. There's been none of that."

I consider it for a moment, then say, "Someone screwed up."

Though I don't really believe it.

I step outside and leave the heavy feeling in Cameo's room. Set my spine straight and march to the lobby, knowing that it won't be long before I get another glimpse of Mena. Which is all I need. It's all I ever need.

"What time is it?" I ask Ruby.

"Perhaps Cameo was right about . . ."

"What time is it?"

"Eight forty-seven."

"See if you can raise the husband."

I opt for the security office rather than my room. I check in with Nik, and he lets me know he's working downstairs with the TEA crew that'll be on rotation.

Ruby floats to the charging port and I'm considering whether I should call Allyn to check in, when the video screen pings me with an incoming call from Jason Simms in Utah. That was quick.

A stocky Black man with disheveled hair and a face covered in stubble appears on the screen. He's a man who doesn't sleep well and when he's awake, he wishes he were sleeping. If he's still burning a candle in the window, then this won't be a pleasant phone call.

"Yes?" he asks. In the background I can make out a wide blue wall, the color similar to the carpets here.

"Mister Simms. My name is January Cole, and I'm the head of security at the Paradox."

He nods. "Been awhile since I heard from anyone out in those parts. How's Cameo?"

"Lovely, as always." I consider asking how his wife is but it seems rude. And also I don't want to know the details. Because knowing about her—and from the weight he's carrying on his shoulders, the answer won't be nice—it's just going to give me a glimpse of my eventual future.

"It's late and I don't want to waste your time, so I'll get to it," I say. "And I apologize if this is an uncomfortable question. I wouldn't be asking it if I didn't think it was important. You assembled your wife's letters and documents for that book about her, right? I was wondering if there was anything you held back. Any notes or information that might have seemed unimportant."

He shakes his head. "No, pretty much everything I had made it in. That was the problem, there wasn't much. The publisher was on me to look for more. But I did the best I could. Everything from her office, from home. That was all I had."

"My understanding is Simms played a role in helping Melody Fairbanks design the hotel," I say. "Did she ever mention that? Anything about her contributions to the construction?"

"She was living out there while it was being built. I barely saw her. And even when I came out to visit, she was always wrapped up in work." He shrugs, sits back in his seat. "I'm a butcher by trade. A lot of that science stuff just goes right over my head." He looks up at me. "Why do you ask?"

"It may be relevant to an investigation."

"What kind of investigation?"

"A complicated one."

"I wish I could help you," he says, though I'm not sure he means it.

"Do you have any notes or correspondence between her and Fairbanks specifically?"

He gives a little chuckle and says, "She told me Dorothy sent her a book. A fancy limited edition. Probably not helpful though."

"What book?"

"*Through the Looking-Glass.*"

My breath catches, but he doesn't notice. He says, "Have a nice night. If I think of anything else, I'll let you know." And he logs off the call, with no intention to ever call me again.

Doesn't matter.

Ruby is already at my shoulder.

"As we investigate, I form a series of data matrixes, trying to connect relevant and similar facts so as to hasten the discovery of information, and often I find that the addition of new data points creates pathways that . . ."

"I hate when you do that. Just say you realized something."

"Kolten Smith said he dreams of impossible things. That's similar to a quote from the book."

I slump down in the chair but it feels like I'm floating. This is the best part of the job. When the pieces start coming together.

And then I remember one more.

"There's a book missing from Fairbanks's office," I say. "I noticed it earlier. Which one?"

After a quick scan, Ruby says: "*Through the Looking-Glass.*"

I clap my hands and jump up. "Damn it, sometimes I am good at this. Okay, I want you to run video, see if you can find who took the book."

"There's more."

"Spill it."

Ruby falls silent again. It hovers for a moment and then says, "'Twas brillig and the slithy toves . . ."

"Stop stop stop," I say. "What the hell is that?"

"What is what?" it asks.

"That . . . thing you keep saying. Slithy toves?"

"You do not have the required security clearance."

"I hate you so much. Okay, one thing at a time. Just run that damn video. I have some plans to look at. And run a diagnostic on yourself."

Ruby returns to its dock, hooking into the mainframe, and I mutter a little prayer that the video we need wasn't lost in the purge. The person doing it could have been covering that up, but if I'm lucky they were hiding something else and this one survived.

Meanwhile I go to the filing cabinet in the corner and find a series of schematics for the hotel. Dig through and pull a pile of them out, laying them over the hologram table at the center of the room, and flip through. Looking at the fifth floor of Atwood, and anything that might be amiss about it.

The prints are all large and old and useless. Nothing out of the ordinary. But if it's a secret room, why would it be on the plans?

Every inch of this place . . .

"Got something." Ruby floats to my field of vision.

It turns to the video screen, which shows an angled, top-down view of Fairbanks's office. Kolten walks on-screen and peruses the titles. He's wearing the same outfit as when we first met, which makes me believe it's from earlier today. I check the date stamp on the corner of the screen but find it's not very helpful because, ha, like I ever know what day it is.

He takes a book off the shelf. Opens the front cover. Places his finger along some text, then puts it back.

"Now watch," Ruby says.

He moves further down the row of books. Out of the view of the book he had picked up.

Which disappears from the shelf. One second it's there, and then it's not, like the video was edited. Except it's smooth. The time stamp doesn't skip. Kolten is still moving as it happens.

"The fuck?" I ask.

"There are no missing frames. This section of video was not subject to any sort of tampering. The book is there, and then it is gone."

Which means we're back to kleptomaniac ghosts. Allyn's going to be very excited to hear this.

I appear on-screen, and Kolten and I start our conversation. I had noticed the gap on the shelf as I was walking up. It must have only just happened.

"Okay, so what was Kolten looking at?"

Ruby rewinds and freezes on the frame, then zooms in on what Kolten is reading. And thank the lord for video enhancement. In small, languid script, it reads: *We will always have A527.*

"So we go on the assumption that this is the book Simms gave to Fairbanks, but the room numbers in Atwood are even, not odd. She's referring to a room that doesn't exist, but it would be directly next to the room with Westin's body." I pace around the table, talking to myself more than Ruby. "Kolten was letting on more than he knew. He had a sense of the location but wanted to see if he could get me to give it up. Then, poof, the book just vanishes."

"I have no real explanation for why that would have happened."

"Of course you don't, because you are not very helpful."

"I am incredibly helpful."

Something is building in my head. Pieces coming together faster than I can process them. I have an idea. I root around in my junk drawer, shoving aside soy sauce packets, thumbtacks, floss, last year's TEA Christmas card, some dead pens I probably should have thrown out, until finally I find it: a tape measure.

Every inch.

At Atwood I breeze past the elevators until I reach the storage closet in the middle of the hallway. The first five floors are identical, all with the same floor plans and room sizes. The closets should stack directly on top of each other. I take out the tape measure and hook it against the doorframe of the first room to the left of the closet. Stretch over to the closet's door frame.

Twenty-seven feet.

"What are you doing?" Ruby asks.

"It's quiet time."

Ruby shuts up, hovering behind me as I cross the hotel, to the storage closet on the first floor of Butler.

Twenty-seven feet.

Next, the second floor of Atwood. And the third. Then on the fourth, where I spook a couple with hair as blue as their blood. They hurry past the weird chick taking random wall measurements in the hallway, like this is all an elaborate ploy to steal their wallets.

Twenty-seven feet.

On the fifth floor I feel the buzz, putting the tape measure against the door of the room with Westin in it. Hoping the guy who's staying here doesn't suddenly come out.

I stretch the tape across and hold my breath as I line up with the same spot I did the previous five times.

Twenty-seven feet, four inches.

Same on the other side.

"That's interesting," Ruby says.

"What did I say about quiet time?"

I run back downstairs. Pick three spots. Distances between rooms. Measure them and tell Ruby to take notes. Then run the same measurements on floors two, three, and four. They're all consistent.

On the fifth floor they're all a few inches off.

Inches though, not feet. Even with the number of rooms, there wouldn't be enough deviation to add another full-size room.

Which brings me right back to the closet.

It looks the same as all the others. I walk to it and touch the doorframe . . .

. . . I press my hand to my chest. I've been standing in the bathroom for maybe a half hour now. Or else it's just been two minutes. Time hasn't really made sense these last few days. I'm wearing the black dress that Mena liked, along with a black blazer and beaten motorcycle boots. It's not dressy, but she wouldn't have cared.

She'd have just wanted me to be there.

A knock at the door. I turn to it, but don't move, just stare at myself in the mirror, tendrils of mascara snaking down my face.

"January, we're about to start," Reg says, his voice muffled through the door.

Another knock.

"Jan, are you in there?"

I couldn't open the door if I wanted to. I'm frozen in place. Physically unable to move. Just staring at that postcard stuck in the mirror.

The little people made of dots.

"Look, you don't even have to come out," Reg says. "Can I just come in?"

With a monumental amount of effort, the kind of effort it would take to move a planet, I tilt my head slightly toward the bed. Mena's side, still mussed into the shape of her. It still smells like her. I've been sleeping on the floor the last few days. I don't know why. I feel like I don't deserve a bed. Don't deserve comfort. Not in a world where Mena doesn't exist anymore.

"Look just . . ." Reg trails off, and I think maybe he's given up on me, as he should, because what is there left in this room? A memory and a dead girl. Which one of those am I? My heart stopped beating in that elevator the night of the explosion. It's like my body is just waiting to catch up.

Then he says, "We'll wait a few minutes to start."

He goes. Still I don't move.

My legs ache. My back is sore. Maybe I have been standing here a long time. Forcing myself to look at me. My face. Wondering what it was Mena saw inside me that made someone so lovely and special spend her time trying to heal me. Those impact craters on my body that, once, I thought were expressions of love.

She fit herself into those grooves.

She did more than that.

Did you know love could reach inside a person?

I didn't. Not until her. It probes your skin until it finds a crack. Then it pours into you, liquid gold that hardens and makes you stronger. That's what Mena told me we were for each other. Kintsugi. The Japanese art of using lacquer dusted with gold to mend broken pottery. So that those cracks are still there, but now they're features. Celebrations of strength.

She would whisper it in my ear as we made love. When we reached those moments where the two of us were so deeply connected we melded together.

Other voices drift through the door, but it's like I can't hear them in real time, I can only recall them. Cameo, saying something about family. Brandon, asking me if I need anything. Mbaye. I don't know what Mbaye says. His voice sounds like static to me.

By the time my perception catches up with reality, it's nighttime. I can tell from the crack in the curtains, arranged in such a way so that the first beams of sunrise would fall across Mena's face to wake her in the morning. Her favorite way to greet the day. Now there's nothing but darkness beyond them, and the service was supposed to be early afternoon, so I must have been standing for a very long time.

I consider lying on the floor again, just to take some pressure off my ankles, which now feel wooden and swollen. Instead I go to the door and lean out, checking first to make sure the hallway is empty before stepping all the way into it. Then cross to the stairwell and take it to the roof, the sound of my boots echoing off the concrete walls.

It's a nice night. Warm. A little breezy. The kind of night we would have come up here with some snacks and stared out at the lights of

Einstein, the massive machines that keep the place running flashing in red and white, with the occasional shock of blue that lights up half the sky whenever a trip takes off.

I watch three flashes of blue from my spot near the door before I make my way to the lip of the roof. There's a waist-high wall in front of me. I feel the rough stone under my fingertips. I look out at Einstein. The place I thought held all I ever wanted. And then I found this.

A job I didn't want, which led me to a love I couldn't have imagined.

Now it's gone.

All of it. Everything. I am just a sad little girl who lives in a sad little room and tells rich people to stop being so sad. I will live here for a little while longer and then, one day, with no warning, my brain will stop working. And maybe the TEA will put me on life support and keep my heart beating on the off chance someone finds a way to fix it.

I should sign a DNR.

But frankly, that feels like too much effort. There are easier ways.

I put my foot up on the ledge.

"What a night."

There's a crunch on the gravel behind me, and I turn to find Mena.

Mena from about six weeks ago. The last time we were up here. Just spring, and a little chilly, so she's wearing my red hoodie zipped tight around her, holding a bottle of wine, looking like she'd rather drink me instead.

That night. We swiped yoga mats from the gym and made love up here, under the dark sky and the blue flashes, even though it got so chilly that by the time we were done, our fingers were stiff from the cold.

"I know the lights are pretty, *mi reina*, but since when are you a moth?" she asks.

It's not her. I know this is a slip. The electricity surging in my brain. I had drifted toward the edge of the roof, the lights of Einstein drawing me closer, to that thing that I loved, and missed so much I felt the ache of it in my chest.

This is an echo of her. The thing she said to me. Worried I was getting a little too close to the edge of the roof.

But right now, does it even matter?

She looks over my shoulder, at the lights of Einstein. "I miss working there. Though admittedly, the view here is much nicer."

My throat grows thick. Eyes well with tears. I reach for her. What did I say that night? What was my response to this? I don't even remember. But damn the rules, what if there's a chance? "I need to tell you something, okay? Please, I need you to listen, because . . ."

She holds up a finger. "Shh." Then points that finger up. "You can actually see some stars tonight."

That snaps me out of it, and I look up and see the sky is overcast, not like that night, the one I saw then, when she was right and there were a dozen stars in the sky, good for a region like this, where the sky is choked by light pollution. That night I marveled at how vast and beautiful the night sky was, but really it was because she was standing underneath it.

When I look back down Mena is gone.

She was never really there.

A home movie playing in my broken brain.

I fold myself to sitting, the gravel scraping the skin of my legs that the dress doesn't cover. I sit there like that for a little while. And even though I still feel like my heart is full of broken glass, the sharp edges have dulled, like beach glass. They take up space and they push, but they don't cut.

It's just an ache now, and I can live with an ache.

My vision goes white, like the end of a spark.

Reg looks away from me, steels his voice. "January, if you cannot get with this, we are going to have your things removed. We don't think it's safe for you to be here anymore. They thought it was. But look at what's happening."

White again. I can smell my brain, like burning ozone.

"Look, I know this isn't pleasant to hear, but after this, I think it's time for you to retire," Allyn says. "You got your ten. You got more than that. It's time."

The next blast sends me to my knees.

"What you need is some kind of professional help," Cameo says. "And I get it, you're a badass, you don't need nobody, but the fact remains, the wound is infected. It's not going to get better if you stay here."

I come out of it, sprawled on the carpet, my face pressed into the fibers.

This carpet. This stupid blue carpet. I hate it. I hate it so much.

"January?" Ruby asks.

What the fuck did I ever do to you, brain?

I go to the door and punch in the code, push open the handle, and step into the closet. Reach up to the shelf and pull it toward me. It doesn't budge. Bolted to the wall. I get a good grip, put one foot on the wall, kicking through a pile of towels, and heave. Something snaps. The shelf groans toward me. I pull my knife out of my pocket, snap out the blade, and jam it into the open spot of wall I created.

It doesn't go very far, just creates a divot that spits out a plume of sheetrock dust. I jab it again. And again. I realize I am yelling, like the wall is an enemy and I am trying to kill it, and Ruby is talking, but I really and truly do not care what it has to say, and then there are a pair of hands around me, pulling me away. I swing back with the knife, hear a yelp.

Find Brandon standing against the wall, holding his arm, blood seeping between his fingers.

He looks at his arm.

Then he looks at me.

"Your nose is bleeding," he says, like his own wound is an afterthought.

And then someone turns out the lights.

All of them.

SPECIAL RELATIVITY

We catch our breath in the shadows of a building carved to ruin by aerial bombings. Searchlights sweep through the sky and I feel like one of them is going to land directly on me. I knew it was a risk, coming along. The collar badge on my itchy gray uniform marks me as the equivalent of a private, a rank low enough that most officers, their eyes will glide right off me. I'm cannon fodder.

Still, the Wehrmacht is not a safe place for a woman. Even with my chest bound, and my hair stuffed under my cap, slightly big so I can tip it down over my eyes. Allyn wanted to bring Scott Houser, whose blond hair and blue eyes give him Aryan vibes, even though he's a touch sweeter than a baby kitten. But I insisted. Give up this chance? C'mon. My only regret is, after we stop this White Power lunatic from trying to warn Hitler that tomorrow his ticket gets punched, I can't turn around and go kick der Führer in the nuts.

Who else in all of history would be able to say they did that? I asked Allyn a dozen times if we could make an exception. If the asshole will be dead tomorrow, what's the harm? He'll just die with a slightly sore set of balls. Or, ball, if you believe the urban legends.

But Allyn is right. Look, don't touch.

That's the whole point of being here.

Allyn is sporting the insignia of the Nazi version of a major general.

He's way more Germanic than I am, and we're hoping the higher rank will give him some leeway. The problem is, we know the guy we're chasing—Richard Sommers—has a huge stash of Nazi memorabilia, and is considered one of the "thought" leaders in the modern fascism movement. Not only does he speak fluent German, he speaks their language.

Which is why we're both out of breath, doing everything we can to avoid crossing paths with anyone. Taking wide, circuitous routes around the soldiers marching through the streets of Berlin, flexing a military might they don't even know is on the verge of crumbling.

According to my watch, we don't have much longer before we have to be back at the rendezvous so we can get home. Miss that, and we live here, and this is not the kind of place I planned on settling down. No air-conditioning. That's some bullshit.

"What's the plan, boss?" I ask.

Allyn looks down at the small tablet he is reluctant to take out too much, since the sight of it will set off alarm bells with the locals. He swipes at the screen a few times before slipping it back into the depths of his uniform. When he does that, the way he moves his arm shows off the red Nazi armband strapped around his biceps, the sight of which gives me chills.

The chills get worse when I remember I'm wearing one too.

Allyn catches me staring. "And they say undercover work is supposed to be fun."

"Who is 'they'?" I ask.

He shrugs. "He's got something on him. Maybe his cellphone. Whatever it is, it's nonperiod tech so I'm able to get a rough location. He's about a half mile due east of here." Allyn cranes his neck to look, through a tangle of bombed-out buildings. "Which is good for us. As long as we can find a pathway through this mess we can stay off the streets."

In the distance there's a shout, and what sounds like a gunshot.

Then another sound. This one closer.

Footsteps.

Allyn grabs my arm and pulls me further into the shadows, and we both remain as still and silent as we can.

"*Guten Abend.*"

There are three of them, and based on their insignias they rank somewhere between me and Allyn. Which I'm hoping will be enough to save our asses. Until I recognize the one in the middle as Sommers. The flattened nose and wispy facial hair. A glint in his eyes like he skins cats as a hobby. He speaks rapid-fire German to the two men with him, and I catch the words *Allies* and *spies* before my earpiece translator shits the bed, spitting static in my ear loud enough it hurts, but I don't want to pull it out and draw their attention. Or the bullets out of the Astra 900s on their hips.

Allyn and I are carrying period-specific pistols too—Browning Hi-Powers. Generally a stunner is enough, especially since our whole "look, don't touch" rule forbids us from killing the two German soldiers. But going into a war zone demanded both protection and assimilation. Which took a ton of paperwork, and then finding a collector to rent them to us, at a steep markup because he could see how much we needed them.

We were supposed to give them back, but it looks like these things are staying. Along with us, in some unmarked grave.

One of the officers takes out his gun and holds it down to his side, and Sommers says something that Allyn understands—his translator must still be working—and he turns, his hands in the air. He gives me an eyeball, like I should follow him.

We march through the ruined buildings, climbing slow over the piles of rubble. I want to ask Allyn where we're going, but figure English might get us into more trouble. I keep my eyes peeled, for something, anything that we might find useful. Something to defend ourselves with.

Then Allyn does something I did not expect.

He speaks German.

I don't know a lot about German but his sounds easy, conversational. I'm sure he doesn't have the accent, but everyone pauses, like they didn't really expect that to happen. Sommers gives an offhand response to whatever Allyn says. Then one of the German soldiers responds with something like a curious question. Sommers gives a terse answer.

And the entire mood shifts.

We're in the middle of a blasted building, the walls still standing but the roof gone, so the only light is from the moon above, soft and diffuse. The two Nazi soldiers step back and away from Sommers, drawing their weapons. Not pointing them yet, but definitely wary of him.

Sommers tries to reason with them. The three of them now locked in a fast and uncomfortable back-and-forth.

I don't want to make any sudden movements but I tilt my head slightly at Allyn. He's eyeing me intently, waiting for me to notice him. His hands are still up, but he moves them down slightly. Then eyes my hip.

I fall backward and reach for the stunner, manage to pull it free and shoot the electric probe into the guard closest to me. I land on my back, tucking my chin to my chest so I don't crack my head, and pray the ground behind me is flat, which it is. I roll to the side and pull the Browning from my other hip, hoping to get a bead on Sommers.

But I misjudge. By the time I get to my knees and I have the gun out, the second guard is down, on the end of Allyn's stunner, but Sommers is standing next to me, his gun against my head. The second the metal makes contact with my skin, my breath locks in my chest. Allyn has his gun out, and a clear shot at Sommers's head, but Sommers has me dead on. One flinch and my brains will be stew.

I play the odds. I know there's one good way to survive this and I hope Allyn is catching my vibe on this.

He just winks at me.

"Very clever," Sommers says. "Getting me to talk about Hitler's suicide tomorrow."

"All I had to do was confuse them. You could have ignored me or written it off as lunatic rambling but you made it sound like you knew it was going to happen. Luckily you're not that clever. It's always the same with you guys. You all think that you're . . ."

As Allyn is talking, I feel it. The pressure of the barrel against my head decreases, just the slightest bit, as Sommers's attention is drawn away. I throw myself forward, away from the pistol, just as Allyn puts three bullets in Sommers's chest.

The cracks of the gunshots reverberates through the space, and we give our hearts a second to ramp down before we get to work.

Sommers's body will stay. We're not supposed to leave anything behind, but, desperate times. Anyway, it's a war zone. He'll be bone before anyone notices. We just need to make sure we strip everything off him that's not period. Which turns into a problem when I pull up his sleeve and find a tattooed portrait of a Rottweiler. Underneath it says: DUKE, RIP, 2049–2064.

I wave over Allyn. "What do you think?"

He shrugs. "Best be safe. Otherwise it's going to end up on some weird conspiracy website."

I take out my knife and get to work carving it off as Allyn extracts the electric probes from the soldiers. I file this one away for the next time I'm at a party and someone asks me if being a timestream agent is glamorous.

Once the job is done I toss the hunk of skin into a shadow and rub my hands on my knees to clean off the blood. Allyn pulls out his tablet and checks it. "We have to go get whatever it is he left to bait us. Probably just his cellphone. Once that's done we can go."

"Hey," I say.

He stops. Looks at me, the two of us standing in the moonlight, the city suddenly quiet.

"Where did you learn to speak German?" I ask.

He smiles. Tilts his head up. "Can you believe we get to do this for a living?"

I can see what he's doing. Searching for some serenity as his insides are being torn up. Sommers was the worst kind of person there was, but there's never anything to celebrate when you take a life. Allyn isn't a cowboy. He volunteers in a food pantry in his free time.

So I give him what he needs.

A touch of comfort. My brand of it, at least.

"Let's see what you have to say about that when you're filling out the paperwork on this one . . ."

My body jolts.

Ceiling tile. Bright light sears my retinas. Brain feels like mashed potatoes. Gloopy and formless and easy to spread across a plate. Move my hands and realize they're shackled.

My body jolts again, so hard I arch off the table.

Droplets of blood pat the blue carpet, turning from red to black as they soak into the fibers . . .

Another jolt.

Mena takes my hand in hers, her fingers lacing through mine and gently twisting my wrist until she's able to place both our palms on her chest and I feel . . .

Jolt.

I'm crossing the TEA graduation stage, glance down at where my parents should be sitting, their seats empty . . .

Jolt.

Mena sits on a barstool next to me and takes my hand and leans over into my ear and she whispers, "Mi reina, my love." And as I'm about to respond . . .

Tamworth. He's holding down my shoulders.

"January, you need to focus."

I'm still with Mena. Still at the bar holding her hand. I know I'm not there, I know it's not real, but I'm there anyway. The smell of the coffee that Mbaye served to a man at the other end of the bar. The warmth of the sunlight spilling through a skylight and falling on my shoulder. The softness of the cushion underneath me.

"I need you to sit up and take this," Tamworth says, holding something in his hand.

Go away, I'm not able to tell him. I hear the words echo in my head but they don't actually make it to my mouth. *Mena. I want Mena.*

"Focus," he says. "January, I'm not letting you die."

I don't want to die. Not yet.

Dying means sitting alone in a room for the rest of eternity.

Need something to pull me back.

Can't swallow a pill right now. Can't get it down. I'll as likely choke.

Pocket, I say in my head.

Not with my mouth.

So I push harder, manage to croak it out.

Tamworth looks confused.

Jolt.

April 10, 1912, I stand on the dock at Southampton, the wind cool on my face, watching the *Titanic* disappear over the horizon, thinking about how I could have just told them to keep an eye out for icebergs and saved so many lives. But that's not what I'm here to do. I'm here to make sure Death does its job undisturbed. Look, don't touch . . .

A hand grips my jaw, forcing my mouth open.

Jolt.

I don't know the date, just that it's nearing the end of the Pleistocene epoch, maybe twelve thousand years ago, and I stalk through patches of brown grass and heaps of snow, land that will one day become Alberta, Canada. An oxygen mask strapped to my face because the air is different, hunting a man who is hunting a saber-toothed tiger for his Florida zoo, and . . .

Jolt.

A little girl walks slowly toward me from the end of a long hallway. The closer she gets, the bigger she gets, until her head's scraping the ceiling, and it blots out the light, hair hanging in her face so I can't make out her features, and I am suddenly seized by a feeling I locked in a chest and threw into the sea a long time ago . . .

My mouth floods with the taste of cherries.

The taste of Mena.

I feel the room now. The table underneath me. The sheet of white crinkle paper. Tamworth is standing back, watching me roll the lollipop around in my mouth. I'm able to center myself. I try to sit up, but the restraints keep me down, so Tamworth struggles to get them undone, then takes the Retronim, breaking it in half, and hands me the two pieces. "Time-release coat," he says, turning to the counter to get a cup of water. I put the pieces of pill on my tongue, wincing at the bitter medicinal taste, and wash them down. Lie back, put the lollipop in my mouth. Breathe long and deep. Filling my chest with air through my nose, then letting it out slowly through my mouth. The way Mena taught me.

Tamworth slumps in a seat in the corner, looking like he just ran a marathon. "The lollipop was smart. Sense memory is a powerful thing." He looks down at his hands, then back up at me. "What does it remind you of?"

"None of your business," I tell him. "How long was I out?"

"You weren't so much out as you were thrashing and screaming. I'm sorry we had to tie you down like that, but you could have hurt yourself, or someone else."

Hurt someone *else*. Brandon. I turn to Tamworth, a look of panic on my face, and he knows the question before I have to ask it.

"Couple of stitches."

Small comfort, but I'll take it.

I run my fingers along the grout between the tiles on the wall next to me, just trying to give my body a chance to relax. Then I push myself up, blood rushing to my head, and swing my legs off the table. Give the room a second to stop spinning.

"How do you feel?" Tamworth asks.

Better, actually. All day, my brain has felt like there was this low-key buzz somewhere at the base of it that I couldn't turn off. For the first time today I feel somewhat settled. Maybe that Retronim tolerance is building up. Which is not good. The lollipop only got me stable enough to take the pill. It doesn't fix the problem.

"Never been better," I tell him. "I didn't say anything too crazy while I was out, did I?"

"Well, you did keep reciting the first stanza of 'Jabberwocky.'"

"The what-er-whatey?"

"The poem." He smiles at the memory. "I used to read it to my daughter when she was a baby. It's all nonsense words. She loved it. Two decades later and I can still remember it."

"Then hit me with that first line, Doc."

"Don't you know it?"

"Humor me."

"'Twas brillig and the slythy toves, did gyre and gimble in the wabe . . .'"

Huh.

"That's actually a huge help."

Tamworth eyes me for a moment, confused, but then shrugs. "Danbridge wants to see you. I told him I would let him know when you were up. But if you'd like to rest for a bit, I can tell him you're sleeping."

"No, I'm good."

He nods and leaves the room. As soon as he's gone, I ask Ruby, "Tell me about that poem."

"It's from a book."

"Is it from *Through the Looking-Glass?*"

"You are correct."

Bingo. For as much as I ride this thing, credit where credit is due. It figured out a way to share classified intel with me. Probably would have figured it out quicker on a normal day, too, but this is the polar opposite of a normal day.

"Well, thanks for taking the long way around on that," I tell it. "So now I have to find a jabberwocky. Whatever the hell that is."

"You don't have the required security clearance," Ruby says, "but that's certainly something you can ask Danbridge about."

"And finally, you are good for something. And speaking of . . ."

Allyn is huddled with Drucker in the security office, and his face shifts from a smile to a frown in record speed as soon as I enter. Drucker's face is already in a frown but I think that's more of a perpetual thing.

"How are you feeling?" Allyn asks.

"High as a kite," I tell him, "and ready to rock."

Drucker smooths out her beige pantsuit. "I was just saying I have serious issues with you being on the premises."

"And I've got nothing else to do to keep myself occupied, so I may as well work. Let's talk postponing this summit."

"Absolutely not," she says.

"Why?"

"Because we're here," she says. "This doesn't impact our ability to work."

"People's lives are in danger."

"They're in danger because you're mentally unstable," she says.

"Why are you so hot to sell this place? What are you getting out of it?"

"Do you even read the news?"

In fairness, not really, but still, rude. "Can you make that sound any less condescending?"

"If you did," she said, "you'd know that the national deficit is on the verge of crippling us. China is coming to call on the debts we owe and we've got nothing to give them. Medicare and Social Security are insolvent. President Everett has tasked us with being creative. This is an opportunity to pump billions of dollars into the budget. It's not a fix, but it's a start."

"I guess it doesn't matter who gets hurt in the process."

"Not my job," she says. "That was your job. And you failed at it."

Allyn looks over at her, then at me, and finally says, "Senator, please give us a moment."

"No."

She is a rock in a river, the two of us cutting around her. So Allyn shrugs and circles the desk, coming for me. "Let's take a walk," he says. I glance over at Ruby in its power station, and I'm about to tell it to follow, but it seems to be depowered, so I leave it.

I hold the door for Allyn and we exit the room, making our way through the lobby. I want a quiet space to talk. We reach Fairbanks's office, which is clear. The book is still missing from the shelf. I sit at the desk, and let Allyn take the guest chair. As he gets settled in the seat he raises his watch and says, "Come over to the Fairbanks office."

"Who was that?" I ask.

"We'll get to that in a second. First . . ."

"First," I tell him, "time to put cards on the table. There's shit you're not telling me and there's shit I'm not telling you. What's a jab-berwocky?"

Every ounce of blood drains from his face. It's not like he ever had a good poker face, but this is certainly a look. He composes himself and says, "I have no idea what you're talking about." But the reek of fear says different.

"Allyn," I say. "It's me. I'll tell you what you want to know, but you have to be straight with me. I know it's something about not being able to change past events."

"Did your little robot tell you?"

I say no. Which is only technically a lie? Either way I have a better poker face.

Allyn lets out a long sigh and sinks back in the chair. "This is like, top security clearance. It's something else Simms developed. Something that never made it to market. The government kept it for itself."

"And what's that?"

"Time cloaking."

"Oh, yes," I say, adding on a pile of sarcasm. "I know exactly what that is."

Allyn sighs again. "I don't totally understand it. Popa can explain it. It's a way to hide stuff from time. Sort of speeding up and slowing down light. Like, on a highway, cars speed up and slow down, right? If cars slow down enough and the gaps between them get big enough, a person can cross, and then when traffic speeds up the people who didn't see it wouldn't have known it happened. So. The fact that the person crossed the street is hidden from time."

"That's the best you've got?" I ask him. "That doesn't help. Like, even a little bit."

"I'm not explaining it right," he says. "The way Popa explains it is better. But basically, we have a secure data collection unit that sits outside the timestream. It's a record of human history. Culture, entertainment, news, stock markets. And we can check against it, so if someone were to change something, we would know. It's a failsafe in case something big slips past the TEA."

"So like a black box. Because if something changed . . . would we even know?"

"Here's where we get into brain-bending territory," he says. "A few years ago, the TEA ran an experiment. They recruited a volunteer who agreed to let us change one small detail about his past. They went back and, before his family moved into the house where he grew up, they had his bedroom wall repainted from beige to green. The experiment was twofold—to see if the timestream could tolerate small ripples, and to see how it would alter his perception of the room."

"And?"

"After the room was painted, they asked him a long series of questions about his childhood. When they asked him the color of his bedroom wall growing up, he said green."

"Well that's . . . I don't even know what that is."

"Yeah," Allyn says, leaning back. "So we learned a few interesting things there. The timestream can handle minor fluctuations. The color of his wall didn't affect anything about his life going forward, so it was a pretty small ripple. We also learned that changes in the past will alter the collective unconscious. Because his family members? His friends? They all said they remembered the room as being green. Hence the Jabberwocky. That's what Simms called it. It sucks up information all day long, and the thing is just huge. Several exabytes, which is like a quintillion bytes each or something. And before you ask, the thing makes Fort Knox look like a corner bodega. It's designed to ping me directly if anything changes, or if anyone tries to tamper with it."

"You and who else?"

"The president. Secretary of Defense. Drucker, since she's on the time committee. Jim Henderson at the TEA. That's actually his main job, handling the Jabberwocky. We call him digital ops, but a lot of the details about what he does are kept vague to prevent"—Allyn waves at me—"exactly this."

It makes me wonder about Westin. The kill that looks fresh, hours and hours later. "What exactly can you hide outside of time with this thing?"

"Looking to take a little vacation?" Allyn asks, smiling. "Someplace no one will bother you?"

"I'm serious."

"It's a computer," he says. "Just data."

"Where is this thing located?"

"It's a little complicated. The main unit is in a TEA facility nearby, on the other side of Einstein. But with the amount of data that's being processed, a lot of it is encrypted and stored in government servers around the world. Essentially, the main processing mechanism is in one place, but we rent out storage units to put the information, with top-level encryption."

"I'm not a computer person but that doesn't sound terribly secure."

Allyn shrugs. "The way they tell me, it's the most secure option we had given the amount of processing power we needed."

"And what makes you think none of the bidders know about this?"

Allyn shakes his head. "No one knows this exists. No one's brought it up."

"Good thing we're dealing with a trustworthy group of people. Henderson runs the day-to-day. Where is he on all this?"

"He's still over at Einstein. So far, no problems. Now," he says, "your turn. I showed you mine. What are you keeping from me?"

Before I can say anything, there's movement from around the corner. Chris, the facilities manager. He's wearing his usual gray polo and jeans and a look on his face like the path ahead of him is littered with land mines. He comes up to the desk, and Allyn waves his hand. "Tell her what you told me."

He looks back and forth between us a few times, then says, "Well, remember we talked about the electrical? We're getting those surges . . ."

As if on cue, the lights flicker.

Chris points a finger in the air. "That. So I've been checking the wiring and boxes, making sure everything is up to snuff, right? And I'm finding a couple of things that are, uh . . . raising questions."

"Like?" I ask.

"Well, for one, I found what looks like cabling buried deep in the wall of Atwood that's unaccounted for," he says. "And then, I ran some data from around the surges and checked it against the meters, and we're not getting any readings there. So . . ."

He takes out a tablet and puts it down on the desk, the proudest he's ever been of anything. We both lean over and look at a mess of numbers that don't make any sense.

"Gonna need you to explain this one, bud," I tell him.

He droops a little, then picks up the tablet. "We've had some humongous spikes in energy use. Especially in the last few weeks, but I can find them randomly going back years. That's not the big problem. The big problem is, something messed with the metering system so those spikes wouldn't be apparent. And I did a little more digging, and talking to Celeste over in accounting? Seems that our electric bill is a lot higher than what we should be paying."

"So what does this mean?" Allyn asks.

"No idea," Chris says. "If the building were on electric heat it would make sense to see a spike like that in wintertime. But we're not. And anyway, there's no pattern or anything. It's like we got a room full of blenders and space heaters that someone keeps plugging in for a bit and then unplugging. But like, a lot." He nods and widens his eyes, desperate to make the point. "A lot."

"And what about the elevators?"

He shrugs. "Nothing wrong that I can find. I looked myself."

Allyn raises his hand at me. "See? Maybe a possible future."

"Or maybe it hasn't been tampered with yet." I turn to Chris. "I want the access hatches to all the elevators locked up, and the elevators themselves inspected every half hour. You see anything that looks shaky, pull it right out of service."

Chris looks at Allyn for approval, which annoys me.

After a moment Allyn nods. "Thank you. That'll be all."

Chris hovers for a second before realizing he's been dismissed, and then he heads toward the hallway. I hold back the laugh building in my chest. Kolten has been on about this secret room and now we know there's something sucking power like crazy in that wing?

"I do not believe in coincidences," I say, before realizing, damn it, I said the quiet part out loud.

"January, it's your turn now. What have you got?"

"Westin is dead," I tell him.

His face shatters at this. Body sags into the chair.

"You knew him," I say.

Allyn nods slowly.

"How?"

"He is a person of interest in an ongoing investigation." He looks up at me, his eyes rimmed with tears. "Where is he? I need you to show him to me."

"Well, about that . . ."

Allyn is in a much better position to get the guy in room 526 to leave, but still, I wait down the bend in the hall, out of sight, just to be safe. It takes a little cajoling—it's getting late—but Allyn assures him it's important.

Once it's clear, I come over. Westin is still there, still dead, still fresh.

"Where is he?" Allyn asks.

I sweep my hand at the far bed. "Right there. Which is the fun part, right? I mean, I can see him. But Ruby ran a scan and came back with nothing."

Allyn walks to the bed, puts his hand on it. Feels the mattress.

"January, there's nothing here."

"Allyn, you know I'm Unstuck. You know I can see things . . ."

"You say the body has been here, what, all day? So what does that mean? He's going to die and we have to stop it?"

"No, I think he's really dead."

Allyn turns and sits on the bed, right on Westin's midsection. He puts his head in his hands. I am making him do that a lot lately.

"January," he says, "what am I supposed to do with this?"

"Are you saying you don't believe me?"

"There's no body here. And the way you've been acting . . . I told you. I told you that you should leave." He shakes his head, gets up, and paces the room. "This is my fault. I'm the one who put you here."

"Allyn, wait, just a second."

"No, just . . ." He sighs. "We found someone with a Jeep, and the roads aren't great, but they think they can get you safely down the road to the Moonlight Motel."

"The Moonlight? Are you kidding? That's the kind of place where you wake up with your kidney missing in a tub full of ice."

"January, the porter found you in a closet tearing apart a wall," he says. "Then you stabbed him. I was trying to get past it. I really was. But now with this . . . if you were in my shoes you would make the exact same decision."

"First off, I did not stab him, I slashed him. They are completely different knife-fighting techniques and I'm disappointed in you for not knowing that. Second, they put a Band-Aid on it and it's fine. Not like he died."

Allyn shakes his head and looks around the room, almost like he's willing the body to appear—something, anything, to back up what I'm saying—and finds nothing. "Go to your room. Pack your things. I'm sorry. Let me get this sorted, and let's get you sorted, okay?"

"Send me to my room, huh? You're not my real dad."

I wait, like he might respond, but he doesn't. He just sits there, his head in his hands, surrounded by a corpse that I'm beginning to think might just be a figment of my time-damaged brain.

I head for my room and swipe my watch, and the latch gives a little red flash. Great. Did Allyn revoke my security privileges already? Now I can't even get into the room? I give the door handle a little jiggle out of frustration and then I'm about to call down to the lobby when the door cracks open, the security bar in place. The room beyond that is dark so all I can see is an eye, peering out.

"Yes?" A male voice.

"What the fuck are you doing in my room?" I ask.

"Ah, oh, sorry, I . . ." The man stutters as he undoes the latch, and when it's clear I push the door open, sending him tumbling to the floor.

He's a sad sight in the sliver of light coming from behind me in the hallway. In a bathrobe—hotel issue, and he had to call down for it because I didn't have any in here. He's not dressed underneath and is grabbing at it to cover himself, to preserve his dignity. His hair is slightly wet, like he just got out of the shower, and his little, sinewy arms make me think of chickens.

"I'm so sorry," he says, sliding back on the carpet. "Did they not tell you? They told me you approved."

"Who told you?"

"I don't . . . the manager, I think? I don't remember. Please, I'm sorry . . ." He points to the corner, at a duffel bag that, presumably, contains my clothing and personal effects, because the room looks like a hotel room again. Not that I had it decked out or anything. But still, it suddenly feels cold and alien, my space having been invaded and wiped out.

I grab the bag, then the wooden beads on the inside knob. The postcard is still stuck in the bathroom mirror. I take that too, press it to my chest and close my eyes and feel it. Then I turn to leave, headed for the stairwell, trying to outrun the feeling like my face is caving in.

When I reach the lobby, the front desks are empty, but there's a group of TEA agents running toward the first-floor hallway of Butler. I drop my bag behind the concierge desk and follow the scrum. They're headed for the end of the hallway, and when I get there it's hard to make out the voices, but I can see Cameo is standing a head above everyone, still in their robe and sweats, and they look furious. Their voice is loud and tight and they are slicing the air with the blade of their hand. I have never seen them like this.

"No, absolutely not. Reg, what is this?"

Drucker is standing there with a group of agents. It's them against Reg and Cameo. The battle lines are drawn. Reg is red-faced, looking at Drucker.

"Look, I'm already sleeping in my office," he tells her. "I am not throwing my staff out of their rooms so that someone can have a bed."

"You can't ask someone with a net worth of a billion dollars to sleep on a cot," Drucker says. "I gave you the chance to find them a more appropriate accommodation and you did not. Since you won't take your job seriously, I'll have to do it."

"That's not how this works."

"It is exactly how this works," Drucker says. "At the end of the day this is a federal facility. And as the highest-ranking member of the federal government here, I'm in charge. Not you."

Reg turns to the side and hails Allyn on his watch, and I step back into the alcove with the ice machine, figure if Allyn sees me here he'll make me leave. But I'm bouncing on my toes, ready for a fight.

So now Drucker is giving away our rooms.

Allyn comes running up and Drucker immediately launches into a spiel about customer service and the needs of the guests and blah blah blah. Allyn takes this all in and turns to Reg and says, "Your staffers will get their rooms back as soon as this is over."

That is not what I expected. And between the pressure of the day and the razor edge my brain is teetering on, I can't even stop myself from stepping out of the alcove and yelling, "What the fuck."

Everyone turns to look at me. Allyn actually rolls his eyes. "I told you . . ."

"Shut the fuck up, Allyn," I say, so hard and so fast it actually works. Then I turn to Drucker. "You know what? I don't care if you are a senator. You are a giant fucking asshole if you think some trust-fund motherfucker who never did a hard day's work in his life deserves a room over the people who actually keep this place running. And putting them ahead in the line is one thing but actually throwing people out of their rooms? Fuck you and your entire bloodline and your pets if you have any."

Drucker's face reduces to a fine point and she is about to speak when Allyn steps between us, looks at a couple of the TEA agents, and says, "Take her to the lobby, right now. Wait for me."

Everyone freezes.

Because he basically just said: *Seize her.*

Three agents—two burly men and a woman roughly my size but with veins in her arms chiseled from rock—close in on me. I could fight them off, and, given the narrow space I can get at least two of them on their asses. It's the third that'd be dicey. But that'll give Allyn more cause to make me leave, so I let them take my arms and lead me toward the front.

I glance back and catch a look on Allyn's face like I think maybe he is sorry? I don't care. It was fun to tell Drucker how I felt. My only real regret is I didn't get to throw a boot at her like I did at Ruby earlier, because she almost definitely would not have dodged out of the way.

The agents say nothing as they lead me to the lobby, and then we stand by the coffee urn waiting for further instruction. I go to pour some, find the thing is empty.

Again. Always empty.

I push the entire contraption to the floor. The smash and clatter of it reverberates through the room and people jerk or dive for cover. A woman cries out from fear. Spent grounds spill across the floor and the space fills with the scent of coffee, which is oddly comforting. Not the most mature thing I've ever done, but it makes me feel like maybe someone will get their shit together and actually fill it back up.

There's a shuffle behind me, and I turn to find Brandon carrying a mop and bucket. His forearm is bandaged tightly. He stares at me as he gets to work cleaning up the mess. For the first time in I don't know how long, I feel an emotion other than anger or numbness. So it takes me a second to figure out what it is. This is a new sensation for me.

I realize what it is: shame.

"Brandon . . ."

He keeps his head down. Very purposely ignoring me. I try to say something else when there's another voice behind me.

"What the hell is going on, January?" Allyn asks.

I turn and find him practically in my face. Almost as red as I made Drucker. She must have reamed him out. I can feel it radiating off him. I don't give him a chance. "The Allyn I knew would never sell people out for a bunch of crybaby assholes," I tell him. "There are few things in this life I can live by, and one of them is that you are a man of integrity. You always have been. And now I feel ashamed to know you. I feel ashamed to have called you a friend, to see you shit your spine out and hand it over to someone like that. And for what? Another little gold star in your file?" I shake my head at him. "You're not the man I knew."

"And you're not the woman I knew," Allyn says, his voice far quieter than mine, but much, much sharper. "Me, the people here, we've done nothing but reach out to you and try to help you and you have pushed us away, with prejudice. I know your loss was enormous, but you let it poison you." His eyes mist up a little, someone else from deeper inside fighting through. "We tried. You did this to yourself."

He turns to the goons. "The Jeep is waiting out front. Take her there now." Back to me: "I'm sure the Moonlight will have whatever you need to get through the next few days. Charge it to the room."

"Just like that?" I ask.

"This is for your own good."

"Allyn, I am fine." I try to hide the desperation in my voice, doing a poor job of it.

He shakes his head and turns away from me. I think because he doesn't want to look me in the eye. The two TEA guys grab me by the arms and pull me toward the front of the lobby, to the sliding glass doors and the darkness beyond.

"Allyn, no," I call over my shoulder.

Then I remember the cell in the security office. I'm supposed to end up in there. Grayson is supposed to shoot me still. Those things haven't happened yet. Can I even leave right now? Or can the future be rewritten?

What if I leave and whatever connection I have to Mena is severed? And then I come back and can't find her?

What if I get to the Moonlight and hit the third stage?

The guys holding me aren't gripping me tight enough, so I drop my weight until I land on my knees. Their hands slip, and I throw a hook punch into the nuts of the guy on my left, because he's the bigger of the two. He doubles over and heaves, which gives me the chance to throw my shin behind the knees of the other one. With the two of them on the floor I manage to get to my feet.

But then the woman with the carved biceps puts me in a blood choke.

Damn it, it's always the third one.

I try to hammer her thigh but she sees it coming and kicks her leg back. I grab the arm that's pressing my airway closed and jerk forward but she's strong. She leans back and hoists me into the air.

She's letting in just enough oxygen I can breathe, but not enough I can struggle. So it's not long before I go limp, my body refusing to cooperate. She drags me toward the door. She'll let her guard down in a second, and then I'm sticking my thumb in her eye.

As I'm balling my fingers into a fist, thumb ramrod straight and perpendicular, yellow lights flash outside the lobby doors. Doesn't look like any of the emergency vehicles we use on-site, and it's enough to slow me down, plus the agent dragging me. The doors slide open and five people in white hazmat suits stream into the lobby, cold air following them as they drag equipment and hoist sensors.

"Who is in charge here?" barks a woman in a stern British accent. The suit at the center, the smallest of the bunch.

The TEA agent drops me and I fall to my knees, breathing hard, trying to reinflate my lungs. No one seems to care about us anymore. Allyn steps to the woman and says, "Allyn Danbridge, TEA."

The woman strides up to him until the faceplate of her suit is nearly pressing against Allyn's nose. "Okay, Allyn Danbridge, TEA. I'm Doctor Liz Gottlieb, CDC. Could you please tell me why you have live dinosaurs on this site and did not think to call me? Or literally anyone?" She is so angry her voice is trembling.

Allyn stammers, his face drops. "How did you . . ."

"Social *fucking* media, you turnip," she says. "Do you know what kind of bacteria or viruses or pathogens those things could be carrying?"

This causes a few people in the lobby to chatter nervously, and frankly it's not a fun thing for me to hear either. One of them bit me. Tamworth seemed to think it was okay, but what if it's not?

"Could you keep your voice down?" Allyn asks, his voice a rasp.

"No, I will not, because I want everyone to know how much of a twit you are. Now, since no one's currently bleeding from their eyes I figure we're okay, but we are still locking this place down and running some tests before anyone will be allowed to leave."

"And how long is that going to take?" Drucker asks, suddenly at Allyn's shoulder.

"As long as it needs to. Until then, no one in or out."

Allyn glances over at me and says, "We have one person who is a risk to security and needs to be taken off-site immediately."

"No one in or out," Gottlieb says, slowly this time, like she's speaking to a child.

Allyn looks like he's ready to argue, but then gives up. Can't help but smile at that.

Eternalism, baby. Saved by the CDC.

"Now," Gottlieb says. "I want anyone who had direct contact with the creatures quarantined in the medical office right now. Everyone else should be encouraged to go to their rooms. We will perform our tests and let you know when we are finished. Until then, I'm assuming control of this facility. Do you understand?"

Allyn nods, and Drucker pulls him aside while Gottlieb goes back to her team. I stroll over, put on the biggest smile that I possibly can, and tell Allyn, "I guess I'll head upstairs then."

He doesn't respond. Just turns back to Drucker and leads her away so that I can't hear what they're saying.

He's still nursing the wound I gave him.

Good.

A man in a hazmat suit uses a long cotton swab to get a sample from inside my sinus cavity, though I think really he's trying to poke me in the brain to see what happens. Then he does a handful of skin tests and takes some blood and without another word he hustles out of the room. At least they're efficient.

The crinkle paper I mussed up hasn't even been changed yet. But I opt for the chair instead of the table. Lean my head back against the wall and close my eyes.

"Ruby, any CDC chatter you can clue me in to?" I ask.

No response. I lost it somewhere in all the confusion. Maybe it was confiscated? I don't even remember. I actually feel a tiny pang of loss at not having it. It may annoy the shit out of me, but it was also reliable.

It was something I could talk to.

And it kept talking to me no matter how I acted.

I get up and go to the door but it's locked.

Fine. I climb onto the table. If I'm going to be locked in here waiting, no sense in wasting the time being awake. I'm dozing when the door opens and Nik comes in. He nods to me and sits in the chair.

"Aren't we quarantined?" I ask.

"Yeah, well. I got the door open. Figure if there is anything to be worried about, we both have it. What's the harm?"

"So are you excited?" I ask. "Soon this will all be yours."

"No," he says. He crosses his feet in front of him and puts his hands behind his head. "I told you, I don't want your job. I want to be in the stream. But I'm playing a long game here. Figure if I step up, Allyn will see me as someone reliable."

"Just make sure to clean off the knife you plunged into my back."

"I tried to convince him to keep you on. Clearly you want to be here." He pauses. "Well, not clearly. You kind of treat everyone like shit. Somehow they're all still fond of you. But I've never seen someone stomp on so much goodwill as you do."

I lift myself to sitting and turn so I'm facing him. "Getting bold now, are we?"

He shrugs. "I have to know who I'm working with. Did you think I wasn't going to ask around? Or that people wouldn't just volunteer information? A lot of them did. Just the way it is."

"So you know me now."

He shakes his head. "Nobody really knows anybody. Your business is your business." He folds his hands in his lap. "I remember the explosion. The woman who died . . ."

"Mena."

"Some of the people at Einstein still knew her, back from when she was a stewardess."

"Yeah, she worked there for a while, before she got the job here."

Nik nods. "Everyone liked her."

"She had that kind of effect on people," I say, choking down the lump in my throat.

"Can I give you some advice?" he asks.

"No."

He stares me down for a minute and scrunches his lip. "Well, I'll say the advice and you can hear it and I guess that'll have to be enough." He clears his throat. "It sucks when people you love die."

I wait for him to continue. I wonder if maybe he's waiting for the next bit, to increase the impact, so I ask, "Is this the point where you tell me that they live within our hearts or some other touchy-feely fucking nonsense?"

"No. I'm just saying it sucks when people you love die."

I lay back on the table. "Yeah. Yeah it does."

After a little bit of silence he asks, "Doesn't it drive you crazy?"

"A lot of things make me crazy."

Nik shakes his head. "What they're doing, sticking people in the wings like that. It's the people who don't do any real work who end up hoarding everything. And the people who do the actual labor have to sleep on a cot in a hallway. It's . . . I mean, I don't even know the right word for it."

"Should be fucking criminal."

"All I know is that I would never consent to sleeping on a damn cot in a damn hallway," Nik says. "I mean . . . these people. Look how much they have."

"There's this saying, about people who are born on third base and think they hit a triple," I tell him. "About the way people inherit wealth and power and think that not only did they earn it, but they deserve it. We deal with a different sort in this place. People who were born on third base and think they built the stadium."

Nik is about to say something else when Allyn's voice sprouts from Nik's watch. "CDC folks still have a lot of work to do but you have the all-clear. Come on down to security."

He gets up, puts his hand on the knob, and lingers. Then he turns and asks, "Want to come?"

It was nice of Nik to break me out. He even offered to let me join him in the security room, but at this point, I just want to get some rest. I'm so tired, thinking hurts. I retrieve my duffel bag from behind the concierge desk, glad that no one walked away with it. On my way to the cots I see Mena stroll across the lobby. She's too far away from me to get over to her in time, and she doesn't see me. I find an empty bed, off in a far corner, with a gulf of empty cots between me and the next person—a flight attendant from Einstein, given the uniform carefully folded and slid underneath.

I drop the bag next to me and stare at the popcorn ceiling for a bit, thinking, Wow, I should really get some sleep. So of course, the more I think that, the harder it is to get to sleep. Doesn't help that, even though the lights have been dimmed in this section, I prefer a complete and total void. When I close my eyes, enough light leaks through that I may as well have a skylight in my face.

Lights.

The electricity thing is weird.

I sit up, wish I had my whiteboard. Try to remember what it looked like, all the names. Maybe I should have added electricity. I knew there was an issue. According to Chris it's bigger than I realized.

Something is getting fed a ton of power. Something that is being used at random. I would ask Ruby to help me break it down, but I don't think I'm getting Ruby back. I would raise Chris on my watch, but when I check my comm link, it doesn't have master access anymore.

Allyn wasn't fucking around.

But he said to work the case. And that's not really what I've done so far. I've been reacting. I did take a little me time to think, but I really need to break this down.

If I can't sleep, there's no sense in staying here.

"You know who I should talk to?" I ask, forgetting again that Ruby isn't hovering at my shoulder, so it just serves to confuse a few people on the cots.

For fun, I complete the thought: "Reg."

Maybe he has some insight on the power issue.

I pull my boots on and head to the lobby, and from the balcony catch sight of a woman with short, curly gray hair in a hazmat suit talking to Drucker. I can't hear them but her mask is off, and she's carrying it under her arm. Doctor Gottlieb? If her mask is off that's probably a good sign.

I'm about to cross down into the lobby when Reg comes wobbling in from someplace underneath me. Probably had too much to drink.

Then he spins around and he's holding his abdomen together with his hands, blood and viscera pouring down his front. He falls on his back and even from here I can tell he's dead before he hits the ground. From somewhere deep within the bowels of the hotel, I hear a sound like a roller coaster makes, that *clack-clack-clack* when it's climbing the tracks.

But it's not a slip.

And this is being made by an animal.

CHAOS THEORY & SPECULATION

My heart slams into my rib cage as I run for the security office. Reg's body is slumped on itself. Staying in the open to confirm what I know will get me dead too, which is not going to help anybody.

As I reach the door I realize my security privileges have been revoked. I'm ready to throw my foot next to the knob when the door opens a crack. I put my shoulder into it, knocking Nik onto his ass. I slide inside and I'm about to slam the door behind me when Kolten and Warwick muscle in too. I ignore them and head for the storage cabinet.

"What the hell is going on out there?" Allyn asks from the other side of the room.

"Give me back Ruby and my privileges, right now," I tell him.

"First you tell me . . ."

I hop onto a desk, reach behind the cabinet, feeling for the hiding spot where I taped the key. "Reg's insides are currently on his outsides, and it looks like an animal attack, and we had three baby dinosaurs in the basement, but with the way time is acting, I do not feel good about any of this. Before you object, don't forget I'm a good shot."

"I want to help," Kolten says.

"And how are you going to do that?" I ask.

"Well, I am the smartest person in the building," he says, with a little smirk that is matched by a look of embarrassment that flashes over Warwick's face.

"Okay, boy genius," I say, momentarily abandoning the hunt for the key. "I believe we have three dinosaurs on the loose and a deficit of dinosaur-catching equipment. Hit me."

His eyes go a little wide at suddenly being called on to actually be smart, rather than just say he is. "We can open the doors. Lure them outside."

"And make them someone else's problem? That's the best you got? Do not say another goddamn word to me."

Kolten looks ready to respond but Warwick grabs his shoulder and quiets him. At least one member of this family has some sense.

My fingertips brush the rough edge of the painter's tape, and I rip away the key, fumble for the gun case, and get it open. Inside is a 9 mm handgun. Use in case of emergency, but there's never been an emergency. I hope the gunpowder still sparks. I cleaned and oiled it, what, six months ago? A year? Can't even remember. As if time means anything at the current moment.

I turn to find Ruby floating in my field of vision like an eager puppy, the plastic googly eyes on its lenses currently walleyed.

"Welcome back, dummy," I say. "Broadcast an announcement. Everyone in their rooms, barricade doors, wait until we give the all-clear."

"Only because you asked nicely."

"What about the people on the cots?" Nik asks.

Great. "Rooms or bathrooms. Anyplace that's safe. Then get some video on the screen so we can see what we're dealing with." I turn to Allyn. "You strapped?"

He opens the lapel of his suit, showing off a holster. "Stunner. One shot."

"Better than no shots."

We move to the video screens as Ruby broadcasts the announcements. Through the door we hear its voice, ramped down a notch to sound a bit more calming:

Everyone please find a safe place and barricade yourself inside. This is not a drill. If you do not have access to a room, find someplace with a sturdy door.

Even inside the security room we hear cries of confusion, but for the most part it's late enough that there aren't too many people out. I watch as the video feeds shrink and separate into small squares, Ruby searching for the most relevant ones for us to be looking at. I know which one I need right now. The most important one. When I see it down in the corner, my stomach flops.

The secured door to the basement is open. "Someone let them out."

"Who?" Nik asks.

"That's a not-right-now problem," I tell him.

A blur darts across one of the screens, appears on another, then disappears again. Ruby reorders the screens so that we can follow the creature's movements.

And there it is.

I thought these were traditional velociraptors, which only grow to the size of domesticated turkeys. Still plenty dangerous, though manageable. I'm not a paleontologist, I just know which species were popular among smugglers.

These look more like utahraptors, which can grow to eighteen feet long.

This one isn't that big yet—maybe my size, a bit bigger. A teenager. But still, not something I want to tangle with.

Just ask Reg.

I tear through the security room, looking for the earbuds I know I have somewhere, and find them at the bottom of a cabinet, next to a set of heavy-duty zip ties. I put the box of buds and the ties on the table.

"We've got two weapons worth a damn," I say, thinking briefly of Grayson, who I know is carrying a gun, but I also don't want him involved. "Allyn, take an earpiece in case we need to split up." Nik sheepishly raises his hand. "You're not going out without a weapon. You stay here and monitor video. Watch our backs."

Ruby whirs to the middle of our little scrum. "I am perfectly capable of tracking video . . ."

"You're coming with us," I tell it. "I need you scouting. You won't look like a meal to them."

"I have a question," Allyn says, holding up the zip ties. "Really?"

"They're like alligators. All the power is on the down-bite. The ties are rated for five hundred pounds. We get them secured, they're not getting out."

"You're sure about this?" Allyn asks. "What if I stun it and you shoot it."

"Yes, I'm sure," I tell him. "You know how many dinosaur assignments I went on. We contain, not kill."

The first part is only a little true. I haven't actually zip-tied a dinosaur, but I think the theory holds.

The second part: they're not my words. They're Mena's.

I remember once—this isn't a slip, it's just a memory, though sometimes it's hard to tell the difference—I saw a caterpillar on the pavement while the two of us walked on a warm summer day. I raised my foot to step on its grotesque, torture-device body, for fear it might find its way into my room and crawl into my ear while I was sleeping.

Mena pulled me back. She bent down and put her hand in its path, letting it crawl onto her palm. She walked it over to the foliage lining the hotel and put it on a leaf, where it stuck its little head—or ass, who knows—into the air. Almost like it was doing a happy dance.

I'm disappointed in you, she said.

Just a bug, I said, trying to play it off, but I could hear the hurt in Mena's voice. I could see that I'd done something she would carry with her for a little while.

We must aspire to end all suffering, she said.

Not even a bug? I asked.

Not even a bug.

What if I stepped on it by accident? Am I dooming myself for all of eternity because I didn't see it?

Her voice took on a slightly exasperated tone. *The intentions that drive the action are more important than the action itself. You were trying to hurt it.*

I didn't think of it like that.

Which is always the problem, isn't it?

I tried to respond, found I couldn't. She saw me flailing and kissed me on the cheek. *Not even a mosquito, my love. But especially not something that will one day be so beautiful.*

Like you? I felt foolish as soon as I said it, in the split second before she rolled her eyes.

I've had about enough with the butterfly metaphors. It's just about being kind.

In that moment, I made myself a promise, that I would leave the caterpillars be. I would carry the spiders out of my room and leave them in the hallway, rather than turn them into smears. Even the big ones.

And if I can contain these things, I will. For her.

I should be scared. I really, truly should be. But my adrenaline is surging. I palm a Retronim out of my pocket and dry-swallow, just to keep me sharp, to stop me from slipping into a memory that'll freeze me for long enough to get myself dead. I throw a look at Kolten and Warwick and say, "Do not leave this room."

Then Allyn and I step into the lobby.

A soft, noninvasive alarm drones. There's no one out that we can see, and hopefully no one is hiding underneath the desks or behind anything. Reg's body is slumped on the far side of the room, in a pool of blood so thick it's more black than red.

. . . droplets of blood pat the blue carpet, turning from red to black as they soak into the fibers . . .

No. I'm in the lobby.

What was that?

Doesn't matter right now.

But why am I slipping if I just took another pill?

I keep an eye out for stragglers. As we move toward the center of the lobby Allyn asks, his voice low, "Maybe it's not the worst idea. Send them outside. They're cold-blooded, right? Won't the snow slow them down? And they'll be easier to track?"

"C'mon, not you too," I tell him. "Set them loose on the closest town? Not happening."

"Just talking it out," Allyn said. "It's your hotel, Jan."

I turn to him, risk meeting his eye. "Is it?"

He sighs. "Do you know what it's like when the president himself personally reams you out? I voted for him . . ."

Clack-clack-clack-clack.

We both fall silent, trying to track the source. It's impossible to pin it down. Too many hard, smooth surfaces. The sound bounces like a rubber ball. I tap my ear. "Radio check, you got me?"

"Loud and clear," Nik says.

"Eyes in the sky," I say. "Tell me what you see."

"One in the basement, one on the third floor, nothing on the third one."

"Anybody downstairs?"

"The CDC had set up shop in one of the conference rooms, but they look pretty well barricaded. It's pacing outside the door but I don't think it'll get in."

"As long as they're secure we leave it for now," I say. "Too many people on the upper levels. Ruby. Get on finding that third one. I want you scanning cameras and moving around. It might be in a blind spot. Allyn, we go upstairs."

Ruby flies off, and Allyn and I move toward the corridor leading to the next level. I press my finger to my ear and drop my voice to a whisper. "Make sure you're tracking us. Don't need one of these things sneaking up on us."

"Um . . ."

"What um?" I ask. "I don't like um."

"Is there something wrong with the cameras?" Nik asks.

"Ruby," I say.

"There appears to be some kind of interference. Individual feeds are blinking on and off."

"Are you telling me we've lost our eyes?"

"Not lost," Ruby says. "But . . . losing. I don't know what's wrong. I need to look into it."

I turn to Allyn, who is putting on a brave face, but not really doing the best job of it. "You better be paying attention," I say.

We step into the corridor, moving toward the second level. My ears are ringing I'm listening so hard. I catch another *clack-clack-clack*, closer this time.

The second level looks clear. Mindful there's a third one of these things running around, we move toward the next level, another twisty corridor with poor sight lines that was not designed for a goddamn dinosaur hunt. We reach the top of the pathway and press ourselves against the wall.

"What's the plan if we . . ." Allyn whispers.

A cry for help pierces the silence.

We both dash into the hallway and follow the noise. My heart drops somewhere into my lower intestine because I know that's where some of the cots were set up. We round the corner to find a group of half-dressed folks huddled in an alcove, a raptor in the narrow hallway, standing on a cot, which is nearly buckling under the creature's weight. Its dark gray feathers with red trim suck up the light. It looks both sinister and beautiful.

There's no way around, and it looks like the group tried to hide inside a storage closet, but no one had the access code. The raptor rears back, ready to leap, and before I can manage it Allyn yells, "Hey!"

It turns and looks at us, tilting its head like it's trying to figure us out, and then swings its attention back to the cowering people. Maybe sensing their fear and figuring them for the easier meal. There's a table to my left with a crystal vase full of flowers. I pick it up and hurl it at the dinosaur, the glass shattering on the wall next to it.

That gets its attention.

It swings around and makes eye contact with me.

I put my hands up and yell, "That's right, come on over here."

The dinosaur hops off the cot and walks toward us tentatively, like it's sizing us up, and then it breaks into a run. I take off like a rocket, Allyn behind me. I feel something in my side and Allyn is handing me the stunner.

"You're a better shot," he says.

"Thanks," I say, taking the gun.

We stop and I check it to make sure the safety is off, then take a calming breath.

Which was stupid. The thing is on us quick.

It lunges, and my mind goes blank. My body takes over. I manage to twist myself to the right and bring my foot up at the same time, planting it on the animal's sternum, serving to both push it away and push myself back.

The problem is I do too good a job, because then I'm airborne. I tuck my chin to my chest and with my free hand slap the floor as I land, dispersing some of the impact. Then I bring my legs up hard over my head, doing a combat roll into a standing position. My abdomen screams. The muscle memory is there, but it's more memory than muscle.

By the time I'm back on my feet the thing is coming at me, and I'm just getting the stunner up and into firing position when Allyn appears, putting his shoulder into it. The two of them go sprawling, crashing to the blue carpet, and then the raptor has its jaws wrapped around Allyn's forearm and he screams.

I go over and give it a hard kick in the side, but it doesn't budge, just whips its head from side to side, with enough force it looks like it could break Allyn's arm. Blood is seeping from the animal's jaws and I don't know if it hit something major, but if it did, speed counts.

So I take aim.

And I say, "Sorry, Allyn."

He opens his eyes and looks at me.

I hesitate.

But then he nods.

I hit the thing in the back and it goes tense. For a second its jaws seem to dig tighter and Allyn screams louder, both from the pain and from the electricity now coursing through it and into him. But then it lets go and gives off a horrifying screech, the air filling with the smell of singed hair and burnt chicken.

Once the thing goes down, I let off the trigger and immediately get to work, lashing two zip ties around its snout, before getting its legs. By the time I'm getting its arms, it's finally coming to, and I have to hold tight to keep it from slashing me with claws roughly the size of my big toe. But then it's done.

I kneel next to Allyn, take the gun out of my pocket, and lay it on the floor, keeping one eye on the dinosaur. Allyn is shaking and gripping his arm. I take out my knife and cut off his sleeve. There's so much blood it's hard to tell where the wound is, but the flow doesn't seem strong. I take the ripped pieces of his sleeve and loop them around his arm.

"Take a deep breath," I tell him.

He does, and I squeeze tight.

He arches his back and yells.

I pick up the gun, hoping the commotion hasn't attracted the other two.

"You ready for the next one?" I ask.

"Lemme at 'em," Allyn says, groaning.

The closest thing with a door I can secure is the gym, so I pull Allyn to standing and duck under his good arm, bracing it over my shoulder. He's shuffling but mostly able to move under his own power. I keep the gun out, not wanting to shoot one of these things if it lunges at me, but not having a choice now.

There's a reedy old man inside, decked out in expensive workout clothes that don't look like they've been touched by a drop of sweat. It takes me a second to recognize him; the guy complaining about the menu in the elevator, from earlier today. As I approach he bangs on the glass. "What the hell was that? Did I just see a dinosaur?"

"Open up," I tell him.

The man moves to the door but instead of opening he grips the handle and leans back. When I swipe and try to open it, I can't. I bang on the window with the butt of the gun. "Are you kidding me right now? Open the door."

"Are there more of those things out there? How do I know it's safe?"

"Open the fucking door."

He shakes his head, eyes wide with panic. I lean Allyn against the wall, and he immediately slides down into a sitting position. I grab the metal handle and pull, get it to budge a few inches, but then the man puts a foot on the doorjamb.

Wants to play it like that?

I press the barrel of the gun against the window, pointed directly at his face.

He puts his hands up and I yank the door open, then grab Allyn and drag him inside. The man backs up against the far wall.

Nik crackles into the earbud. "What's going on? I can't see anything now."

"Allyn is down," I say. "Ruby, where are we?"

"I've located one of them, in the Tick Tock," it says. "But I still don't know what's wrong with the cameras."

"Nik, do what you can on your end." Then I turn to the old man and point to an expensive-looking pair of noise-canceling headphones sitting on top of the towel cabinet. "These yours?"

He nods, so I pick them up and crack them in half. He doesn't protest and it serves to make me feel a tiny bit better. I pat Allyn on the good arm. "You okay, chief?"

He nods. "Go get 'em."

I check the gun to make sure it's loaded. Pat my pocket, full of the zip ties. And realize that I have nothing to contain the last two but my wits. Can I shoot one in the leg? Is suffering pain or is suffering death? Why do Buddhists always have to be so fucking obtuse?

I step into the hallway, ears on alert, and check in with Ruby. "Still in the Tick Tock?"

"Toward the bar."

"Anyone up there?"

"Not that I can see and . . . oh, it sees me."

There's a stretch of silence. "And?"

"It's . . . curious, for sure. I'm trying to distract it. Moving back and forth to see if it'll follow me."

A plan knits together in my head. "If you can get into the kitchen and find something it wants to eat but stay out of its reach, you can keep it distracted long enough that maybe, I don't know . . ."

"The freezer," Ruby says. "If we can lure it inside we can lock the door."

"That's brilliant," I say, moving toward the ramp that'll take me up to the next level. "Finally pulling your weight."

"In fairness it's from the classic Steven Spielberg movie *Jurassic Park* . . ."

"You could have just said nothing," I tell Ruby, "and I would have been impressed. How high can these things jump?"

"Roughly ten to twelve feet."

"Then get in the kitchen, latch onto something tasty, and be thankful we have high ceilings."

"One problem. I lack the dexterity to open the freezer door."

"Yeah, that's why you're going to distract it, dummy. I'll get the door."

"That does not sound like a smart plan."

"Then come up with a better one. Until such time, this is it."

Ruby cuts off and I move up the ramp, listening for the sound of anything that might tip off an approaching raptor. I'm hoping the one in the basement stays fixated on what's down there.

As I approach the glass doors of the restaurant I say, "Getting close. Cutting off contact. Keep an eye on me and make sure I can loop around to the freezer."

"I found a pork loin," Ruby says.

When I peek my head around the corner I see Ruby floating about twenty feet in the air, a raptor a tiny bit smaller than the last one—this one with more orange in its feathers than red—scrambling onto a table to grab the chunk of pink meat dangling from Ruby's chassis. And the first thing I think is: how am I going to clean raw pork off of that thing?

Another not-right-now problem.

I creep through the doors, sticking close to the far wall. Ruby locks on me and backs up, creating a wide berth. Still don't feel good, and I keep the gun out, wondering how quickly I'm going to have to go back on my moral stand.

Wondering also, do these things hear very well?

Which doesn't matter, because I'm being so careful sticking against the wall that I nudge a chair, and the metal leg screeches so loud, the sound rips right up my spine. I duck behind the hostess table as I hear something crash behind me.

Then silence.

I hold my breath.

The light changes, and the space fills with the blaring sound of "Walk Like an Egyptian" and movement and clatter and plates and bodies.

Then, just like that, it's gone.

Is someone really playing the Bangles right now?

I lean out and the raptor is looking around in confusion.

I'm about to ask Ruby what's going on, when it happens again, but this time I see it. The restaurant is suddenly filled with that party from earlier today, with the guests ready for their trip to Egypt. Kolten, Warwick, and Drucker are just about to take their seats.

The raptor lunges for an old woman in a cream-colored robe, but then the scene is over, all of it gone. Back to a quiet restaurant. Just it, me, and Ruby.

God, couldn't they have been listening to a better song?

Also, why the hell can the dinosaur see it too?

That helps me right now, but doesn't bode well for pretty much anything else.

Worse is, in a couple of minutes I'm going to come crashing through those doors to save Kolten. I think about the test pilot who visited himself as a kid and had a brain aneurysm. Would this count as crossing my own timeline?

The cacophony returns, and this one seems to be going on a little longer, so I risk getting up and moving toward the kitchen. It won't be too far to get there. I stick to the tables, keep low, an eye on the raptor, which is snapping its jaws but not sinking into any of the people around it. As soon as I hear the music stop, I throw myself to the floor.

This is like the shittiest game of musical chairs ever.

And as soon as the music starts again I'm back on my feet, weaving through people who aren't really there. Closer to the bar, where, as soon as I get behind it, I'll be out of sight.

Of both the dinosaur and, hopefully, myself.

The ghost party resumes, filling my head with that damn piece of shit song.

So close to the bar. Twenty feet. Ten.

Five.

I drop behind a table as the music stops, and I expect the room to be empty save Ruby and the dinosaur, which I can just make out from my vantage point, through the chair legs. But there's more movement, from the kitchen.

Something peeking around the side of the bar.

It reveals itself slowly, and it takes me a second to register.

The little girl.

Damn it. The dinosaur is straying from Ruby a bit, moving closer toward us, and if it sees the kid then it will probably abandon that pork loin for a more accessible snack. I wave to her, trying to get her to move back into the kitchen, but she just stares at me. She's crouched down, looking at me through thick strands of dark hair. Through them, I can just make out her eyes, where they catch the light. She is so scared.

The music starts again. The kid ducks away, and I use the cacophony as a chance to move forward, try to get the girl someplace safe in the kitchen while I handle the dinosaur, but even though the musical interludes have gotten longer, I am relying too much on that, because I'm still on my feet when the music stops, and when I drop I knock against a chair that squeals across the floor.

The raptor snaps its head around, making direct eye contact with me. Its talons strike the floor. Then it rears back and the *clack-clack-clack* of it calling out to me echoes through the room.

I'm sorry, Mena. My love.

I tried. This one little thing, I tried. But if it gets through me it might get the kid next. I want to strangle her right now but I'm not about to let her get eaten.

I grip the gun tighter and I'm about to stand and get a bead on it when Ruby zips into its field of vision.

"Hey, look at me," Ruby says, its voice booming, flashing multicolored lights. "Don't you want some of this delicious pork?"

The raptor returns its attention to Ruby, and man, I've got to stop being so hard on that thing. I bear-crawl toward the kitchen, making sure to not hit any more chairs.

At the bar I stop.

I haven't been past here since the night Mena died, and I knew this was what I was suggesting, but suggesting it and being on the threshold are two different things.

Afraid for what I might find, I take out another Retronim, knowing it's probably thrashing my kidneys at this point. Not like I'm going to need them much longer, with the path I'm headed down. I take the pill, then get into a crouch, make sure the raptor can't see me, and step inside.

The kitchen is dim. No sign of the kid. Hopefully she got smart and hid somewhere.

The room looks different. The tile has been replaced. It used to be a sea green with black accents, but now it's subway white, and there's more chrome. The configuration has been changed too. The fridges are moved to the other side of the room, next to the walk-in freezer, on the far side. The ovens are still there, but there are more of them and they look more modern.

The ovens . . .

. . . It's late. I don't know what time it is. Late enough the place is empty, so I make my way through the kitchen and pat my pockets, looking for my lighter so I can bang out a smoke on the roof, with enough time to wash up before Mena gets back. Even though she caught a bad cold a few months ago that shot her sense of smell, she still knows when I've smoked.

But I realize I forgot my lighter so I head over to the stove and . . .

No. Don't slip now. Focus.

What the hell. I'm taking Retronim like candy. I should be good.

Got to move fast.

"Ruby, get this fucking thing in here," I say.

I move toward the freezer . . .

. . . when Mena calls out behind me, "Babe, seriously?"

I turn, the cigarette dangling from my mouth, reaching down to the pilot, where I know that if I light it and inhale hard as I hoof it across the room, I can make it to the roof access door without exhaling smoke in here, which I know is against the rules, but fuck it, sometimes you have to live a little.

With Mena watching me, I can't do it. As much as that nicotine craving is clawing at my center, I can't smoke in front of her. I tried it, once, and it was worse than someone seeing you naked for the first time. She never told me I couldn't smoke, but I also knew she didn't like it.

She didn't like it when I did things to hurt myself.

I hold the cigarette out to her. She crosses the room and takes it out of my hand with a little roll of her eyes and tosses it in the closest trash can. Then she leans into me, snaking her arms around my waist, pulling me in for a kiss, and I taste cherries.

It feels like I'm forgetting something. This little itch.

"There," she says. "Isn't that better?"

"It's nice, sure, but it doesn't change the feeling like I want to throw a chair through a window."

Mena frowns. "I'm going to tell Alexi to stop stocking your brand in the gift shop."

"I can always switch."

"My love . . ." Mena says, trailing off.

"What, *Mom*?" I ask.

"Don't you dare," she says. Then she looks around the kitchen. "I need to tell you something. Now seems like as good a time as any."

There it is again. What is it I'm forgetting?

I take her around the waist. "Tell me."

"You can be a real asshole sometimes."

I throw my head back and laugh. "Well yeah, but that's why you love me."

Mena sighs. "There was once a teacher . . ."

"Hey," I tell her. "No kōans. You have something to say to me, say it directly."

Mena nods, the way a parent might smile at a student who got a passing grade on a test. "You know what that was like for me, my mom convinced I was some kind of demon. I mean, when I first came out, she went to a priest to have him perform an exorcism . . ."

"Your mom was an asshole."

Mena nods. "And I know you don't have a good relationship with your parents, even if you haven't said why. We share that. But these people have always been here for me, no questions. And because they're my family, they're your family too. You don't treat them that way. You think it's funny, but it's really not."

"My sense of humor is my best quality."

"Stop making jokes," Mena says. "People reach out hands to you and you bat them away. Sooner or later they'll stop reaching. And you might find that when you need that hand, it's not there. Have you even gone to check on Brandon?"

"Good god, what's wrong with Brandon now?"

"See, the fact that you don't even know is part of the problem."

Mena wraps her fingers around the back of my neck, fingertips coming to rest in the dips and folds of the muscles. "There's a painting I want to show you," she says. "It's in Chicago." And she pulls me close, kisses me softly . . .

. . . Something big and heavy slams into me, throwing me against the stove. It hits so hard it takes me a moment to remember where I am. I scramble for the freezer door, hoping I'll get there before this thing gets its footing.

As I'm doing it I see Ruby shattered on the floor.

The ceilings in here are too low. I want to yell at it, to tell it that it should have stayed outside. Stayed safe.

The raptor is on the other side of the room, having slid on the floor, and it's getting up now, focused on me. I yank at the freezer door, trying to get it open, but it's stuck. There's a bolt holding it closed. I pull that out and crack the door, turn to see the raptor bearing down on me, coming fast, and I reach my hand up but I am no longer holding the gun. Must have gotten knocked free when the raptor barreled into me.

So, here we are. I am going to be dino food.

I put my forearm out, thinking maybe it'll clamp down and I can drag it into the freezer with me, when something flashes out from behind the fridges. Grayson, wearing gray sweats, a T-shirt, and sneakers, swinging a fire extinguisher. He hits the dinosaur hard, and it goes flying against the wall. With the raptor clear of me, he pulls his gun out of the holster and is training it on the scrambling reptile when I yell, "No!"

He turns to me, confused, but then shakes his head and aims. The raptor is already darting at me, so I jump up and grab an outcropping on the inside of the fridge, the cold burning my hands, but the frost is coarse enough that I'm able to maintain my grip. As it bears down I tense my core and just before it can dive for my midsection, I throw my legs up, let it pass underneath me and slam into the shelving on the far wall.

Then I drop, slam the door closed, and reinsert the bolt.

With that done I turn to Grayson, who is now holding the gun out, pointing in my direction.

And I wonder if this is it.

But in the slip he was wearing a suit.

Though he could be changing his mind.

I hold my breath. Waiting for what's next.

He lowers the gun. I slide into a sitting position against the door of the freezer, then pee myself a little when the raptor slams into it from the other side. The door shudders but stays secure.

"Why didn't you let me shoot it?" he asks.

I consider telling him the truth, but know that won't be good enough for him, so I say, "CDC said capture and contain."

He nods. "CDC is a bunch of idiots if they think that's the safest way to handle that."

"Well, government, what can you do?"

Grayson strides over and offers me his hand. I stare at it for a second. Mena said something about hands. I take it. His grip is tight. Too tight, like he's trying to make a point. But I let him pull me to my feet. We stare each other down before he says, "That was a sick move, flipping up like that."

"Thanks."

"How many more of those things are there?"

I stoop to pick up the gun I dropped, then cross to Ruby, and over my shoulder say, "One." Pick up the drone and set it on the stainless-steel countertop, and find that one of its rotors is busted, both of its bulbous lenses cracked. One of the googly eyes is missing. I click the button on the side, thinking if I turn it off and turn it on again, it'll come back to life, but it doesn't.

"Nik," I say, pressing my ear.

"Yeah."

"Ruby down there with you?"

"Not that I can tell."

I thought maybe it would start spouting out of the computer system. I guess not. I poke at the drone a little more, feeling a dip in my stomach. I hated this thing.

Always talking to me. Always by my side.

Hated it.

"Still nothing on video," Nik says. "I'm flying blind down here."

"So if there's one more of these things out there, what's the plan?" Grayson asks.

I force down the lump in my throat, which I don't even know why it's there. Because what a stupid thing to be upset about. A goofy little robot that I liked to throw my boot at. What is even the point of being upset? It's a flying smartphone.

"We uh . . ."

I breathe deep. "Last one was downstairs. We get down there and we contain that one too."

"How do you propose we do that?" he asks.

"We're going to be clever."

He walks to a large plastic bin of the mixed nuts we put out on the bar, dips his hand in, and sticks a big helping of it in his mouth. "I'm coming with."

"You're staying here."

"You going to stop me?"

"Why do you want to help me?" I ask.

"I'm not helping you," he says. Then he steps to the sink and pours himself a glass of water, which he downs most of, and I can hear his throat working as he swallows. "I'm here to protect my boss and end the threat. You're all alone right now. It would be crazy to turn away an extra set of hands."

"No one ever said I was smart."

He comes to my side and checks his gun. Seems satisfied with the state of it. "Let's go."

The cameras are out. I could kill you right now. Who's to say you didn't attack me? I could scare up a pretty reasonable case of self-defense. No one would ever have to know. Maybe that's the smartest thing I could do right now. Protect myself from what's coming.

My hand tightens around the gun.

And he sees something in my eyes, because he takes a little step back.

But then I hear Mena's voice again.

End suffering.

"You can come with me," I tell him. "But I don't want you shooting. There are a lot of thin walls in this place. I will not tolerate someone catching a bullet. This isn't going to be easy but we are going to do our best, okay?"

He thinks about it for a long moment.

Then he nods. "Okay."

I don't believe him. But what choice do I have?

———

We move slow, flanking each other, listening for the sound of the third and final raptor. Far as I know, it's still in the bowels of the hotel, but no sense in getting cocky now.

"So what's your plan if your boss wins?" I ask, my voice low. "You aiming for my job?"

Grayson doesn't respond for a second, and I think that maybe he doesn't feel like chatting, but then he says, "Not exactly."

"Way I hear it, I'm not even sure he can afford it."

Grayson gives me a sharp eyebrow. "Don't believe everything you read in the news. That *Forbes* thing? He beat the owner in golf a few months ago and the guy lost his shit. Said he'd get him back. How do you hurt someone like Teller?"

"Take away their Confederate flag bedspread?"

"Make them look weak," Grayson says, ignoring the jab. "Money is a construct anyway. It's all meaningless. What matters is influence. And Teller has more of that than anyone on the board."

"Right," I say. Wanting it to sound slightly unimpressed, because I want him to talk more. And nothing makes a tough guy want to talk more than a woman who is not impressed.

"I guess it doesn't matter," he says, his voice dripping with condescension. "Everyone thinks you're a nut anyway so I'll just tell you. This is his retirement plan."

"I thought it was a money pit," I tell him.

He laughs. "Oh, Teller doesn't care about that. He's done with the game. He's going to pick a place somewhere in the past, retire there. Somewhere that his money goes a little further. Someplace that he feels a little more . . . comfortable."

The way he leans on the word makes me ask, "What? Jim Crow era?"

"Far enough back that it predates America being a shit show," Grayson says.

"You can't just move to the past, you know. There are rules."

Grayson shrugs. "Not if he owns the place. By this time tomorrow, he's going to be your boss. Trust me, if I were you, I'd be a little nicer."

"You're a bagman. Why would I trust you?"

"Because, like I said, the real measure here is influence. I just wish Drucker would stop playing her fucking games."

That pings my radar. "What games are those?"

"We all know the government isn't going to sell to the Saudis, or to Smith. Putting American technology into the hands of a foreign power was never going to happen. And no one trusts Smith, not with the way Axon does business. This is a horse race between us and Davis, and frankly I think Drucker brought in the others to drive up the price."

Drucker again. Though I'm slightly less interested in her all of a sudden. "Why is Kolten toxic? Aside from the obvious, what's so wrong with Axon?" I ask.

"Where do we start," he says. "Privacy issues, the way they dodge government regulation, the way they influence political campaigns. Not to mention that literally the entire government stores its information in their cloud services. Give them this place, give them access to all of time? May as well just put them in charge. The United States of Axon."

All government information is stored in their cloud servers.

Does that include the Jabberwocky data?

"Whatever," Grayson says. "Let Drucker play her games. When she gears up her run for president and comes to us looking for help, we'll just remind her of all this."

Another puzzle piece.

What did I overhear Drucker say in the elevator?

Something about "can you make this happen for me"?

Was she cutting a deal with someone?

I guess it wasn't so bad that Grayson joined me after all. But should I suspect him and Teller more or less, especially since he's being so open about all of this?

Not the time to sort it out.

We make it to the bottom level and press ourselves against the wall. I think, furiously, for some kind of plan. The best I can come up with is to try to lead the thing down into the bunker below the hotel. It's twisty down there. If I can outrun it and lose it, then make it back out and shut the door, it'll be trapped. I could plant Grayson by the door and have him ready to close it behind me.

But what if Grayson decides to just close it and walk away?

Again, cameras are off. Cover stories are easy. I'll be nothing but rag and bone.

I feel a little twinge in my back pocket, and pat it to check that the zip ties are still there.

And they aren't.

I thought I just had them. Did I check before we made our way down here? Not that I was going to wrestle this thing to the ground, but it felt good to know I had them. Must have dropped them and didn't notice. I consider another Retronim, but figure at this point I'm just asking for an OD.

"What's the plan?" Grayson asks.

"Lure it into the basement, try to lock it in there."

"That's a dumb plan."

"*You're* a dumb plan."

"If I have a clear shot I'm going to take it."

"You will not."

"Hey." He makes eye contact with me. "Try to stop me." Then he stalks off down the hall, and I move after him, eyeing the hallway with the basement door, which is sitting open. That part of the plan, at least, is still on the table.

At the next corner Grayson stops, throwing himself against the wall, and gives me a harsh look. Guess he found it. I slide against the wall too and listen. I can hear it. Something heavy padding on the carpet.

Grayson peeks around the corner and sets his grip on the gun. I grab his arm, try to stop him, but he's fast—throwing me off him at the same moment he dives into the open space. He gets a bead with both hands and fires, the gunshot making my ears hum.

I turn the corner just in time to see the dinosaur collapsing into a heap on the ground. Looks like he got it right in the head.

"Like I said, dumb plan," he says. "This one was better."

In response, I smack the gun out of his hand and put my fist into the soft part of his throat.

End suffering my ass.

He falters, coughing, and I step back and throw a push kick into his sternum, hard and high enough to knock him off his feet. He hits the ground and I move toward him but he puts his foot up, throwing jab kicks to keep me from getting too close. He nearly catches me in the knee and I hop back, which gives him enough time to scramble to his feet as he clutches his throat.

"What the fuck?" he asks, hacking.

"I said we weren't firing guns in here," I tell him.

"You said no firing guns where it would put someone at risk." He points to the dead raptor. "There was no one at risk with that shot."

I feel the weight of the gun in the back of my pants. And again, I think that maybe I should just put one in his head. Save myself the trouble. I can feel it bubbling inside me, that want, to destroy him, to see him bleed, and even Mena's voice can't get through.

I'm reaching for the gun when I hear "What happened?"

It's Doctor Gottlieb and a group of scientists from the CDC. Probably—and somewhat stupidly—drawn from the security of their room by the sound of the gunshot. I remove my hand from the gun, but I'm pretty sure Grayson sees that I was going for it, which doesn't help my case.

Gottlieb marches up to me and demands a status update. So I tell her that we've got one dead dinosaur down here, another lashed upstairs, and a third in the freezer. Which Mbaye is going to be pissed about because that thing will probably have started eating through the supplies.

"Good lord," Gottlieb says, pressing her hands into her face. Then she turns to a young woman with a severe ponytail. "Go get the tranq kit."

"The CDC carries tranqs?" I ask.

"Brought one along just in case," she says. "I thought you said these things were babies."

"They were. But with time acting the way it is . . ."

"What do you mean?" she asks.

I tell her about the clock, the ovens, the sun setting. She listens intently, nodding her head along, and finally shrugs. "I'm not a physicist. Someone else can figure that out. We just have to secure these things."

"What are you going to do with them?"

"I've had three research labs call already asking that we hand them over," she says.

"Pick someplace humane," I tell her. "Someplace that isn't going to rip them apart, okay?"

She gives me a long stare, and then a little nod. Who knows if she'll follow through on it? At least I said it. Grayson is already gone and a few of the CDC scientists are kneeling around the dead dinosaur, examining it, taking swabs, so I leave them to it and head upstairs. People are outside now, some TEA agents, a few guests and staff. There's a cloth over Reg's body, already soaked with blood. Brandon is standing over it and gives me a little side-eye as I walk past.

There are a lot of things to say in this moment, but looking down at the body, one thing springs to mind, and even though I know it's wrong, it's the thing that comes out of my mouth: "That's going to be hell to clean up."

He turns to me, his face twisted. "Really?"

"Look, just, calm down, okay . . ."

Brandon takes one of his little candies out, undoing the crinkle paper around it, and pops it in his mouth. He shakes his head. "You just can't turn it off," he says, as he strides away, dropping the wrapper on the floor.

Fine. Whatever. Let him go. I head to the security room, where I find Nik and Allyn. Doctor Tamworth is wrapping Allyn's arm in gauze, a med kit upended on the holo table.

"How's the arm?" I ask.

Allyn shakes his head. "Still wondering if I need a rabies shot or something."

"All the CDC tests thus far have deemed everything to be safe, but I'll run a full blood workup," Tamworth says.

"I know, I know, I'm just being funny," Allyn says. Then he looks at me. "Thank you for shocking me nearly to death."

"You're welcome." I stroll over to the video array, which Nik is reviewing. "We back on?"

"Yeah," he says. "No idea what happened. You and Allyn went out and it blanked on me. I'm sorry, I didn't know what to do."

Ruby's voice fills the room, coming from the video console. "It seems the raptor got the best of me. I'm pleased to see that you're still in one piece, January."

I have to turn toward the wall so no one can see the smile that erupts on my face. "Way to get yourself killed, dummy. Is there another unit you can download into?"

"Handling the data transfer now."

"Good."

I move toward the center of the room, pull out my favorite beaten roller chair, and flop down into it. I'm sure within moments I could fall asleep if left alone, and I kind of wish I could, but then Allyn snags me from the edge of it. "We're canceling the summit tomorrow."

"Someone finally came to their senses," I say.

"Whatever's going on, we don't have a handle on it," Allyn says, getting up and stretching his arm back and forth, to check the flexibility of the bandage. "It's late but the snow stopped, so I'm sending facilities to start clearing out. We're going to hunker down tonight and hope we get through it in one piece. TEA agents will be on walking patrols all night."

"And what about the big meeting?" Nik asks. "Does it get bumped a day or two?"

"No, I'm telling them to do it somewhere else. Let it be someone else's problem. If it costs me my job"—he looks down at his arm—"then it costs me my job."

I stand, suddenly so tired I feel a little drunk. "That's a good idea. Someone else's problem. Listen, I know you want my ass out of here, but can I at least crash on my luxurious hallway cot for an hour or two?"

"You know this isn't how I wanted it to go."

"Yeah, yeah. I get it. For my best interest."

I think he wants to respond but I don't let him. I step into the lobby, and Ruby's voice is calling over the speaker system, telling everyone that the lockdown is ended, they're free to leave their rooms. Seems Allyn was the only injury we incurred besides Reg. I take some small comfort in that as I weave my way through the hallways, up to the second level, and the cot I had claimed earlier, which is still free. I fall into it and feel my body relax as the pressure to keep standing comes off my feet.

It's nice, but when I close my eyes, the light fixture above me drills down, so bright I can hear the buzz of it.

I reach back for the gun but there's nothing in my belt. Must have left it in the office, so I stand up, take my boot off, and wing it up at the ceiling. I miss the first time. And the second. But on the third I manage to smash it, and the light sputters out, shards of glass falling to the floor. A few people jerk up in their cots and I just wave at them.

"Good night," I say.

I get back into bed, and there's still too much ambient light—not the dead blackness I prefer—but it's manageable. I lie there, my brain spinning off the rails, because of course now that I'm finally here I can't sleep. Wondering who let out the dinosaurs. Who's messing with the hotel. All the nonsense with the ghosts. Plus, god, the kid again. And Axon's access to government servers, Drucker's presidential campaign.

God, at this rate I will never sleep.

So I do the same thing I always do on restless nights . . .

. . . snake my hand over the sheets, running it across Mena's sleeping hip and onto her chest, searching for that *thump-thump* of her heart, the vibration of which will travel through her and into me and lull me to sleep.

When I find it, her skin warm and soft, she intertwines her fingers with mine.

"Still awake?" Mena asks.

"Always awake," I tell her.

"It does seem that way, doesn't it?" She slides a bit under the covers, pressing her body against mine.

"I'm sorry," I tell her, pulling her close.

"For what?" she asks.

"Does it matter? I feel like I'm usually due someone an apology."

"Why is that?"

I stare at the ceiling that I can barely see, through the sliver of light cast underneath the bathroom door by the night-light.

"Seriously," Mena says, nuzzling into my neck. "Tell me."

"I've told you."

"But you've never told me the truth."

She turns a little and places her hand on my chest, and I can feel the *thump-thump* of my own heart against it.

"I'm serious, January," she says. "If you're capable of regret then you're capable of understanding the weight of your actions. So why do you persist?"

I shrug. "Dunno."

She presses harder on my heart. "It's right here. Right under the surface of your skin. I can feel it. I know your family . . ."

"What about my family? I don't remember them."

"Stop that."

"What do you want to hear?" I ask, and I can feel my pulse increasing against the smoothness of her hand. "That my parents didn't give me the courtesy of hating me? That they were just indifferent? That they didn't know what to do with a queer little nerd they thought was going to be a doctor or a lawyer and give them a bucket of grandkids? Do you want me to tell you how I was a lonely kid and I found the only way to get people to like me was to get them to laugh? And I just stuck with what works?"

"Sure, that," she says. "There's something else. Something deeper. I can feel it. You have to let it out, *mi reina*. It's poisoning you. It's a thing I know you want to say but you're afraid."

I put my hand over hers, knowing exactly what it is I want to say, exactly the thing I have almost told her a hundred times and never could find the courage to come out with. "It's embarrassing. If you know I'm afraid, why not leave me to it?"

"I love you," she says. "Tell me."

"That," I tell her, the word slipping out.

"What?"

"That," I say, turning my face away from her, afraid for her to see it, even in the dark. On the off chance the tears might catch a stray bit of light from the bathroom. "You're the first person to ever tell me that you loved me. The first time you said it, it just overwhelmed me. But I also felt the vacuum of what my life had been like without it until that point. And I just felt so stupid. Like, this little tiny thing is what fucked me up so bad?"

"Oh, my love." She wraps her arms around me then, cradling me like a child, and it makes my face hot, reveals to me exactly why I held this inside, because the wound has met the open air. "Not even your parents?"

"That just . . . wasn't them. They weren't the touchy-feely type, I guess . . ."

"Hey," Mena says, her voice sharp. "It's not about being 'touchy-feely.' It's about being a kind and loving person."

"Well, I just . . ." My voice catches in my throat. "I don't want to talk about this anymore."

"Close your eyes."

"It's already dark."

"Close them."

I close my eyes. Nothing changes. All that darkness. Filling the room, filling me. She takes my hand and twists her wrist a little so that both of our hands are pressing my heart.

"Breathe in through your nose," she says. "Feel your chest expand. Get to the top and hold it. Count to three. And then just let go through your mouth. Let it all flow out."

Even with my eyes closed, even in the dark, even as quiet as I manage to stay, I am crying. But only ever in a place where no one can see me. I want to hide it from her and she knows I want to hide and she won't let me. She pulls me tighter.

"Do you think . . ." I start, but my throat seizes.

She doesn't respond. She waits for me.

"Sometimes I think I don't want to be like the way I am," I say. "Do you think one day I'll be like you?"

"Who am I?" she asks, her breath warm on my ear.

"You're kind. And you're on a path. You're working toward self-betterment. Toward nirvana, I guess. And I'm still just . . . treading water here in my own bullshit."

Mena laughs a little. Not at me, I know it's not at me, but still, it makes me feel vulnerable. And she says, "Babe, nirvana is a tough nut to crack and I might still have a few more lives to go before I get there. I wouldn't sweat it too much though. You just have to know the trick."

"What's the trick?"

She repositions herself so she's looking at me. "The thing about nirvana is, it's about escaping the cycle of reincarnation. That karmic revolution of reward and punishment that you've accumulated over the course of your existence. When you achieve nirvana, you stop accumulating karma. Once you've fully escaped it, then you've achieved parinirvana, which is actually beyond human comprehension . . ."

"Is this all just karma, then? Am I being punished?"

She sighs. This time, at my expense. She nestles into me tighter, until her body is fitted to mine. "The only one punishing you is yourself."

I let the weight of that sit on my chest for a minute. Breathe in and out some more.

"Mena?" I ask.

"Hmm?" It's soft. She's dozing.

"You said there's a trick."

"To what?"

"Nirvana."

"Right, sorry." She yawns, speaking through it and stretching out her words. "So, the secret to nirvana is that the path to achieving it is a paradox. Like any goal, you think you should be working toward it. But to truly achieve nirvana you have to let it wash over you. You can't fight for it or struggle over it. You get there by surrendering, not by trying. One of the base tenets of Buddhism is to end suffering. Struggle is suffering."

"So struggle is the root of suffering?"

"Well, sort of," she says. "Suffering comes from desirous attachment or craving. It's easy to point at other things and say, 'That's the reason I'm sad.' The truth is this: to find the true source of your problems, you have to look inside. The suffering you experience is related to how you process it."

"So we're back to it being my fault?"

"Yes," she says, kissing me on the lips. "And no."

I laugh at her, sniffling away the tears. "You and your riddles."

"It'll make sense one day," she says. "When it matters the most, it'll make sense. I promise."

"So when do you think you'll get there?" I ask. "Nirvana?"

I feel the movement of Mena shrugging against me. "You can't set a time frame. And anyway, I'm not exactly seeking it. There's too much work to do first." Her voice is tired, and she doesn't say anything for a few moments, and I wonder if she's fallen asleep, but then she asks, "Have I ever told you about the bodhisattva's vow?"

"I don't think so."

"It's delaying your own nirvana to save other people from suffering. To help others achieve it before you achieve it yourself."

"Is that what you're doing?"

She kisses me again, longer and harder. I feel a wetness between our skin. Is she crying too?

"Hey," she says.

"Yeah?"

"You are loved," she says. "More than that, you are worthy of love."

She grips my hand tighter . . .

. . . and then my hand is empty. I'm just here, alone in the hallway of the hotel I will be leaving tomorrow.

And no one will be sad to see me go.

Rather, this place will probably be better off without me.

This time when I cry I don't try to hide it.

NOBLE TRUTH

Green carpet runner, worn down until the piles are smooth as glass. It cuts a pathway through a narrow hall of worn wood and faded floral wallpaper. As I walk down the hall, the creaks sing a symphony of my childhood.

I look into the oversize mirror interrupting the wallpaper. I see myself. Not a scared little kid who felt alone and isolated, but as I am now.

January Cole, house detective, perpetual fuckup.

Is this a dream or a slip?

Does it even matter?

I continue down the hall, toward my room, the hallway filled with the smell of garlic and chili paste frying in the kitchen. The knob catches and I have to turn it hard, then push the door open from where the wood has swollen against the frame. I expect that when I open the door I will find myself. Sitting alone on the bed, back to the door, a book open on my lap. *The Bell Jar* or *Little Women* or *Kindred*.

My timeline will cross itself. I will die. In a place that I did not experience hatred or cruelty, but something far worse. Something that left me permanently hobbled.

Gentle but persistent indifference.

The room is empty. The bed is a mess, as always, blanket and sheet rumpled from where kid-me threw them off. Morning sun streams through the window. The room smells the way it always did. Freshly laundered with an undercurrent of old wood.

I sit on the bed and fold my legs underneath me, wondering if I should take my boots off, but do I need to? Is this even real? I lay back on the pillow and stare at the ceiling. At the water stain in the far corner, from where the radiator leaked in the attic. At the popcorn ceiling, that I would try to divine shapes and figures from when I couldn't sleep.

I blink, and find myself on my cot in the hallway of the Paradox Hotel. Quick as that.

Getting toward the end now. I can feel it.

I've also got a killer headache. I stand and stretch, feel my spine pop. My whole body is sore. Dinosaur hunting will do that, I guess. Everyone is still sleeping. No way to tell what time it is. There are no windows. I check my watch and phone, find them both dead. The TEA watch is working. Seven in the morning. I consider heading to the security office, but I can find chargers in the medical suite, which is closer. Plus it'll have something for my headache.

After that I can start the process of whatever comes next.

There's no one at the front desk in medical, so I go around and find charging mats for my electronics, then rifle around for a bottle of acetaminophen or ibuprofen.

No, that's not what I need. My brain is buzzing. That constant Unstuck static, the volume still getting louder. Even louder than it was yesterday. And when I think about the last twenty-four hours—so many weird slips. More than usual.

What I need is a Retronim.

I dig a pill out of my pocket and I'm about to toss it back when I give it another look. The pill is a shiny little oval, slightly pink, and a bit bigger than the one I used to take, which was a robin's egg blue.

Tamworth changed my prescription yesterday.

I head toward his office, and luckily he's already at his desk, poking at something on a tablet.

"January," Tamworth says, barely looking up. There's a bandage on his forehead, just on his hairline. "What can I do for you?"

I don't bother sitting. I put the Retronim pill on the desk in front of him.

He leans in close and squints at it. "What is this?"

"I got it from you," I tell him. "Yesterday morning, you upped my dose."

He takes it between two fingers and holds it up to the light. "This is not Retronim."

The record playing in my head scratches. "Then what have I been taking, Doc?"

He cracks the pill in half and touches a piece to his tongue. "Sugar pill."

"Why did you give me sugar pills?"

"I know you have a low opinion of just about everyone here, but I do take my job pretty seriously," he says, placing the pill half on the desk. "So the only thing I can think is that someone switched out your prescription. Which begs the question, how have you been feeling since yesterday?"

Since yesterday.

Not good. More slips than normal, and different kinds, too.

Except when I had my breakdown and slipped back to Germany before hopping around on my own timeline. Tamworth gave me a pill and I felt better after that, for a little while at least.

"The dose you gave me, in the afternoon, that was from your stash, not mine," I say.

He nods as gravity pulls me deeper into the floor.

"Then shit, yeah, I think someone switched out my prescription."

He gets up and goes out of the office, where I am left to wonder why a ghost wanted to fuck with my medication. Tamworth returns and puts another pill bottle on the table. I take it, crack it open, and down one.

"Keep this one safe," he says.

"Will do. Thanks, Doc."

He laughs.

"What?"

"Funny to hear you say thanks for anything."

"Am I that much of an ass?"

He doesn't laugh this time. "Yeah, January, you are."

"Okay." I lean back in the chair. "So what's on the agenda today? When do I get dragged out kicking and screaming?"

Tamworth sighs. "Who knows. Cameo had wanted to organize some kind of group session or service for Reg this morning, and then it got bumped for that summit meeting, so . . ."

"Allyn canceled the summit last night," I say.

Tamworth shakes his head. "The senator says it's back on. Apparently last night was calm. After the dinosaurs, of course."

I tap my forehead, gesturing to his bandage. "If it was calm what the hell is this?"

He seems to forget, and then shakes his head. "I got up in the middle of the night. I had to, you know . . . relieve myself. And I tripped. It felt like a piece of luggage, but when I turned around nothing was there. I don't know what it was."

"Why did you think it was a piece of luggage?"

"I don't know. Just, felt and sounded like a roller suitcase." He folds his hands together and stares into them. "I thought I saw it, but when I looked up . . . I don't know. Maybe I was hallucinating."

"No, Doc. I don't think you were." I get up, leave the office, and head to the railing, where I see a group of staffers standing around Cameo. There's a funereal feel to it, and from the downcast eyes and hands on their hearts, I realize they're taking a brief moment for Reg.

So of course Drucker, nightmare bitch that she is, stomps over snapping her fingers, telling them to get back to work. Lucky for her, by the time I get down to the lobby, she's gone, or else that would have ended badly. For her immediately, for me in the long run.

Outside the front doors, a plow is pushing a large pile of snow around the front loop. The lines at the concierge desk are long, the staff back to struggling to keep up. I don't know if people are trying to stay or leave or see about their trips being rebooked. Everything on the board still reads *canceled*. I don't really care right now.

No one pays me any mind. This time I'm the ghost.

It's like they've all finally agreed to just give up on me and move on.

That January, can't be saved.

Which, rightfully, I have earned. But now that it's finally here it feels like there's a little piece missing from my inside.

Whatever. Now is not the time for a case of the sads. There are bigger issues to tackle.

The biggest being: the early sunset, the aging dinosaurs, the oven timers, and now Tamworth tripping over a piece of luggage that wasn't there. Maybe it was a piece that was there before, or will be there.

The sunset, that was something everyone saw. It could well have been an optical illusion, which is what most of my slips are. Except this, he was able to interact with. It had weight. It existed in that moment.

Are physical objects now moving through time and space at random?

It's a question I wonder if I should pose to Popa.

But then I remember someone else who might be able to help. Someone I'm really due a conversation with anyway.

Brandon is pushing a luggage cart across the lobby, laden with designer suitcases, as an old couple trails behind him, berating him to keep steady. I catch up with him and he stops.

"Hey," I say.

"Hey," he says, not meeting my eyes.

"Excuse me," the old man says. "We need to get to the terminal because apparently our driver can't make it up here with all the snow and . . ."

I point a finger at him. "Shut up." Then I see a TEA agent nearby. Young guy, shaved head, built like a fridge. I wave him over and tell him to handle the old couple. He's not happy about it, but he recognizes me, and apparently hasn't heard that I shouldn't be giving anyone orders right now. He hustles off with the couple as they mutter about the service.

"How's the arm?" I ask Brandon.

He gently rubs the fresh bandaging. "You care?"

"I care," I tell him.

"Funny way of showing it."

"Brandon, look . . . I'm not going to sit here and give you some kind of song and dance routine and make excuses. I'll just say I'm sorry. I am."

He nods, drops his arm to his side. "Tamworth offered me painkillers but I had some stuff in my own stash that was a little better, so I went with that. Feeling okay at the moment."

"I fucked up. I know."

He nods. More like he's agreeing and less that he's accepting the apology, but that can be enough for right now. He glances around the lobby, like he's looking for an excuse to go. And part of me now feels like the apology was not good enough, like I need to try a little harder, but there's a task at hand too, so I tell him, "I need your help on something."

I wave him over to the coffee urn, which is, for once, actually full, and I nearly want to do a dance, then dip my head under it and pour coffee directly into my throat. Instead I take a mug, fill it, and I'm about to walk away from it when I realize, no, let's try this whole being-nice thing. I offer him the mug and he accepts it, then fills it with creamer and sugar. *Wuss*, I want to say, but I don't. I take my mug, black, the way it's supposed to be, and lead him over to a little circle of leather chairs and couches that are currently free from people.

We sit and he asks, "What's up?"

I tell him about Tamworth's fall. The more I speak the crazier I feel but I stick with it until I've got enough out. He sits back and takes a sip of his milkshake coffee and says, "I guess the question that I've had is why is it localized to here. Why was the sunset thing an issue? I mean, has anything else happened over at the timeport?"

"I think Allyn would have brought it up," I tell him. "But the weird thing is, Popa said none of the sensors on the outside of the building are picking anything up, and the building is shielded anyway, so . . ."

"Did he do any readings on the inside of the building?" Brandon asks.

I try to answer, and can't. Wouldn't Popa have said that? Do we even have sensors on the inside? And anyway, wouldn't it have made sense to check? But sometimes very smart people miss very obvious things.

"I'm going to look into that," I tell him, standing up. "Thanks . . ."

"Wait," he says.

I sit back down, but he doesn't say anything. I put my hand up, prod him to go on.

"Reg is dead," he says.

"Correct."

"A lot of the people who are close to him, they wanted to take time off, so they could mourn. But the senator refused. She says she's in charge now and is telling us we have to be here. All hands on deck."

"I don't know how it works, but technically it is a federal facility . . ."

Brandon shakes his head. "Reg was like the dad of this place. He held it together. Say what you will about the guy, but he knew how to lead. And now we're all just . . ." He looks around the lobby. Cameo at the desk, drowning. Chris arguing with someone. TEA agents marching around like they own the place.

"You've always had a good rapport . . ." I tell him.

"It's got to be you, January."

This earns a deep belly laugh from me. "Right. I'd be a great mom. That's me. Nurturing by nature."

"I'm serious," he says. "You're carrying what you carry. And we all look up to Cameo, but even Cameo looks up to you, okay? Not that they'd ever admit it. You're like . . . maybe not so much a mom but like . . . I don't know, an angry nun?"

"Angry nun. Nice."

"Just, like, a stern authority figure who scares the shit out of everyone but at the end of the day you know they have their shit together."

"Kid," I tell him. "If you only knew . . ."

"You're all we've got right now, January. Someone needs to be there for us." He points to the lobby, at all the richie-rich guests, stomping around like they're ten feet taller than they really are. "These people aren't here for us. And I know that however you feel, that still makes you angry."

"Why does it have to be my responsibility, huh?" I ask. "No one was there for me. I had to learn to protect myself. That's all any of us can do. Because if you open yourself up too much, you know what happens? Do you know what it's like to find someone . . ." My throat grows thick. Face hot. I don't want to be on this train anymore. I take a deep breath and bail between stations.

"Nah," he says, shaking his head. "Nah, you don't believe any of that bullshit. Mena wouldn't have loved you the way she did if you weren't capable of showing love in return." He gets up, slightly exasperated. "Or maybe that's just gone now. Whatever. I've got work to do."

I try to respond. There are words in my mouth and I can't pick the right ones.

That new feeling, back again.

Shame.

Brandon leaves and I slug the last of my coffee, then head to the security office and bang my fist against the door until Allyn opens, wide-eyed and exhausted. Dude could use a shave, a shower, and probably ten gallons of coffee.

"You," he says.

"Me," I tell him. "Where's Popa?"

"Not here."

"You need to ask him if he's done radiation scans on the inside of the building."

Allyn looks around, shakes his head, and says, "Walk with me."

He steps out of the office, headed for the ramp that leads down-stairs, and Drucker is pulling alongside us. I give her a little side-eye and then say to Allyn, "I need to speak to you alone."

"And we have to get this thing started," Allyn says.

"Fine. You know why I was out of my mind yesterday?" I ask. "Be-cause someone messed with my Retronim prescription. They wanted me off the board, Allyn."

Drucker stops at the edge of the ramp, which is being guarded by two TEA agents. She squares to Allyn and puts her hands on her hips. "We're due to start soon. Let's go."

Allyn turns and sighs, then drops his head. To the TEA agents he says, "She's not approved to go down."

"Allyn," I tell him. "C'mon. After everything."

"We'll talk later, January," he says, and he and Drucker go down the ramp, toward Lovelace, where I am fairly sure some not-so-great shit is about to happen.

The two agents, both of them like football players gone to seed, but not so long ago they can't still rumble, both cross their arms in unison, like they planned it. It makes me laugh a little, which makes the guy on the left laugh too. Not that they're giving me an inch. So I salute them, give them the finger, and turn back toward the lobby.

Fine. I still have a way in.

But I do need to clean myself up and put on a fresh pair of clothes. If I'm going to bust in there, it's not going to help my case if I smell like a homeless person. So I jog up to my cot, where my bag is stashed, and pull it out from underneath.

I settle on a pair of jeans, a dark T-shirt, and a red blazer. I pull off my boots, and the stench reminds me how much I need a shower. It's bad when you can't tolerate your own BO. I drop the boots to the floor and pull on a pair of canvas sneakers, then stop in the bathroom to freshen up before I make my way toward the security office. See if I can't rope Ruby into this.

The door is locked and my privileges are still revoked, so I pop my knife out of my jeans, make sure no one is looking, and jimmy the lock. Which I'm pretty sure I break in the process, but I don't care. There's no one inside so I head over to the main console, find a freshly charged AI unit, and press the button on the top. It wakes up, but it doesn't move.

"Hello, January," it says.

"C'mon," I tell it. "Time to work."

"Unfortunately I can no longer assist you," it says.

"What, did I hurt your feelings one too many times?"

"No, Allyn has prevented me from responding to your commands."

"I thought I hacked you."

"I could probably get around it, but if all it's going to result in is a lot of name-calling, I don't feel particularly inclined to do it."

"God, you too. Fine, I don't need you."

I pull out my roller chair and log in to my laptop—that much at least still works—and stare at the screen for a moment.

Work the case.

Someone here wants to own this place. They're willing to hurt people to get it. At this point I will assume Drucker is playing along.

Four trillionaires. Four men used to getting what they want.

But even if they get what they want, they won't get what they want, because of the Jabberwocky.

I still feel like that's the ultimate prize here. Having access to all of time is one thing, having unrestricted access is another. Why they aren't more concerned about the potential destruction of reality, I wish I knew, but that's a not-right-now problem.

What do I know about the Jabberwocky?

It's a mix of physical and cloud computing.

It exists outside time and records human events.

Jim Henderson runs it.

Where the hell has he been in all this? I seem to remember Allyn trying to get in contact with him, but shouldn't he be here? Or is he troubleshooting in another location?

I'm sure I've met the guy. I must have. But I can't conjure his face in my brain. Probably just another pasty middle-aged white man, same as a lot of the TEA admin. He was probably on the Christmas card, though. Allyn puts one out every year with the bigwigs, all of them in period Christmas hats. Every year, he asks me to join. I have yet to appear on one.

It'll be on Allyn's Axon page. I log in to my account and click over, scroll through his photos until I find it, and yeah, there's Jim. Bland as a beige wall, not much of a chin to speak of, vacant-eyed smile that looks vaguely homicidal. So, a boilerplate government bureaucrat. He's standing two people over from Allyn, and they're all wearing knitted, Victorian-style Christmas hats.

At least now I know who to look for. If he's here maybe I can brace him a little.

Something about the photo is screwing with my head though. I look at Allyn, standing in the center, smiling that TV-ready smile of his.

Allyn, my old partner.

Allyn, who saved my ass in Germany.

If something had been changed, how would you even know?

What did I say to him in that cell?

I don't even know if I can trust you. I don't even know who you are.

"Ruby, what can you tell me about Allyn Danbridge?"

"He's our boss."

"Has he always been our boss?"

"What are you getting at?"

I don't know. I truly don't know. I wish I could say I was confident about my own brain, my own memories, my own history.

At this point, I can't be.

I glance at my watch. Time to go. My train ride into the summit is probably getting ready to leave the station.

I know MKS is staying in the penthouse suite of Atwood, because there's no way they were going to stick a Saudi prince into anything less than a penthouse. And since he's royalty, he's the biggest security risk. The Atwood elevator is the only one that goes all the way to the basement.

Lucky for me I know how to exploit security in my own hotel.

I make it to the elevator bank and the TEA agent there eyes me until I press the up button. I give him a little smile, put my hands behind my back, and wait for the doors to open. I'm so hopped up I almost knock over the people trying to get off, and I jab at the button for the top floor until the doors close.

I make it into the hallway just as the penthouse double doors open. Eshe steps out, followed by a few members of the entourage, all of them forming a protective scrum around MKS.

Eshe clocks me right away. As I'm trying to come up with some kind of excuse to get close, MKS looks over and raises his hands. "Ah, the detective." He waves me toward him.

The entourage stops and I approach, but no one makes room for me to reach him. He steps forward and extends his hands. I offer both of mine, and they disappear in his huge mitts. We do a weird double handshake. His grip is firm and warm and he makes strong eye contact with me. It's easy to see why he's a prince. It's like he was built for the role, forged out of gold and other precious things. I have to remind myself about Nura Fayed, that missing dissident. It makes me wonder where these hands have been. Around whose throat.

"Please, accompany me downstairs," he says. "I've been wishing to speak with you."

"I'm glad we ran into each other," I say, giving Eshe a little glance. She quickly looks away.

We make it to the elevator and Eshe presses the button and the prince turns to me.

"First I wanted to thank you," he says. "For this misunderstanding with Eshe. I appreciate that you were able to see through it. Do you have any suspects?"

"Honestly, no," I tell him, feeling a little silly for not chasing that lead down, but the truth, which I tell him, is, "The dinosaurs threw me off a bit."

"Well, when I assume control of this hotel I would like to keep you on. Unless you have aspirations beyond this place. I would appreciate having you for the transition, given your expertise. You will be well compensated."

"Thanks," I tell him. "But I have to ask, what makes you so sure you're going to win this thing?"

He gives a little smile, like I'm a toddler asking him how the sun stays in the sky. Him and Drucker did seem to be friendly the other night during their dinner. Maybe Grayson is wrong and she's playing Teller.

The elevator door opens and we climb on. A few people have to stay behind, and it seems like there's a pecking order to who gets to come. We're all crushed in now, and as the doors close I can't help but ask, "What's your endgame?"

MKS smiles. "My endgame?"

"Sure," I tell him. "The point of all this. What do you plan to do with this place?"

The elevator stops, the doors open, and there are a few people waiting. They are grumpy about the fact that there is no room, and we wait in awkward silence for the doors to close. When they do, MKS says, "You understand how many people died during the bombing campaign against my country."

"I am aware, yes," I tell him.

"Women and children."

The images are impossible to forget. No matter how much the U.S. media tried to downplay it, we all saw what happened. The havoc one childish president could wreak with the press of a button because he thought it might lower the price of oil by a few bucks, and at the same time boost his poll numbers. "Yes. I am aware."

"I plan to undo it."

"That . . ." I find I can't respond.

The doors open at the lobby. More people looking to go down, and again, no one can get on, but we have to stand there and wait for the doors to close. When they do, I say, "The consequences . . ."

MKS gives a little wave of his hand, like the risk of destroying reality is a gnat buzzing around his head. "I've spoken to several experts who assure me that the timestream will be able to handle it. There will be some adjustment, but how can you weigh that against restoring the lives of so many people who died? Who suffered so needlessly?"

He locks eyes with me, daring me to answer. Daring me to say that, no, when presented with the means you shouldn't try to save innocent lives. No, you should let people die screaming instead.

How do you tell someone that?

"Do you really think the U.S. government is going to sell to a foreign nation?" I ask. It feels a little rude, but at this point I'm flustered, and want to keep him talking. "I saw you with Drucker the other night. But she seems pretty friendly with Teller."

"I do not trust Drucker, but I never really did. You understand this sale is happening because this entire location is underfunded, correct? And who writes the budget to fund this place?" He holds a gold-ringed finger in the air. "The committee that Drucker sits on. There is only one language she understands, and lucky for me, I speak it as well.

Better than a cut-rate businessman who would be living in a ditch if not for his father's money."

Before I can say anything, the doors open on the lower level. There's a group of TEA agents standing there, and they eye us, but no one stops me. Which annoys me, even though I'm not technically in charge anymore.

We move into the hallway, heading for the summit room, and MKS asks, "You do not believe me, that the timestream heals itself?"

"I think we're seeing firsthand what happens when you mess with the timestream," I tell him. "The hotel . . ."

"The hotel was here and it will be here," he says. "So will the timestream. I appreciate your concern. It makes me respect you all the more. I can see why Eshe likes you."

I glance at Eshe and I am sure that if I could see her face, her cheeks would be red.

"But remember, I have hired the best experts, and this is what they have told me," he says. "That the timestream can bear it."

"Right," I tell him. "But did they say that because they're the best, or because they're the best at telling you what you want to hear?"

He takes my hands and shakes them again. "Thank you for your dedication. It is not lost on me. We will speak again when this is over."

And he takes his entourage down the hall, leaving me there, finally understanding how bad this is going to end up being.

I thought these men were just greedy. But no. It's worse than that. They're zealots, and the only thing they believe in is themselves. They're so used to getting what they want, to being told yes that the word *no* doesn't even exist in their language, at least not when directed at them. The very idea that they could want something and not have it is something they can't process. All light, all gravity, bends around that.

They've been conditioned by their own success to believe they can't do anything wrong. And because of that they're going to kill us all.

The lights flicker and my stomach bottoms out. A Pavlovian re-sponse. It takes me a minute to realize why. I don't even need Ruby to confirm it for me. Every time something bad has happened, the lights tend to flicker first.

I figured Allyn would miss the southern door of Lovelace. It leads into a maintenance hallway, which leads into a kitchen, which I assume is not being used right now, because we never talked about there being food service at this. So I duck through some back hallways until I emerge in the ballroom, and lo and behold.

The place is a mess of activity. They are definitely breaking the rule I had set about how many people could be in here at one time. The place is packed—the most important people crowded in the middle, and everyone else backed off. It works in my favor; no one notices me, so I move to the side, into a shadow, so maybe I'm not as noticeable.

In the center of the room is Drucker, surrounded by the four tables with the bidders, all of whom are sitting by themselves, their various team members scattered throughout.

Warwick is talking to some guys from Saudi Arabia. Grayson is hovering over Teller's shoulders. Davis, as always, is alone, smiling serenely. The only person I don't see here is Nik, but I imagine he's back up in the office, or over by the scanners. They probably figured out the issue with the cameras by now. I go to ask Ruby if that's the case and realize, again, it's not here with me.

Drucker is holding a wireless microphone, and she taps the top of it. The sound booms through the room, and most of the conversations stop, attention turning toward her. She adjusts a knob on the side of the mic until it's down to a more acceptable level. "Welcome, every-one. For those of you who don't know me . . ."

That makes me laugh a little. Self-centered bitch.

". . . I'm United States Senator Danica Drucker. And we're here today to accept bids for control of the Einstein Intercentury Timeport and the Paradox Hotel. You've all read and consented to the terms and conditions in the briefing documents. President Everett wanted me to pass along his best wishes for a fair and orderly process. He regrets being unable to attend, but as you can imagine, we've had to be a little flexible in order to maintain security, and I want to thank you all for your decorum and your patience throughout this bumpy process . . ."

Bumpy? A guy got killed by a fucking dinosaur.

". . . And I would like to give some special recognition to Allyn Danbridge of the TEA for his hard work in putting this together . . ."

Aww, not going to thank me?

". . . As well as the hotel staff, for their selfless sacrifice in impossible conditions. They are the true heroes here."

Selfless. Right. Because they chose to get tossed out of their rooms. My new life goal is to fistfight this woman.

"So," Drucker says, "as we all discussed, we will begin by . . ."

"I would like to start the bidding," MKS says, "at one trillion dollars."

Everyone stops cold.

The words hang in the air, a monolith MKS has dropped into the center of the room and now everyone else has to navigate around.

Then the crowd erupts into chaos.

"That's not how this . . ." Drucker says.

"How dare you . . ." Teller says.

"Now it's a party!" Kolten booms into his own mic.

Osgood just smiles and laughs.

There's more, but the words drown out for me.

Across the room I catch a weird stutter. Like there's something in the fluid of my eyes, and I'm about to blink and rub them when I see it again. Something warping the air and the light around it, but then it's gone.

Then back again. A flicker.

It's hard to focus on when I'm looking at it directly. I have to look at it out of the side of my vision, and even then, it gives me a bit of a headache. But whatever it is, it's moving.

Flashing for a moment, then blinking away.

Flashing again, closer to the middle of the room.

Gone.

Then closer again.

My head is pounding now, but it seems to be moving toward Teller and Grayson. No one else sees it. No one else is reacting. Teller is now ranting into the microphone about foreign powers being given access to our great American-made technology.

He's completely unaware of this thing that seems to be bearing down on them.

I move closer, and get into Allyn's field of vision. He glances to the person he's talking to and then back at me, doing an exaggerated double take.

Then Grayson sees me. His look is more angry than confused.

Another flash. Closer still. Nearly on top of them.

I break into a run, dodging between people, and just as the shimmer seems to reappear right next to Teller, I lunge at it. I land on the table, hard, pain ripping through my shoulder. The table splinters and cracks, splitting in the middle—of course we used the cheap shit for the trillionaires—and then there are hands on me, pulling me off and away. Voices yelling. No one is happy about this. Least of all me.

I manage to get my bearings, struggle back to my feet, and I'm staring down Grayson. The light catches his silver tie clip as he pulls a gun from the inside of his jacket. It must have looked like I was attacking Teller just now.

The gun clears and I know what's coming next.

I saw it.

But that gives me the edge.

I duck to the side, away from the line of fire. At the same time, I put one hand against the gun and the other in the crook of his elbow, folding his arm back. All I mean to do is direct the bullet into the ceiling. In a crowd like this, it's the only way to make sure no one gets shot. The bullet won't ricochet or travel through to the lobby. It'll embed safely in the ceiling.

Instead the bullet embeds in Grayson's chin, blowing out the back of his head.

As he rag-dolls to the ground, the room explodes. A body slams into me, knocking me to the floor, and black fabric fills my vision. It takes me a second to realize that it's Eshe, her burka draped over my face, as she presses my hands together across my chest.

The floor of the holding cell is cold and hard underneath me. It makes me feel bad for all the people I've put in here. Not that it's been a whole lot of people. Mostly just drunks who need a little while to cool off, or that one time, that guy we found beating on his wife at three in the morning, and we needed to keep him contained until the cops showed up.

Not just cold and hard, but gritty, too. Like someone spilled sand in here before painting over it. It makes me wish there was a bench. Even just a chair. I should put one in here. I reach my hand out and press the white painted wall, find there's blood on the back of my hand. Still crimson red. Fresh.

The blood matches the color of my blazer.

The green door at the far end of the holding room opens and Allyn comes in. The look on his face is so grave it may as well be etched. *Here lies the career of January Cole.* He stands for a few moments, unsure of what to say. He keeps his distance, like I'm a wild tiger chained to the wall. After a beat he steps forward and leans down so he's more on eye level with me.

"I need to know why you did that."

"I don't even know if I can trust you. I don't even know who you are."

Allyn's shoulders slump. "January, it's me. I am here to help you.

But after what you just did, I'm not sure if I can. You've been holding shit back since I got here. I know that you have been, and I let you, because I trust you. Now I need you to trust me."

"You didn't see it?" I ask.

"See what?"

"The ghost," I say. "It was going after him. It was going to kill him. I was trying to save him."

"January," Allyn says, starting a thought, then dropping it. He looks away, and his face falls. He's resigning himself to some level of defeat, and I can tell that I've let him down. That something he believed about me has been broken. It hurts in a way that I haven't felt hurt since the day Mena died. I know I can be a prick but Allyn and his trust in me was always a rock. Something to be sure about. I've worn it down to a grain of sand, and the tide is taking it away.

Which makes me think that, yes, Allyn is real. Our memories are real. Why else would it feel like I'm drowning?

"It was going to kill him," I say, my voice dropping, to a place where it sounds like I'm not even sure I believe myself.

"This is my fault," he says, pressing his hands to his face, standing. "I knew you were in the second stage. And I figured—you're January Fucking Cole. You'd handle it. That's what you do. But your behavior the last few days. We should have pulled you from this when we found you tearing up that wall."

"Allyn, I know this is hard to understand," I tell him. "I know I've been . . ." I drop my head. "I know I've been me. But you have to believe me. There's something at play here and I think I'm finally seeing how the pieces come together."

"Just cool your jets here for a little," Allyn says. "I'm going to do everything in my power to protect you. I feel like that's what I owe you. I feel like I failed you." The corner of his lip curls, like he's about to offer a smile, but then he pulls it back. "I'll do the best I can."

He crosses to the door and leaves.

I touch the floor. Remembering this moment. Not really thankful knowing that my perception finally caught up with my timeline. Should have put a key in here or something.

I get up and pace. Touch the walls. Peer out through the small security-wired window into the office, where Allyn is talking to Nik. The panel is soundproofed so I can't hear them but Allyn is doing most of the talking. They both leave. I walk the four walls of the room, looking for something, anything, but there isn't even a window. It's just a box.

I do remember something. Something I may have left behind.

On the far end of the room is a little crack in the stonework, high up, near the ceiling. I put my hand inside and find what I'm looking for—three strike-anywhere matches. I take them in my hand and sit back down.

Useless, really. Can't exactly burn my way out of this place. I used to stash them up here because sometimes, on rainy days, or lazy days, I would sneak in here for a cigarette, when I didn't want to cross the lobby. I tried to limit it. Not smoking indoors and all that. Plus, the circulation in here isn't great, so the odor would just linger.

I strike a match against the floor. It erupts and I hold it out in front of me. Watch the little oval of red and orange and blue on the end, the movement of my breath making it dance.

And then there was Mena, always on top of me for it.

Mena, who even when that cold knocked out her sense of smell, always knew when I smoked.

The fire creeps down the wooden matchstick.

Mena, who couldn't smell the gas that had accumulated in the kitchen.

That smell isn't even real. Natural gas is odorless. But they add a chemical called mercaptan, which simulates the smell of rotting eggs, so that you know there's a leak.

There was no way for Mena to tell the place had filled with gas, that it should have been evacuated. No, she was just in there working late as the gas built up. In a hotel like this, where a full spa package can run ten grand or more, we didn't have a better system for gas shut-off or detection. Boggles my mind.

The flame continues its slow march toward my pinched fingers, leaving a black, mangled shape in its path.

Every night, I remember that night. Going into the kitchen. Looking to light a cigarette off the pilot on the stove before scurrying through the back door. One more smoke before ending my rounds, then heading to the second-floor bathroom for a scrub, followed by the bottle of mouthwash I kept in my office, which I would swallow since there was no place in there to spit it out.

Then Mena. Who despite all that would still know I smoked. And she'd give me that little shake of her head and say, "My love, what about your beautiful lungs?"

There's a knock at the door but I'm lost in it now. It's not a slip. It doesn't need to be. I remember it more vividly than I remember my own name.

Leaning over the range, tipping the cigarette toward the blue flame.

I feel the warmth of the flame on my fingers. Not much untouched wood left.

The stove flame snuffing out, and me thinking, there must be some kind of shutoff. I'm sure it'll be fine. And then going and having my smoke and hustling off to something else. Not even bothering to ask Ruby, or let Mbaye know, even though I should have. Because minor shit like that tended to work itself out, and I was more worried about getting to Mena, and making sure no one knew I was sneaking cigarettes inside.

There's a knock at the door.

It was me.

I'm the one who did it.

Two people I've killed now.

The flame reaches my fingers. Singeing my flesh. I hold it there, feel the pain travel through my arm, up my body. Overwhelm me. I close my eyes and clench my teeth. Take all the pain I can, because I deserve it.

The door opens, and it's Mbaye.

I throw the match, stick my fingers in my mouth, then lean forward and land on my knees, hands spread, palms up.

"It was me," I tell him, choking out the words.

He's holding a plate of food, his eyebrow arched in confusion.

"It was me. I did it."

He crosses the room slowly and puts the plate down on the floor next to us. It's a bowl of the thieboudienne. My favorite dish. And that makes my heart wrench all the harder. Because he's kneeling there, looking at me, with my favorite meal that he cooked for me, and I lose it. How could he do this to me? I fall into him, sobbing. Burying my face in the hard muscle of his shoulder. He wraps his arms around me, unsure of what's happening.

That he would even do this for me makes me sick.

So I tell him everything.

That I accidentally blew out the pilot light. That it must have been me who created the gas leak. That it was me who killed Mena. That I was sorry. These are the words I think I'm saying but frankly I will be impressed if he understands any of them because they're just coming out in a jumbled mess of snot, coughing, and tears.

And this man, who I have hurt, who I have let carry the burden of Mena's death, he leans back from me and puts his thumb under my chin, tilting my eyes up to his. And he does the worst possible thing he could do in this moment.

He smiles.

His eyes well with tears as he says, "I would like to tell you a story."

That calms me because it's so unexpected. My brain just completely resets.

"Sit back," he says. "Let me tell you this story."

I fall back against the wall, and he sits down, legs crossed, and puts his hands on his knees, sitting in lotus position. He takes a deep breath.

"There once were two monks," he says. "A young monk, and an old monk. They were walking somewhere far away. And they came across a river, where they found a woman." He holds out his hands, palms up. "And the woman said, please will you help me across? The water is too deep. The young monk said"—he shakes his finger—"it is against our vows to touch women, I am sorry. But the older monk . . ." Mbaye offers his hands. "He took the woman and put her on his shoulders, and carried her across the water."

I'm about to say something about how I don't miss being told things in riddle format, when I realize that is not constructive.

God, even now I can't help myself.

"So," Mbaye says, pressing his hands together in prayer, "they get to the other side, and the older monk sets the woman down, and they continue on their journey. The younger monk, he is upset. The older monk broke his vow. There is a tension in the air between them. Until finally, later in their journey, the young monk asks, 'Why did you touch that woman, when it was not allowed?' And do you know what the older monk said?"

"What?" I ask.

"The older monk said, 'I set her down hours ago, so why are you still carrying her?'"

He sits back and waits.

I ask, "Mena tell you that?"

He smiles. "Of course she did." Then he leans forward. "We don't know what caused the gas leak. It was an accident. We just have to accept it."

"Why?" I ask, holding the words down, and it feels like I'm wrestling something trying to tear its way out of my chest. "Why do we have to accept it?"

He pauses, puts his hand on my knee. "What else can we do?"

"We could change it. If we wanted."

"You know we can't."

I am suddenly washed with such an intense and bracing wave of shame it makes me want to vomit. I have tortured this man. Publicly humiliated him. All for what. To make myself feel better? To share the burden of how I felt, so it would be lighter on me? I struggle to breathe. The words that I owe him.

"You should hate me," I say, looking down and away from him, wanting to disappear into a crack in the wall. "I almost wish you did."

He doesn't respond for long enough that I have to look at him, and when I do, he's smiling again. He gets onto his knees and takes me under my arms, pulling me into the firmest hug I have ever felt.

"I forgive you," he says, and the words make me go limp.

"Why?" I manage to ask.

"Because it's what Mena would have wanted," he says, his breath warm on my neck. "Because it's right. For you as much as it is for me."

That takes me apart, and I get lost in the fold of his neck, sobbing until I've got nothing left.

And when I'm able to regain my composure, I tell him, "Something really bad is going on, and people are going to die."

Mbaye leans back and looks me in the eye and says, "Tell me what you need."

My heart soars. A sensation that is incredibly unfamiliar, and there-fore somewhat uncomfortable, but also very, very welcome.

"Okay, you are smiling now," Mbaye says, patting my back. "Cut it out before someone sees you."

"I need to get out of here," I tell him.

"Hold on," he says.

He crosses to the door and looks out the little window, surveying the office. "Danbridge is still here."

"Okay, well, you can't hang out in here all day, so . . ." I pick up one of the matches. "You walk out now, I'll put this in to keep the lock from engaging, and you try to get him to leave. Easy enough?"

"Easy enough."

Mbaye opens the door and I take it from him, close it, and get the match into the slot. The lock doesn't click.

I watch from the window as Mbaye crosses to Allyn and says something to him. They talk for a few moments, and Mbaye keeps glancing back at me. C'mon, man. Allyn looks annoyed, not so much that he thinks something is up, but he definitely can't be bothered with whatever this bullshit is. Finally Mbaye's shoulders slump and he heads for the door.

Great. So I have to hope Allyn leaves and the office is cleared out before someone comes back in here to check on me.

The smell of the stew draws me away. My stomach is an empty void; I haven't eaten since I don't precisely know when. And as I shovel the stew into my mouth, dipping in the bread, savoring the nose-watering spice Mbaye added because he knows I like it face-blasting hot, I play through what I know.

I'm chasing a ghost. This ghost successfully killed one person and tried to kill several other people. It knows about my condition, considered me a threat, and tried to sideline me. It's getting desperate, too. The attempt on Kolten was subtle and could have been written off as an accident. Letting out the dinosaurs was a bold move.

So does the ghost want to stop the summit, or no? If they wanted to stop it, they could have just started slitting throats, mine included, and it'd be done. What would any of us have been able to do to stop it?

But I have more data now, and data is good. It seems like the thing I saw—whatever it was—was going after Teller. Another escalation.

But now that means attempts have been made on all four bidders.

So far I've been a step ahead of it. Changing things that were maybe supposed to happen. Or maybe just could have happened and now they didn't. Except space-time is supposed to be a four-dimensional block that doesn't change, we just move through it and witness the moments.

Moments like dots of paint.

Like on that painting that Mena showed me.

I finish the stew and down the small bottle of water it came with, then check the window again. Danbridge is puttering around, talking to some TEA agents. I cross the room and it takes twelve steps, and I swear on the next time across it's eleven. Then ten. I count it again and it goes from ten to eleven. My mind playing tricks. I walk heel to toe, trying to get an accurate count of the square footage of the room, because it's something for me to obsess over, something to push away the realization that I murdered someone.

Is it murder if it's self-defense? I don't know.

I looked, and I touched.

Worse than that, I didn't end suffering. I created it.

Before I can get too lost in my hole of self-reflection, there's commotion from outside. I make it to the window in time to see Allyn rushing out of the office. As soon as the door closes behind him I pull the cell door toward me, the match falling to the floor, and move across the room.

Then I think better.

I run back toward the main console and find Ruby, still asleep. I turn it on and it winks to life and hovers up to my eye level.

"I need you," I say. "Please. If you can work around whatever locks are in place, work around them."

"Say something nice," it says.

"Are you serious right now?"

"I'll know if you mean it."

"Fine. I miss talking to you. And I felt really sad when the dinosaur killed you . . ."

Ruby hovers up and moves a little closer to my face, probably tracking my pulse and facial tics. Finally it says, "I will accept this.

". . . But only because I don't have any more googly eyes."

Ruby floats back down to the desk.

"Fine," I say. "The reason humans process pain by inflicting it on

others is because it's a really shitty and childish way of asking for help."
I drop my head. "They want to be seen, but at the same time, they're
terrified of what it is people are going to see."

"Thank you," Ruby says, floating up to my shoulder.

I take a breath, center myself. "C'mon, we have work to do."

I throw the door open and find the lobby under construction.

The place is gutted. No carpet, just hard concrete floors. There are
men wandering around in construction hats and my eye is immediately drawn to a woman standing on a ladder, fiddling with a lighting
fixture.

Fairbanks, highlights of gold catching in her brown hair. She looks
around the vastness of the lobby—empty, without its clock, without
the desks, without anything. And she gives a little smile, like she can
see the entire thing laid out before her. I follow her line of sight across
the room, which lands on a Black woman with a shaved head, in a
white blouse and navy pencil skirt.

Simms, coming out of the Atwood hallway.

And she returns Fairbanks's little smile, like it's a fragile object
passing between them. A tender moment, which stands in pretty
strong contrast to the guests and employees from now, who are freak-
ing the fuck out.

But I can't stop looking at Simms and Fairbanks.

Because, holy shit.

They weren't colleagues. They weren't even friends.

They were more than that.

It's the blue. The carpet. That one horrible design choice made by
someone who should have known better. It matches the paint I saw on
the wall of Simms's home, when I was talking to her husband.

Fairbanks made that choice *for* her.

The past people—Simms, Fairbanks, the construction crew—can't
see us, but we can see them, and no one is handling it well. Allyn is
standing in front of a construction worker who is wiring something in

the floor, waving his hands in front of the man's face, getting no response. Before he can look up and clock me, I duck behind a pillar.

"You seeing this, Rubes?" I ask.

"I'm not sure exactly what it is I'm seeing."

"Everything's slipping, the way I do," I tell it. "Whatever the problem is, it's getting bigger."

"January?"

I step out from behind the pillar. Everything is back to normal, except for the clear disorientation of everyone in the room. Mostly people are just wandering in circles, checking to make sure everything
around them is real. A few people seem to be clutching their noses,
sporting nosebleeds. That's not good. I actually feel pretty okay. Not
like my usual slips. No spark in my brain. I don't know if that's better
or worse.

Allyn is yelling into his watch, "Get over here *now*." I stay where I
am, out of view, and after a few moments, Popa appears.

"Ruby, amplify."

The drone gives a little whir and then their hushed conversation is
buzzing out of its speakers.

Allyn asks, "Have you finally managed to do what I asked?"

Popa says, "Well, they're not handheld devices. Do you know how
hard it was to get one of the sensors over here from Einstein?"

"What did you find?"

"She was right. Radiation levels in here are off the charts."

Allyn asks, "How the hell are you just realizing that now?"

Even from here I can smell Popa's flop sweat. "The only radiation
should be coming from the timeport. There's no logical reason that
something in here would be generating it."

"Do we need to evacuate?" Allyn asks.

"I mean, not immediately," he says. "It's a problem for people who
are in more progressive stages of being Unstuck. But we need to find
the source."

That's right.

We need to find the source.

And I know what it is.

Atwood 527. The room that shouldn't exist.

I stand there, staring at the keypad of the storage closet.

"In the garden of memory, in the palace of dreams, that is where you and I shall meet," I say to Ruby. "Simms and Fairbanks were in love."

"That seems to be . . ."

"Ruby, what year was *Through the Looking-Glass* published?"

"Eighteen seventy-one."

1-8-7-1.

The pad lights up red and gives an angry buzz.

"The edition we had downstairs. It was a reproduction of the original?"

"Published in two thousand twenty-two."

2-0-2-2.

Red.

The frustration gets to me. I start punching in combinations, wondering if I can just smash the keypad and if that'll do it.

Then Ruby floats a little closer and says, "Try one-one-oh-four."

1-1-0-4.

Still nothing.

"What's that?"

"I've been running possible number combinations related to significant instances in the book since I realized what you were doing," Ruby says. "The book opens on the fourth of November. So it seemed like the most logical but not too obscure . . ."

"Okay, it's not correct but you're on the right track. It's going to be something personal. Something between the two of them."

I think back. Dates. Times.

Fairbanks's journal, which I've flipped through. I haven't read all of it. Neither have I read the book about Simms. As I'm about to ask,

Ruby says, "I am currently scanning the writings of both Fairbanks and Simms to see if I come across anything significant."

Anything significant.

The photo on the desk. The groundbreaking. And what did Simms say in that interview? It's when they first met.

"What was the date of the groundbreaking?" I ask. "Month and day?"

"October fourteenth."

I punch in 1-0-1-4.

And the buzzer goes green.

"Hey, Ruby, power down rotors," I say.

It does, and I catch it just before it loses its buoyancy in the air. I forget how heavy this thing is.

"What are you . . ."

I look deep into its circuitry and give it a little kiss on its right lens.

"My vision is now partially obscured," it says. "Again."

I use my thumb to wipe it off.

"You're making it worse."

"*You're* making it worse. Engines on," I say, letting go, and it drops a few inches before hovering back up to its usual eye-level position.

I take a deep breath, turn to the door, grasp the handle, and push it open.

EMERGENCE

Static electricity buzzes across the folds of my brain, moving in waves that are not unpleasant, but are still persistent in a way that troubles me. It feels like this when I slip, but never for more than a couple of seconds. Now it's like I can't turn it off.

The storage closet is empty. The shelves and supplies that are normally here are gone, replaced with nothing but four gray walls. I take a step inside it and turn back toward the hallway, and there's a keypad on the inside now. Was that there before? Blocked by a shelf and I didn't notice?

I step to the threshold. The air feels . . . wrong. When I move my arm it's like being in a pool, that little bit of drag as you move it through the water. Like when I touched Westin's body.

"Ruby, run a scan," I say.

No answer.

Ruby is suspended in the air in front of me, frozen. The sight of which freezes me. The individual blades of the rotors that keep it aloft are completely still. I reach up to touch it but then pull my hand back, unsure if I should even do that.

"What the Cincinnati fuck is this?" I ask, like Ruby is going to respond.

The waves in my head grow in intensity. Not painful, not yet, but what started off like a massage now feels like the masseuse is getting a little too deep, sliding sharp fingertips between the muscles.

I look down at my watch. The TEA watch. The second hand isn't moving.

And the pressure in my brain is increasing.

The room next door. I should check the room next door. My gut is pulling me there, but after a few steps, there's a throbbing through the roof of my mouth, like a shuddering blood vessel. Then I feel something wet on my nose and reach up.

Blood.

The pressure of the hotel's gravity increases. Pulling me down. Or maybe that's me just passing out? I don't know. But I need to not be here.

Another burst of pain. Getting worse.

Am I trapped in here? How do I get out?

The keypad.

I pull myself across the wall, back to the storage closet, past the frozen Ruby. Inside the room now, I try to remember the code, but my brain is sparking, not making connections. Like when you mean to do something, and forget what it is, and then your whole mind goes blank.

Worse than that, there's a sound behind me. A shuffling. Something is moving now, and it's moving toward me. As much as I want to look back, I can't. There's something deep and primal telling me: don't turn, don't look.

Don't.

What was the code? And how screwed am I if the code to turn it off is different from the one that turns it on?

Focus.

1-1-0-4.

Red. No.

Whatever's behind me gets closer. I can almost feel the air behind me moving now, like it's reaching for me.

The day they met. What was the day they met?

1-0-1-4.

The keypad turns green.

The door opens and I nearly collapse into the hallway, the pressure coming off my brain immediately, like a clenched hand letting go. I look up and Ruby is still suspended above me, but its rotors are moving. I can hear the dull electronic hum of them. I check my watch and the second hand is skipping, but at least it's moving.

"January, what just happened?" Ruby asks.

I breathe deep, collect myself. Ask, "How long was I gone?"

"You weren't," Ruby says. "You stepped into the room and immediately fell out with a nosebleed."

That must have been three or four minutes for me. Maybe a little more. Hard to tell with my brain puttering back to life.

"January, I suspect you may need medical attention," Ruby says.

"No, I'm good, let me just . . ." I push myself onto my elbow and before I can even register the rumble in my stomach, I vomit on the carpet.

"You were saying?" Ruby asks.

"Fine, okay, get housekeeping here but don't tell them it was me," I say. "And have Brandon meet me in Fairbanks's office. Right now."

By the time Brandon shows up, my stomach and brain are both settled. Ducking into a bathroom to douse my face and gargle with some water helped, but my mouth still tastes like the bottom of a dumpster. I need to brush my teeth. At least a breath mint.

Brandon sits across the desk from me and folds his hands in his lap, looking at me like he has no idea if I'm going to hug him or strangle him.

"I need your help."

He's a little dumbstruck by that and doesn't respond.

"I should go to Adrian Popa, but TEA resources are not really on the table for me at the moment," I say. "Lucky for me, I know someone with a degree in particle physics or whatever. I just found some-thing . . . weird. And I need help figuring out what it is."

He nods and leans forward, and I explain things the best I can: that there was a device embedded in the wall that made everything freeze, from Ruby to my watch. He listens, nodding along, looking at the top of the desk, and when I'm done he sits back in his chair and looks up at the ceiling.

"That's some wild shit," he says.

"Let's call it that, yeah."

"It almost sounds like you stepped outside the timestream. Or, like, you were hidden from time? There's a term for that. It's called 'time cloaking' . . . "

"Wait," I say, putting my hand up.

The same tech they use for the Jabberwocky.

Brandon is eyeing me now, wondering what's gotten me so turned around. And I feel like I should not tell him, considering how top se-cret it is, but at this point, I don't even know if it matters, so I give him the rundown of how the Jabberwocky works. But I stress that Allyn said it could only hide data.

When I'm finished Brandon sits back in the chair and looks around and says, "Wish I could smoke in here."

I raise my hand to him, and he pulls a vape pen out of his pocket. He takes a hit and exhales a huge plume of marijuana smoke scented with blackberries. He offers it my way but I wave it off.

"So," he says, "yes, obviously, time cloaking as we understand it is not sophisticated enough to move physical objects outside of time." He holds up the vape pen like a pointer, takes another hit, and ex-hales. "Simms was a once-in-a-generation genius. She invented fuck-ing time travel. So what's to say she didn't invent some other stuff and just keep it to herself?"

It makes sense. I don't know what Fairbanks's deal was, but Simms was married, and if even Cameo, the monarch of gossip themselves, didn't know they were together, then they did a damn good job of keeping their relationship on the DL. And what better way to do that than with a secret room outside of time that only they could access?

"Allyn used some kind of car analogy for me that didn't really work," I tell him. "I couldn't even repeat it if I tried."

"It's sort of like an invisibility cloak, right?" Brandon waves his hands around like it's supposed to mean something. "An invisibility cloak works, in theory, by bending light around it, so you see what's behind it. Same thing here, except you're bending time around events." Brandon lurches forward and makes more shapes with his hands. It is not helpful, but he seems very intent on providing a visual component. "Imagine you're sailing down a river. That's the time-stream, right? You're constantly moving with it and on the banks of the river are the events that are happening. You see them as you go along. The gateway lets you get out and stand on the bank, between the moments. The river stops too. You can get back in at the same point, and then it starts moving again."

I stare at the ceiling. Things are taking shape, slowly.

"Ghosts," I say.

"What about them?" Brandon asks.

"The ghosts, the ones in the hotel. The presences. Could it be people moving around after passing through the gateway?"

Brandon clears his throat and smiles. "Could be, yeah. Someone moving between the seconds with all the time they need. And given your condition, it could be giving you some kind of extrasensory perception."

"Ruby," I say, and the drone hovers closer to my shoulder. "I assume you've been checking the hallway. Anything jumping out on video."

"I already checked," it says. "Nearly all the video we lost was focused on that door."

"Then do this: I want you to run every incident we know about. Today with Teller, Kolten's near-death, the elevator I pulled out of service. Around the time of the dinosaur attack, plus anything that syncs up with the hotel's electricity going wonky. Then I want you to analyze the video in the rest of the hotel. See who is not accounted for. Or who seems to be moving in the wrong direction, toward At-wood."

"That'll take time," it says.

"Then get started."

I stand up, brush off my pants, and turn to Brandon. "You still have all your clearances, right?"

"Well, yeah . . ."

"Good," I tell him. "Time to go break and enter."

Allyn knows I'm not in the cell. He's storming around the lobby, cut-ting through crowds, stopping to talk to people, his head on a swivel. Brandon and I stick to the shadows and alcoves. I try to keep things between me and Allyn's line of sight, and am mostly successful, man-aging to make it around the circumference of the lobby without so much as a curious glance.

I pass near Teller, who is tucked in a dark corner, his eyes darting like the rest of the building is full of zombies and he's a second from being found and devoured.

"Just get me someone . . . who cares," he whisper-barks into his phone. "Oh, whatever, send his family a fruit basket, I just need some-one here now . . ."

Asshole.

Still, sucks to know Grayson had a family.

I let Brandon get ahead of me and open Reg's office. He steps in-side and closes the door, but not all the way. I move a little more, get behind a large potted plant just as Allyn is turning his gaze toward me and—shit.

He looks in my general direction and pauses. Did he see me? Does he see Ruby? No, it's hovering behind me. I peer through the gaps in the leaves, hoping Allyn doesn't follow his nose on this, and just as I think he's going to turn toward me, someone grabs his attention, and he's off, heading toward the security office.

"He's scanning the camera feeds for you," Ruby says. "Since we've already been experiencing a great deal of interference I'm blocking them, and it should appear as though whoever infiltrated our system is still inside."

"Good job."

I wait for Allyn to close the door, and then scurry into Reg's office, where Brandon is sitting at the computer, tapping away.

"Don't know the password," Brandon says.

"Perhaps I can be of some assistance," Ruby says. It floats onto the desk, hovering over the large, uneven piles of paperwork on the surface, looking for a safe spot to land. Nothing to be gained by keeping tidy. I push everything to the floor and it perches next to the terminal. The screen turns red and shakes, and Ruby says, "This is interesting. The security features on this have been increased. Normally I'd have access to all the computers here, but I'm locked out."

"Can you get around it?"

"It still requires a password, and three wrong guesses will wipe the drive. I can't brute-force it, so I'll need a little time to dig around the system."

"How long?" I ask.

"Twenty minutes, maybe."

"Don't make me get my boot."

"You know what's funny?" Brandon asks.

"What's that?" I respond.

He shrugs. "Not having enough time. Maybe you should use the door."

"Not going in there again unless I have to," I tell him. "And who's to say electronics even work in there?"

"Fair, fair . . ." he says. Then he leaps up and tears for the door. "I have an idea."

While I wait, I look around the office. At the clutter and the dust and the lesbian Sicilian flag, which has been up so long that, even in here without any sunlight, it's starting to fade. The lotto ticket, the lucky one he figured was going to change his fortune, still taped to the bottom of the screen. I pull it off and hold it.

Wouldn't it be funny if it won? Well, not funny. Ironic maybe. Would that count as irony? What would I even do with the money? Did Reg have family? I should find out. I'd give it to them. I'm about to ask Ruby if Reg had any next of kin when the door opens and Brandon comes in with Cameo, who pauses on the threshold and throws up an eyebrow at me. "A lot of people are looking for you."

They enter the room tentatively, and I stand, tell them, "I apologized to Mbaye. I apologized to Brandon. And now I'm apologizing to you. I know it doesn't erase my behavior and I have a lot to make up for. But I'm going to try."

Cameo says, "It's a start."

They maneuver around me and fold their lanky frame into the seat, type at the keyboard, and the desktop opens.

"Just like that?" I ask.

"Have you ever seen the man type? He pecks at the keyboard with two fingers. It was 'Sicily' with ones replacing the I's."

"Lord," I say.

"Time to get to work," Ruby says, then windows cascade across the desktop, until finally it stops on a series of pages that look like bills. "So we have a series of pretty serious issues here. I know who was messing with the video system."

That lands like a hard fist on my ribs. "Are you serious? It was Reg?"

"Not directly, but as manager he had full admin access, and he handed over his security key to someone."

Brandon and Cameo look at me like I'm supposed to say something, but I got nothing right now.

"There's more," Ruby says. "I reviewed the electrical bills, which, yes, are nearly triple what we're supposed to be paying. But there are numerous other irregularities. Other bills that don't match up with official records. While we've been led to believe the hotel has been losing money, it's actually been turning a profit. It seems Reg was using creative accounting to make the hotel look like it was in financial trouble."

I sit on the corner of the desk, stare at the wall. "Why did he make it look like the hotel was tanking?"

"Because if it wasn't, there would be nothing to sell off," Cameo says.

"Who was Reg communicating with?"

"I can't say," Ruby says. "I have detected the remnants of encrypted messages. I can't locate the source or read the content. His personal financial records don't indicate any large infusions of cash. Rather, he barely has a thousand dollars between his personal checking and savings."

No infusions of cash.

But if Reg was gaming the system for someone, there had to be a payoff.

A payoff from someone who has already proved themselves adept at messing with time.

I look down at the lotto ticket, the paper now getting slightly damp in my sweaty palm. I check the date on the ticket, then hold it up so Ruby can scan it. "This is from a week ago."

"It's a winner," Ruby says. "There was only one other winner on this pot, which means Reg would have been in line to receive approximately five hundred and fifty million dollars. Before taxes."

Brandon lets out a low, impressed whistle.

He must have been waiting to cash it until all the nonsense around here settled. It makes my heart hurt. Because it means Reg was a part of this conspiracy. I get that the guy had his flaws, but I liked him. Hell, I looked up to him. He had a tough job and he got through it without murdering anyone, which is definitely something I've struggled with myself.

As if on cue, Reg comes walking in.

I know it's not Reg. I know it's a slip. That familiar little buzz in my brain. So I barely notice it. But then I look at Brandon and Cameo, who are staring, wide-eyed, mouths open.

Reg doesn't regard us. He crosses the room and goes over to a file cabinet and starts rifling through it. Cameo and Brandon look at me, and we share a brief glance, only to look back and find that Reg is gone.

"Jesus," Brandon says. "Is that what it's like? When it happens to you?"

"All the time."

Brandon nods, and Cameo folds their hands in prayer. I think they get it. What it's like to constantly be surrounded by the dead. What it means when they seem to follow you.

How can you let go when you're given a choice?

I almost want to say this out loud. But I'm not ready. Not yet.

The greater concern here is why is this happening?

"January," Ruby says. "There's something you need to see."

A web browser comes up, playing a news report. Cellphone footage of soldiers in period garb shooting muskets at each other amidst tombstones, smoke curling into the air. The camera shakes and has a hard time focusing and the battle rages for a couple of seconds before disappearing into thin air.

"The world is baffled by the events that took place in Green-Wood Cemetery in Brooklyn today, where it seems visitors were witnesses to the infamous Battle of Brooklyn. But this was not a reenactment. It seems as though the battle, which took place in August 1776, was happening in real time, before vanishing."

The sound drops out and Ruby says, "This isn't the only report of time slipping. I'm scanning the news and finding reports around New York, and into neighboring states. It seems as though whatever is happening here is spreading."

"Yeah, that's not good," Brandon says.

"This is it," I tell them. "Someone made changes that were too big, and now they're rippling out."

"How do we fix it?" Brandon asks.

"You're the one with the degree."

"Shit, man, we never covered this one . . ."

I exhale. "We kill the alligator closest to the boat. Someone paid off Reg to make sure this hotel was tanking, and Drucker is involved to some degree. These things we know."

But there's something else tugging at me. Scratching at the back of my head. I keep thinking about the storage closet. The world beyond it.

And the room next door.

Westin.

Schrödinger's corpse.

Which I could see, and no one else could.

Yes, the slips in the hotel are becoming that much more extreme. But what if there's a reason I can more easily see the ghosts? Why am I the only one who can see Westin's body?

I know what the answer is here. I don't want to say it but I know what it is. I rattle the bottle of Retronim in my pocket. Take it out and remove a tab, break it in half and touch an end of it to my tongue. Tastes like aspirin, not sugar.

"What are we going to do?" Brandon asks.

Him and Cameo both look at me, eyes wide, faces wrapped in fear. I do know the answer. I feel it pulsing in my heart. A place where I thought I had no feeling left.

We aren't going to do anything.

"Brandon, find Adrian Popa, and the two of you are going to put your heads together on how we fix this," I say. "Ruby, I need you to broadcast an evacuation order. Allyn should have done it by now and I don't know why he hasn't but I assume it's because Drucker doesn't want to spook the clientele. Fuck them both very much for that." I turn back to Cameo. "You need to round up the staff and get them someplace safe. Some of them might be tempted to stay behind, but impress upon them that this evacuation order is for them too."

I don't tell them the rest of the plan. I can't. Because it's risky. I pat the bottle of pills in my pocket again, try to remember how many Tamworth said I was allowed to take in a day. That was yesterday, and so long ago. Three? Four max?

"Ready to broadcast," Ruby says.

"Good." I clap my hands. "Break."

I move to the door, all charged up, ready to get this shit done, so when I yank it open and see Allyn standing there, reaching for the knob, I don't even wait, I just duck down and dive past him, running for Atwood.

"Damn it, January!" he calls from behind me, which I know is because he does not like when perps make him run. Too bad. As I'm weaving through the pockets of people toting their luggage, Ruby's announcement comes over the speaker.

Attention please. We kindly request that everyone check out of the hotel and proceed to Einstein to await pickup. Please remain calm, this is a nonemergency situation, but it is in the best interest for guests and staff to temporarily close the hotel.

Please remain calm.

It was cute of Ruby to say that, like it was going to work.

This sets off a panic, which sends a whole bunch of people running around in circles. I nearly barrel over an old man who wanders into my path, and manage to turn enough that I go sprawling instead of him. I hit the floor hard and skid across the surface, come to a stop against a desk.

There's not supposed to be a desk here. I get a better look and it's the concierge desk, but it's unfinished, just raw wood. Like maybe it is just being moved in. I turn to check behind me, see Allyn coming up on me with a TEA agent next to him, and turn back to find the desk is gone.

I run again, being a little more watchful for what might be popping up in my path. When I reach Atwood there's no elevator open, and all the lights indicate they're on upper floors. I push into the stairwell and start hoofing it.

As I'm running I come across Mena, sauntering down the stairs. She's wearing her work uniform—black slacks and a white blouse. I stop and she stops too and we stare at each other.

She says, "Almost there, my love."

What?

There's a slamming sound from behind me. The door opening, hurried footsteps.

I look up and Mena is gone.

As I climb the stairs I shake a bunch of pills out in my palm. I don't bother to count them. I don't think it matters anymore. I crunch them between my teeth, breaking the time-release coating, and nearly gag on the taste. Work my mouth full of spit and do my best to get the raw, chalky mess down my throat.

On the fifth floor there are a handful of people in the hallway and I duck and dodge around them until I get to the storage closet. As I'm punching in the code I hear Allyn burst out of the stairwell door, and I realize, shit, I don't have Ruby. It probably got lost in all the confusion. I turn to look at Allyn just as the door lights up green. I duck in and slam it closed behind me.

When I open the door and duck into the hallway, it's like I stepped into a frozen frame of film.

Allyn is closer than I thought. Another few seconds and he would have grabbed me. Him and his TEA guy are just hovering there. I touch Allyn's arm. Gently at first, because I don't know what's going to happen, but I feel a little resistance, and then I manage to move it a couple of inches. No reaction from him.

My head seems okay. It doesn't feel like it's going to burst, which is a good sign, that the medication is working. I try to remember the side effects Tamworth warned me about. Irritability? Sure. Something like that. And my kidneys.

I move to room 526. Swipe the door and it opens. Electronics work here, and I guess Ruby got all my privileges back? Still, that's weird. What are the rules? You can hurt and kill people. Does machinery still operate? What if you call the elevator and there's already someone in it?

A not-right-now problem.

The smell hits me immediately. The dead smell. It's not rot. I've smelled rotting bodies and this isn't that. It's more of the open body smell, like when you first open a package of raw beef. Blood and exposed skin.

Westin is lying on the bed, throat slit, blood still fresh. It's been, what, more than a day?

At least he's real. When I stand at the side of the bed, careful to not step in the pool of blood on the carpet, I can feel him when I touch his shoulder. My fingertip doesn't continue through to the bedspread.

Which means I can finally examine the scene.

Not that forensics is my expertise. I know some basics. But I also know I don't have to worry too much about crime scene preservation at this point, so no need for booties and a Tyvek suit. The first thing I do is walk a grid of the room, see if there's anything I might have missed, or anything that's in here and I wouldn't have seen on the other side of the gateway. After covering the room back and forth, I've found nothing.

The medicinal taste in my mouth is making me sick, so I go to the sink in the bathroom. I twist the faucet but nothing comes out.

I'm struck by a funny thought. I feel like I should rush to get this done and get out of here, but besides the possible overdose, I really do have all the time in the world. So I guess I may as well use it productively and desecrate a body.

Rigor hasn't set in, so I move Westin's limbs, trying to get a better look at identifying marks or tattoos. It's easy enough to maneuver him around. If time really is on pause in here, that makes me think he was killed outside, before being dragged in. It's a small piece, but that's all this is. Adding up small pieces until you get a look at the whole picture.

Next I pull out his wallet, flip through it. I'm surprised at how sparse the contents are. There's some money, an ID card, a credit card, and that's it. No health card, no coffee discount card, no receipts, none of the weird personal stuff people cram into their wallets. Could be he's tidy and a minimalist, but his slightly unkempt hair and worn jeans and tattoos seem to speak against that narrative.

I take out the ID and turn it over a few times.

Fake.

High-level work. Nearly every feature is on point, except for the reflective band at the top. On a real New York ID, that band shines in a rainbow when you tilt it a certain way. This strip isn't as reflective, not as colorful. It's subtle, and you probably wouldn't notice it if you weren't the kind of person whose job it is to obsess over IDs.

But the ID says John Westin.

And he came up in the system as John Westin.

So why would he have a fake ID that matches his name?

He wouldn't. His name isn't John Westin.

Okay, another piece.

God, I wish Ruby was here. It's so much easier when I can talk through this stuff.

I pat him down again, starting with the pants and working my way up. Looking for a weapon, or anything hidden on his body. I consider taking his prints and running them but I feel like I need to come out of this room with a more definitive answer about who and what this guy is, because otherwise Allyn isn't going to give me a chance. And it's not exactly like I can wait him out.

When I get to Westin's leather jacket, I roll him back and forth until I can get it off fully, nearly sending him tumbling off the bed. The jacket is a constellation of tiny zipped pockets, so I check them, one by one, and find they're all empty—until I get to the inside breast pocket. Inside of which is a smaller pocket. There's something round and hard inside, and I pull it out.

It's a watch. The band has been removed and the hands are frozen.

But it tells me who John Westin is.

Well, maybe not who. But at least what.

Allyn comes to a halt outside the storage closet, his face twisted in confusion. Which makes sense because from his perspective I must have stepped inside and then right back out.

"What the hell is going on, January?" he asks.

I hold up the watch. The one in Westin's pocket. The exact same one I am wearing on my wrist. The one they give TEA agents at graduation.

"So you never forget the importance of time," I tell him.

"What's that supposed to mean?"

"Westin, or whatever the hell his name is. He's one of us, isn't he?"

Allyn turns to the TEA agent and says, "Take a walk."

The agent offers a look of confusion, and then a resigned shrug, and heads off down the hall. Allyn turns back to me and says, "Where did you get that?"

"From his body," I say. "The one I told you only I could see. Which, fair, fine, that was weird. But I managed to get to it and examine it and I found this hidden in the pocket. So, you've got some truth-telling to do, buddy."

Allyn looks around nervously, and then nods to the storage closet. I punch in the code—the regular one, the one that takes us to the linens, not some bizarre time-stopped dimension—and bring him inside. We shut the door and we're plunged into darkness and he sighs, pulls out his phone, and uses the glow to hunt for a light switch.

He clicks on the light and says, "Westin's real name is Frank Olson.

Yes, he's TEA. Deep undercover. There were signs that someone was trying to game this process, and yes, it's related to the Jabberwocky."

"You could have just told me that," I tell him. "So someone got inside?"

"That's the problem. We have no evidence of that. But ever since the Aztec incident, we've been seeing ripples that have only ever aligned with changes in the past. And now we're seeing more of them, so whatever it is, it's getting worse. Something must have changed, and whatever it was, it was big."

"What does Henderson say?"

"The last I talked to him, he was looking into it," Allyn says. "Been trying to get him on the phone for a half hour now . . ."

Henderson.

How is this guy not here?

Why was it so hard for me to remember what he looked like?

Our paths must have crossed, more than a few times. I think of the Christmas card I found on Axon and I can't even remember the face. I know he was bland, but still. It's like when I call it up in my memory there's just a gap where he should be.

No, not a gap.

More like one picture laid over another.

It comes on like a slip. That buzz, except deeper, in my brainstem. There's an image in my head, stuttering and re-forming, like a bad video conference connection. But the more I focus on it, the more it smooths out.

I'm a rookie agent, sitting in the briefing room, for a rundown on our new comms system, and the man standing at the podium . . .

"Shit," I say. "Shit shit shit."

I grab Allyn by the arm and drag him down to the lobby, my brain knitting pieces together, like a broken pane of glass reassembling.

We reach the security room, where I push him inside and shut the door. Take a breath. The images keep coming. Now that I know the truth, the parts of my memory that got overwritten by the collective unconscious are coming back together.

Osgood Davis, standing at the podium.

Sharing a friendly nod with him as I passed him in the hallway.

Visiting his goddamn office on the third floor of the TEA building to pick up a new tablet after I broke my old one.

That's why he felt familiar when I met him.

I already knew him.

"It was Davis," I say. "He was our digital ops guy."

"January, what . . ."

"I remember now. I don't know why. Maybe I can still access the memory because I'm Unstuck. But, the reason we didn't know someone got into the Jabberwocky is because Davis was the guy in charge of it. He was our digital ops guy. Of course he knew how to manipulate it."

"But then . . . but I know Henderson. I *know* him."

"Maybe you don't. Maybe he's part of it. Someone Osgood slotted into the role as part of his plan. And then that collective unconscious thing just took over."

Allyn presses his hands to his face. "I figured it was an inside job. Another TEA agent gone rogue. That's why I was keeping this so close to the vest. Had you been at full capacity, you would have been the one chasing it down. Olson was the second-best choice."

"Someone got the drop on him."

"January, explain to me what is going on."

So I try, and still, his eyes are going a little crossed halfway through, and I'm sure this sounds like the ravings of a lunatic. But the longer I talk the more he listens and then finally he's nodding along, like, *okay, this makes some kind of sense.*

"Where is it?" he asks. "This doorway or gateway or whatever?"

"It's built into the wall around the storage closet. Simms must have developed it without telling anyone, and I guess it was just their little thing. And I'm starting to think it was supposed to stay a little thing."

"Is it safe?"

I shrug. "It fucked me up good and I had to take a whole bunch of Retronim to handle it. But I'm second-stage Unstuck. I could take you in and you'll probably be fine."

He hesitates. Starts to say something and then stops. Looks away.

"Jesus, Allyn," I say. "When?"

"A few weeks ago. My secretary walked into my office five minutes before she actually walked into my office."

"Okay, well, maybe we can go in real quick, just so you can see the body . . ."

"I don't think so."

"Why not?"

He sighs, rubs his face with his hands. "I'm close to retirement. I can't risk this getting any worse."

I want to call him a coward. Tell him that the Allyn I knew would say, damn the consequences and let's get the job done. But I also see the example I have set. How I've made this look. And how it can't be pleasant to know what's down the road.

And in that I understand. Why he pushed me so hard, why he wanted me out of here. Why he wanted me safe. My anger dissipates a little. No matter how many times he said it, I didn't want to believe it, but he was trying to protect me.

"Where did you learn German?" I ask.

He shrugs, exhausted. "I just liked the language. There was an app for it."

"Simple as that?"

"Simple as that."

"I'm sorry for what a complete pain in the ass I've been," I tell him.

He smiles. "You think a simple apology is just going to wipe all that away, you got another thing coming. I'm going to need dinner and a round of drinks. At least."

"Deal," I tell him. "After we get out of this. I know Popa said the radiation is leaking into the hotel, and presumably it's from the gateway. We know Davis is the guy. Drucker is working with him. We have to figure out who else is compromised. Because someone staged an attack on Davis to throw suspicion off him, so clearly he's not working alone."

"We need to solve this soon. Popa just let me know, the time distortions are starting to ripple out . . ."

"The Battle of Brooklyn," I say.

"There was just a woolly mammoth in Ohio. Killed three people before it disappeared. This is not good. And we have no idea how to stop it."

"Well let's make sure no one is standing in our way first. Who else is compromised? I mean, for a hot second I was worried about you. Who else is there?"

Timing. Think of the timing. Think about who's been close to this.

And who doesn't seem to be around when the fan gets struck by a handful of shit.

The lightbulb in my head blinks on.

"Where did Nik come from?" I ask. "Are you really grooming him?"

Allyn frowns. "I wouldn't call it that. It was more, I guess he knows people because Drucker's office put in a good word for him, and then this assignment came up, and I pulled his file . . ."

He stops. We don't even have to say it. We look at each other and we know.

Then Allyn's body goes rigid and he cries out.

Nik is standing on the other side of the room with a stunner in his hand, pumping volts into Allyn's back. He's got a second one, and he's bringing it up to point at me, so I grab a mug off the desk and wing it at his face. He ducks and it misses, but it gives me time to cross the room before he fires, and I get my foot into his midsection. He goes sprawling, letting his finger off the trigger, and Allyn falls into a heap.

I pull the barbs out of Allyn's skin and check his pulse. He'll be okay. I turn my attention back to Nik but instead of him I see a desk chair swinging toward my head. I manage to get my arms up and twist a little into the blow so it doesn't land too hard. But it still hurts.

Nik tries to get around me but I kick his legs out and he launches facefirst into the door, and as I'm getting to my feet I find the chair he discarded, which I pick up and throw at him, just to slow him down. It misses and he makes it out of the room. I follow him into a lobby that no longer resembles the lobby I know. It's decrepit now. The blue carpet is faded and ripped and in desperate need of cleaning. The astronomical clock in the center of the room isn't working, and seems covered in a layer of dust. So do the desks, which are now chipped and dinged. The place smells moldy.

I chase Nik into the hallway of Atwood, where he's headed for the elevators, and by the time we reach them, everything is back to normal. He passes them and heads for the staircase, and I know exactly where he's headed, so I follow along, a few landings below, until I hear him curse loudly, and then a door bangs.

At the next level I find a handful of people maneuvering their luggage down the stairs, and there's no easy way around them, so Nik must have opted for the third-floor hallway, which he'll take to the far end, and the other stairwell, doubling back around to the supply closet.

As I push into the third floor I catch the slightest glimpse of him disappearing around the curve of the hallway, so I pour it on a little, trying to catch up.

And then the hotel is gone.

I'm in freefall. Tumbling through the air. Nik is too, about a hundred yards ahead of me. We're in the middle of a field, the land virgin and untouched, and my stomach lurches as the grassy ground rushes up.

But then it's back.

I land hard on the second-floor hallway, my face full of carpet. I roll over and catch my breath, the wind knocked out of me.

The actual building is slipping in time now. Great.

I get back to my feet just as Nik is making it to the stairwell, and I get to the fifth floor without any further disruptions. As we're headed to the gateway I reach in my pocket for the Retronim and find it's gone. Must have dropped it. Hopefully the last dose is enough to keep me straight in there.

Just as I'm getting to the closet, Nik disappears inside. The door slams shut and I get to it, punch in the code, and step through.

And as soon as I step inside I feel a searing pain behind my eyes.

I stumble out of the storage closet and the hallway is clear. Who knows how long he's been in here? He disappeared from my view seconds ago and he could have been wandering around in here for hours.

I head for the lobby but my knees buckle. I take a deep breath, try to center myself, but crumple into a heap.

Droplets of blood pat the blue carpet, turning from red to black as they soak into the fibers. The drops come slow at first, before turning to a trickle as the bones of my skull squeeze like a hand around my brain. My body yearns to release the tension in my shoulders, to let the pressure off my knees, to lay down and go to sleep.

Except it won't be sleep.

It won't really be death either. Something more in-between.

A permanent vacancy.

This moment has been chasing me for years. The third stage, when the strands of my perception unravel and my ability to grasp the concept of linear time is lost.

More pats on the carpet. But the blood from my nose has stopped flowing.

Heavier, from the other end of the hallway, getting closer.

Footsteps.

Maybe I can fight this. A handful of Retronim. A cherry lollipop. What if I scream? I open my mouth but no sound comes out. Just more blood.

The footsteps get closer.

This is the moment when my brain will short-circuit. That's the third stage of being Unstuck. No one really knows why it happens. The prevailing theory is your mind finds itself in a quantum state, and can't handle the load. Others think you witness the moment of your death. I don't give a shit about the why of it. I just know the result doesn't look pleasant: a glassy-eyed coma that'll last as long as my body holds out.

The pressure increases. More blood. Maybe I'll bleed to death first. Small victories.

In a moment I'll be gone. Probably reality too. The timestream is broken and I'm the only one who can fix it but instead I'm dying on the floor. Sorry, universe.

I slip again, memories rattling around my brain like rocks in a tin can. Sitting in my bed, the smell of garlic and chili paste frying in the kitchen, wafting upstairs, turning something over in my hands that I can't quite make out.

Except now I know what it is.

I feel it, the displacement of air, the gravity of another person, standing there, watching me writhe on this dumb blue carpet. Nothing I can do now. It's over. But I'm not going to die on my hands and knees.

It's time to face myself. Is there anything worse?

Because that's the third stage. I know it now. Your timeline crosses on itself. You see yourself, and it's not that your brain can't handle the mental load. It's that you can't handle seeing yourself as you are.

And what's worse than admitting who I am and what I've done? I've watched four men ready and willing to light a match that'll burn down reality, because they can't see how their own sphere of influence extends beyond themselves.

But am I really that different? I tore down the world around me because I thought doing that might cushion the sharp edges, but all I did was create more shrapnel.

With the last of my strength I push myself up.

Expecting to see myself.

But it's not me.

It's Mena.

SANGHA

For a moment, the briefest and most beautiful moment, the pain racking my body dissipates, and I know this is not a slip.

Mena is standing in front of me.

Her love like the warmth of the sun.

She looks so different, but the same. Her features glowing, blurring at the edges, so I can see who she has been and who she always was simultaneously. The most beautiful I have ever seen her.

The pain creeps back in and I try to speak, but my mouth is full of blood. She reaches her hand out to me and I take it. When she touches me I feel stronger, like she's channeling energy through her skin. Giving it to me, providing me with the power I need to stand.

The whole time smiling like she was waiting for me and I was just running a little late.

"You're dead," I say, my eyes welling, throat growing thick. "You died."

She takes my hand and turns it so my palm is pressed against her chest and I can feel it. That *thump-thump* that I would reach for on restless nights, running my hand across her sleeping hip and onto her chest, where the vibration of it would travel through her and into me and lull me to sleep.

"How can I be dead if you carry me in your heart the way that you do?" she asks.

"I don't . . ."

The pain comes back. Stronger this time. Tearing at my head.

And I hear it again. The footsteps behind me. I can feel myself standing there. I can feel the pain and the anger and the rage that I have carried inside myself. It's humid. It has a smell. Something old and festering.

But Mena holds my gaze.

She says, "I need to show you something."

And she twists my wrist so that both of our hands are pressed to her heart.

I slip.

That buzz on my brain, the electricity making my muscles tighten.

It's dark. I can see the outline of a person. I might be standing in front of a mirror? There's a smell like soap, and hard, cold tile under my feet. I reach up and flick on the light.

The person I see in the mirror is not me.

It's Mena.

But not the version of Mena I know, or even one that I've seen before. This Mena is just a child. Hair buzzed to stubble, but sloppy, like someone did it to her. I see her in there, those eyes, that heart. But they're dim, like a fading star.

And in that instant I am struck by a feeling of regret and sadness that reaches my core, at seeing myself like this. This image in the mirror that does not at all reflect the person I am on the inside. It's like suffocating slowly in a buried coffin. Wanting to claw my way out, and not knowing how.

I watch as Mena reaches her fingers up and touches her face.

There's a banging sound, outside the bathroom. A woman screaming in Spanish.

Mena's eyes well with tears. She digs her nails into her arm, raking it like she's trying to tear it off, leaving long red marks on her skin.

And then I hear her voice. It's not this Mena speaking. It's her, but it's coming from someplace else.

You don't know what it's like. It's like you don't have a future. Your body is so foreign to you, you don't know what you'll grow into. Who you're going to be. The very idea of growing old in a body that doesn't belong to you is horrifying. It feels like a life sentence for a crime you didn't commit.

Mena reaches into the medicine cabinet and takes out an orange bottle of pills.

And worse, for your own mother to treat you like a monster for trying to be who you are.

Mena gives the pill bottle a little shake. It sounds full. More screaming from outside the door. More pounding.

When you met me, I did not look like this, did I? But if the Mena you knew could have traveled back in time to that moment, this scared little girl would have recognized herself. She would have known there was a future. She would have truly seen herself for the first time.

Mena, sobbing, taps a handful of pills into her palm.

Had I known I had a future I wouldn't have tried to kill myself that day. Or all the other days after, until I was able to get away safely.

The room goes dark again.

I think, to spare me the sight of what comes next.

Probably to spare Mena, too.

And then we're in the Art Institute of Chicago.

Except it's different from the last time we were here. Empty of people. Just long, desolate, blank hallways. The only thing here is that painting, hanging in the vastness of the empty space. *A Sunday Afternoon on the Island of La Grande Jatte.*

Those little dots of color, those people standing on the waterline, staring off into the distance.

I can still feel the presence behind me, but there's something about standing in this space that's making my brain feel a bit more clear.

"You're Unstuck," I say.

She nods, proud of me for finally getting it. "Remember, I was a stewardess at Einstein before I moved to the Paradox. And that was back before they improved the shielding. Turns out"—she taps her head—"I was very susceptible to the radiation. It happened before I even met you." She laughs. "It's funny, I almost gave it away. The first time we met, I told you to take the job here before you told me it'd been offered to you. You're usually sharper than that. I think you were just gobsmacked by my beauty."

"But if you could see what was going to happen, why didn't you just not go in the kitchen?"

She sighs. "Even if I had the words to explain it, I'm not sure you'd understand. Sometimes I don't. All I know is, some things, it's not that they *must* be, it's that they *should* be. Sometimes the universe decides."

"I'd like to have a few words with the universe."

"You will," she says. "Before this is over, you will."

"How are you here now? How are you showing me this?"

She leans into my ear, presses her body against mine. Keeping me from falling before I even knew I was going to fall. "Being Unstuck isn't a disease, *mi reina*. It is an evolution." She holds me tighter, almost like she's pulling me inside her. "I was forged in a fire of self-acceptance. I had to fight to be the person I am. Facing myself? I already did that."

"But how are you here? Right now? What is . . . this?"

"Places like this"—she looks around and smiles—"they hold on to energy. I died, yes, and it was an accident. Not your fault. After it happened, part of me stayed here. It suits me. Remember the bodhisattva's vow? Even in the acceptance of my own fate, I knew there were ways I could still be of service."

Mena takes my hands in hers, and holds them in front of us. She nods toward the painting. "All those little dots that make the bigger picture. That was the best way I could think of to explain time. Time is a collection of moments. Put them together, that's you. That's your portrait. Being fully Unstuck means being able to step back and see more of the picture." She turns, showing me the expanse of hallway. As I turn to follow her gaze I feel the presence behind me shift, staying out of my line of sight.

"I was so terrible to so many people," I tell her. "They all cared so much and they tried so hard and I just pushed and I pushed and . . ."

"Hey," she says, pulling me in for another hug. "You loved hard and you lost hard. And no, my love, you did not handle it right. You were a big-time dick."

At this, I am able to muster a little laugh.

And I'm noticing that, the more we talk, the better I feel.

She takes my hand and we walk. The presence follows but gives us space. There are paintings on the wall now, or maybe they're photographs. Young January sitting on her bed, the room so huge and empty compared to her small frame. Not true to scale, but that's how it felt.

January walking across the stage at the TEA graduation, but instead of her parents' seats being empty, it's all of the seats.

January standing in an empty hotel lobby.

"I know that you took the loneliness you felt as a child and turned it into a way to protect yourself," Mena says. "Think about how much you struggled, pushing away connection. Especially after I was gone. It takes a lot of effort to be angry."

She stops in front of another picture. The two of us, standing at the railing, looking out over the lobby. She's kissing my neck, and I'm smiling.

"I found a family in this place," she says. "I found you. And I knew that after I was gone you'd be in safe hands because these people are your family too. The Paradox is our sangha."

Just like that, we're back in the hotel. Standing on the blue carpet dotted with my blood. There's still that presence behind me. That feeling of looking at myself. But it doesn't make the hair on my neck stand. It doesn't make me so anxious.

"We're not outside time," Mena says, caressing my collarbone. "We're beyond it. In the place where we can face the things we need to face. I'm here to do it with you."

She puts her hands on my shoulders and turns me around.

Before me is the little girl.

It's funny, the way memory works. The way you can bury things and then pave over them. They're still there, and you might even truly forget them, but then they come back and it's like they were never gone.

My favorite pair of sneakers, that I wore into the ground. That green sweatshirt, the color of which I didn't like, but it just fit so well, like a gentle and constant hug.

It's almost silly to me now, how I couldn't recognize myself.

I take a step forward and lower myself to one knee. The little girl flinches for a moment, and I shush her, tell her everything is going to be okay, and I brush her hair aside to reveal her tearstained face. In it, I see the anger and the fear that came to define me. I see myself at the moment when I decided the world around me was hostile and the safest thing to do was hide from it.

I take the girl in my arms, press her face into the crook of my neck, and tell her, "I'm sorry."

And when I do this, all the buzzing in my brain, all the pain in my body, it just goes. Like I've been walking around for years tensing every muscle and just decided to stop. In this moment I see the portrait of my life.

January Cole, wanting so desperately to touch and be touched, but believing it's a weakness, when really, our vulnerability is the greatest strength we have.

"They're in trouble," Mena says. "Our family. Plus everyone who ever was, and will ever be."

My arms are empty now. I stand and turn to her. "The timestream is coming apart."

"Hmm," Mena says. "It is."

"What's going to happen?" I ask. "If you can see the picture, tell me I can fix this. Or has the universe decided already?"

"What was the other question I asked you, that day in the museum? About the painting?"

I think back. It takes a second. There's a lot to process right now. "You asked me what the people in the painting were looking at. In the water, off the frame."

Mena laughs. "Time isn't a painting. It's just a way to help explain a concept that, truthfully, our brains aren't able to comprehend. Yes, I see more than you, but I only see a fraction of the sheer immensity of it. The majesty of it. What those people are looking at, the things beyond the edges, those are the parts I can't see."

"Eternalism is bullshit then?" I ask.

Mena shrugs. "It's all another kōan. The past is written. The future? That's written in pencil, not pen. And no, the universe is not inclined toward destruction. It helps to think of entropy as part of a cycle of growth and rebirth. But hey, I could do this all day. And there's work to do now."

"So there is a chance," I say.

Mena smiles. "Not chance. Choice."

"For me, I mean. There's a chance for me."

Mena locks her eyes with mine. "You are the kindest, most loving person I know, January."

"How could you say such a ridiculous thing?"

"Because of the choice you are about to make."

The strength returns to my spine. I feel the way I felt traveling the stream. Saving people. Righting wrongs. Doing the thing I always wanted: providing people with the safety and protection I never really felt.

"I love you so much," I tell her.

"*Mi reina,*" she says, and she presses her lips to mine, and I am flooded with the taste of cherries, but also, the knowledge that she has fulfilled her vow.

I am alone, but I'm not alone.

I never really was.

The pain is gone. There is only one thing ahead of me.

I click the button for the elevator and nothing happens, which I guess is fair, so I head for the stairs. As I make my way toward the lobby I'm amazed at how good I feel.

Lighter. Transformed. Energized. Whether that's my body releasing the tension of being Unstuck, or just releasing the tension of being a prick, I do not know, but otherwise, I should have tried this sooner.

The lobby is still packed with people, everyone frozen in place. Which, on one hand is good, because it means with this place stuck in time, it's not going to disappear on me again. What I don't like is how much potential there is for collateral damage. Nik—or even I—could still hurt these people. I slow down a bit, wanting to catch Nik by surprise if I can.

No movement. I can't hear anything. I move to the edge of the room and make my way slowly around it, trying to figure out what he might be up to. I think he knows we're on to him. Could he be going after Allyn?

No, Allyn is running toward the stairwell, probably headed up to the gateway.

Maybe Nik is downstairs. Are the trillionaires still down there? Is he going after one of them now? I move in that direction, toward the ramp that'll take me down, moving between the crowds of people, careful not to touch them. No need for anyone to suffer a heart attack because they were nudged by a ghost.

It's creepy though. All these glass eyes. People midstride so they've got one foot in the air. Cameo is arguing with a woman, their hand stuck out, gesturing midsentence. An old woman is filling a cup of coffee from the urn, but she lost control of the mug, so now it's tumbling through the air, halfway to shattering on the marble floor, drops of coffee suspended in space. I want to go over and grab it, move it to safety, just to save Brandon from having to clean it up.

But then there's movement beside me.

And Nik slams into me, knocking me across the floor.

We hit a couple of people on the way down. I do a rear breakfall, trying to keep myself from taking too much of the impact, and scramble to my feet before he gets too close. He's pushing people aside, their bodies moving slightly but not really reacting, and I square myself, next to a man pulling an expensive, solid-looking roller suitcase.

"Really?" I ask.

Nik pauses. "C'mon. You know the pay is shit."

I grab the suitcase and arch my body, using my weight to swing it his way, and it connects, distracting him enough that I can rush in and throw a kick into his midsection. But he manages to move a little and my foot glances off. I tumble into an old woman carrying her tiny dust-mop dog in her arms like a baby. The dog is knocked free from her hands, and will probably go flying when time restarts.

Nik manages to land a shot on my back, and I move with the momentum, trying to stay on my feet, and land on a young frat guy. It's like hitting a wall. He doesn't go down, doesn't move the way a normal person does, which works to my advantage because I'm able to regain my balance and turn around.

Just as Nik charges me again.

We go down, and he's on top of me, swinging at my face. I get my arms up, trying to block, but he's straddling me, the weight of his body pressing down into my hips. He's slamming his fists into me and it's all I can do to protect my face and I'm not doing a great job.

I tense up, brace my body, and buck my hips, at the same time managing to turn him to the side, so that I'm able to reverse our stance and climb on top of him.

And then it's my turn.

I pick my shots, waiting until I have an opening, and then crash my fist into his forehead. A bone cracks in my finger. The back of his head dings off the floor and his eyes go a little fuzzy. Guess he's not as good at BJJ as he thought.

In the process of my hitting him, something clatters to the floor. I hear it. I don't know what it is. I don't really care. All I know is that this is my chance to incapacitate him. He drops a hand, which opens his face up a little more, and I focus in, go for broke, and by that I mean breaking his skull.

But then pain screams through my side.

I roll off him and reach for the source of it.

Find my knife.

My lucky knife, having betrayed me, sticking out of my flank now.

Pain blinds me, and even as I'm yanking it out, I know I should not be doing this, that the blade is wedged in, holding things in place, and when I take it out the floodgates will open. But pain makes you do stupid things.

The bloodstained knife clatters to the floor and I wait for my life to leak out of me but it doesn't. There's blood, but it's not gushing. I must be lucky, for once.

Nik comes at me again, lumbering now, feeling the hurt I put on him. My pain crystallizes my focus. Or maybe it's something else. It feels like I'm tapping into something, and as he reaches for me he seems to slow down. I move to the side and grab his wrist, twist under his arm, and the momentum and torque send him spinning onto his back. With my free hand I jab straight down into his face. Once, twice. On the third shot he stays down.

I let go for long enough to grab the shawl off a young woman standing next to me and spin him onto his stomach, lashing his arms behind his back. I get it tight and knot it a few times and once I'm sure he's properly secured, my body takes it as permission to collapse.

I touch my side again. Still not too much blood. I move back against the concierge desk and the two of us sit there, breathing hard, our ragged lungs the only sounds in the entirety of this crowd of people.

"Okay," I say, "let me see if I worked this out."

He doesn't acknowledge that I said anything.

I try to move myself into a more comfortable position, and finding none, just settle on laying on my back. "Davis figures out a way to alter the Jabberwocky. He teams up with you. You go back in time, make whatever changes to make him filthy rich, and put him in the running for this. He covered the tracks so no one would notice. You must have a third man on this—Henderson, the guy everyone thinks was TEA the whole time. You needed a plant, otherwise you wouldn't be able to maintain control of the Jabberwocky. So you pulled the trigger, what, around the Aztec incident? So just a few days ago then? Which, wow. That's wild to even think about. That's why they overshot on the trip, and that's why the time issues have been increasing since then. Allyn knew something was up and that's why Westin—or Olson—was coming after you. When Olson got too close you killed him and stashed him through the gateway."

He doesn't say anything, but I'm on a roll, and talking gives me something to focus on.

"So you get yourself put on this, and you mess with things a little, just to sow some chaos. Maybe get one of these guys out of the running. I imagine after all the changes you made on the setup and getting that lotto ticket for Reg, you didn't want to risk going back in time to game the summit too, right? Anyway, you step things up, going so far as to maybe poison Kolten. And you realize as things progress that you should make it look like someone went after Davis, which was sloppy, but sloppy enough it might throw suspicion on Teller. Which I guess was moderately clever."

"You kept seeing it happen," he says, grumbling.

"If you just wanted to scare everyone away, why did you let out the dinosaurs?"

"The CDC lockdown screwed with my plans, so I had to improvise."

"Right, because you knew Drucker wasn't going to cancel. It was kinda dumb, but I'll give you credit for one thing. You started off with a really smart move. You swapped my pills so I'd be less stable. Take me off the board by making everyone think I was nuts."

Silence, which I accept to mean I am correct.

"And I guess word about the gateway was getting around. Kolten knew about it. That's why you swiped the book. Make sure more people didn't find out about it."

More silence.

"How long has Drucker been party to this?"

Nik rolls onto his side and laughs. "Actually, I found out she cut deals with everyone. She didn't care who won. But she made sure everyone promised to get her elected. She's a snake." He shrugs. "We finally assured her we were the ones to make it happen. Well, I was the one to make it happen."

"To what end? What does Osgood even want? It wasn't enough that he made himself a trillionaire in the course of a few days?"

"What does anyone with power want, January?"

That's an easy one, at least.

"More," I tell him.

Silence. Another answer.

"Nice to see you got something out of the job. You asshole, you know the rules . . ."

"Fuck the rules. All these scientists are like, well we think this or we think that. If any of this 'look, don't touch' bullshit was real, the timestream would have torn itself apart by now."

"Have you looked outside?" I asked. "There are anomalies rippling across the planet."

Nik struggles with the bindings, twisting like he's going to try and get up. "The timestream heals itself. It'll settle down."

"How do you *know* that?" I ask.

He doesn't answer.

And it's the same as the other idiots.

If it's true, it runs counter to what he wants, so how could it be true?

I push myself to standing, lurch over to my knife, the blade still marred with my blood. I grab the shawl and yank him up, being sure to hold the knife close enough he can see it, and walk him toward the Atwood stairwell.

As we climb the stairs he asks, "Doesn't it ever make you mad?"

"Lots of things make me mad."

"We bust our asses, day in and day out, and look what it gets us? What are we even doing it for? We like to think we're playing by the rules, but meanwhile the rules are being written by someone else."

"Don't get all high and mighty right now," I tell him. "You picked your side."

"Well, maybe that was my mistake."

"Why, because I got your ass?"

"No, because I finally figured it out. I didn't dream big enough."

"Yeah, well, hope you're ready for some nightmares."

"That's a shitty line."

"I'm bleeding. Shut up."

"I'm serious though," he says, almost pleading. "Just across the way is a machine that will let us go anywhere, do anything. Think about what we can do with that. We can go there right now. We don't even have to go through the door. We have all the time in the world. I can fix this whole thing right now. Hell, I could put us in charge. Are you telling me you're not even tempted?"

We reach the fifth floor and I push him into the hallway. "Every day I was tempted. Every fucking day. And I didn't do it."

"Well, maybe you just lacked the courage."

I consider kicking him out behind the knees and stomping his head into the carpet, but I'm supposed to be ending suffering, so I don't.

When we reach the storage closet, I push him inside, then hold the knife to his throat as I punch in the code. I open the door and shove him out, time moving around us again. Immediately, I feel a rip of pain in my side and collapse to the ground. I press my hand to it and bring it back and it is shiny and wet, drenched with blood.

Chaos erupts. Hands grab at me. Nik dodges away. Someone gets knocked over. I don't even know who is here. All I know is: there was something holding in that wound.

Time.

Or the lack thereof.

Then Allyn is there, on his knees now, his hand pressed to my side, trying to hold me together.

"January, what happened in there?" he asks.

"Just, I . . ." I'm struggling to get the words out.

His watch erupts with reports of disturbances in the lobby. People knocked down and not knowing why. A dog flying through the air. And then one drowns out the rest.

Danbridge. Danbridge, respond. We found Osgood Davis down in the ballroom. He's been killed, sir . . .

"January, what the fuck . . ." Allyn says, before his back arches and he cries out, and then he tumbles off of me, my knife now sticking out of his back. He hits the floor with a thud and before his body even stops moving, I can see that the light is gone from his eyes. I try to reach for him, like there might be something I can do, but I'm losing too much blood.

There's a ripping sound, and then there are hands on my torso. Something wrapping around and around and then tying tight. I cry out just as I hear a door slam. I look up and fight through the pain to focus and see Brandon is over me.

"January," he says. "That guy just went back in."

"How do we fix this?" I ask. "Did you talk to Popa?"

Brandon nods toward the gateway. "If Davis is dead half the job is done. He was the source of the biggest change. Now we need to shut down Einstein and destroy that. Between all the changes in the past, and the frequency that thing is being used, it's creating a rebound effect. Once it's destroyed we just have to tuck in and let everything even out. At least, we hope."

"Shit," I say, pulling myself toward the door. "Shit. Nik said . . . something about going to Einstein. Traveling to someplace, but from the other side . . ."

Brandon's face goes slack. "January, if he does that . . . traveling through time from *outside* the timestream? That's like leaving a spaceship through the airlock and getting back in by punching a hole in the hull. That could just break it outright."

"Help me," I tell him.

"There's no time . . ."

"There's plenty of time. Help me get back in there."

"No," Brandon says, his eyes welling. "You're dying."

"Better to make it count then," I tell him, and if he won't help me then I'll just drag myself there. But when he sees I'm not giving up, he lifts me under the shoulder. I get to the door and Ruby floats in front of it.

"I'm coming with you," it says.

"You're staying here," I tell it. "You're going to make sure Drucker goes down for this. Use your fancy data matrixes and I'm sure you'll figure it out."

"You can't go in there alone."

"Sure can," I say, as I reach up to punch in the code.

"January, I know as an artificially intelligent construct I don't experience emotion the same way a human does, and I know our time together has sometimes been tense, but I think it's fair to say that I have developed a level of fondness for you, and . . ."

"Yeah, yeah," I say, giving it a little grin. "Don't get all weepy on me now. You'll rust or something."

I give one more glance down at Allyn, dead on the floor, and I use some of the anger to propel me forward to finish the code. Brandon steps back. "We'll be waiting right here."

"Thanks," I tell him.

As I'm opening the door I feel a body beside me, and then I'm shoved to the side. I fall backward, away from the door, someone darting in past me.

Kolten.

Warwick is calling out, trying to get him to stop, and I'm pushing forward, the door still open, and beyond it I see the closet, but I don't see the closet. It's like seeing two things at once, both a full room and an empty room.

As I fall backward my body lets go, and I know when I hit the floor I won't be able to get back up, but then I feel a strong pair of hands grab me around the shoulders, and Cameo whispers, "I have you, darling."

And they shove me forward through the doorway.

I tumble to the floor as the door slams behind me and I feel it immediately: the blood stops flowing. It hurts and I'm woozy, but I'm not leaking anymore. I roll to my side, taking a second to collect myself, and see Kolten, his back to me.

He's standing there like he's looking at something, but there's nothing to see.

At least, I don't think there is.

But then a groaning sound comes up from the middle of him, and his hands float out to his sides, reaching up for his face. He turns, like he's trying to get away, and blood is pouring out of his nose. For a flash, I see a younger version of Kolten, but darker, radiating a terrible energy. As I'm trying to focus on him, the Kolten I know falls to his knees, his eyes blank, and he slumps over.

Some people are more susceptible than others.

I leave Kolten where he fell. Not much I can do at this point. But before I go looking for Nik, I take off my boot.

Family.

It was a dream, once. And then I convinced myself I could never have it. Maybe that I didn't deserve it, or it wasn't actually out there. A fantasy concocted to sell movies and greeting cards and shit. Mena showed me that wasn't true, but I wasn't all the way there. I got part of the way but it wasn't enough. I needed to get there on my own.

If I have one regret, it's that I won't be able to make good on all the apologies I need to make. To say the goodbyes I am suddenly wishing I could deliver.

I use the heel of the boot to smash the keypad.

It sputters and goes dark.

I check to make sure the blood has really stopped flowing, and then gallop-slash-limp toward the lobby.

I find him in the tram station under the hotel, trying to figure out how to work the controls to take a car over to Einstein. As I approach he gives up and hops down onto the track. I'm walking like a zombie, practically dragging myself his way. He hears me coming well before he even sees me.

He's ready. Worse, he's cocky.

Because I took a chunk out of him before, his face a collection of cuts and bruises, but he can see that I'm seriously hurt, and even with the time-stopping properties of this place, my body is basically moving on adrenaline at this point.

"Thought you were dead," he says. "I should have taken a moment to finish the job."

"I broke it," I tell him.

His face twists up. "Broke what?"

"The gateway. The panel. Smashed it up good. So basically no matter what you do, we're stuck here."

He laughs. It's a very unsettling laugh. It echoes and grows deeper the longer it goes.

"I have access to all of time," he says. "I'm sure I can figure something out. And once I'm done, fuck it, *I'm* going to own this place."

"So that's the plan? What happened to feeling bad for all those poor people on their poor cots and all the rich assholes who put them there?"

His shoulders slump a little and he sighs. "This is just how the world works. It's built so that the people at the top stay at the top. There's no way to climb anymore. If you want something, you have to take it. I am tired of my shitty apartment and my shitty paycheck and my shitty life. I'm going to climb the ladder. If I have to do it by their rules, then so be it."

"Too bad I'm going to stop you," I tell him, not entirely convinced, but with enough conviction that he appears momentarily worried.

And he comes for me.

As he does, time seems to slow, like it did before. I hear Mena's voice in my head. She's telling me about nirvana. About how you achieve it by not trying to achieve it. That you just let it be.

So I let it be.

Knowing that this is where I'll die, and that's fine.

Because I saved my family and found my sangha.

THE THEORY OF EVERYTHING

The Paradox Hotel, once, was a grand place.

The blue carpet is worn and in desperate need of replacement, or at least vacuuming and cleaning. The astronomical clock in the center of the room doesn't work anymore. The top is covered in a layer of dust, along with most of the desks, which are now chipped and dinged. The air is permeated with a damp smell.

Cameo stands at the desk, checking their nails. They're now responsible for pretty much everything at all times, but wasn't that always the case? They look terribly bored and yet comfortably content, presiding over their own little fiefdom.

Brandon refills the coffee urn, his pockets stuffed with candy wrappers, but carefully compressed so they don't fall out. Chris looks bothered as he paces across the lobby, like there's too much to fix and not enough time to do it. Tamworth stands at the railing outside his office, looking down into the lobby, not much for him to do at this point, now that his office has been converted to a general practice and he sees patients from the nearby towns, which are mostly empty anyway.

Next to Reg's office there's a framed picture of him, taken at a staff party in the Tick Tock. A drink in his hand, an arm around his shoulder. The woman he's standing with is cut off but it's a long, slender arm with a nude painted nail.

He's still watching over the lobby. Because in the end, there are some things that are better to set down than to carry.

Most of the shops are closed. The ramps need cleaning too, but they still lead up, up, all the way up, to that spot at the top floor, where if you stand at the railing and you squint, you almost can't tell that things are different. It could just be a quiet day.

The Tick Tock still shines. There are only two guests in the entirety of the restaurant: a young white couple, sitting at the bar, dressed for the summer heat in shorts and T-shirts and sandals. The kind of outfit that once would have disqualified them from entry. They are looking around the cavernous space with wonder and awe.

Mbaye comes out from the kitchen, hefting a pair of heavy plates. He places them down, and they clack against the expensive marble bar top. Basic burgers and fries, each flanked by an oversoaked pickle. The kind of meal you'd find in a diner that was all neon and chrome. Not something that would have been in regular rotation when Mbaye had his way—and an unlimited budget—but at this point he probably can't afford the jamón ibérico anymore, and neither can the clientele.

"So," the boy says, leaning forward, like any second him and Mbaye are going to be best friends. "Is this place really haunted?"

Mbaye smiles. His hard muscles have softened a bit, and there's more gray in his hair. But his eyes still shine with that bottomless well of patience.

"You could say that."

"What happened?" the girl asks. "When they shut down Einstein. Didn't a couple of people get"—she looks around and drops her voice—"killed here awhile back? And that senator got arrested? It was a big scandal. Were you here for that?"

As a response, Mbaye shrugs, picks up a sweating metal container of water, and tops off their glasses.

The girl looks worried, like she might have offended him. "If I could go anywhere," she says, "I'd want to see Johnny Cash in concert. Just once."

"I'd go back to when they were building Stonehenge," the boy says. "And ask them why." He turns to Mbaye and asks, "Where would you go?"

"I like it here just fine," he says. "Turns out, there are things people are not meant to meddle with. Time travel being one of them."

"We tried to go over to Einstein," the boy says, his voice rising. "You can't even get near it before security is on you. I know they supposedly dismantled everything, but still, it's wild. Have you ever been?"

"No," Mbaye says. "Above my pay grade."

"But, back to the hauntings . . ." the girl says.

Mbaye raises an eyebrow. "Let me guess. You saw them? On the fifth floor?"

The couple freezes. They look at each other.

"That's exactly right," the girl says, nodding. "It was the craziest thing. Two women. One of them was bleeding." She touches her side as she says this. "But she was smiling? We only saw them for a second."

Mbaye nods. "There are many ghosts here. But those two are my favorites. We call them the Lovers."

The boy and the girl look at each other very seriously when he says this.

"Who are they?" the boy asks.

Mbaye picks up a clean glass, pulls a towel off his belt, and polishes it. "They were two people who passed through this place a long time ago and found something special together." He puts the glass back down. "This is the thing, about places like this. There's something about enclosed spaces that hold on to energy. And a place like this receives so much energy, with all the people who pass through here. Because it doesn't matter if you're here for a night, or a week, or you work here and spend most of your time here." He points toward the lobby. "Everyone who comes through those doors is looking for the same thing. Do you know what that is?"

The boy and girl look at each other and shake their heads, entranced more than stumped.

"Comfort," Mbaye says. "That's all. A little comfort. A little feel of home. With home comes family. With family comes emotion. That is the energy a place like this absorbs. Our emotions are the way our hearts call out to each other, and those echoes remain after we're gone. And a place like this"—he gestures toward the ceiling, hands spread, almost as if in prayer—"a place like this holds so many different kinds of energy. It's up to us, to choose which of those energies we respond to."

They wait for more, like Mbaye has something else to say, but he doesn't. He asks them if they need anything else, and they say no, chewing slowly on their burgers and more slowly on his words. Mbaye gives a little nod and continues to tidy the already tidy bar, and when they're done eating, they sign their tab and leave, eyes darting around the restaurant, like if they're quick they might see a shimmer out of the corners of their eyes.

Or maybe they do see the shimmer.

When they're gone Mbaye comes over, picks up their plates, and places them in the wash bin under the bar. He looks around to make sure there's no one around, then goes back into the kitchen. He comes out with a steaming bowl of thieboudienne, and places it on the top of the bar. Next to it he puts down a napkin and utensils, then a glass of water. After the arrangement is set he puts his hands on the bar, on either side of the bowl, and closes his eyes, breathes in slowly through his nose and exhales through his mouth.

When he opens his eyes, he smiles.

Then he returns to the kitchen.

From my seat at the other end of the bar, I reach over and take Mena's hand.

ACKNOWLEDGMENTS

Thank you to Alina Boyden, Emma Johnson, Blake Crouch, Elizabeth Little, Chantelle Aimee Osman, Alex Segura, John Vercher, Amanda Straniere, and Todd Robinson. Also: Chris Betz at the TWA Hotel at JFK; Tim Bevan, Eric Fellner, Katy Rozelle, Dylan Harris, Jordan Gustafon, and Jacob Chase; Lucy Stille; Josh Getzler, along with Jon Cobb, Soumeya Roberts, Ellen Goff, and the whole team at HG Literary; Julian Pavia, along with Caroline Weishuhn and the whole team at Ballantine/PRH.

ROB HART is the author of *The Warehouse*, which is available in more than twenty languages. He also wrote the Ash McKenna crime series and the food-noir collection *Take-Out*. His short stories have been selected for Best American Mystery Stories, and he is the online writing workshop director for LitReactor. He lives in Staten Island, New York.

This book was set in Goudy Old Style, a typeface designed by Frederic William Goudy (1865–1947). Goudy began his career as a bookkeeper, but devoted the rest of his life to the pursuit of "recognized quality" in a printing type.

Goudy Old Style was produced in 1914 and was an instant bestseller for the foundry. It has generous curves and smooth, even color. It is regarded as one of Goudy's finest achievements.